Globalocity
The Adventures of Raymond

A novel by DC Leberknight

Globalocity - The Adventures of Raymond

Print Edition ISBN 978-0-473-29863-0
Cover art by Johnny Murphy

Dedicated to Space Aliens
For Lili

If you go on the road hoping to find it, you might discover you've had it with you all along. That which you seek is yourself. *-Raymond Love Jr.*

Around the World in 80 Chapters...

01 : The Terrorist
02 : The Third World
03 : Good Fortune
04 : Dodgy Delhi
05 : The Beggar and the Sikh
06 : More Rules Less Free
07 : Home Away From Home
08 : The Yogi
09 : The Spiritual Quest
10 : The Goddess of Magic
11 : Untouchable Pie
12 : Indian Tibet
13 : Too Safe
14 : Angeline
15 : Messing with Fate
16 : The Theory of Everything
17 : A Gift from Hanuman
18 : Beach Bliss
19 : Yin-Yang Universe
20 : Animal Instincts
21 : Roi du Monde
22 : The Epicenter of Globalization
23 : Good News Bad News
24 : Small World
25 : Dusty Food
26 : Copulating Statuary
27 : Women are Smarter
28 : The Most Holy River
29 : Speaking in Globish
30 : Maoists
31 : Freak Street
32 : A Rolling Stone
33 : A Swiss Bank Account
34 : Lost in Lhasa
35 : Monkey See Monkey Do
36 : Travelling Light
37 : Old Man Chan
38 : Ki Gong
39 : Husband and Wife
40 : The Oldest Profession

41 : Full Moon Party
42 : Not Lucky, Blessed
43 : Travellers versus Tourists
44 : You only Live once
45 : Aloha in Aloha out
46 : No God but Allah
47 : The Happy Hippie
48 : Escape to Sumatra
49 : Globalocity
50 : The Jungle
51 : Not Tarzan
52 : Marvels of Evolution
53 : Culture Shock
54 : General Lipshitz
55 : The Most Holy Neighborhood
56 : Dinner with Gay Iranians
57 : Tea with Suicide Bombers
58 : Doing God's Work
59 : High Stakes Poker
60 : Survival Tactics
61 : Space Aliens
62 : Goat Meat
63 : The Historic Circuit
64 : The Genius of Lalibela
65 : Doctors without Medicines
66 : Beauties and a Beast
67 : Trained Apes
68 : Peace and Love
69 : King Congo
70 : The Girl from Ipanema
71 : The Africa of Dreams
72 : The Lion and the Buffalo
73 : A Marvelous City
74 : Seven Sins
75 : The Postcard View
76 : The Love Illusion
77 : Another World
78 : Flowers for Yemanjá
79 : Ze Violão
80 : The Land of the Free

1 - The Terrorist

Pedro dropped me off at Terminal Two. My best friend since high school, his last words were, "Cuídate, cabrón!" That's Spanish for, "Take care of yourself, big goat!" Pedro dropped me off and so it all began, a mind-expanding odyssey impossible to plan. I was so happy that I never could have imagined my imminent arrest.

This was the first time airport security ever searched my luggage and it caught me unprepared. I expected them to pass my backpack through an x-ray machine, never to comb systematically through all my stuff, but I was "on the list."

A security officer escorted me to a special search zone, a temporary construction sandwiched between two check-in counters. Tall and muscular, the officer reminded me of Frankenstein's monster (without the electrodes) and he was rude, but I was not worried. Instead I was puzzled why the only passenger they called out to search was me. I got worried when Frank smelled my shampoo bottle.

He asked, "What's this?"

I mumbled, "Huh? Um. It's... It's shampoo, sir." Then I began to sweat. I had a joint, one joint stashed near the bottom of my pack, one joint to smoke in Central Park in New York City. There was no escape; Frank would find the joint. When he uttered the word "marijuana," everyone in our vicinity turned to stare, then the big man clamped on handcuffs, then he led me away, into an elevator and down.

Frank handed me over to a California cop who shoved me into a cell and told me to wait, as if I had a choice. My cage consisted of concrete and metal and bullet-proof glass, not an inspiring sight, so I closed my eyes to visualize a grand adventure to elsewhere and beyond, but those handcuffs were too tight and this overwhelmed my fantasy.

Hours later, a different cop interrupted my boredom. His wrinkled face showed signs of wisdom, but his voice was angry. He demanded, "What the hell is this?"

The cop was carrying the book and the note. I laughed out loud.

Pedro gave me the book to deliver to his friend Dan in India, because I was on my way to India. Written in three languages, the text referred to esoteric concepts of Tibetan Buddhism, but the illustrations depicted demons, some bathed in fire. Pedro wrote the note to his friend on a CD label, unremarkable except that the CD's artwork depicted an airplane engulfed in flames, about to crash. The note said, "D, Decipher and report back. Love P." Pedro also gave me the joint, he said, "to smoke as soon as you're away and free, to imagine exotic women and endless possibilities." I packed these gifts, and I did not think much about them again until Frank smelled my shampoo bottle.

The California cop glared as if I was a terrorist. He reminded me that my name was on the list, that I had a book about fire demons written in unintelligible languages, plus a cryptic note written opposite a picture of an airplane engulfed in flames, about to crash, and furthermore, I had marijuana.

The cop's eyes focused on the airborne inferno so I explained, then much to my relief he unlocked my handcuffs. He quizzed me about my plans. He said, "If I bust you, the system will probably set you loose by tomorrow afternoon. Or not, because I'm gonna set you free now. There's just one detail: do you mind if I confiscate the marijuana?" He smiled. "I'm actually jealous. It sounds like you're in for quite an adventure! You should go to Brazil." The cop filled my head with visions of sun, samba, and "pretty girls in string bikinis," then he escorted me to freedom.

I queued to see a ticket agent, hopeful to get on my way without delay. The woman typed into her computer, then she said, "I see you had a little excitement today..."

"Yeah," I answered. "Is it possible to get to New York tonight, please?"

The woman typed some more. "Yes," she said. "I'll book you, but first we need to search your luggage. Please go with the officer."

Frank searched my backpack again without saying a word, and as he flipped through my spy novel, page by page, I laughed the whimsical laughter of a free man. I saw the incident as a warning, a bump in the road, the unfortunate confiscation of Pedro's joint, but never as something that would radically alter my destiny, perhaps even more than a one-way ticket to India, perhaps even more than falling in love.

2 - The Third World

My hotel wasn't in New York's nicest neighborhood but it had the advantage of being cheap, and conveniently located near a subway station. I entered a world which at first seemed dodgy, because I was trained to think that Brooklyn after midnight was dodgy, but I sensed no danger. Indeed, I was delighted to inaugurate my cultural odyssey. I ditched my backpack then went straight back outside to explore, but first I put a twenty-dollar bill into my shirt's secret pocket, enough cash for a taxi ride home.

My father taught me to sew secret pockets, and to carry a decoy wallet too. Pops was paranoid. Once a soldier, he sadly grew fat and lazy as he squandered his inheritance on five-star hotels and chic restaurants. I resembled more my grandfather, and this made me smile as I wandered in search of beer. I planned to travel for years, and like him it was in my nature to be frugal. Gramps loved India. His passionate stories of adventure had everything to do with my going there first; and New York City was on the way.

I entered the first bar on my random path, an Irish pub. The rustic detail screamed authenticity but the clientèle did not. I was the only white guy. I ordered a pint of Guinness, then I noticed the woman sitting next to me staring into an empty bottle. I saw her as depressed, perhaps lonely, so I ordered a second pint.

She looked up from her trance to say, "Thanks."

"You're welcome," I said. "I'm Raymond, and you must be somebody else."

The woman introduced herself as Sasha. She almost smiled.

Hoping to brighten her mood, I burst with enthusiasm, "You're not gonna believe what happened to me today!"

Sasha's eyes indicated curiosity, so I told her the story of the joint, the book, and the cool cop who let me go, concluding, "Frank searched my backpack, again, as if he figured I somehow managed to score another joint since I left the cell."

The bartender served our Guinness.

Sasha raised her glass with friendly glance, then she said, "If you were poor and black, you'd be in jail." Her stare was intense but not unkind.

I put my beer down and stared back. "What makes you so sure?" I asked. "I mean, that cop was pretty cool. Maybe if I was poor and black, he'd have felt sorry for me and let me go just the same."

"Maybe," she said. "Who knows?"

My celebratory mood transformed, I made a toast to freedom, then I asked my fellow traveller why she was out at one o'clock in the morning.

"I'm a social worker," she said, "but my funding just got cut off."

"Oh."

"Yeah. I help unwed, pregnant girls; that is, I used to. I can't do it for no money!" Sigh. "I don't want to beat up on you, but a lot of the fathers are in prison for drugs, so when a white kid gets away with a slap on the wrist, well that pisses me off. Nothing personal."

I encouraged Sasha to talk about her girls. Lacking stable family environments, she had been their mentor, sometimes their only adult friend and confidant, but the country's priorities changed.

"So Raymond," she said, "What brings you to New York again?"

"Today's the first day of my world tour. Remember? The joint? Pedro's book?"

"Oh yeah."

"Yeah! I fly to Delhi the day after tomorrow!"

"Well, I hope you have fun."

"Thanks."

"Funny isn't it? I always thought of India as the third world. You know? But it's probably nicer than Brooklyn."

"I don't know. I've heard they have some pretty extreme poverty over there."

"Yeah. I shouldn't complain on a full stomach."

My drinking buddy hit her beer and stared at me, so I hit mine too, scanning faces. I felt surprisingly great, because I was elsewhere and on my way.

Sasha broke the silence by asking me if she could ask a

personal question. I nodded my approval so she queried, "How you gonna pay for this world tour of yours? Sorry, I know it's none of my business, but no young men I know are going on extended overseas holidays..."

I told her I was a lucky bastard. I told her, "When my grandfather died, Pops bought himself a new house with the inheritance money, then he gave our old house to me, and I just sold it."

"I see," she said. "You are a lucky bastard."

"Yeah."

I told Sasha about my ex-girlfriend Maia. I always wanted to travel the world and Maia gave me the excuse to go. All I had to do was sell the house. I told Sasha, "I caught her sleeping with another guy, and then we got into a fight, and then she dumped me, so... I thought I was in love but... I'll forget about Maia soon enough. I'm on my way to India!"

Sasha smiled. "Good for you! Sell your house and go learn about the world. Fly to Delhi and get your mind blown away. I admire that. Most people wouldn't do that. You have courage. Eat some interesting food for me."

"Thanks," I said. "I will... So what about you? Where's the old man?"

"Prison."

"Drugs?"

"Nah. Johnny fancies himself something of a messiah, sent to Earth to save our souls. He wasn't on drugs, but there were times when it sure seemed like he was. The police busted him once breaking into the Humane Society to free all the dogs. Another time they caught him trying to steal holy water from a Catholic church. He's a little loco."

"He sounds like he's missing some marbles, but not necessarily criminal."

"No, he's a criminal. The messiah shouldn't have to work, you know?"

"Oh."

"Yeah. Johnny's got a big heart, but I'm gonna divorce him. I'm not giving up on love."

Sasha and I enjoyed another round of beer, then we left together to the New York night. I went left and she went right.

I walked boldly ahead pondering my good fortune, but after a few blocks I noticed a posse of punks lurking in a dark corner, so I changed course, feeling fear. Sasha said I was lucky and courageous but I knew the opposite of cowardice was reckless stupidity, so I made haste to my room and locked the door. I put my decoy wallet on the bedside table, I recalled my most eventful day, I pondered the nature of adventure, and I wondered why my name was on the airport's secret list. Then I felt overwhelmed by a simple sense of joy because I was finally on the road, finally free. I fell asleep smiling.

3 - Good Fortune

I woke up disoriented, half dreaming that I was locked in a cage but nevertheless laughing about the idea of a messiah named Johnny. I devoured a big breakfast in a neighborhood restaurant, then I navigated the city subway to fulfill a childhood dream, to see the view made famous by King Kong. I was delighted to finally be on the road, to be a tourist, to break in my new camera, and to stand atop the Empire State Building pretending to be the greatest of all apes ever.

I walked to Wall Street where I admired the grand façades, then I sat to watch businessmen buzz as if their buildings were hives filled with money instead of honey. I was curious to glimpse inside this capitalist culture by meeting some locals, but the money bees all seemed too busy to buy me lunch.

I bailed in the direction of the Statue of Liberty.

The tourist ferry also stopped at Ellis Island, the point of arrival for immigrants in the time before airplanes, so I disembarked to explore the museum. One exhibit made me wonder why Gramps changed his surname upon arrival from Syria. I always assumed he wanted to avoid prejudice (certainly Love sounded more American than Alzahabi), but I never asked him. I wished that I had asked him.

On the ferry back to Manhattan, I stood next to a man wearing a diamond-studded wristwatch, and I could tell by the fancy cut that his suit was also top quality, a garment of power. With Lady Liberty dominating our view, Mr. Suit spoke with his companion about a business issue. By eavesdropping I learned that the smaller man's name was Budi, he just arrived from India, and therefore I inferred that their touristy voyage was the boss's way to welcome his new worker to his new job and new country.

Budi beamed optimism, an unshakable belief in the American Dream. I welcomed him, then I told him I was poised to visit his country. He replied by passionately describing Darjeeling, the tea, and the benefits of yoga.

Mr. Suit introduced himself as Robert. We shook hands. He said he was going to India soon also, "to expand the Bangalore office." He said, "Why don't you join us for lunch? I'm buying. Do you like Chinese?"

I said, "I like free. Thanks!"

Over lunch we discussed my travel plans, Budi's new job, and Wall Street's capitalist culture. Finally Robert glanced at his wristwatch, he said that time was money, then he asked our waitress for the bill. He gave me his business card.

Along with the bill, our waitress delivered three vanilla cookies individually wrapped in plastic. Budi looked perplexed so Robert explained that if Budi cracked a cookie open, he would find a prophecy inside.

Budi cracked a cookie open then proclaimed, "If I work hard, I will be justly rewarded!"

His boss agreed that sounded right, then he read his own fortune with a smirk. "I will be extremely successful in my next career," he said.

I cracked my cookie open then read aloud, "You will travel far and return with great riches." Then as I contemplated the nature of those riches (spiritual wealth perhaps, or maybe a hidden stash of gold and jewels), I munched that cookie, and it was good.

Robert asked rhetorically, "Did you know the ancient Chinese used to add the words 'in bed' to the end of their cookie fortunes? They were wise. Yours, for example, should read, 'You will travel far and return with great riches in bed.' Budi will be justly rewarded for his hard work in bed. And we all know what my next career is supposed to be."

First I laughed, then I thought of Sasha. I said, "Maybe your next career should be politics. Don't you think improving schools in Brooklyn, say, might provide a more impressive legacy than working as a porn star?"

Robert answered with a smile, "Please don't underestimate my talents in bed."

Soon thereafter, my companions got into a taxi and sped away. I was mindful that travelling alone meant being alone, a lot, so I took a deep breath and walked in a random direction, straight to the site where terrorists destroyed twin towers with airplanes. I paused to watch workers prepare a new foundation, then I walked to Times Square, then to my favorite Irish pub.

There was no sign of Sasha, so I rested my feet while

pondering the nature of life, luck, and love. Sasha, Robert, and Budi were all smart people who rolled life's dice. Robert was the wealthiest but Budi seemed the happiest, because like me I figured, he was embarking on a grand adventure.

In Central Park the next morning, I reclined under a giant oak where I closed my eyes to imagine exotic possibilities. There was no need for Pedro's joint. I imagined my heroic return from far away with great riches in bed.

On the subway to the airport, I listened to musicians playing the blues. When they passed the hat, I gave them a dollar. I was never more excited. I was on my way to India!

My check-in agent informed me that I was "on the list" and thus flagged to be searched. He didn't know why, so I went through the process then I sought out a manager. She said, "The system says you're a security risk, a person of interest. That's all I can say."

4 - Dodgy Delhi

"Namaste," said the customs agent, no questions asked, no search imposed. "Welcome to India." Sweet! I changed one-hundred dollars into rupees, then I put my passport away, then I walked to where taxis waited. Beggars dragged themselves after me to plead for charity so I gave my coins to the most crippled one, not anticipating that his companions would pursue me with intensified expressions of desperation. I avoided eye contact and quickened my pace to the taxi queue.

"How much to the Shiva Guest House?" I asked. "Near the main train station."

"Two-hundred rupees," said the driver. "Five American dollars."

"Three dollars."

"Four."

Our deal done, we sped away.

The moon's light was sufficient to see scenery more shocking than the beggars. Women and children slept under cardboard boxes. Armed guards patrolled gated enclaves. Cows chewed on garbage oblivious to the traffic whizzing by. Worst was the foul stench of burning rubbish.

My driver stopped on a dark street then he turned to address me. I noticed a scar on his face and missing teeth. "Sir," he said. "This hotel is very good and inexpensive too. Only forty American dollars. Best value in Delhi, at this time of night especially."

Tempting as it was to get a shower and a bed, I said, "Please take me to the Shiva Guest House... Now, please."

"I'm sorry sir, but I do not know Shiva Guest House."

"Why didn't you say so at the airport?" Sigh.

I retrieved my hotel's phone number from my guide book, then Scar-face made a call, speaking in Hindi. Finally he said in English, "I'm sorry sir, but Shiva Guest House all full, no vacancy."

I had considered booking a room in advance but I didn't bother because I expected to arrive during the daytime. I did not expect that grueling twelve-hour delay in London. Sigh.

I asked Scar-face to call another cheap hotel but he refused, saying, "All of Delhi city is most full now because of international conference. I have taken you to the best-value hotel available, at this time of night especially. Only forty American dollars."

I didn't believe him. I wondered how many tourists fell for his scam, and I wondered how he got his scar, but I figured if he had a gun he would have used it. I estimated that he was a coward, so I tried to look mean and I stared him down.

Finally he said, "Sir, there is tourist agency open twenty-four hours. They will find one room for your good self."

I nodded, and he put his taxi in gear.

In a dilapidated office suspiciously nearby, a man sat at a desk covered with maps and brochures. He seemed to be expecting us. Something other than the sewer outside didn't smell right, but despite feeling frustrated and exhausted, I was excited. I was in India!

I asked the mustached man to please find me any cheap room near the New Delhi train station, a landmark surrounded by a backpacker neighborhood according to my map, and a safe place to wait until sunrise in the worst case.

The man made two phone calls, speaking in Hindi, then he said to me, "I am so sorry sir, but every hotel in Delhi is fully booked now because of very big, international conference. It is crazy! So many people in Delhi now. I recommend you take the forty-dollar room that your taxi driver is recommending. You are lucky it is available. Indeed, this room is excellent value for money, at this time of night especially."

Tempting as that was, I did not want to fall for a scam, so I asked Scar-face to please take me to the New Delhi train station. Instead he drove me to a small, neighborhood station not far away. When I saw that he was playing me for sport, I snapped, "Take me to the main, central train station, the big one, now! Please."

Scar-face insisted that my bill just increased to nine dollars, then he put his taxi in gear. Later as we approached the central station, I ordered him to stop and he obliged.

Incredibly, I saw a sign down an alley that said Shiva Guest House. The alley was deserted except for some night workers hauling cargo, and I sensed no danger, so I put one-hundred-and-sixty rupees on the taxi's front seat, then I marched towards the sign. Scar-face chased after me, demanding more money. He grabbed my arm and yelled in Hindi; this was annoying. He threatened to call the police.

The door to the guest house was locked but a night guard was on duty. Scar-face started to say something but I cut him off to ask for a bed. The guard quoted prices in rupees, about seven American dollars for a room with a private bath.

I stared into Scar-face's unsteady eyes. "Look," I said. "At the airport you agreed to accept four dollars to take me here. Not nine, four. I paid you. Now go away."

I looked to the night guard for support. He put his hands together and bowed. "Namaste," he said. "I bid you welcome in the name of God."

5 - The Beggar and the Sikh

I awoke in the afternoon laughing at myself because I was still wearing boots. Excited, I splashed water on my face then raced down to the street.

My neighborhood was set up for tourists, with restaurants, hotels, and shops selling accessories for the spiritual seeker. The gritty lane was packed with humanity living at the edge of chaos, with women in colorful saris avoiding cow dung as they walked near crumbling buildings plastered with hand-painted advertisements, with spaghetti wiring keeping the lights on most of the time, with rusty motorbikes speeding past children peddling bangles, incense, and fruit.

I sat down to take in the scene, but a beggar girl found me, her legs so disfigured that she had to drag herself across the madness and filth, her beautiful eyes pleading for help. I wanted to give her money, but I didn't want to attract attention, especially given the other beggars on patrol. As I wondered what to do, the girl touched her grubby hair and said, "Shampoo."

Inspired, I entered a shop that sold shampoo. The girl followed. Her smile warmed my heart, so I made the purchase.

As I stepped back outside, other beggars grabbed their hair, yelling, "Shampoo! Shampoo!" They swarmed to me, so I lurched away while protecting my wallet, then I looked back only to see my crippled friend selling her gift back to the store for money.

Confused, I sought calm, so I followed a sign to a rooftop restaurant where I enjoyed a panoramic view and a shockingly inexpensive curry, but I couldn't get my mind away from the beggar girl. I knew that giving her shampoo wasn't going to help her plight in life, but at least the money provided her with a moment of happiness. I decided to always keep small change handy in case I encountered a situation where my heart wouldn't allow me to give nothing.

With my belly full and my attitude adjusted, I procured an Internet outlet. First I emailed Mom to tell her I arrived safely. Then I emailed Dan to confirm my imminent arrival in Dharamsala. Finally I emailed my best Mexican friend to narrate the events at LAX.

To Pedro I typed, "I bet the cool cop took your joint home and smoked it himself. I hope it helps him find enlightenment :-) Anyway, please ask your computer-guru friend to look into my red flag, you know, that Hawaiian guy with the crazy tattoos (I forget his name). I bet he can break into the airport's database or something. He told me that hacking is what he does for fun, and I really want to know what the Feds have on me, so it's worth a try. Thanks! Meanwhile, it's great to finally be on the road!"

As I stepped outside to the busy street, I felt a rush of excitement. I was in India!

I hired a bicycle rickshaw for a tour, paying a man named Ganak to take me through the alleys of the Old City. Ganak pontificated about poverty as I marveled at the sights and sounds and smells. On a street that specialized in used books, I saw a man feeding a cow with a potato. I saw cows eating plastic too, but the rats fascinated me more, or rather, the way in which the magazine wallah ignored them. I didn't see children begging from locals, but I did see them smiling and playing, only to put on pathetic faces with their hands out for money the instant they saw me.

Ganak stopped several times to show me interesting sites by foot, every time paying a boy almost nothing to watch his rickshaw. We entered a hardware and electronics market, but instead of wandering around, my guide took me straight to the rooftop for the view. From high above the city I could see a billion souls scrambling to survive, but I was no longer surprised by the crowds and cows and filth, but by the density of happiness. I didn't expect the smiles.

After Ganak's tour I entered a Sikh temple, a sanctuary in marble, where I met a man wearing a turban and a most-impressive mustache, a man who offered me food, insisting it was free. Feeling no hunger, I declined. The Sikh explained how his temple was a place where anyone could eat. "It is the way of the Sikhs," he said, "to treat all people equally, with yellow hair or balding, Hindu or Muslim, it does not matter."

I asked him why all Sikh men wear turbans, to which he replied that he wore his turban as a traditional tactic to protect his long hair, which he never cut. He said, "The turban also benefits for keeping warm in winter, cool in summer, and for shielding face from sand storms in the desert. The turban also increases hygiene, most important in food preparation."

We continued to a great hall where perhaps a thousand people sat eating chapati bread and dal. Meanwhile my guide explained how Sikhism grew out of Hinduism but rejected the caste system, an ancient organizing principle whereby everyone inherits their occupation at birth.

The Sikh said, "The priests and power brokers are traditionally of the Brahmin caste, whereas the backward-class people do the filthy and menial labor. Many Hindu people consider the lowest of these backward-class people to be untouchable, branded as impure from the moment of birth, but please never say the word *untouchable* to refer to human being, nor *dalit* either. Ganhdi-ji himself outlawed these words in favor of *harijan*, this word meaning, children of God."

My turban-wearing, mustache-bearing companion asked me to sign a guest book, insisting that all donations would go entirely towards food. I gave generously, smiling as I imagined the little beggar girl enjoying a meal with all her *harijan* friends. To understand India, I decided, one must meet a beggar and a Sikh; one must go to India.

6 - More Rules Less Free

I was surprised to find myself the only backpacker on the tour to Agra. My companions were like Mom and Pops would be if they were ever to visit India. (As if. Mom wouldn't last ten minutes in Delhi; she'd freak out the first time she had to step over cow droppings or stare into a crippled girl's eyes.) My companions complained a lot. To them India was too dirty, too poor, too noisy, and too uncomfortable. They did agree that the food was good, except that one could never find a steak.

My companions did not bother me though, because visions of India demanded my attention. I saw farmlands obscured by a brown haze, crowded towns built with minimal help from machines, and ox carts causing traffic jams. I saw an ancient civilization struggling to survive an unrelenting transformation to modernity.

To enter the Taj Mahal cost fifteen American dollars, yet the total my tour-mates and I gave to the beggars outside was zero. I asked the cashier for small change so that I could pass it around on my way back out.

I previously hadn't known that the Taj Mahal was a Muslim design, nor that there were two red mosques symmetrically positioned as part of the site. I admired the aesthetic of the Koranic script that bordered marble walls adorned with stone flowers. This exquisite craftsmanship made the mausoleum worthy of its fame as the eighth wonder of the world, the symbol of India, the greatest monument ever constructed for love.

My grandmother died before I was born but Gramps always spoke of her as the love of his life. He was Muslim and she was Christian, so it must have taken courage for them to marry. I was sad that Gramps was dead, and I was sad that I didn't ask him more questions, but remembering his living spirit gave me confidence to run with my instincts, to explore Agra on my own, so I blew off my tour group.

It occurred to me that despite the countless photos I had seen of India's masterpiece in marble, I never saw one taken from the other side of the river, so I walked in the direction of a distant bridge. Around the first corner I saw camels; I hadn't expected to see camels.

A man ran after me. "Mister, mister..." He insisted, "Where you from?"

I conceded, "California."

"I love California," he said. "I show you Agra. No worry. No money. I take you to my brother's store, yes? Very nice."

Despite my desire to meet locals, I said, "No thanks. I like to walk by myself. OK?"

He said, "No problem. My brother's store is very cheap, almost free!"

I darted into a nearby restaurant with a sign in English. I was hungry after all. The hustler peered through the window but he did not enter. Meanwhile I ordered a thali plate, an all-you-can-eat vegetarian meal. It was fabulous.

Away from the tourist area, I was unmolested by beggars and salesmen. My walk was filled with the sights and smells of ordinary people, cows and camels, plus the odd ancient fort. This was the first time I ever wandered the streets of a city unable to read the urban wallpaper of billboards and advertisements, which was strangely liberating. I wandered for hours, enchanted by an India I never imagined, that India where marketing majors invented creative ways to sell toothpaste.

I wanted to get my photo at sunset, so I flagged down a tuk-tuk, a three-wheeled taxi decorated with cartoon drawings of Shiva. My picture turned out great, a surreal image of the Taj Mahal's reflection in water that flowed to the sea, a metaphor for life and love.

My tuk-tuk driver, Abu, drove me to where I could catch a bus back to Delhi. The bus was so cheap and the local people were so interesting that I made a rule for myself to never travel with a tour company again. I wanted the freedom to do whatever I wanted whenever I wanted, with Indian locals and not Western tourists. Then I changed my mind. Maybe some day I would go on another touristy tour after all. I wanted freedom, and the more rules the less free.

7 - Home Away From Home

I asked Dan via email how long the bus took from Delhi to Dharamsala. He replied, "Twelve hours but maybe twenty-four hours, and if it's twenty-four hours that's good, because this will help your karma as you learn to be more patient. PS: Welcome to India."

The bus journey took eighteen hours, and despite Dan's pronouncement, I felt no detectable change in my karma. The man who sat next to me spoke passable English but not enough to answer my questions about the culture outside our window, so eventually I gave up the dialog and tried in vain to sleep. I wished that I spoke Hindi.

Finally off the bus, I followed Dan's instructions to navigate away from the wanna-be guides and hustlers to a quiet place where I adjusted my backpack for walking comfort, then I clambered up uneven stairs, smiling in the realization that my world tour had finally begun in earnest. Next I walked to Chuki's Café from where I telephoned Dan as arranged.

My hosts were colleagues of Pedro's from university, and it was nice to finally meet them. Dan was taller than I imagined, and Dana shorter. We hugged as if we were old friends. While Dan ordered beer from Chuki, Dana insisted that I stay at their house. I accepted. We swapped stories about Pedro, then we all drank beer, then we discussed the impending rain, and I felt happy.

I told my new friends about the beggar girl and her shampoo scam, still in shock at the unimaginable suffering. Dan's answer shocked me more. "The girl's parents probably broke her legs when she was born," he said.

I gasped. "No. You mean on purpose?"

"Yup. This way she'll be ensured survival as a beggar. Welcome to India. Poverty is part of the scenery. For many people here, that girl simply has bad karma. Why else would she be born into such misery, if not to pay for her sins from one of her past lives?"

We all drank. I felt sad, and then despite my ethical confusion I felt happy. India!

Dan said, "I don't give anything to children, well maybe food sometimes, but never money. You'll hear them ask for school pens, but it's better to give directly to schools. Give pens not money. If you give money, the teachers will just keep it."

Dana said, "If we stop to cry for every injustice, we'll spend our whole lives crying. Instead, we should work to reduce injustice." Her eyes met mine, and I knew she had seen suffering that I had yet to imagine. I knew that I knew nothing about suffering.

We took a taxi uphill to a village known as McCloud Ganj, then proceeded by foot. We walked past an apple orchard, a yoga ashram, and wild marijuana plants, pausing only to give a cow the right of way.

Dan and Dana's lair was decorated with thangkas, scrolls, and mandalas, all with a Buddhist theme that radiated tranquility. As Dan showed me around, he explained how he and Dana got five-year-resident visas, renewable in Kathmandu, how the exchange rate made some things impossibly cheap, including their live-in cook Vijay, and how if he lived in America, he'd have to work a full-time day job, but with positive cash flow in India, he lived like a king.

Dana served tea then her expression turned serious. She said, "There are only three house rules..." I gave her my undivided attention. "One: no toilet paper. The toilet will get clogged up, and we'll make you clean up the mess, and it's just not a good thing when it overflows. Two: if you want to smoke marijuana, fine, but do so only in your room. Sometimes monks visit without calling first. And three: don't be an asshole."

I laughed. "Good rules. About the toilet paper though, what do you use to wipe?"

Dana explained, "Use the bucket by the squatter for water. Pour with your right hand and wipe with your left, then wash up with soap. You'll get used to it. And be careful with your left hand in public. Any questions? Good. You know it's funny. Americans always think it's disgusting to clean your ass with water, but Indians think toilet paper is gross. Water cleans better, and you don't have to leave smelly shit paper lying around. But be careful with water in India. Tourists do get sick from ice, for example, or they swallow water from the shower. We boil and filter our own drinking water. Anyway, regarding yoga, if you want to go tomorrow, I'll wake you up at seven."

"Yes," I said. "I want to go."

Dan said, "Good. And if you want to learn about Buddhism or yoga or anthropology, I have some excellent books."

I said, "Cool. Speaking of books, I'll go get that book from Pedro..."

Dan and Dana sat on their sofa to inspect Pedro's gift, admiring every illustration while discussing esoteric points of philosophy that I failed to grasp, but they did not answer my most basic question: "What's the deal with the fire demons?"

Dan flipped to a page with a particularly fierce-looking spirit. "This fellow predates the arrival of Buddhism in Tibet," he said. "Pedro's book explains how the ancient pagan beliefs were incorporated into the new religion from the south. These fire demons (as you call them) have since been transformed into protective deities, more or less the guardians of Buddhist dharma."

I asked Dan to explain the meaning of the word *dharma* (the eternal laws of the Universe), then I chronicled the story of a humble every-man who got busted with a joint. Dana found it hilarious that California cops might consider a book about Buddhism to be part of a terrorist plot. She asked, "So, why do you think your name is on the list?"

8 - The Yogi

Dana and I passed through a gate designed to keep cows away from the herb garden. We removed our shoes then entered a studio where we encountered a man sitting alone reading a book, his beard as if he never shaved, his robes colored orange, his posture perfect. Dana introduced me to Swami Raj. The yogi said, "Namaste."

A woman appeared, her robes colored white, her smile endearing. Dana introduced me to Lilavati, Raj's wife. She also said, "Namaste."

Other students arrived and sat on mats. Soon we were all chanting *OM*.

My introduction to yoga was awkward, but I was happy that Swami Raj knew his stuff. After just one class I knew he could help me strengthen both my body and my mind. Raj was a real yogi, a guru, a man of wisdom, and whenever one finds oneself in India with a guru, I figured, one should search for enlightenment, because why not?

Lilavati and Swami Raj invited Dana and me for tea after class, and of course we accepted. As Lilavati put water to boil, Raj explained how yoga's benefits were many. In addition to the stretching postures called asanas, there were breathing exercises called pranayamas, with meditation practice too. Raj offered me the same deal he made for Dana: one American dollar per class if I promised to practice every morning. I accepted.

My new guru asked me about my dietary habits. He asked me if I drank or smoked. He asked me if I had a girlfriend, if I played sports, if I believed in God.

I asked him back about the swastika painted on his wall. I had seen the *OM* symbol repeatedly since my arrival in India, but I was surprised to see anything that reminded me of Nazis. Raj explained that the symbol was ancient and auspicious, meaning, "Let goodness prevail." Dana added that Hitler was a master of propaganda.

Regarding *OM*, Raj explained, "This symbol represents the primordial vibration. This is the essence of the eternal way. This is our mantra."

I had never spoken to a real yogi before, only California girls who taught yoga, not the same, so I was unsure how to respond. Fortunately Raj seemed to rejoice in sharing so I went with the first question that came to mind. "I'm not sure how to ask this," I began, "but um, what's the deal with the cows? I mean, why are they holy? With so many hungry people in India, I would think that, well, that some of them would become beef?"

The yogi answered, "The cow is the vehicle of Lord Shiva. The cow is the holy mother. The cow provides milk during famine, and dung for fire to cook and to repel mosquitoes. The cow helps to plow the fields... Lord Krishna taught us to love and protect the cow."

"Ah," I said. "OK. Thanks."

Lilavati said, "Now it's my turn to ask a question... Since you two are both American people, you can help me to understand one thing. I mean, America has great universities and freedom of speech, and every American person I have met has been a kind person, so how on Earth could you re-elect a president who lied to start a war? I do not understand. Why not vote for the other guy?" She looked at me.

I answered, "Yeah, good question... Um, I hate to admit this, but at first I supported the invasion of Iraq. You know, the evil dictator had weapons of mass destruction. But now I don't know. The media doesn't teach facts, it sells debate, so... I know I'm supposed to vote, I know, but I didn't vote."

Dana said to her friend, "Did I ever tell you that I used to work for a television news program? Not for long, but I did get to see how the game is played. My boss was hired to keep the advertisers happy, and his boss only cared about money. Our 'news' reports were designed to manufacture approval for the president and for his war, because this was profitable, and this worked. We manufactured approval. Propaganda works."

"Yeah," I added. "In other words, we the American people are gullible."

Lilavati nodded her head to show understanding. "Corruption," she said. "I should have known. We have that here too."

Raj said, "Children of families who have television, I notice they get fat. It must be that the television promotes the junk food.

Yes?" The yogi never watched television, ever. He knew little of the outside world, but he was refreshingly free from corporate influence.

We moved on to talk about cows. Lilavati loved cows, but not so much when they munched on her herb garden.

I went for a walk in the cool mountain air, delighted by all the welcoming people I met. I discovered a vegetable market, temples of several faiths, and a backpacker district with restaurants, bars, and Internet cafés. Over a cappuccino, I read an email from Pedro lamenting the confiscation of his joint. I reminded him to ask his hacker friend to look into my red flag. Then I had lunch with a wanna-be monk from Canada.

Every morning after yoga I went for a walk, sometimes up a mountain, or into the forest, or into a coffee shop with fellow backpackers. There was a busy commercial district down the hill, but where I hung out things were shanti, the opposite of stressful.

I picked some wild ganja flowers and put them under my bed to dry. This way I could smoke the odd joint and watch trees grow in the forest; I also watched monkeys play which was more interesting. Sometimes I let my mind wander to exotic places far away. I could go to Africa if I wanted, or Rio de Janeiro, or Syria. I wondered if I would stay alive long enough to see these places, and I wondered if I would fall in love.

Thinking about religion made me think about Mom because she taught me to have faith, or else the Devil would corrupt my mind. I did my time in church quietly to avoid her morality lectures, and I did not pray, but I secretly wondered if maybe she was right, if ignorance was bliss, if science was irrelevant. I did not know, but a big part of my dream to travel the world was to investigate such matters for myself. I was searching for a deeper understanding, to know the truth, because I wasn't sure.

The next time I was alone with Swami Raj, I asked his opinion. "Do not worry about enlightenment," he answered. "Too difficult. Most important is to know yourself. With this you control your body and your mind. With this you control your thoughts. If you know yourself, you know joy and bliss!"

The cosmos had spoken; aside from adventure and truth and love, the thing that I sought was myself.

9 - The Spiritual Quest

Dan and Dana's mountain lair was a magical place where monks, backpackers, and ordinary Indians competed for my attention. Hindu mystics with their tridents and dreadlocked hair were cultural curiosities *extraordinaire*. I loved walking to waterfalls, and I rented a Royal Enfield motorcycle to explore the hills beyond. I also read books about yoga and Buddhism.

Upon finishing one such volume, I found Dan sipping masala coffee in the sun room. "Great book," I said. "To know yourself is to know joy and bliss."

"Yup," he answered, putting his newspaper aside.

A former anthropology professor, Dan was a great teacher. He did not practice yoga because as he put it, "I just don't bend that way," but he knew a lot about the philosophy. He said, "To know yourself you must know your thoughts, and to consistently achieve joy and bliss, you must be able to choose which thoughts to think or not think."

I replied, "That's easier said than done."

He said, "Correct, therefore practice. That's where meditation comes in. When people desire something they cannot have, say a new television or a high-paying job, then they'll suffer for the lack of it. We cannot take every sexy woman we desire to bed, but we can dominate our inner voices."

This made me think about Maia, my ex-girlfriend, and that made me feel sad. I was better off thinking about the cute girls in yoga class. I queried Dan, "Are you saying the secret to happiness is low expectations?"

He laughed, "Yup." Then he explained Buddhism's four noble truths: the reality of suffering, the fact that suffering arises from unfulfilled desires, the possibility of the cessation of suffering, and a path to achieve the requisite thought control with practice.

He explained, "Sit in a quiet place and try to not think. Focus on your breathing. When a thought comes, put it aside. With time you'll train yourself to go longer with a clear mind. Not only is this relaxing, but you'll arrive at a state of consciousness where you can dismiss negative thoughts. Select positive thoughts, as these lead to positive speech and positive actions, creating positive karma. Buddhist philosophy is consistent with science by the way. There is no deity. The mind is the creator. Control your mind."

I said, "Conscious self-control seems like a good idea. But Buddhism is a religion, right? Reincarnation? Prayer? So what do you mean, consistent with science?"

Dan said, "Reincarnation and prayer *are* religious beliefs, but I'm talking about Buddhism's core philosophy, which *is* consistent with science. The idea of somehow surviving death does not follow from the teachings of the Buddha but from the cultural influences of Hinduism. The Buddha, the sage Siddharta Gautama, he taught us that our perceived human reality is an illusion, so therefore reincarnation must also be a fabrication of the mind. If there is no ultimate self, then what is there to be reincarnated? This point is widely misunderstood."

I grew up with stories about God being the son of a virgin so I respected Dan's scientific worldview. I said, "Interesting. What about being reborn as an animal?"

"That's another Hindu thing. I can imagine a feudal lord telling his minions, 'Accept your status and be happy, and if you are a good person like me, then you can be rich like me in your next life, but if you're bad, then you'll come back as a snake or a dog.'"

"After I die I want to come back as a ten-eyed flying monster on another planet."

"Nice one. Do a good deed and become the species you deserve. But seriously, this fear of being reborn poorly seems to keep people from behaving poorly, so maybe the idea of reincarnation does more good than harm."

Our prolonged eye contact confirmed that our newly formed friendship was strong.

I said, "Define karma."

Dan answered, "Cause and effect. For example, if you endure an eighteen-hour bus ride, you'll improve your karma if you become a more patient person, because this will help you to promote happiness in others. It's all about human interactions. People with bad karma piss other people off, and this usually comes back to haunt them, or maybe they get reborn as pigs; I don't really know."

"Nice one. And who is the Dalai Lama exactly? The Buddha

reincarnated?"

"No, he's just a monk."

"What?"

"Yup, a monk, but a special monk. Some people believe he's the Bodhisattva of Compassion, and as far as I can tell this does nobody any harm. Bodhisattvas are enlightened beings who postpone their own nirvana to serve humanity. That's why people refer to the Dalai Lama as 'His Holiness' but the man's claim to fame is mainly that he's the leader of the Tibetan government-in-exile. I've met him. He's a really nice guy. It's possible for you to meet him too, but he's out of town now. He travels a lot."

"Cool. Good to know."

"By the way, Hindus dress up their ideas with Gods and Goddesses in order to explain them to Joe Public, but their core philosophy is similar to Buddhism. For example, Hindus believe that cosmic energy is manifest by Lord Brahman, the deity whose essence is the Universe. Hindus also have a Goddess Maia who has the power to create the brain's illusion of reality."

I coughed. "Maia?"

"Yeah Maia, the Goddess of Magic. Kali is the Goddess of Time and Change."

I smiled with the realization that my former girlfriend existed merely as a fabrication of my own mind.

Dan and Dana both loved to ponder the grand philosophical questions of life and everything. Indeed, most Westerners I met in Dharamsala seemed to be on a similar trip, a quest for spiritual knowledge, a phrase Dan called an oxymoron because the implied spirits could not be known. He told me that if my intellectual quest was to know myself, then I should focus on understanding humans, not spirits. "What is our intrinsic nature?" he asked me. "And what is culture?"

Dana added, "And what is that mysterious thing called love?"

The cosmos spoke to me again. Aside from adventure and truth and love and myself, I also sought an understanding of absolutely everything. I wished that I paid more attention in school, but better late than never. My inner curiosity was never more awake.

10 - The Goddess of Magic

Swami Raj and Lilavati often invited Dana and me for tea after yoga, and I looked forward to these encounters. My growing collection of random backpacker friends were fun to hang out with, but they were not gurus. Raj was a strict vegan, avoiding even onions and garlic, he said, "because these inspire carnal desires." He never smoked or drank alcohol, and he was poor financially, but he was happy. Despite the fact that we had so little in common, he and I got along great. I was inquisitive, and he devoted his life to teaching the ancient wisdom.

Swami-ji's shrine was devoted to Lord Ganesha, the God with an elephant's head, a broken tusk, and a pet rat, *vehicles* invented in antiquity to provide meaning to life's myriad mysteries.

When I asked my guru to explain the half-human hybrid, he stroked his beard. "Lord Ganesha is the God of Wisdom," he said, "and the remover of obstacles. He is the son of Lord Shiva with his consort Parvati... One day, when Ganesha was a boy and still human shaped, Parvati ordered him to guard her private bath, but Shiva wanted to enter this bath, and Ganesha refused him, so Shiva, he removed the boy's head. When Parvati saw this, she became angry. She made Shiva find a new head for the boy, and the elephant was the first animal he encountered. This is how Lord Ganesha acquired an elephant's head."

"Do you believe this really happened?"

"I am not certain. There are other histories to explain Ganesha's head but this one I like the best. This history is from several thousands of years ago, so it is hard to know what really happened."

"Interesting," I said. "And why does Ganesha always appear with a rat?"

"Ah. Ganesha is the remover of obstacles and rats can chew through obstacles, so it is for this reason that the rat is Ganesha's vehicle. Whenever Ganesha appears in a shrine, there are always reminders of his history and purpose."

"What about his broken tusk?"

"Lord Ganesha is also the God of Learning, and he needed a pen for writing the Mahabharata. In his enthusiasm, he broke his tusk and used it to write." My guru stopped for eye contact. "I follow Lord Ganesha because I desire wisdom and knowledge," he said. "I desire to remove obstacles for myself and for others. This is why I have my shrine, to remind myself of these virtues always."

"Swami-ji," I said. "Thank you. You inspire me. I will buy a statue of Lord Ganesha to remind myself of these virtues also."

"Good. Everyone desires to know God and the meaning of life, but most important is to know yourself."

"Thank you. Can you tell me also about Ganesha's father, Lord Shiva?"

"Of course. Lord Shiva is the most auspicious God of Destruction! His consort is Parvati, the Goddess of Disintegration, of course, because disintegration is required for complete destruction."

"Interesting. I'll have to think about that. Meanwhile, what about Maia?"

"Ah Maia! She is the Goddess of Magic! It is through her magic that cosmic consciousness becomes individual consciousness."

"Do you mean the illusion of individual consciousness?"

"Yes. Because of Maia we all have the illusion of individual consciousness."

After a moment of silence, I had to ask, "Swami-ji, do you believe in reincarnation?"

"Yes."

"But if everything we imagine is Maia, isn't there a contradiction?"

"No. I believe the ground is solid, but it is Maia. I believe the sky is blue, but it is Maia. I believe in reincarnation, but it is Maia."

Mom told me that I should never debate religion or politics because this led to arguments, but Mom was argumentative; she proselytized. With Raj I knew I could disagree peacefully so I asked him, "But if there's no ultimate self, then what is there to be reincarnated? Shouldn't Maia's magic include reincarnation also? Isn't this concept therefore a fabrication of the mind?"

My guru answered, "You might be right, but I do not eat meat because it could be my father, peace be with him."

I knew this wasn't why Raj avoided meat. I knew he was trying to be funny so I laughed with him, then I asked him about Lord Vishnu. He asked me back about a thing he recently heard of called *the Internet*, so I took him to a cyber-café where he could see the technology with his own eyes. He was most intrigued. He asked me how it worked. I answered of course that it was just another manifestation of the mysterious magic of Maia.

11 - Untouchable Pie

Vijay was an excellent cook. He also cleaned the house and ran errands to earn his minuscule salary, half of which he sent home to his mother. At first he called me *Sir* even though we were the same age. When I insisted that he should use my birth name instead, he thanked me repeatedly for showing him so much respect. I never witnessed greater humility. My new friend said he loved America, the land of the free and Hollywood movies. He said he loved me too after I called him a harijan, a child of God.

Dana shocked me when she said that soon after she hired Vijay, some of her so-called friends refused to come over for dinner. They would not eat "untouchable" food. I knew such attitudes were common in India, but Dana's story still shocked me.

The newspapers frequently reported violence against people from "the backward classes." So-called "honor killings" were also common. I read that a Dravidian woman was killed because her shadow touched a Brahmin man; her shadow! This superstitious mayhem made me appreciate why the Sikhs founded their religion on rejecting the caste system, their premise being equality and tolerance.

One crisp autumn day, as Vijay and I walked home from the vegetable market, we stopped to watch workers harvesting apples, and this gave me an idea. I called my mother to get the recipe, then I taught Vijay how to make American pie.

While we worked my companion told me that he loved Dan and Dana, his bosses. When I said they were lucky to have him, he seemed so happy that I thought he might cry. He said, "My family is so poor that my parents' most prized possessions are their honor and their dignity. My family is so, so poor, well, let's just say that they do not know what it is like to have extra money, but every day they find moments of happiness. And thanks to my bosses trusting me to cook and clean for them, I can now ensure my family always has enough to eat! For this I will be forever grateful."

Just as our creation emerged from the oven, filling the house with the smell of pie, Dan and Dana arrived with their friend Rinpoche, a man whose name meant "reborn monk." Rinpoche resembled the chubby Buddha of the tourist statues, so I was not surprised when he said, "I am too fat to eat pie, but this looks too good! Mmm. Thank you!"

We all sat down to eat except Vijay who set the table then cleaned the kitchen. We all ate a delicious pie, a pie that many Hindus would refuse to eat because Vijay touched it.

Dan said, "This is the power of not-science. Apple pies should only be untouchable if they're friggin' dirty, covered in cow-shit dust or something like that."

Rinpoche laughed, then he invited me, along with Dan and Dana, to visit his monastery in "Indian Tibet." I envisioned peaceful monks in a mountain hideaway, one with nature and pure of spirit. I accepted his offer excitedly.

Rinpoche did not invite Vijay because of limited passenger space in his vehicle, but Vijay was delighted to stay home alone, happy that his bosses trusted him so much. I marveled at the fact that Vijay was the most outwardly happy person I ever met, and also the person with the least amount of stuff. Vijay had low expectations. All he wanted was to help his family eat every day, nothing more, and he achieved this, so he was never disappointed. Vijay taught me that when it comes to happiness, attitude is everything.

12 - Indian Tibet

Magnificent mountains provided a picturesque background to the Tibetan capital-in-exile. The landscape was green with many waterfalls, but as Dan, Dana, Rinpoche and I drove up and away, the colors changed to rocky shades of brown. We stopped at every Buddhist stupa along the narrow track to stretch our legs and watch prayer flags fluttering in the wind. In several places we saw grim reminders of vehicles that didn't survive the journey, resting like skeletons below. I was happy that Rinpoche had a sturdy jeep, but I was even happier that he was a slow and prudent driver.

At the top of one mountain pass, with grand vistas of snow-capped peaks, we encountered a military checkpoint. While we waited for soldiers to scrutinize our documents, ethnic Tibetan women peddled handicrafts to the few tourists who made it so far from the beaten track. I bought a miniature statue of Ganesha from a woman with no teeth, then my friends and I sampled yak-butter tea from the restaurant across the street.

Arriving into a village along with the last light of day, Rinpoche drove straight to his favorite guest house, a place with no shower and dusty blankets. He said, "When one lives in a cold, dusty, and windy place, one learns to live with cold, dust, and wind."

Our guest house provided buckets with hot water so we washed up, then we dined on yak meat and barley soup. I previously thought all Buddhists were vegetarians, especially monks, but Rinpoche devoured his yak. "Up here," he explained, "there are few options. People grow barley and herd yaks, so that's what we eat."

The next day we pushed onward and upward, eventually arriving at Rinpoche's monastery, located majestically above a remote valley. The resident monks could see us long before we could see them, so they greeted our arrival.

Rinpoche escorted Dan, Dana and me to a guest suite, then he left saying he'd be right back. Meanwhile a boy monk served three cups of tea, then left. My friends and I shared a moment of silence as we looked out our window to see the commanding view. Then Rinpoche returned with an elder monk, but before he could make an introduction, Dan leaped to his feet. "Tenzig," he said. "Nice to see you! Namaste!"

Tenzig bowed. "Dan and Dana," he said. "Nice to see you!"

He looked at me. "And you must be Raymond. Hello!"

I bowed then said, "Namaste."

The monk shook my hand, then said, "Listen everybody. This is fascinating. Rinpoche lost weight!" He asked his friend, "The nuns in Dharamsala stopped feeding you good?"

Rinpoche answered, "I'm on a diet for health reasons, but the truth is, I like my fat. It keeps me warm. Raymond however, is too skinny." He looked at me. "You must be cold! The nuns here make excellent momos. Do you want some momos? Fatten you up..."

I said, "Actually, I'd love some sea bass please. Or cod. Any ocean fish. Thanks."

Rinpoche laughed. "How about some momos? The nuns here make the world's best momos. Seriously, let's go eat."

Jovial nuns served us steamed dumplings filled with cabbage and spice. They did not speak English so I non-verbally conveyed gratitude. They non-verbally insisted that I eat more. The momos were yummy so I ate heaps.

My Tibetan hosts never complained, except when the topic turned to the plight of their cousins across the border in China. Tenzig went off on an rant, the only time I ever saw a monk get angry. He wanted all Tibetans to have cultural autonomy from Beijing so that they could live traditional lives, free from militarized intimidation. He told me about the Dalai Lama's efforts to get the Communist Party to negotiate. Then Dan told me it was illegal in China to have a photo of the Dalai Lama. If the government mentioned him at all, he said, it was to call him a traitor or a terrorist. Rinpoche then asserted that the Dalai Lama worked hard to promote happiness in others, creating a virtuous cycle called karma.

After dinner, Dan asked me if I wanted to go sample the local drink. I asked him back, "Don't the monks have a vow against alcohol?"

"Yup. But I know for a fact that not all monks keep all of their vows all of the time, and there are different levels of vows, so let's go get some chung!"

"Let's go," I said. "What's chung?"

We descended to the monastery's kitchen past paintings of fire demons, the mythical guardians of the Buddhist dharma. Dan said something to a monk in Tibetan, something like, "Hey. How's everything? Great. Say, do you guys have any chung?"

The answer was negative so we proceeded outside to the Himalayan night, walking by the light from more stars than I previously imagined possible. Dan said, "Coming here helps me understand that I am just a spec in the infinite cosmos. It helps me to humbly accept the prospect of my inevitable demise."

Just then a shooting star streaked by, leaving us both speechless because words could not match the majesty of the moment.

We walked into the village where Dan knocked on the door of a house that seemed random at first, until an old man answered who remembered Dan from a previous visit. My friend explained that we wanted some chung (I recognized the word chung), so the man beckoned us inside to a musty smell of yak. We followed him up a ladder into a room with one woman and three children illuminated by a kerosene lamp and a wooden fire. Conspicuously absent was television. Dan made conversation while the woman strained two liters of white intoxicant into a plastic soda bottle. Then, with our transaction completed, we hurried back to our room. We drank chung. It did not taste good, and I did not care.

My new friend was twice my age with heaps of international experience, so I encouraged him to give me practical advice about specific scams and how to defeat them. He advised me never to advertise that I was American given the bad war karma. "I used to see myself as an ambassador of good will for our homeland," he said, "but now I care more about keeping my costs down, and not getting kidnapped. You can always say you're Canadian. Only borders, banks, and hotels will ever ask to see your passport."

Later I dressed warmly to sit outside, admire the Milky Way, and put my journey into perspective. I had many ideas (such as exploring China and South America) but no plans. As I drank the last of the chung, I never felt a greater thirst for adventure. Nothing from California mattered to me any longer, and I did not know what day of the week it was, and squat toilets without hygienic paper seemed normal. This was a great start to any world tour, I figured, but I knew that whatever I was looking for, it lay ahead of me, down the road.

That night I had a dream, a high-altitude hallucination, and in my dream people were judged not by the country of their passport, nor by the pedigree of their caste, but by the content of their character. In my dream I was a ten-eyed fire demon on another planet, but a kind and gentle fire demon on a mission to protect Buddhist yaks. When Dan's snoring woke me up, my magical illusion disappeared, so I looked around and thought, "Where am I?" Then I fell back to sleep with a smile.

13 - Too Safe

Rinpoche's monastery was a fascinating place to hang out, and the price was free but it wasn't really free because we felt obliged to make a donation. Dan, Dana and I slept in a guest suite near the monks' dormitory, an annex built from concrete like a cheap hotel but colorfully painted in meticulous detail. For me the highlight was a room filled with statues that escaped the Chinese takeover of Tibet during the 1950s. I loved how the vivid colors of the precious artwork contrasted with the brown and gray of the top of the world.

My friends and I tramped to a cave where Dan once resided during a three-month meditation retreat. He said it was therapeutic to live without modern amenities, with ample time to think. Dan's cave was located in a valley with no visible green, but it was not as stone-aged as I imagined; it had a door, a window, two chairs and a table. Dan explained how he met daily with a senior monk named Lama to discuss his experiences and to eat.

Dan wanted to visit Lama, so we tramped to the man's village several kilometers away. We found him sitting with male friends while women worked outside harvesting barley. After an emotional reception, Lama sent his youngest friend to fetch a woman to make tea.

As Dan and Lama laughed about the past, Dana and I talked about yoga while two other men lay together on a bed, holding hands and caressing each other. I couldn't understand a word they said, but I thought, "These guys are gay."

As we walked back to the monastery, I asked Dan what he thought. He said, "They're not gay, or maybe they are gay, I don't know and I don't care, but their behavior, men caressing each other, that's common here. It's a cultural thing."

I said, "They sure looked gay to me. Not that there's anything wrong with that."

Dan replied, "Yup."

Then I asked Dana, "And what's up with the women doing all the work?"

She answered, "This is one area where the world still looks up to America. Our women can vote. They earn nearly equal pay.

They can have an abortion. They can wear whatever clothes they like. They can file for divorce... Most American women take this stuff for granted, but over here..."

Dan added, "Our life is comfortable, nobody hassles us, but as foreigners we don't have the right to speak out. India does not have the same law and order that you're used to. We live on a delicate edge between order and chaos. All we have to do is piss off the wrong person and..."

Dana interrupted, "But we love it. Too much order takes the spontaneity out of life."

Arriving back at our room, we took hot showers, but this required burning precious firewood so we took short, hot showers. As I bathed I realized that despite Indian chaos lowering my life expectancy, I felt safe. Plus I was hanging out with monks in a Tibetan monastery. Awesome.

I asked Rinpoche, "Your name implies that you have been reincarnated, yes? So does that mean your soul is the same as a human being who lived before?"

The fat man answered, "What is a soul? If you're asking, have I been reborn? I say yes. But if you ask, do I have the same soul? There is not a simple answer to this question."

Dan offered, "Your soul is that piece of cosmic energy that keeps you alive."

Rinpoche said, "That's a fair definition, Dan. And then there's karma. The idea of reincarnation encourages us to make good causes for good effects. It helps us to understand that everything is interrelated. Even the human spirit is made of the same energy as the rest of the Universe. It will be carried forward forever."

I saw no reason to convert to Buddhism because there was no Hell for the unbaptized, but I liked the embedded wisdom. After many conversations about the philosophy, I realized the important thing was not to memorize a set of beliefs as a child, but instead to create positive karma through conscious self-control and mindful living. No religion was required.

Rinpoche drove us to the village where he was born. As we arrived, dusty locals gathered to meet their native son. A ceremony ensued whereby Rinpoche sat on a carpet under an umbrella next to a stupa, then villagers lined up to offer him silk scarves.

Rinpoche touched each person's forehead and uttered a chant.

Soon thereafter, women prepared a meal for us in a nearby cave, complete with candles, incense, and yak-butter tea. We discussed world affairs until a monk interrupted to announce that the season's first winter storm was on its way quickly. This was a serious concern because it implied that our road home might become impassable until spring, so we departed back towards Dharamsala that same day.

In Indian Tibet, I saw no computers or mobile phones. The children seemed to have more fun playing with old bicycle wheels than kids at home with expensive video games. The Tibetan children also bonded noticeably more with their elders. This was a simple culture, a pure culture, a land uncontaminated by excessive stuff and all the stress that goes with it. This was a place where I wanted to spend a lot more time, so I was disappointed that our excursion got cut short, but delighted by the awesomeness. The drive home was long and uncomfortable in the bad weather, but I was happy that at least I improved my karma as I slowly transformed myself into a more patient person.

Back home, back in my invigorating yoga routine, something was missing, a girlfriend yes, but I craved adventure, so I rented a motorcycle. One day, despite the fuel gauge showing fuel, the bike ran out of gas. I hitch-hiked to where I could buy a liter of petrol then I hitch-hiked back, but by then it was dark and my headlights didn't work. Feeling bold I rode home anyway. I followed a truck to protect myself from the obstacles ahead, and this worked. I was not an experienced motorcycle guy so I drove on full alert as I engaged the night. This was dodgy but I loved it, the adventure, India. Back home, back in my comfortable room, I suddenly felt too safe, and so I knew that it was time to leave Dharamsala.

14 - Angeline

A saddhu approached me. He carried a walking staff, his hair was knotted into dreadlocks, and he wore many necklaces. I was generally suspicious of strangers bearing gifts, but when this guy reached into his satchel, produced a flower, and offered it to me, I accepted.

The man bowed with his palms together. "Namaste," he said. "My name is Hari."

I returned the gesture. "Raymond."

He asked me where I was from and I replied honestly.

He said, "California? Then you rich. Please give me baksheesh?"

"I'll think about that," I said, still contemplating my rose.

Hari told me that he walked to Dharamsala from Rishikesh, which if true would have taken him months. He said he was about to attend a special saddhu gathering. "You are invited," he said. "All welcome."

"Thank you," I replied. "And what does one do at a saddhu gathering?"

"We make puja. We talk philosophy. We smoke charas." He whispered, "If you want charas, I have. You want to buy charas?"

Dan told me about pseudo saddhus, also known as bogus babas, con men dressed in orange robes. I also knew about charas, the local word for hashish. I did not trust Hari so I walked away, impressed by the large number of people staring at me. At first the Indian stare made me nervous but Indians stared at each other too, a lot, leading me to conclude that the idea of personal privacy must disappear wherever there are a billion people. At that moment however, there seemed to be more staring than usual. It must have been the flower.

Back home I asked Dan about the saddhu gathering. He said, "It's big. I mean, it's not just saddhus running around naked; there's a Durga puja too, um, a festival including a parade for the Goddess Durga. But I'm not going. I've seen enough naked saddhus in my life already. But you should go. The festival is actually pretty cool."

I searched for Durga on the Internet. She was the Warrior

Goddess who could vanquish great demons. Riding a ferocious lion, her cosmic energy was lethal when directed against the forces of evil. She was the Goddess one wanted on one's side when times got tough. Thus the puja (prayer session) was a celebration of the triumph of good over evil, and the goal for devout practitioners was to tap into Durga's energy to eradicate the evil tendencies of their own minds.

Lilavati announced during yoga class that she and Raj were planning a puja ceremony of their own, and we were all invited. After that Lilavati planned to hire a minivan to drive to the village hosting the Durga festival, about thirty kilometers away. She said, "A few students from the afternoon class want to go too, so if we share the cost, the van will be inexpensive and convenient."

I said, "Sign me up."

My yoga buddy Dana said, "Me too."

On the day of the puja, Dana and I walked into the ashram as usual, but on this day the sweet smell of incense permeated the air. Raj was not sitting still as usual, but instead he was preparing an altar for a ceremonial fire. Meanwhile Lilavati attended to the many guests, including two women from Israel, another from Holland, Pierre and Angeline, plus an American guy named Ed.

I first met Angeline two days prior while sipping tea with Raj. My guru and I were discussing life on other planets when she arrived to discuss something else. I watched her approach, admiring her practical fashion and sturdy walking shoes. As she bent over to remove those shoes, I noticed a Yin-Yang tattoo on her lower back that accentuated her feminine curves. When she said, "Hello," I blushed.

"Where are you from in France?" I asked.

"I was born in Paris," she answered, "but I live in Cern. How did you know I am French?"

I didn't know. I guessed. I figured that if I was wrong, she would have said something else and either way, we had the beginning of a conversation. I answered, "Your accent." Her accent was delicious.

"Ah yes," she said. "Where are you from?"

I answered, "California."

Her eyes said, "American huh? Oh. Too bad for you." This was easy to understand; America's president started a war with dubious objectives based on false pretenses, capitalist imperialism gone berserk. She said, "I wouldn't have guessed that."

I knew Angeline had a private appointment with Raj, so I finished my tea then made my exit, but this encounter was just long enough for me to become hypnotized. When I saw her again at the puja she gave me a warm greeting, her eyes captivating, her smile intoxicating.

I introduced her to "my friend Dana." She introduced me to Pierre.

Raj lit his fire while a Hindu priest muttered chants, then we all threw ceremonial fruit and rice into the fire as an offering to Durga, to tap into her great energy and to eradicate the evil tendencies of our own minds, or so we hoped.

When the ceremony was over, Lilavati drove us to the village hosting the festival. For the ride home, we all agreed to meet back at the van by seven pm sharp.

Together we watched the parade, perused exhibits, bought trinkets, and laughed at all the crazy people we saw. We also enjoyed a spirited conversation about pujas and politics. The festival was fascinating not just for the parade but also for the tribal groups in attendance, the women in their best saris, the police in their smart uniforms, plus the usual riffraff.

I saw Hari sitting inside a large tent with other saddhus. None were naked. Hari saw me too then he waved, inviting me and my group to join him. At this moment Hari seemed like a peaceful man of philosophy, not a hustler, so I encouraged my colleagues to check out the scene. We all entered the tent and greeted the various swamis and babas, but when it came time to have a smoke, only Ed and I stayed. Of course I wanted to spend more time with Angeline but she was with Pierre after all, so I was compelled to sit with the saddhus, an easy choice because these holy men radiated a uniquely charming positivity.

Hari prepared a chillum, a pipe for smoking hashish mixed with tobacco. I hadn't had a puff of tobacco since eighth grade because I didn't like the buzz, but given the circumstances I gave it a go. Hari passed me the chillum and I took a hit, then Ed took a hit, then he passed the pipe to a saddhu named Sage who shouted,

"Boom Balinath!" Sage took a hit. Meanwhile I quietly dealt with my quickly changing head space.

Ed and I bought some charas from Hari thanks to his charismatic sales pitch. The convivial baba expressed gratitude as he exchanged our cash for his hash. I divided my chunk in two, half to smoke immediately and half to try later without tobacco. I wrapped the sticky blob in a scrap of paper which I put into my pocket.

Just then an Indian man I recognized from Dan and Dana's neighborhood arrived with a tribe of Westerners. They sat in our vicinity. We greeted each other warmly (the man's name was Guto). Together we sometimes smoked, sometimes laughed, and sometimes quietly contemplated our exotic surroundings.

After a spell, Ed noticed it was time for us to head back to the rent-a-van. Guto offered us a ride home with him, and I was in the mood to stay, so Ed took off alone. He promised to tell Lilavati and Dana not to worry, then he disappeared into the festival crowds.

Hari prepared a chillum. He said that when I die, I will lose everything but my karma so therefore I should not worry about money. He said my good deeds were my only wealth. Then he claimed he could perform miracles. "For example," he said, "I can transform you from a sexard and a drunkard into a saintly person."

I called him on that. I admitted that I liked beer but I was not a drunkard. Then I looked up and saw Angeline enter the tent. Our eyes met. She waved at me and smiled. She walked towards me and sat down. "Hello," I said, delighted.

The French beauty said hello, then she surveyed her surroundings: stoned saddhus sharing their spirituality with Western backpackers and with God. She smiled into my eyes, then she asked, "Where's Ed?"

I explained.

Angeline told me that she got "lost from Pierre" and then couldn't find the van. It was hard to concentrate with so much charas on the brain, so I smiled while considering a clever reply. Hari saved me. "Please my lady," he said. "Please join us for pipe of peace."

Angeline declined the smoke at first, but I talked her into it. I told her, "We're all stoned so you'll be in good company, and besides, smoking with these guys is a fascinating cultural experience, and don't worry, we have another ride home."

I introduced her to Guto.

Angeline took a hit from Hari's chillum, then she said as if there had been no delay since my previous comment, "Well then, I won't worry."

I looked into her eyes long enough to see them smiling back.

Hari interrupted, "You two boyfriend girlfriend?"

Angeline answered, "No." Then she said to me, "I'm actually leaving for Goa tomorrow, um, with Pierre. I only have six weeks left in my holiday, and I need to get all the way to Bangalore for my flight home."

I tried to hide my disappointment. "I'm going to Goa too," I said, "but not tomorrow. Well anyway, if you have to go you have to go. That's life. Así es la vida."

Angeline seemed happy to change the subject. "You speak Spanish?"

"I'm not fluent," I replied, "but some of my best friends are from Mexico."

Hari interrupted to indicate that it was my turn to hit the chillum, and as I inhaled I wondered, what was the deal with Pierre?

Angeline steered our dialog towards the pros and cons of English as the universal language. I steered it back towards my new favorite subject, her. I learned that my alluring associate once worked in London as a waitress with a goal to improve her English, then she studied physics at the University of Paris. She and her father both worked at the Large Hadron Collider in Cern, a world-class science lab.

"I have no idea about Hadron Colliders," I said, "but that does sound impressive. I'll ask you about it the day after tomorrow, when I'm not so stoned."

"But I'm leaving for Goa tomorrow," she said.

I was at a loss for words. Blame it on the charas. My brain wandered until I remembered the moment we met. "I like your Yin-Yang tattoo," I said. "It suits you. Sorry, but I couldn't help notice it the other day."

She feigned displeasure. "You mean you were checking me out?"

"Well yes," I said. "Every man on the planet who's not blind or gay checks you out."

She blushed, "I'm glad you like my tattoo."

"I do, and I plan to ask you all about it, and its connection with Hadron Colliders, the day after tomorrow."

Angeline's smile betrayed that I scored a point, but there was a conversational dead end. My brain froze. I watched Hari clean his chillum. Finally Angeline asked me, "Do you think people are worried about me? I mean, I didn't show up for our ride home at seven."

I thought, "Yes. Pierre is worried." But I said, "Ed knows that I have a ride home, and he knows that you know this place here, so there's that. Furthermore, you are obviously capable of taking care of yourself. It's easy to get a ride to McCloud Ganj from here."

"True," she said. "But I'm not sure Pierre thinks I can take care of myself. Maybe people are looking for me."

"If people were looking for you, they'd look right here."

"That's true. Do you know what time it is?"

I turned on my digital camera. "Yeah," I said. "It's almost eight."

I took her picture.

Hari asked to see the result so I showed him, then he showed another saddhu. They had never seen a digital camera before so I let them take pictures of each other. A few of the shots turned out great, and this caused my beautiful new friend to smile with delight. This helped me relax with her, and thus our conversation flowed like smoke from a chillum. We sat together talking and laughing until Guto asked if we still wanted a ride home.

With that, along with four other stoned Westerners, we followed Guto through the festival crowds to his van. Angeline and I sat together and our energy was great, but I grew nervous because I didn't know where she stood with Pierre, she was leaving the next day, and we had zero privacy.

When I asked about Swami Raj, her eyes lit up. "Raj is great," she said. "He's a devoted yogi, and he loves people. I practice with him every day. Why do I never see you in class?"

"I go to the morning class every day," I answered.

"Oh. You should go to the afternoon class too."

"But I'm leaving for Goa the day after tomorrow."

"With Dana?"

I laughed. "No! Dana's married. She and her husband are friends of my friend Pedro back home. He's an anthropologist."

"Oh. So you are travelling alone?"

"Yes."

"And you are going to Goa?"

"The day after tomorrow."

Angeline studied my face. Meanwhile other backpackers filled the conversational void. My companion seemed tantalizingly available so I looked for any opportunity to confirm a new travel plan, but the other backpackers were chatty.

Angeline asked Guto to please drop us off near the yoga ashram, to check in with Lilavati in case she was worried. Guto obliged, and so Angeline and I stepped out to the street together, but we were alone for only one moment before Swami Raj saw us and waved.

He walked towards us quickly. "I am so glad to see you," he said. "Lilavati is searching for you with Pierre. They have police looking. They made announcement at festival. They checked hospital."

Angeline said, "Oh no. Really? Oh no! I am so sorry. Merde!"

The yogi invited us to drink tea while he called his wife from his old-fashioned telephone. He explained that Lilavati just bought a mobile phone, because she was a modern woman, because she had vast experience with Western tourists.

The three of us discussed yoga asanas until Lilavati and Pierre arrived, a moment I seized to immediately explain how the confusion was all my fault, that I convinced Angeline to have a smoke with Hari, then I explained about Guto.

Swami Raj looked at me disapprovingly, then Pierre said something to Angeline in French.

She seemed angry. Maybe she said, "Why don't you trust me? I am a big girl. I can take care of myself."

The awkward silence that followed indicated that it was time to depart, so Angeline, Pierre, and I left the ashram together. After another awkward silence, Pierre said to me, "Good night."

I kicked myself for having failed to confirm a plan with Angeline while I had the chance. I blamed that on the charas. Meanwhile I pondered a clever way to correct my mistake.

Angeline said to me, "Good night."

I said, "Cheers! I'm glad we got to hang out. Maybe I'll see you in Goa in a few days, at the chill-out beach furthest to the north."

We waved goodbye, then the couple turned to walk away. I kicked myself some more. I wanted to chase after this very special girl, but I did not know how to reset our situational dynamic. Then just before she turned a corner, she looked back to me and said, "Maybe I'll see you the day after tomorrow!"

15 - Messing with Fate

I awoke from my dream disoriented, forgetting where I was until I opened my eyes, then I remembered what happened the night before and the implications. I jumped out of bed on a mission to seduce a beautiful French girl and take her to Goa.

As Vijay made coffee, I announced my imminent departure.

Dan asked, "You're abandoning your home away from home for some girl you just met?"

"Yes."

"OK. I can see that."

I blew off morning yoga to prepare myself. Compared to other backpackers, my pack seemed bulky so I went with the motto, "When in doubt, leave it out." My hammock was heavy but I was going to the beach, so it stayed. My mp3 player and speakers were also bulky, but I loved music so they stayed too. I kept my Frisbee because it was a multi-purpose tool that I could use to collect water, or fan a fire, or capture spiders, or protect small things from sand on the beach, or play catch. I also kept Hari's charas; the risk seemed to be approximately zero I figured, because if there was any sign of trouble I could eat it. I gave Dan my extra shampoo because pharmacies in India carried shampoo, and I gave Vijay two shirts and a pair of shoes; they fit him perfectly and he was delighted.

I went to afternoon yoga class for the first time, a detail that Raj noted with delight. He said, "Welcome to afternoon yoga, Raymond-ji."

I greeted my guru, then my eyes found Angeline sitting quietly alone. Her eyes indicated that we should wait to talk until after class to avoid a show (she had expressive eyes) so I sat in the front near Raj. Other students arrived and soon we were all chanting *OM*.

After class, the instant we were alone, I said to my friend, "Let's go to Goa!"

She said, "Yes! Why not tonight?"

We walked straight to the bus station and purchased tickets as far as Delhi. Then we walked to Dan and Dana's house because I had to collect my backpack and say goodbye.

Vijay served American pie.

Dan said that our timing was perfect to go south because it was about to get cold. He then described his ongoing negotiations with his landlord about who should pay to install a wood-burning heater. With that we said goodbye.

Angeline and I visited Swami Raj and Lilavati briefly, to bid them peace and love.

Then we boarded our bus.

Backpackers from Japan, Israel, and Europe engaged in blissful banter. All were going to Goa, a yearly migration for Westerners at the change of seasons. Several had dreadlocked hair including the Japanese guy, which seemed odd. None emanated from a poor country, because travelling requires cash even where the exchange rate makes everything cheap; there's still that plane ticket to buy.

The Dutch guy, Bastiaan, had been to Goa before. As our bus barreled down the mountain road, he provided insights about party beaches, resort beaches, package-tour beaches, and hippie beaches. One beach had a flea market every Wednesday, and another had a rave every Saturday night.

When our bus stopped for dinner, Angeline and I sat alone. We looked over the menu, we decided to head to Bastiaan's favorite hippie beach, then we ordered curry. That's when my new best friend asked me why I travelled the world.

I told her about Tijuana, the place where I first fell in love with another culture. I was seven. "Mom hated it," I said. "To her Tijuana was unsafe and dirty, but I loved it! Mexico had mariachi bands, exotic food, and cool stuff for sale, plus it's always fun to practice my bad Spanish. Now I've been to Mexico several times, but I've never had enough money to travel the world until recently... My grandfather died, and he left money to my father, who... Pops bought himself a new house, a mansion really, then he gave our old house to me, and I sold it."

As I grinned happily, Angeline seemed shocked by my good fortune.

I added, "Yeah, Pops was furious." Then I imitated his most-stern voice. "'You need to work boy! I didn't give you that house to squander on some foolish adventure!' ... Yeah well, that's Pops.

Anyway, now that I'm finally on the road, my plan is to go with the flow, with you. You're the flow."

I quizzed Angeline about her, and she quizzed me back about me. I told her that I didn't study much in school except for Spanish. I told her that I worked as a carpenter, hung out with friends playing music, or playing soccer, or drinking beer, because I believed that the most fun won. I told her that selling my house bought me several years of freedom with which I could decide what to do with my life, but meanwhile I was still a newbie to the open road, and I had no idea whatsoever about the future.

As we savored our curries, I quizzed her about Hadron Colliders. Fascinating stuff. I understood little but I respected Angeline's fact-based worldview. I respected her big brain. She convinced me to start reading non-fiction.

Angeline confessed that she met Pierre on the plane to India, and this made it easier to ditch him at the festival. "Sometimes travellers can become close very quickly," she said, "but then comes the day when we all must go our separate ways."

As I contemplated the implications of this sentence, searching for a witty reply, Bastiaan sat with us, just to make sure we were satisfied with our curries, or so he said. We got to talking about Goa and then the world beyond. Bastiaan insisted that we call him Bas even though he had just introduced himself as Bastiaan, because we weren't friends at the time, and his friends call him Bas. He said jokingly that this was how he knew who his friends were.

By coincidence, he and I both had to pee at the same time, so we stood up together, agreeing to meet Angeline back on the bus. The happy hippie and I took care of business then we loitered outside to watch the scene.

As he lit a cigarette, two local men approached, one fat, one short. The fat man asked if he could borrow a lighter so Bas obliged, then we all engaged in small talk until the short guy flashed a policeman's badge saying, "Please come with us. We have reason to believe you are smuggling drugs."

I had Hari's charas in my shirt pocket.

I understood why cops might select Bastiaan to search given his hippie dreadlocks and his cool vibe, especially as most of the charas smuggled into Goa from Himachal Pradesh had to pass through this strategic location. Hoping my adversaries would focus on my new friend instead of me, I remained poised to eat my charas, but the short cop never diverted his eyes long enough for me to make a move.

The fat cop led us to a police outpost around the corner while the short cop brought up the rear. I considered my options; none were good.

We arrived into an interrogation room where Fatty told Bas to take off his clothes.

While the cop investigated my friend's pockets systematically, I tried to maintain outward calm as I brainstormed tactics. The man told me to get undressed so I took off my boots, then as I slowly stood up, I prepared myself to grab the charas while removing my shirt.

Just then another cop entered our room speaking in Hindi. His gibberish was unintelligible but Shorty was distracted so I grabbed the charas. The man turned and stared at me, so I froze. Meanwhile the third cop rambled on excitedly.

Shorty wagged his head and said, "We must leave now. Have a nice evening."

Just like that, I was free. "Have a nice evening." Ha. Awesome.

I showed Bas the charas as we made our exit, laughing all the way to the bus. He sat across the aisle from me snickering, "Have a nice evening!"

Angeline looked at me quizzically so I told her, "Fate is trying to tell me something. I just quit smoking charas." To be emphatic, I gave the blob to Bastiaan.

He said, "Thanks, but what if you meet a guru high on a mountaintop and he offers you a smoke? You're going to smoke, yes?"

"Yeah," I said. "I would. You got me. Maybe I didn't just quit, but I hereby pledge to never travel again with illegal contraband because... Don't mess with fate."

Angeline said, "You can never mess with fate because if you do, that's because fate wanted it that way. Twist your brain around that."

As my brain tweaked, our bus departed. Meanwhile Angeline asked me what happened to cause my delay, so I told her about the search. The happy hippie embellished the bit where he had to stand around in his underwear.

Angeline hit me for being stupid, the kind of smack only a girlfriend can deliver. Then Bas said, "In Holland, ganja is tolerated officially. We understand it is much like alcohol and tobacco, only less harmful. So why lock up the peaceful pot-heads? Maybe the lesson here is: legalize it."

I said, "Maybe the lesson is, never travel with illegal contraband."

Bas agreed, "Yeah man, don't mess with fate."

As our bus motored into the night, Angeline, Bas, and I swapped stories until the time came to sleep, poorly, mostly not-sleeping with our eyes closed, lost in thought. That's when I put my arm around my still-unofficial girlfriend, and we cuddled together for the first time.

16 - The Theory of Everything

Our bus screeched to a stop because of a traffic accident. From my window I watched a swarm of people investigating the scene, plus cows and vendors promoting chai and nibbles. The accident was shocking Indian chaos but it seemed far away and surreal, like watching a movie. As the bus resumed speed, I studied Angeline's eyes in hopes of gaining insight into her soul. I found beauty, intelligence and humor. Lucky me.

She asked me, "Do you believe in fate?"

I decided that instead of debating a philosophical topic, I should spin our dialog towards flirting. "Fate brought us together," I answered. "If I hadn't thought it interesting to hang out with Hari and the saddhus, we never would have hooked up."

"That's true," she said. "But do you think it was our destiny?"

"You and me together? Yup. It couldn't be otherwise. My good luck."

"Luck yes, but do you think humans have free will?"

I explained my naïve understanding of free will as an illusion created by the Goddess Maia, then I asked my new girlfriend what this had to do with her job. She explained how centuries of scientific experiments have demonstrated conclusively that the Universe always obeys forces that act precisely according to known physical laws (except for known variations that are the subject of much debate). Therefore, she asserted, the human brain must obey these same universal laws, and this was proof that we only have an illusion of choice, because everything is always caused by the dynamic interplay of natural forces in action.

She said, "Einstein was right. God does not play dice with the Universe. There are no supernatural powers over human existence. The physics is not random, it's chaotic, and that seems random, like rolling dice. Do you see? The biggest illusion of them all is time."

I told Angeline that it seemed like a good job, trying to deduce the order of the Universe. She agreed it was fun, and it paid enough to travel. She went on to explain how scientists were finally pulling together a robust theory of the mind.

I asked, "But if there's no free will, doesn't that take some of the fun out of life?"

She answered, "I have fun with the illusion. Anyway, true freedom would imply that the human spirit is supernatural, that the brain operates independently from the laws of physics. I believe we can prove otherwise."

"All right then," I said. "Prove it."

Angeline smiled. "OK. Life began billions of years ago, right?"

I interrupted her for sport, faking a serious expression. "No," I said. "God created Adam and Eve in the Garden of Eden, and that was only about seven-thousand years ago, plus or minus a few hundred."

Angeline looked incredulous until I added, "Just kidding." Then she laughed. Perfect.

I said, "I remember when my parents told me that Santa Claus was real, and I believed them until my little friends made fun of me. That's when I first realized my parents didn't know everything, and of course now that's obvious. My mother believes that when she dies, she's going to live again in Heaven. She believes in *the rapture*. But not me, so please continue."

"OK. Well, we can never be certain of the precise details because there is no fossil record, but one-hundred percent of the scientific evidence is consistent with the idea that life began as a simple molecule that could copy itself (by bonding with its chemical opposite) and then split in two. These copies could then make more copies and so on. Eventually these molecules had to compete for food, and thus began the struggle for survival. Nature invented the cell because the cell survives, but this took billions of years, and another billion years for single-celled organisms to evolve into multi-celled organisms, and another billion years to produce us, but this is key to the proof. Did that first self-replicating molecule have a soul?"

"No," I answered. "This was all chemistry, all physics."

"*Voila!* And did that first multi-celled organism have a soul? Do fish have souls or only mammals? Do you see? Life is an unbroken chain of chemistry going all the way back. At what point can you say that the laws of physics stopped working in order for humans to acquire a supernatural spirit? It doesn't follow. Humans are natural, not supernatural. We are biological machines with super-complex brains, nothing more."

"That makes sense," I said. "But might there be some undiscovered physical law? I mean, haven't scientists been proven wrong many times? How can you be so sure?"

"I'm sure that the scientific method is a reliable way to acquire knowledge. But you are right, there are still many mysteries, and all scientists are human and therefore we sometimes make mistakes, and sometimes we find new evidence that breaks a long-held assumption. But after five-hundred years of scientific inquiry, we now know many things with certainty because all of the evidence agrees, for example evolution. This is a fact. Also, there are some things we can safely say are impossible."

I replied, "I agree that evolution explains how life came to exist on Earth, yes, but if this is a proven fact, then why call it a theory?"

She answered, "In science the word *theory* has a strict meaning. In science one needs evidence or one has no game, and the evidence for evolution is overwhelming and incontrovertible. Evolution is both a theory and a fact."

"Ah," I said. "OK."

Angeline explained that quantum mechanics and general relativity were both perfect theories in that every scientific experiment has confirmed them precisely, thus proving conclusively that the Universe has a mathematical structure. "But these theories remain incompatible because they describe different aspects of reality." She explained to me that the "holy grail" of physics was therefore to create a new mathematical system, a *theory of everything*. Then she admitted that she worked on this with her father as a side project. "And we have an idea..."

She smiled nervously, and I sensed this was because she didn't think I would understand, so I said, "That's very cool. Your spiritual quest is nothing short of understanding the mathematical language of God. You'll have to explain your idea to me later. For now though, I'll assume that you are right; I'll assume that science is good at explaining the *how* of existence, but what about the *why*? I mean, God or whatever you want to call it, the Universe, Brahman, OK, it's mathematical, but why? Why is there something rather than nothing?"

"I don't think science can ever answer that."

"Then that's the divine mystery."

"Yes! I think this is the only theological question worth asking. Why like this? The best answer I can give is that things are the way they are because that's the way the math works. But please keep in mind, the truth might be a cold, hard mathematical truth, but that doesn't make me a cold, hard woman. Anyway, I think math is beautiful."

"I think you're beautiful."

I wanted to kiss her, but fate did not allow me that chance. I hesitated and the moment was gone. Angeline finished her point. "Therefore free will is an illusion," she said. "And all those people searching for meaning and truth should study evolution if they really want to know, plus chaos theory and astronomy... But that's the mathematical truth. There's also the human truth..."

Angeline's smile provided an opportunity to cuddle, but I did not kiss her because she started talking again. She did so however with humor, intelligence and grace, and as she explained the meaning of life I imagined flowers in her hair. I was hypnotized. I was smitten.

17 - A Gift from Hanuman

We arrived in Delhi sweaty and tired and happy to get off the bus. Angeline and I invited Bastiaan to join our continued journey to Goa by train, so he shared a taxi with us to the Shiva Guest House. We checked into our respective rooms, then we agreed to meet later for dinner. Angeline suggested that maybe our new friend was a gift to us from Hanuman, the monkey God. I didn't know about that, but I was happy he joined us. He was a funny guy.

As my foxy companion took a shower, I paced the floor anxiously. When she emerged wearing only a towel, I said nothing so that I could focus on remembering the moment forever. She walked to me, each step slower than the previous until she stood an inch away. She brought her lips to mine. We kissed for the briefest of moments, then she jerked away saying, "Take a shower. You stink!"

I washed myself in record time, then I slid myself under the bed sheet. Angeline said something in French. I caressed her feet then her thighs. When I got to her mouth, the intensity of our passion grew until I felt like I might explode...

Hours later Bas knocked on the door. "Are you guys awake?" I opened my eyes and saw with delight that my fantasy had not been a dream. Yes! The happy hippie from Holland insisted on buying my official girlfriend and me a nice dinner for our zeroth anniversary.

Next we walked to the train station to buy tickets to Goa. We walked past the place where a beggar girl convinced me to buy shampoo, along the lane where Scar-face threatened to call the police. This urban chaos made me appreciate the mountain serenity of the Tibetan monks, but this was dodgy Delhi, agitated and rough, where the eyes of the pavement people displayed not even hope. I was happy that I was born me.

As we walked, Bas explained how the Indian railroad was a positive legacy of British colonial rule, good trains that sometimes ran on time. Following his advice, we bought second-class-sleeper tickets, reserving upper bunks for enhanced privacy. Technically Bas bought all three tickets because he knew how to queue Indian style; with no organized line, he used his relatively large body to gently push his way towards the clerk.

As our train cruised towards Mumbai, my friends and I listened to music and swapped stories. Bas described a place in Rajasthan he called, "the temple of the Holy Rat." He said, "You might think that it's just a touristy side show, but no... People honestly believe that these particular pests are the reincarnated followers of the Goddess Karni Mata. You have to remove your shoes to have the privilege of having their poop stick to your feet. It's auspicious if they bite you." Quintessential India.

The first thing I noticed about Mumbai was the noise pollution, excessive honking, enough to make any city resident dream of moving to the countryside. I did not see even one cow in the old British neighborhood, but I did see cockroaches and rats, big rats like I had never seen before. Next I noticed that hotel rooms were expensive, but as India's cultural and banking metropolis, the whole economy was elevated, a rich city in a poor country.

Angeline and I arrived into our room exhausted from the long journey, but all the city stress melted away as she went into the shower. I sensed déjà vu as I sat on the bed and smiled incessantly, the luckiest man alive. Ahhh...

The next morning after breakfast, Angeline stayed at the hotel while Bas and I ran errands. First we walked on the beach until we came across a human shit, then another, then we saw a human taking a shit. Bas said, "There's no hope for India."

I asked him, "What do you suggest we should be hoping for, exactly?"

My friend said that this was a good question, adding that maybe he was hoping for Indians to learn how to shit into toilets, and to clean up their plastic garbage, and to stop having babies they can't afford to feed.

With that we left the beach on a mission to make custom trousers from khadi cloth, the fabric that Gandhi advocated all Indians should wear instead of British textiles as a sign of unity and self-reliance during their struggle for independence. Bas knew of a good store for buying khadi fabric, so we went there. I bought enough fabric to make trousers too, with secret pockets, a project to be completed later in Goa with a tailor.

Bas had a clever scheme for protecting his belongings while sleeping on trains: metal webbing internal to his pack plus a wire loop for locking it. His theory was that thieves would look for an easier target, for example my pack. I wanted to copy his technology but we couldn't find the gear, so I bought a wire loop and a padlock instead, sufficient to deter a snatch thief and better than nothing.

We walked by the Gateway of India, a grand monument where we stopped for ice cream. When the salesman gave us the wrong change on purpose, Bas told him, "Bad karma!" Then he said to me, "That's the number-one way to steal from tourists, or they give you the wrong bill. Always check the math. This is a good mental exercise anyway."

I suddenly felt a cramp that mandated a bathroom immediately, or else! When I mentioned this to Bas he said, "Being white has its advantages. We'll have you in a five-star crapper within a minute." As we were in a touristy area, there was a luxury hotel across the street, so we walked in as if we owned the place. Sure enough, the concierge directed me to a men's room with marble walls, shiny brass fittings, and classical music playing. There I had the most luxurious diarrhea of my life.

Back at our hotel, Angeline surprised us with French wine, Gorgonzola cheese, bread, and olive oil. We had a picnic in our room. Then we went out to see a Bollywood movie, in this case a musical with sweeping cinematography. There was just enough English to follow the plot but that didn't matter; it was all about escaping into a fantasy world filled with singing and dancing, plus beautiful people falling in love.

Leaving the cinema, we witnessed an obese Indian child eating American fast food. Bas commented, "I was in America once, yes, but only for a couple of hours. I had to change planes in Miami on my way to Jamaica. Anyway a fat cop searched me. I mean really fat. It was horrible. But I never met an American like you, Mister Love."

"Thanks," I said. "I think. USA! USA!"

Angeline said, "Americans are fat. It's true. America is the fattest country of the world after Tonga and Samoa (I think) so it's true. Americans also have too many guns. But I do not like stereotypes. These can lead to racism, or (how would you say?) culturism, and this is important because cultural differences, not racial differences, cause misunderstandings and problems. I guess what I'm saying is that Raymond is not fat."

Bas said, "Good insight, my fair lady. But in order to really understand cultural differences, you have to travel the world, but most people stay home. They see the world only through entertainment, and the truth is not entertaining. Poverty and corruption... No, I take it back. The truth is entertaining. I find India to be very entertaining."

Angeline said, "To me the truth is that which physicists aspire to describe with mathematics, and this is entertaining to me. But you're right, there is a separate truth, the human truth, and yeah, it's entertaining too."

Bas said, "The truth is also blissful ignorance, televised sports, and singing competitions. Actually, football is truth, or uh, what do you Americans call it? Oh yeah, soccer. Soccer is truth. Gorgonzola cheese is truth."

Thanks to chaos, destiny, or luck, and whether we discussed culturism, cheese, or king salmon, Bas always found humor, a gift from the Monkey God, Hanuman, perhaps.

18 - Beach Bliss

We shared our second-class-sleeper cabin with an Indian family. I trusted them but I inaugurated my new security system anyway, to lock Angeline's pack to mine while investigating music emanating from the next carriage, a jam session with a dozen odd backpackers banging on things and getting into the groove. Hours later, we crawled into our bunks to let the train's rhythms lull us to sleep, but not for long. We arrived in Goa.

A taxi from the train station delivered us to Bastiaan's favorite hippie beach. He knew a nice hotel that was so cheap it was almost free. The only downside was that this hotel was a kilometer down the beach from the action, which I did not see as a downside at all. We checked into this hotel, then Bas departed on a mission to track down an old friend.

Angeline and I went out to explore, and soon we found ourselves eating chocolate cake and sipping coffee at the Danish bakery. We adapted to life as fish adapt to water. I loved the cool, hippie, beach vibe but mostly I loved falling in love. This was easy with Angeline because there was nothing to not like. To prevent getting too attached, I reminded myself often that nothing is permanent.

Angeline and I made love often, and we never quarreled, but we always laughed as we discussed a world of topics. Whenever we played chess, she whipped my ass. We usually woke up early enough to be alone on the beach for a swim, but we were never alone for long because India is crowded. No worries. We enjoyed watching the weird and wonderful people too.

We sometimes practiced yoga on the sand, but also in our room for privacy. Angeline taught me how to practice to music, transforming the asanas into something like a dance. This was fun and better exercise than I ever imagined possible for yoga. I never felt more fit. Angeline practiced with a local guru too, because this was her top priority for her visit to India. She had planned to study at a famous ashram near Bangalore also, thus her flight home from that city, but she decided to blow this program off in order to spend more time with me on the beach. Lucky me.

Along with a growing circle of random friends, we often

watched the sunset at the place where a drum circle cranked out primitive beats, with pretty girls practicing fire dancing and hula-hoop, with tourists snapping photos and hippies chilling out. I was tempted to buy a drum but I didn't (when in doubt, leave it out).

Bas often joined us for sunset, but the first time was memorable for his rant about how his favorite beach had grown beyond recognition. He explained the history: when the Portuguese left Goa in 1961, hippies flocked in to take advantage of cheap prices, liberal attitudes, and a general tolerance for diversity, but Goa since evolved. Instead of hallucinating to the sweet notes of a traditional sitar, backpackers listened to electronic trance, dancing like Shiva to mp3 rhythms. "This mix of hippies, Israelis, and locals became normal in a good way," Bas said, "but now there are Russians too, a lot of Russians. Russians!"

Angeline said that she envied the hippies, especially the freedom they found as they avoided the trappings of work, television, and the consumer rat race. She said that she envied me. And I envied her. She earned her place in a fascinating program of research, she was never bored, and she only seemed unhappy at that certain time of the month. Mostly I envied her superior understanding of the truth. She knew how to separate facts from opinions. She knew her place in the cosmos with scientific certainty. She was a genius.

During the heat of the day, I often lay in my hammock and read. Sometimes I played Frisbee with Bas, and he taught me how to juggle oranges too, a skill I practiced because it was fun exercise that also increased my general dexterity. My juggling improved.

Bas and I found a tailor to make trousers from our khadi cloth; they came out great.

I called Pedro. He told me that his computer-hacker friend, Shepherd, was keen to investigate my red flag because it related to America's tragic response to the tragic events of September eleven. I only met Shep once at a party so I had forgotten his name, but as a hefty Hawaiian with impressive tattoos, his character was easy to remember. "Shep breaks into government computers for fun," Pedro said. "And he's on the case! So stay tuned, cabrón."

I didn't seriously think I would learn why my name was on a government watch list, and even if I did find out, I didn't figure such information would have any practical use, but I was still happy that Shep was on the case. We were all curious, but not concerned.

The day of the full-moon, Bas introduced us to Violetta, his new best friend. They invited Angeline and me to join them at a secluded beach for an all-night rave. Bas added that he just scored some ecstasy pills. "Pure MDMA," he said.

I had never been to a beach rave so I did not know, but I would have guessed, that a major ingredient was illegal narcotics, so Bas's announcement seemed normal. He sold the idea by explaining that the "love drug" made people extroverted and alert, and that the chemical was even used for clinical psychotherapy before it became illegal. After a moment of apprehension, my lover and I agreed to see what all the fuss was about. But first we needed a motorcycle.

As Bas planned to stay in Goa for the whole season, he bought a Royal Enfield bike, a cool ride, but as I planned to visit China after delivering Angeline to Bangalore, I rented a less-cool bike from a guy down the beach named Shashank.

Getting to the party beach required cruising the Indian highway, which seemed dodgy compared to the back roads. Freight trucks passed on blind corners honking, *get out of the way!* If they honked a second time, it meant, *or else!* Sometimes they didn't honk at all. Most shocking were the drivers who accelerated into these situations as if their goal was to reduce the pain of death incurred while flying through their windshields, or perhaps to hasten their arrival as reincarnated beings with better lives. Anyway, we arrived safely, then we sat on the sand, then we took the stuff.

The chemical washed over us like a tsunami. After a bizarre body buzz, we all began talking too fast and grinding our teeth, then a second wave of extroverted energy enabled us to dance for hours at a bar somewhere not on the beach. I remember not being able to remember how we got to this bar. Strange stuff. Mesmerized by wild colors and freaky hippies undulating to rhythmical vibrations, at this bar we tripped our brains out.

Many hours raced by too quickly to remember, but sitting on the beach with Angeline later was unforgettable. Together we laughed and shared intimate secrets, talking for hours through the night. The sunrise was incredible, then the music stopped and the party ended. By this time I felt mostly normal and alert, so I drove home no problem.

Back in our room, as much as we were high the night before, we were low. I was happy that I packed my hammock.

Bas came around offering a joint that would make Bob Marley proud, so I told him to have a seat, thinking the ganja would help my hangover or at least help me ignore it; and indeed, the wacky weed did seem to help my head while simultaneously increasing my laziness to an extreme level, laziness like I never felt before or since.

Bas explained how he paid for his travel habit by working odd jobs. He said he never worked at a desk and never would. My friend knew how to weave coconut leaves into hats that he could sell to tourists (I watched him do this one day with great skill). He also picked fruit and flipped hamburgers, he said, to top up his stash of cash. I was inspired by how he managed to travel the world with little more than a good attitude.

When I asked him what he planned to do when he got old, he answered, "Marry a rich girl, then sit around the swimming pool sipping lemonade."

Angeline joined us to puff on Bastiaan's joint. She thanked our furry friend for the party pills, then she said, "I found the trip fascinating, more proof that our perceived reality is just an illusion. Change the chemistry just a little and the mind's illusion changes dramatically, but the true nature of reality does not change."

19 - Yin-Yang Universe

One morning as Angeline and I were swimming in the calm waters of the Arabian Sea, I watched her Yin-Yang tattoo dancing in harmony with her body's curves and the ocean's waves, so I asked her to explain her tattoo further, because I wanted to know everything about her, especially as time was running out before she had to go home to France.

My lover explained that Yin and Yang represented obvious opposites like male versus female, God versus the Devil, Order versus Chaos, and also the ocean's waves (Yang energy versus Yin gravity). The surf made her point emphatic.

"Yin-Yang is a metaphor for the Universe," she said, "including all the laws of physics. The amazing thing is that this becomes accessible to us through mathematics. Did you ever study Trigonometry, for example, the functions Sine and Cosine?"

I did not lie. "Math was never my strong suit."

"Math is beautiful," she said. "Like Yin and Yang, the mathematical functions Sine and Cosine are half-opposites and also half-identical. They are separate but inseparable. Yang, having reached its maximum, retreats in favor of the Yin."

I watched the waves with a new perspective, perfect harmony, an elegant Universe.

"What do you know about imaginary numbers?" she asked.

I hesitated so she insisted, "If you want to understand how Yin-Yang applies to physics..."

"OK," I said. "I'll bite. I know nothing."

"Don't panic," she insisted. "It's easy! Imaginary numbers are in the mathematics for nearly everything. This is how physicists model light for example, as electro-magnetic waves phasing in and out of the imaginary plane. The electric is Sine and the magnetic is imaginary Cosine." She made rhythmical whirling motions with her hands. "The real and imaginary numbers are like Yin and Yang also, separate but inseparable."

Angeline's tattoo was different from the classic Yin-Yang design in that it wasn't black and white, but just black, with no circular line to contain the skin that would normally be white. I asked if her ink represented Yin or Yang.

"It's Yin," she said, "the feminine. Black is Yin and white is Yang."

"Doesn't that imply that your skin is Yang the masculine? Sorry, but that's wrong. My skin is Yang the masculine, therefore I should have the Yin tattoo."

She giggled, "Oh yes. You have a point!"

We went straight to our room, took showers to rinse away the sand, then we made love with our bodies as Yang and Yin, separate but inseparable.

Hours later, we walked to our favorite beach bar looking for orange juice just as birds flew over the waves looking for fish. I suddenly remembered our previous conversation, so I asked, "What's an imaginary number?"

My angel answered, "It's an anti-number, something fundamental to the laws of physics. But don't worry! There's only one tricky detail: there's a special number called i that we define as the square root of minus one. That's it. I know this doesn't make sense intuitively, but it's in the math and it's in the physics."

I could see in my lover's smile that she loved her life, her job, and the elegant beauty of the Universe. She explained, "I know it seems bizarre, but this simple idea allows mathematicians to model light and chaos and quantum mechanics. The metaphor with Yin-Yang also holds up under scrutiny. In other words, there is an 'imaginary' dimension that connects the Yin to the Yang. Papa and I are trying to prove this, and we're making progress!"

"Really?"

"Yes. Thanks to the brilliant work of many dead philosophers, God's laws are now accessible to us through mathematics. Papa and I are working on a new topology, a new coordinate system, one that follows the Yin-Yang metaphor. And it works! We have results that confirm we're on the right track."

"That's awesome!"

"Yes. We are excited, because our new system explains how quantum mechanics can twist space to create gravity for particles with mass. Our breakthrough came when we redefined the speed of light to be the maximum rate of change of energy with respect to space. Running with this idea, we derived a completely new model for space, a new topology. In our model, mass is real and energy is imaginary. The speed of light becomes the square root of *i* times *pi*."

I stared at her quizzically so she said, "I know, I know, bear with me... All we had for years were crazy ideas, until Papa came up with a way to transform our simple equations into infinite series that computers can calculate. Now he and I are redesigning the computer code in order to simulate a perspective that mirrors our human point of view, and then we can publish! We're optimistic because our equations do create dynamic fractals with the right fractal dimension, things that look like trees and galaxies. We are close!"

While Angeline grinned proudly, I sipped my orange juice, hoping the refreshment would help my brain. I said, "I'm glad you understand that, because well..."

"Yeah I know," she said. "But to explain further I need to make some drawings, visual aids. Anyway, now you know something about my Yin-Yang Universe theory. Thus the tattoo. Papa and I have a lot of work to do, but if we succeed in proving our result, then this will have profound philosophical consequences."

I tried to not think about my best friend going home, but I could not help myself. Sometimes I told myself *bad brain must meditate*, and this worked somewhat. Other times I got sad. Meanwhile I wished that I could understand her genius. I knew this was impossible, but at least I came to appreciate that there are objective facts, they matter, and therefore my spiritual quest should include understanding science, so I asked my lovely lover to teach me the calculus, the language of God.

20 - Animal Instincts

Despite meeting tourists with broken bones from horrible crashes, Angeline and I explored Goa by motorcycle. The side roads were easy to cruise for fun, but the highways were always sketchy. Actually it was all sketchy. Every blind corner meant the potential for an imprudent truck driver, an angry bull, or an avatar of Shiva. Perhaps most dangerous were those tourists just getting used to motorcycle gears for the first time; at least the farm animals were somewhat predictable. One time I had to bail off the road at medium speed thanks to a surprising squeeze in normal traffic, almost losing control as I skidded to avoid a tree. Angeline told me to slow down repeatedly after that, until I built back up her trust.

One day we discovered a foot trail that led to a special banyan tree where a tribe of hippies called home. We joined them to discuss the wind, the rain, the male's fascination with female boobies, and other topics. Just after we sat down, a gringo named Ben offered me a chillum filled with tobacco and charas. I asked if he had any pure ganja instead, and a minute later we all got whacked in the head with a tasty buzz.

Ben said that Angeline and I should check out a certain restaurant in town, so we did. Crowded with Indians and with zero tourists, it was cheap and delicious, our new favorite place to have lunch.

Despite our delight in discovering these hidden places, our favorite activity was watching the sun rise from the beach, the time when we most relaxed and enjoyed our togetherness.

One morning Bastiaan appeared out of nowhere, purposefully surprising us. "Good morning!" he announced. "How are my favorite love birds?"

We bid our friend good morning, then he sat with us on the sand.

Angeline told Bas that we were discussing philosophy, then she asked him what he believed.

The happy hippie looked perplexed. "I don't believe anything," he said. "No. Wait. I believe that we're sitting on the beach. How's that?"

"Good. Do you believe that $1 + 1 = 2$?"

"Yes. You got me there. Yes, I believe that $1 + 1 = 2$."

"Good. How about $E = MC$ squared?"

"Ah yes, Einstein... Do I believe? Um. No."

Bas produced a joint before adding with a mischievous smile, "Do you want to know what I believe? I believe that I'm about to light up this joint. It's natural, super-natural. Yes, that's it. Thats it! I believe in the supernatural. Praise Hanuman!"

Bas lit his joint, took a puff, then he said, "Philosophy huh? OK Angeline, then please answer me this: what does Einstein have to do with the human condition? Isn't $E = MC$ squared all about making bigger bombs with nuclear energies? How is this a good thing?"

Angeline's eyes brightened. "Einstein taught us fundamental truths about our Universe, a good thing because only factual knowledge can explain how *you* came to be human, Bastiaan, unless you prefer to believe in one of those funny old creation myths, you know, the ones written long before we learned how to analyze the light from distant stars..."

Bas puffed his joint. "Good answer, but that's just your opinion, and now you're talking about evolution anyway, and everyone knows that's just a theory, and furthermore, science changes all the time. Why should I believe something that changes all the time?"

The happy hippie handed his joint to Angeline with a wink. She took a puff, then she silently stared at the ocean. She took another puff, then she held the joint up in the air dramatically, high above the sand. She said, "If I drop this joint, it will fall towards the Earth. That's a fact. Do you agree?"

Bas looked alarmed. "Yes! But please don't drop my joint. I don't want to have to smoke a sandy joint. Thank you."

Angeline said, "*Voila!* Gravity is not an opinion. Gravity is a fact that existed before Newton discovered her physical laws, and gravity still exists despite Einstein's improvements to the maths. Nothing alters the fact of gravity."

Angeline passed the joint to me, then she elaborated, "Evolution is also a fact (it's a theory and a fact), but I see your point. Sure there is speculation in science but at least it's constrained by the empirical evidence. Everything else is just a guess. The scientific method is a reliable way to grow humanity's knowledge base, and the proof is computers and modern medicines and robots on Mars. Sure you can turn to religion if you don't care about evidence, but if you really want to understand the human condition, then you must start with the facts."

Bas countered, "What about the eye? It's a fact that evolution cannot explain the eye, because nothing so complicated can possibly arise by chance."

Angeline said, "Sorry Bastiaan, but you are wrong. Evolution *can* explain the eye. Even the most simple plants grow towards the light! This is not a random process. Mutations are random, but natural selection is not. Sorry, but you should not talk like an expert about something you really know nothing about."

Bas frowned. "OK," he said. "Good philosophy. But just to be clear, are you saying that I'm related to a fish?"

I interjected, "You look more like a monkey to me, brah."

Angeline laughed, then she asked me, "Do you know why sex evolved?"

I answered, "No, but I am glad that it did!"

She said, "Me too! Sex is fun. And thanks to this process, animals can mix some mama DNA and some papa DNA to become something different, and this diversity enhances survivability. Better breeding boys! Life is about the survivability of organisms that survive because they are good at surviving. Sex is so successful that even plants do it."

I said, "Yeah, but I'm sure they don't enjoy it as much!"

My girlfriend laughed, then she explained how DNA was yet another example of Yin and Yang in nature, a molecular structure called a double helix that functioned as a chemical self-replicator, something scientists can witness directly in laboratories using modern technology.

Angeline addressed Bas. "The meaning of life isn't some divine mystery. It's all about the survival of successful DNA. We know this now, as a fact. In other words my fine furry friend, you are related to a fish."

Bas said, "Good! Because I want to swim."

My friend knuckle-walked to the waves while imitating a chimpanzee, then he dove in, and as he splashed around I suddenly realized that by choosing to believe in evolution as a fact, I better understood my animal instincts, my survival instincts, hard-wired impulses that I could sometimes tame with conscious controls, the essence of living as a rational ape. For me this was an intellectual turning point, the moment when I rejected my previous belief in humanity's inability to understand the mysteries of the Universe. This belief (which I acquired from my mother) suddenly seemed like a cop-out, an intellectually lazy way to avoid the hard work of analyzing the evidence, then testing and refining theories over centuries.

I sat thinking until Angeline asserted, "You don't have to take my word for any of this, you know. Nothing is stopping you from getting a university degree. There are some good courses in physics on the Internet, but there's nothing like a well-equipped lab to see for yourself. Anyway, do you think it sounds arrogant for one to admit that one knows something?"

21 - Roi du Monde

I found Angeline contemplating a book. "What are you reading?" I asked.

"The words of the Buddha," she answered.

"Oh. And what does he say?"

"Cease negative actions. Cultivate positive actions. Calm your mind."

I tried to look at the bright side, cultivating positive thoughts. Angeline's work was important, the only constant was change, and I needed to continue my trek alone.

The hardest part of leaving the beach was saying goodbye to Bastiaan. He planned to stay in Goa until the end of the season, sell his motorcycle, then head to Thailand and beyond. I gave him my hammock, I said, "to contemplate Angeline's philosophies in comfort."

He gave me his hat.

Angeline and I travelled to Bangalore by bus, then by taxi, then by train, a grueling journey. We checked into our hotel, took showers, then went out for a nice dinner, but the evening was most memorable for our time spent atop our king-sized bed. Sometimes it's good to splurge on a quality room. Ahhh...

I fell asleep with Angeline by my side, but in my nightmare she was missing. I panicked and looked for her, but she was too far away. Then we were swimming, and it was cold. I spoke her name but she stayed away, swimming. I flew to her but I could not reach her. She was drowning.

The real Angeline woke me up. "What is it?" she said. "You called my name."

"Sorry," I said. "It was only a dream."

Later, as I boiled water to make coffee, Angeline asked me about this dream so I told her. She asserted, "You're afraid to lose me and I understand. I don't want to lose you either! I love you Raymond. Vous êtes le *Roi du Monde*, the king of the world. So you mustn't worry about your dream, and you mustn't worry about me. Worry instead about having an amazing adventure! Explore this world... and visit me in France!"

"Of course I will. You know I will. I love you."

We hugged for a long while, a deeper hug than usual.

Angeline broke the silence. "Your nightmare says nothing about the future, you know. We cannot know the future. Your dream last night was produced by billions of neurons discharging the day's electro-chemical energy; that's all. It's like we're watching a five-dimensional movie, more like a hologram, with the conscious output of the thinking process, the thought, becoming an input into the next thought. This feedback loop allows us to hear our decisions and see our dreams, and this (hearing our decisions) is fundamental to the illusion of consciousness."

I said, "That's fascinating stuff but... But at this moment..." Sigh. "My dream last night really freaked me out, OK? So you be careful. Don't you go dying on me, OK? Did you hear me?"

I suddenly felt like crying.

Angeline said, "I'll try my best not to die my lovely, but of course we all die, and anyway, death isn't so bad. You already know what it's like to be dead."

"Huh?"

"Yes. You don't remember the dinosaurs, do you? No. Because you were dead. And all those people who haven't been born yet, they're dead too. Birth and death are part of the natural order. It's another Yin-Yang thing."

"OK," I said. "But let's change the subject." I paused to think of a topic. "OK, tell me... How do you reconcile your pursuit of hard mathematics in Europe with your love of soft mysticism, yoga and meditation et-cetera, here in India?"

My lover smiled. "That's easy. We humans all share the selfish delusion that we are the conscious actors who drive our lives, but that's an illusion. To understand this intellectually is not enough. Practicing meditation and yoga with bona-fide gurus helps me to experience the unity of all things, and to act accordingly. This is where the mathematical truth and the human truth converge. In other words, there are two approaches to knowledge: the scientific method and introspection."

Angeline gave me a present, a necklace with coconut wood surrounding a shell that swirled into the eye of Shiva. She said that Shiva would protect me from evil. I knew she didn't believe this, but it was a nice gesture. I gave her my miniature statue of Lord Ganesha, the God of Wisdom and the remover of obstacles. I said that with Ganesha's help, she and her father would sort out their theory of everything.

We took a taxi to the airport where Angeline checked into her flight. I escorted her to the security gate, then I told her and myself that all good things must come to an end.

Angeline said, "Raymond my friend, my love, you are a good and courageous man. Have so much fun, and remember everything you see, because whatever you forget is gone forever. And stay safe. I want to see you again. Come visit me in France!"

We hugged for a long moment. She began to cry.

I tried to look at the bright side. Angeline had to work and I had to continue my trek alone. I told her, "I love you, my friend. Good luck and good skill. I'm going to miss you a lot, so of course I'll visit you. Besides, what world tour would be complete without seeing France?"

"Good," she said. "Au revoir. Visit me soon!"

"The day after tomorrow?"

Angeline laughed and then she was gone, and I was alone.

22 - The Epicenter of Globalization

I sat outside the airport watching travellers coming and going, some rich some poor, but none super-poor. I laughed at three businessmen dragging identical wheeled luggage, but I was not happy. My best friend was gone and I felt sad. I felt the weight of responsibility too, because whatever I did next, my fate, was entirely up to me.

I wandered in search of the friendliest-looking tuk-tuk driver. As I approached a guy with a big mustache and a bigger smile, he said, "Welcome to India's number-one tuk-tuk!"

I climbed aboard.

The guy asked me where I was going so I told him, then we motored away. I also told him about Angeline because I needed to vent. "My girlfriend just flew home," I said. "And you know when you leave a true friend when you feel sad."

India's number-one tuk-tuk driver asked me, "Did you have sex with her?"

I still wasn't used to India. Can anyone ever get used to India? I snapped, "That's none of your fucking business!"

The number-one tuk-tuk driver apologized. "Sorry sir," he said. "I was not wanting to be rude. I was only wanting to know about foreigners having sex before they marry."

Sigh. "Well, we do. It's normal."

"Sorry sir. I never have experienced sex before, so I am curious to talk to foreigners. I am still waiting for my parents to find a suitable wife for me."

As we motored away from the airport, I missed Angeline but I knew I would be OK. I would have to be. She was gone. In her stead, the Universe brought me a horny tuk-tuk driver named Tarik.

"Why don't you go out with girls?" I asked. "Go find your own wife, for love."

Tarik wagged his head. "Sorry sir, but my parents say that to marry for something as fickle as love is folly. They say it is more important to share cultural values and to have good social connections, because love is unpredictable. But for me, I am wanting to understand love as it is in the Hollywood movies."

"Look, Tarik," I said. "I'm no expert in love, but I do advise you not to rely on Hollywood. And I don't agree with your parents. Sex is an animal instinct but love is beautiful, an important part of being human. One should only marry for love, I think."

Tarik replied, "Sir, my parents insist that emotions should not influence logical decisions, and they are older so they have a broader vision. They say I can have a love marriage if I want, but then I will be on my own, and I agree with them. Another benefit of an arranged marriage is that if I have problems, I can always complain to my parents because they found the girl for me."

"I guess that makes sense," I said. "By the way, please call me Raymond, not sir."

"Oh, sorry sir. I mean Raymond, sir. You are from America, yes? India is not like America. It is not so easy to meet girls, and I do not have the freedom to go against my parents' wishes. Furthermore, all of my money I spend to study so that some day I can work as an engineer. This will help my parents to find a better wife for me."

As Tarik casually swerved to avoid a couple of pigs that suddenly decided to mate in the road, I looked around to see people mixing cement and deep-frying samosas. The buzz of motors rang in my ears.

I said, "Tarik, you are not shy! There must be girls in your engineering classes..."

"Yes, but..."

"Invite one of them out for coffee! Tell her you like her taste in clothes, you know, compliment her shoes. Go for it. Flirting is fun."

"Thank you sir. Do you want to see where I go to school? We are close."

Tarik drove me by his technical college free of charge, then he showed me a business campus with manicured lawns and smartly dressed workers. He spoke about his dream to secure one of those air-conditioned jobs, "at the epicenter of globalization."

We were surprisingly close to abject poverty. Tarik wanted to show me that too, he said, "because if your eyes don't see it, then your heart doesn't feel it." He turned down a dirt road lined with rubbish, where the children walked barefoot and the adults looked skinny. The worst imaginable stench of a dead animal made me want to vomit. I saw harijan men working to remove the corpse. This was followed by a glorious whiff of incense emanating from a colorful temple.

As we returned to the lair of the merely poor, I asked Tarik to take me home.

I watched TV in my room, first a Bollywood musical, then an American news channel to catch up on the war. I watched an interview with a politician promoting specific military tactics, followed by poll results selling those tactics as popular, manufacturing consent. I switched the TV off.

I missed Angeline. Her English skills were so good that they inspired me to become more fluent in Spanish, so I made for myself a priority to travel to Spanish-speaking countries on my world tour, starting with Spain, because Spain was close to France.

I decided to visit Hampi next, formerly the capital of the Vijayanagar empire and, according to my guide book, "a site with impressive ruins and gigantic boulder fields that together create a surreal and energetic landscape." After Hampi I planned to visit Varanasi, "the holy city on the river Ganges, and the most auspicious place for a Hindu to die."

I called my mother. She was relieved that I was OK because in her mind India was dangerous. I loved her despite her avoidance of evidence. I said, "Mom, the last time I sensed danger was in Brooklyn, USA. It's both easy and safe to travel in India, and I've found the people to be well, pesky sometimes yes, but dangerous no. And it's good to see poverty first hand, because if your eyes don't see it, then your heart doesn't feel it."

I took advantage of being in Bangalore, the epicenter of globalization, to eat a cheesy pizza and watch a Hollywood movie about an action hero. This was the first time I ever saw my home city of Los Angeles through the eyes of an outsider. The gun culture seemed dangerously unnecessary. I missed Angeline.

I studied my digital photos, wondering if my far-away friend and I had a future or merely a fling. I wanted to fly to France immediately, but I also wanted to explore China and beyond. China! Travelling the world allowed me to contemplate life's mysteries undistracted by television and routine, it provided opportunities to meet beggars and businessmen and horny tuk-tuk drivers, and this helped me to discover my true self, because I was free from the expectations created by past behaviors and familiar faces. I felt lonely but free, free to be me.

That night I dreamed Angeline was the star of a Hollywood movie that got rolled into a bottle of soda pop. I woke up and looked for the bottle, but the illusion disappeared as soon as it was subject to logical scrutiny. What a funny organ, that brain. I went back to sleep, happy about the existence of love.

23 - Good News Bad News

Pedro sent me an email with the subject, "Good News Bad News." The message said, "Call me." I calculated that my friend was likely home at that moment, so I made haste to my room where I had a telephone. Pedro answered, "Cabrón! You got my email!"

"I did," I said, surprised he knew it was me. "Pedro, mi hermano, dígame! Tell me. What's the good news?"

I could hear my friend smile. "Our esteemed brother Shepherd figured out why you got searched. I told you man, Shep's the man. But first he told me to make you promise to never tell anyone, and especially never put any mention of this into writing. Shep's paranoid."

"OK," I said. "I promise."

"Right. Well, the good news is that you're clean. But you have an evil twin."

"What?"

"No. Ha! Well, sort of. You match up with a different Raymond Love on the so-called *selectee list* because you have the same birthday and birth city, and when in doubt, search. We looked the other Raymond up and he's an outspoken critic of the government, so we figure that they're keeping an eye on him. Anyway, just expect to get searched every time you go through airport security. That's the bad news."

"That does explain..."

"Now for the interesting part!"

"Yeah? Go on..."

"Your father is on the selectee list too, and the *no-fly* list... No airplanes!"

"What?"

"Yeah. Pops is on the no-fly list! His name came up in the same search as you, junior, ha! In other words, Shep discovered this accidentally. But that's it. We don't know why Pops is on the list, except for one clue: Shep said that he found a data dump on one of the hacker networks, data from the Terrorist Screening Database (unclassified data), and Pops's name came up there too, but again with no explanation as to *why*?"

"Damn," I said. "No shit?"

"Yeah. Shep said that there is another database with more information, um, the Terrorist Identities Datamart or something like that, and he wants to hack into this next. 'There will be gaps,' he said. 'There are always gaps, and that's where hackers play, in the gaps.' So stay tuned, cabrón. Shep is on the case. That's good news too! So is Pops a terrorist or a spy or what? Didn't he used to live in Israel?"

"Yes he did, but a terrorist? No way. That's crazy talk. A spy? No. Pops is by the book, you know, he follows the rules, and he's a friggin' super-patriot. So I don't know, but hopefully Shep can find out! I mean, Pops is on the no-fly list?"

"Yeah no shit, right? Meanwhile Shep insists that hacking is what he does for fun, especially when it's related to something important in the real world, like for example the no-fly list, so you never know, he might come up with something... Why don't you call Pops and ask him?"

I said, "No way. I can't just say, 'Hey Pops! Why are you on the no-fly list?' I don't have that kind of relationship with him. And also, let me put it this way: if this turns out to be a poker game, then I don't want to give away my hand."

My curiosity spiked. There were things I never questioned about my parents that suddenly seemed weird. For example, they met in Jerusalem then moved to Tel Aviv, but aside from the fact that Mom was with a church group and Pops was a soldier, I knew surprisingly little about what they did over there. Then there was the Syria connection; Gramps emigrated and changed his name, and he was eventually killed in a hit-and-run car accident. This suddenly seemed nefarious. I was damn curious, but also happy to know something about Pops that he did not know that I knew. Pops was on the no-fly list?

24 - Small World

I walked into an American-style coffee shop just as a man wearing tights arrived on a full-suspension mountain bike. I sipped a cappuccino while contemplating the revolution in progress: younger generations were embracing far-away ideas, and not just coffee and spandex but politics, technology, even cultural notions of love and sex.

I looked up and I could not believe my eyes. I mumbled to myself, "No way." Budi and Robert "Mr. Suit" Onassis entered the coffee shop. Seeing these men seemed ridiculously improbable, and this made me happy. Budi and Robert both waved at me, all smiles. Robert shook my hand then he introduced me to Haji, the best-dressed Indian I ever met, and the head of the Bangalore office. Haji looked marvelous. The men all sat with me declaring, "Wow! What a coincidence!" and "Small World!"

The three men prodded me to tell stories from my adventures, and I did so gladly.

Robert ordered coffee including a fresh cappuccino for me. He said he was envious of my freedom because he flew all the way to India and it was all business and all luxury. He said, "It sounds like you're having fun!"

"Yeah," I said, "and I'm just getting warmed up. I'm going to Hampi next, once the great capital of the Vijayanagar Empire, a site with impressive ruins and gigantic boulder fields. Why don't you join me? When you're done with your meetings, of course. Take in some culture. Take off your suit. Hampi is only about eight hours away from here by bus."

"That's tempting! Really! Thanks. But I must be back in New York next Monday."

"Suit yourself. But you're the boss right? Can't you call in sick? Just say, 'Sorry, I had a change in plans.' You can afford to change your flight, right?"

Robert's smile seemed sincere. "No, but thanks, really."

"OK," I said. "Suit yourself."

I asked Budi, "You too? Are you going back to New York on Monday?"

"Yes," he beamed. "I have a big responsibility to the

company!"

My coffee colleagues explained their business model which I found fascinating. Robert said, "We're moving our operations here, not just because the exchange-rate voodoo makes labor so cheap, but because we can always find the staff we need when we need them. Have you ever heard of an American kid dreaming about working in a call center?"

I previously thought of outsourcing jobs to India as bad, as increased unemployment in America, but Budi called this economic liberation, and Haji said, "I am not sad for America. I am happy for India."

I asked Robert to please explain the exchange-rate voodoo.

He said it was a legacy from World War Two. "America won the war! And so the dollar became the world's reference currency. The dollar used to be backed by gold but now it's backed only by confidence. The game is rigged. Did you know the Chinese currency's exchange rate is not set by a free market? Nope. The Chinese set the rate to ensure that their exports are cheap, but we let them into the World Trade Organization anyway... And India has to compete with China, so..."

"That explains a lot."

"It does."

Haji summarized, "Political systems do not work according to the rules of logic. They work according to the rules of greed."

I said, "Greed is logical."

This led to a discussion about Wall Street, the grand casino. Banks borrowed from other banks to bet on derivatives, creating a web of debt worth hundreds of trillions of dollars, highly leveraged loans from phantom wealth. I was shocked to learn that my government did not create its own money supply, but borrowed money instead (with interest) from "the Fed," a privately-owned bank with special powers.

Robert explained, "Abraham Lincoln proved that government banks can play by different rules. He printed *greenbacks* to fund the Civil War, with no debt, and I think that's why he was assassinated (not because of slavery). The modern financial system is fairly new, created by corrupt lawmakers in 1913, and since then Wall Street has become dangerously powerful, a banking monstrosity that thrives when every country and every human is in debt."

I reminded Robert about our fortune cookies in New York, and I suggested again that he run for political office. I said, "We need people in government who actually understand how the system works, people who will look good on television too, people who can actually win elections, and (this is crucial) we need people in office (like you I believe) who will fight for their grandchildren ahead of their shareholders."

"That would be good sport, wouldn't it? But no, my company needs me."

"In bed?"

My unlikely friends and I ordered another round of coffee, and this was great for my morale, but eventually they had to go to a meeting. Robert gave me his business card and told me to stay in touch. I borrowed his flash pen, wrote my email address on his card then gave it back to him. I told *him* to stay in touch. He told me to keep the pen.

When my well-dressed friends departed, I stayed behind to contemplate globalization. I discovered my curiosity to understand that mythical beast known as "the economy."

Leaving the coffee shop I encountered a boy. He asked if I could exchange a ten rupee note for ten coins so I obliged him, then he asked if I could spare a coin, so I gave him one, and this made me feel good, but I knew that if I wanted to help eradicate poverty then giving away the odd rupee was futile. Intrigued, I asked a tuk-tuk driver to take me to the city's largest bookstore where I bought books on the history of philosophy, science, and economics. Later I also went online to research the Fed and the derivatives bubble.

This was the first time I ever embarked on an independent research project because I wanted to understand my crazy, modern world at least as well as Angeline and Mr. Robert Suit. I needed facts I figured, because no matter how logical my brain might be, if I didn't start with facts, I would reach the wrong conclusions. Fortunately I had plenty of time to read.

My epiphany came when I realized that Socrates was wrong when he said that wise men know that they know nothing, because

Socrates lived long before Galileo, Einstein, and Angeline. I realized that to make progress in my spiritual quest, I had to abandon my prior belief that it was wise to plead ignorance of the divine mysteries, because thanks to the scientific method, humanity has learned a great deal. I concluded that despite science being incomplete with respect to understanding everything, when it came to the truth, it was better to be approximately right than completely wrong. I began to question everything that I previously thought I knew, including the nature of knowledge. The wise man knows not that he knows nothing, I reasoned; instead he knows the limits of what can be known.

25 - Dusty Food

I travelled to Hampi, a village with magnificent ruins from a former empire plus gigantic boulder fields that together created a surreal and energetic landscape. I loved exploring the boulder fields at sunrise, and I relished the opportunity to be alone with my thoughts. I also hung out with other backpackers, read my books, juggled rocks, practiced yoga, remembered happy moments with Angeline, and I wondered why my government might prohibit Pops from flying. Tempting as it was to call him out on that, Shepherd the hacker was keen to investigate further, and this seemed like the best way to proceed. I had no idea.

Wandering around the ruins from a lost civilization made me realize the inevitability of America's decline, but I saw myself as a citizen of the world, caring not so much about the fate of one country per se, but humanity in general. This was an intellectual step forward for me, because my parents raised me to be a patriotic nationalist.

I found especially interesting Hampi's temple devoted to Lord Narasimha, half man, half lion, and an avatar of Vishnu. Swami Raj once told me that Lord Vishnu was the Great Protector, and that Vishnu's consort Lakshmi was the Goddess of Wealth. This made sense because as Raj put it, "Wealth is required for complete protection."

Angeline sent me an email saying that she made it home safely and that she loved me. I replied saying that I loved her too. Remembering that she predicted the fall of America because Yang, having reached its maximum, must retreat in favor of the Yin, I asked her, "If the current regime of macho capitalism is Yang, what's Yin?"

I sat atop a giant boulder to practice meditation, but not for long. I saw saddhus walking with an elephant so I raced down to join them. We walked together as far as the river where we enjoyed a charas-infused conversation about grand metaphors and supernatural beings. My companions translated these metaphors into wisdom, a model for living well according to their ancient traditions. Fascinating stuff.

One of the gurus, Willow, convinced me that my aura was

perfectly prepared to depart northward, so the next day I boarded a bus towards the nearest town from where I could catch a train to Varanasi.

My hotel bill seemed too expensive so I checked the math. The gold-toothed administrator added a zero, asking for ten times the fair price. When I showed him the error, he pretended it was an honest mistake. I paid the correct amount then told him, "Nice try, but I'm not stupid." He frowned a guilty frown. With that I was on the road again.

My bus to the city of Gooty broke down twice, turning my six-hour ride into a ten-hour ride, and so I missed my train. The station manager would not refund my money so I bought a new ticket, then I waited for another six hours, then two more as my new train was late. This was grueling, but then it became surreal as the station's annoying computerized voice repeated over and over, "The inconvenience caused is deeply regretted."

Feeling hungry, I bought a fried samosa. I took one bite and it tasted good, but dusty. I knew better than to eat dusty food, so I threw the rest away, but it was too late...

As I boarded my train, I saw a blind man struggling to orient himself so I attempted to help him. I touched his shoulder but instead of following my lead, he hit me with his cane repeatedly. As I ran away, I heard other passengers laughing.

When I arrived at my designated berth, I encountered two blond-haired, blue-eyed backpackers, Kenny and Barb from Australia, en route to Tadoba National Park, they said, because they wanted to see a tiger. From there they planned to visit Bodhgaya, the place where Buddha allegedly achieved enlightenment.

As our train reached speed, as we looked upon India's agricultural heartland, Barb asked me where I was from, so I answered, "California."

She said, "Oh, I thought you were American."

I checked her expression to see if she was joking (she wasn't), then I asked Kenny what he did for a living. He said, "I'm a surfer."

I didn't pry. Instead I prepared my upper-bunk nest for security sleeping, then I put on some music and we all played a card game.

I asked Barb if she believed in reincarnation. She answered, "Of course. I feel that I have a purpose, a path I must follow. In my previous life I was a nurse. In this life I'm supposed to be a healer. I can feel it, you know, the energy."

I decided not to debate her. Instead I reminded myself why reincarnation was incompatible with the fact of evolution and therefore impossible. Kenny asserted that he believed in reincarnation too, so I asked him how a soul gets transported from a dying person's last breath to a sperm.

That's when I felt the first cramp. I sprinted to the bathroom where I aimed my ass towards the hole in the floor, but with the train bouncing down the tracks, I made a mess. Fortunately the toilet had a bucket for water designed for ass-washing so I was able to clean somewhat without using the last of my precious toilet paper. Then, with sweat dripping down my brow, I told my comrades to avoid the toilet on the left.

That's when I got the urge to vomit. I made a hasty retreat to the bathroom and puked up my lunch. Then a painful cramp invoked another squirt from my back side. I tried to practice my aim, but improved little.

I must have looked as bad as I felt because Kenny and Barb seemed genuinely worried about me. That was the end of the card game. I had anti-diarrhea pills in my first-aid kit, so I took one. Barb said that she studied *reiki* healing in Goa so I let her pass her hands over my gut while transmitting healing energy. I didn't believe in reiki magic but I felt better. Maybe all I needed was feminine attention? Or maybe it was the anti-diarrhea pill? I didn't care. I felt better.

I asked Barb about her other beliefs: lucid dreams being good predictors of the future, specific knowledge from past lives, long-distance telepathy, and spiritual agency. I asked her if she believed in fate. She answered, "I do. It helps me to bear life's suffering, with conviction that life has purpose and design. Everything happens for a reason."

"That was well spoken," I said. "So what do you think is the purpose of my diarrhea?"

At the next station stop, Kenny left to buy chai from the chai wallah. I asked him to keep an eye out for bananas too. He returned with chai, bananas, and a bill for twenty-five rupees. I didn't have exact change so I gave him twenty rupees. He seemed oddly disturbed so I said I'd get change and pay him later.

That's when our new bunk-mate, Rajat, arrived. A gray-haired gentleman wearing a worn-out suit, he asked the usual questions about where we were from and where we were going. Then he lay down to sleep.

I quietly observed my Australian colleagues as they planned the hotels where they would stay, the restaurants where they would eat, and how much they were going to spend each day. I had a different philosophy: I preferred cheap hotels and local restaurants, so there was no point in monitoring my budget. I never made a schedule (that seemed too inflexible) and I did not try to see everything listed in my guide book (that seemed like work).

Despite intense cramps, I managed bursts of sleep. It was horrible, but in a crazy way I loved it, the adventure, India.

As Kenny and Barb stirred, preparing to depart the train, I awoke to the realization of how desperately I had to go to the bathroom. When I returned, the three of us stood in our compartment rather awkwardly. Remembering that I owed Kenny five rupees, and that he once commented to Barb that he wanted a music system like mine, I gave it to him. I decided this spontaneously as a way to force myself to pay more attention to the sounds of India, and to rid myself, at least somewhat, of my materialistic tendencies. Kenny thanked me repeatedly, then Barb gave me a hug, then they disembarked into the night.

Rajat looked up from his bunk and smiled.

I was strangely happier without my music system. As I tried and failed to sleep, such was my intestinal discomfort, I vowed to give away most of what I stored in Mom and Pops's basement too, whenever I got home. Living out of a backpack taught me that I did not need all that stuff. I preferred to travel lightly because this allowed me to focus on things more important than stuff. Without that music in my head, I had thoughts instead.

I awoke to Rajat tapping on my shoulder. "Excuse me, Raymond," he said. "I do not desire to intrude upon your rest, but I get off at the next stop. My son will meet me there, and then we will drive to a place called Khajuraho. I thought that given your condition, you might want to ride with us. There are wonderful ancient temples in Khajuraho, a tourist attraction, but primarily I say this to you because I have a friend who owns a hotel there, and I think this might be the perfect place for you to recover from your sickness."

I vaguely remembered Khajuraho from my guide book as a place that looked interesting, so I told Rajat that I would be foolish not to accept his generous offer.

"Good," he said, wagging his head in that uniquely Indian way. "In this case you must get your good self organized quickly. Our train will be arriving at the Satna station soon."

I took another anti-diarrhea pill and trusted in the kindness of a stranger.

26 - Copulating Statuary

Rajat's hotel-owning friend, Shivendu, escorted me to a room where I promptly passed out, but I had cramps, diarrhea, and I was dehydrated so I slept poorly. I had nightmares. One had something to do with Angeline, something bad, but I couldn't remember. When the roosters crowed, I woke up delirious thinking, "Where am I?"

I stayed in my room for three days watching Bollywood movies on a black-and-white television, plus music videos and a dramatization of Hindu Gods and Goddesses in a tele-novela. Shivendu visited me every morning to deliver water, bananas, and plain rice, all easy on the stomach. I told him the story of my sickness, skipping the messier details, concluding, "The moral of the story is: don't eat dusty food, especially when it's cow-shit dust."

Shivendu agreed, then he told me about Khajuraho's ancient temples, famous for their detailed sculptures of daily life, but especially the sexually explicit scenes. As soon as I felt strong enough to walk a few miles, I went to see for myself.

The site was fascinating, and indeed the temples did include carvings that Mom would describe as pornographic, even sinful (as if I could ever get Mom to visit India), but I saw nothing obscene (except for one statue of a guy shagging a horse). Despite the overtly Hindu themes, the Khajuraho temples celebrated human sexuality in a time before modern taboos. I could imagine the ancient priests carving their artwork to confirm with the villagers that their carnal pleasures were officially sanctioned. Other temple carvings seemed to convey that it was OK for soldiers to attack enemy cities with elephants. To me however, the most remarkable aspect of the site was the striking sensuality of the celestial nymphs, carved from stone but so seductive that they were capable of making men feel horny just the same. I missed Angeline.

One of my new favorite activities was wandering around the ruins of lost civilizations, especially grand monuments built not for banks but for magical spirits, but one can only do so much wandering in a day, so eventually I retreated to town for food and rest. I ordered aloo dhum (potatoes with spicy sauce) plus garlic naan (bread) and chai, all cheap, delicious, and healthy.

While I savored my meal, I contemplated the vast differences between modern Indians and their great-great-great-grandparents. The ancient people made monuments with incredible craftsmanship, whereas modern people made cheap towns that began to all look alike, such was the general lack of concern for creative aesthetics. I enjoyed the fascinating culture, but I was starting to feel jaded by so much poorly-educated inattention to quality. It did not help that I was still feeling sick and therefore grumpy, but India was finally starting to wear me down.

The modern people I met were mostly charming, trying their best to cope with their society's cruel imperfections (even while accidentally overcharging me for my aloo dhum and chai on purpose), but some people were quite annoying, especially in touristy towns like Khajuraho where hustlers waited on every corner trying to make a dishonest living.

I got into an argument with one drug dealer just as I left the main temple site. The guy wouldn't leave me alone so I went off on a rant. I said, "Look at the magnificent, beautiful work of your ancestors, and then compare that to the shit you have here, an ugly little city with dirt and noise, overpriced tourist shops, and nothing of beauty (women don't count). Seriously, with all the money that flows through this town every day from tourism, you have no excuse to still have such a crappy main road. It's a muddy mess! Half mud, half shit. Pave the road, man, pave the road! And why does everybody have to honk their friggin' horns all the time? That's noise pollution, man! And where's the art? Show me anything interesting here that isn't at least two-hundred years old."

I sipped my chai and tried to relax, and as I contemplated the implications of wide-spread ignorance, I suddenly realized that my mediocre education (by California standards) was actually pretty good. For many years I learned basic facts plus an ability to think critically and creatively that I previously took for granted. And now I was a student at the University of the Open Road, an institution of higher learning where travelling alone especially, I had the luxury of time to conduct research and to contemplate.

The open road also forced me to continuously analyze my personal likes and dislikes in a chaotic environment, unbiased by previous habits and the opinions of others. For example I learned that I liked aloo dhum with garlic naan.

I decided to improve my attitude, to ignore the persistent hustlers and wanna-be guides (because ignoring them works) while always being prepared to respond to a sincere smile or a genuine *namaste*. I also decided to appreciate all the Indians who worked hard to make things better, especially those people who spent a little more money on their construction projects to make them look nicer. I decided to appreciate paint.

A group of Japanese tourists entered my restaurant excitedly taking photos of everything including me. They ate their meals and then departed except for one woman. She didn't have a camera. I asked her why she didn't leave with her group. She replied that she wasn't with a group.

Her name was Mutsuko, and she had a delightful smile. Like me, Mutsuko was poised to depart to Varanasi, so we walked together to buy train tickets from a suitably-authorized travel agent.

When I asked her why Japanese tourists were so obsessed with cameras, she answered, "Japan has technology culture and we love gadget, including camera. But I think every tourist love photo from holiday. You have camera, yes? But I no have camera. Instead I buy postcard and mail home. I travel light. I am fifty-year-old woman. I cannot carry heavy backpack anymore."

Regarding the Japanese tourists, Mutsuko noted, "They are work group. They are boring. All tatemae and no honne." Next she explained *tatemae* and *honne*, Japanese words that contrasted one's public face (smiles and small talk) with one's true feelings. Mutsuko said that the work group never discussed their true feelings, at least not with her. We laughed as we imagined them showing images of copulating statuary to their friends back home.

Mutsuko was an avid traveller, having visited more than one-hundred countries. I wouldn't have guessed this from her conservative clothes nor her diminutive demeanor. She told me that she studied artificial intelligence at university, then worked as a researcher which was interesting but didn't pay well, and then she went to Bali on holiday. She loved travelling so much that she mastered marketable skills in order to make more money, so that she could take longer sabbaticals. She had no children and she worked hard, so she succeeded.

Mutsuko was an expert in programming computers to understand human languages. She described syntactic parsers, semantics, artificial neural networks for pattern matching and learning, plus models of context. She said that this was a difficult area for researchers, "because computer no have common sense."

I said, "I know people who don't have common sense either. Artificial intelligence is no match for natural stupidity."

Mutsuko laughed before saying, "Every human have common sense. If I throw ball, you catch. You no think. You just catch. If you go underwater, you hold air."

"Ah," I said. "By common sense you mean animal instinct."

"Yes, but robot no have instinct."

"Do you think future robots can be conscious? In other words, can they be aware of their own thoughts?"

"This question depend on nature of conscious."

I paused to consider the implications. "I can see that," I said. "If consciousness is an illusion, like a hologram, then maybe there's an electro-chemical component to it, some property of the physical brain that cannot be simulated in silicon."

"*Sugoi!* This question is still not decided, but I think conscious illusion must be sensory input into brain originating from brain. In other words, similar to sight and sound we have thought. We think with words and visual symbols."

"Yeah," I said. "We hear our decisions."

"Yes."

Mutsuko explained how humanity's superior intellect compared to chimpanzees was a question of neural-network complexity, not chemistry. Then she explained how AI researchers were writing computer code to create artificial neural networks in software, powerful technology that was poised to go mainstream.

"Interesting," I said. "But what about the chemistry? A brain simulated in software could never feel the effects of drugs, right? Of altered brain chemistry?"

"That would be big simulation! Too big, perhaps... Our model for neuron today is very simple, and we get good results! But real neuron is very complex."

"What about emotions? What about robot love?"

"I think Robot cannot love. Too much chemistry from human biology, too much emotion. Love is human. Robot love must be different somehow..."

My new friend and I chatted about the possibility of robots having fun, the glories of world travel, and the wisdom of the ages. We discussed the difficulties involved in touring India too, agreeing that the most important thing we had to enjoy the trip was our sense of humor, something still too difficult for an artificially-intelligent learning algorithm to master.

Upon checking out from my hotel, to my surprise Shivendu told me to keep my money. He said my bill was zero. I said, "No way. Do you mean free? No. I want to pay you for your fine hospitality, my friend. I insist."

"No, no," Shivendu said. "But thank you. I promised Rajat to take care of you, so please now, go with God."

Instead I went with Mutsuko. Then I realized that the question of whether I went also with God depended on my definition of the word *God*. I asked Mutsuko if she thought this word had any meaning outside of our mostly-shared network of semantic associations, as speakers of English, and so we talked for hours.

27 - Women are Smarter

Rebecca was tall. She was also African by race which made her stand out against a crowd of Indians. I saw her get into a tuk-tuk near my hotel. I saw her again at the train station. Given her exotic beauty, I felt compelled to observe her, and I observed that she was a professional at ignoring Indian men while simultaneously smiling for the women. As Mutsuko and I boarded our train, she followed. Rebecca was our bunk-mate in our first-class, air-conditioned sleeper carriage. She introduced herself as a Brazilian who lived in Rome on her way to Goa via Varanasi. She confessed that she was supposed to be studying at university but she blew that off to travel the world. She spoke good English because all the rich children from São Paulo studied English, she said, but she preferred Italian.

As we settled into our respective bunks, I was enchanted as I observed this beautiful backpacker asking Mutsuko her opinion of Khajuraho's copulating statuary.

Mutsuko answered, "Oh I like very much! Japan also have erotic statue, but not so much creative positions! Not so much detail or beauty either."

Rebecca said, "Yes! Why should we be ashamed of our sexuality? Let's carve it into stone for eternity! Let's celebrate our passion!"

Mutsuko said that she understood Rebecca's cultural perspective because she visited Brazil twice including for carnival. She said it was easy to imagine Rebecca as a bare-breasted carnival queen dancing samba. I had to agree.

Rebecca's smile was festive and she spoke with musical rhythms. "Carnival music is sexy," she said. "But Brazil is also very conservative. You will not see naked women at the beach for example. Very small bikinis yes, but topless no. Did you know Brazil has more Catholics than any other country? But there's nothing wrong with sex for pleasure. The Khajuraho pagans understood this, until the holy warriors killed them all."

I had just read the Kamasutra, the ancient Hindu guide to virtuous living including sex, and I witnessed within myself how this recent memory helped to inspire my lust. I felt loyalty to

Angeline also, so I was conflicted. I contemplated my animal instincts.

Meanwhile Rebecca asked Mutsuko about women's rights in Japan.

Mutsuko answered, "In ancient time, man hunt and woman raise babies, of course as with all animal. And now in Japan man have office job and woman raise babies. I think house-wife in Japan have better life than salary-man. Man work too hard, always tired. Woman stay home, walk in fresh air, make nice dinner, spend all the money. Woman are smarter than man. Woman think with one head, but man distracted by second little head."

We all laughed, then as I looked into Rebecca's smiling eyes, I thought, "It's true." I was distracted.

Just then, Mutsuko pointed out elephants dragging tree trunks along a dirt road. Seeing this made me feel adventurous, far from home.

My train-mates and I discovered that we all spoke Spanish. Rebecca spoke the best because Spanish was similar to her native Portuguese. I found her accent to be delicious. My animal instincts pushed me towards seducing her, but my logical brain insisted that my love for Angeline should prevail. I knew this would be a temporary dilemma however, because I would eventually give into temptation, I would flirt with other girls, and if the flow was right, I would take them to bed. Angeline had to work and I had to travel, and therefore I had to flirt as this was my nature. My sex drive was built into my lizard-brain, programmed into my DNA.

I prodded Rebecca to teach me practical Portuguese, because as I told her, "What world tour would be complete without visiting Brazil?"

28 - The Most Holy River

Mutsuko, Rebecca, and I ditched our backpacks at a cheap hotel (they shared a double room, and I got a single), then we walked in search of the Ganges river to find the famous *burning ghat*, the place where the faithful would be gathered. This was surprisingly difficult given the labyrinth we encountered, a maze of narrow lanes and Indian chaos. As we explored we paid close attention so that we could find our way home later. We heard drums, then singing. The noise got louder then saddhus appeared carrying a corpse wrapped in colorful textiles. They moved towards us chanting a mantra while skillfully avoiding a bull with sharp horns chewing garbage. Mutsuko said, "If we follow them, we find river."

She was right. We followed the saddhus to the sacred site where we watched in morbid fascination as death professionals prepared firewood then laid the corpse on top. One man lit the fire which quickly became an inferno. Meanwhile the victim's family and friends (entirely men) looked solemn, and nobody cried. My friends and I watched, mesmerized, until the fire burned completely and the wind blew the ashes to eternity.

We wandered back to our hotel via a temple inhabited by monkeys where we stopped to chat with the men who guarded the temple's treasure, then we wandered around some more, getting completely lost for what seemed like ten minutes, then we ate yet another fabulous thali plate in an open-air restaurant surrounded by chicken wire to keep out the monkeys.

I found an Internet portal in a bazaar beyond my imagination, crowded and noisy and fun to explore. I was anxious to hear from Angeline so I was disappointed. I asked her to please send me some news. In the same note I told her about Willow, the guru who said that plans are what make the Gods laugh. I typed, "I want to keep the Gods happy so my current plan, ho ho ho, is to visit you. But first I'm going to China. Don't worry, I'll be careful. I traded some sugar-beet seeds with Willow in exchange for eternal illumination. I happened to have some sugar-beet seeds with me (long story) and Willow seemed like a real guru."

The clerk asked for two-hundred rupees, many times the fair price for ten minutes of Internet. When I argued, he called two friends to join him from a back room. I decided it was worth five dollars to avoid a fight, but I felt indignation as the hustler pocketed my cash. I wanted to slap the smirk off his face. As I was leaving I told him to fuck off. I wondered what Willow would have thought about that.

Later I told my friends about the scam. Mutsuko summarized, "This was small injustice. Imagine if he kill your brother?" She went on to describe injustices she witnessed during the civil war in Mozambique on her second African tour. Then she described the Japanese Yakuza, a group Rebecca compared to the Italian Mafia, a secret society who mastered the art of murder and intimidation to pursue wealth and power. Stealing two-hundred rupees was child's play.

My friends and I set our alarms to wake up early, following another backpacker's advice to go on a river cruise at sunrise. We walked to the river in the darkness.

Our first mission was to witness the twenty-four-hour spectacle at the burning ghat. We sat to watch a funeral long enough for the fire to highlight humanity's fleeting existence as small beings on just one of trillions of planets, each spinning through one of quadrillions of galaxies, all spanning infinite time; we are star dust.

Meanwhile on Earth, my Khajuraho buddies and I befriended three New Zealanders who were also looking to go for a sunrise cruise, so we joined forces. Micah was a ginger-haired man who spoke Japanese, and his boys Johnny and Floyd had Asian eyes.

Micah and Mutsuko hit it off instantly, and to me they seemed perfect for each other. Micah once had a Japanese wife but she died, then six months later, he took his boys out of school to travel the world, to literally move on. Sharing a boat with them was a fun adventure, and it brought the price down per person.

As our captain rowed into the darkness, we witnessed the birth of a new day on the world's holiest river. Floating past the burning ghat, with the flames standing out against the cold calmness of the black water, he explained that the death workers did not burn saddhus, pregnant women, nor people who died from cobra bites, and for those who could not afford wood, there was an electric crematorium. He smiled. "Ceremony of death is joyful because the holy Ganga carries soul to eternity."

As the sun rose, I marveled at the faithful bathing in water polluted with sewage and industrial waste. It was a peaceful experience until a corpse floated by, which was shocking.

Micah said that in contrast, New Zealand was the cleanest country on Earth, with managed fisheries, renewable timber, and happy people. He said the government was the world's least corrupt, the result of simple design, a single house of parliament. To me this analysis was fascinating because I was trained to believe that America's democracy was the perfect model for the world to follow, that the separation of powers was brilliant, but I since learned that complexity was a recipe for dysfunction. Keep it simple, stupid.

Micah admitted that New Zealand was lucky because the small population was coupled with abundant resources. "I'm not a salesman, I'm a citizen," he said. "And let me tell you, we have a lot of work to do! Inequality is growing, and so are the people. We are becoming obese, and that's bad. But nowhere is perfect because everywhere has human stupidity. Anyway, I prefer to live in a clean, green land where fairness trumps freedom, where equality leads to stability and reduced crime (at least that's our goal). I prefer to live where the government is mostly there to help. I'm also a fan of Japan; the culture works. Just look at the low crime rate in Tokyo."

Micah seemed like a good person, so I was happy when Mutsuko left with him the next day, first to Agra to see the Taj Mahal, then to Rajasthan for a camel trek. I was not so happy when Rebecca decided to go with them. She was anxious to go to Goa, so she left too.

Suddenly alone, I missed Angeline more than ever, especially given that I hadn't heard from her since Hampi. I called her at work to surprise her, but she didn't pick up, so I left a message, then I called her mobile phone and left another message, then I sent her an email. Then I aggressively explored Varanasi, a holy city filled with culture and beauty, plus a fair amount of crap and annoyance too.

Pilgrims travelled from afar to bathe in the sacred waters alongside pseudo saddhus trying to swindle rupees from hapless tourists. All of this provided fine entertainment for the casual observer, me. The bogus babas added color to the scene. So did the monkeys and snake charmers and at least one elephant. I couldn't imagine a place further from California.

Because of my own poor cash management, I had to pay for lunch with a five-hundred rupee bill. The waiter could not make change. None of the customers could make change either. So the waiter asked a beggar outside. The beggar made change. When I asked the waiter what he thought about this, he replied, "That guy makes more money than I do! And you see that woman over there?" He pointed to a beggar mother. "That's not her baby. She rents the baby by the hour. This is a very good corner for begging. We get too many tourists."

On a whim, I engaged the next street shark who asked me, "Where you going?"

Sharky seemed harmless, just a kid trying to make small money by guiding foreigners. His dark eyes seemed somewhat honest, so I answered his questions about me, then I asked him questions about him. He said that I was different from other tourists. "Most foreigners only try to ignore me," he said.

"Walk with me then," I said. "Let's go to the river."

"Good idea. Let's go for a swim!"

"Are you crazy? Sorry, but I'm not into toxic chemicals and infectious diseases."

"You must swim! The water will purify your soul!"

"Sorry, but I'd rather have a purified body. And by the way, if the river is so holy, why do you treat it like a toilet? Clean it up, man. Clean it up!"

As Sharky and I watched a cremation, he explained how the flames all came from a single source that burned continuously for thousands of years. I saw a corpse's head explode, oozing brain through the funerary cloth. Sharky laughed, then he said this family did not buy enough firewood, so the victim would not burn completely. He was right. One of the death workers stirred the fire, causing a blackened arm to fall to the ground. A dog grabbed the arm and dashed away. Sharky laughed, then he explained how the death workers were from an "untouchable" caste but they were proud of their role in society. "In India," he said, "each person has a job to do."

When the fire died out, part of the victim's torso remained in the ashes. I watched in awe as a harijan worker gave the charred heap to the victim's widower at the edge of the river. The man said a prayer, then he threw the heap over his head into the water. He walked away and never looked back. I was deeply impressed by the stark symbolism, but for Sharky this was life and death as usual.

When I explained that in my culture we buried people, Sharky asked, "For who? Whenever the people who know you also die, whenever there is no memory of you left alive, then nobody will ever visit your grave." I knew he was right. My great-grandparents were all anonymous dead people. I did not even know their names.

Sharky's comment caused me to remember my previously-most-exotic cultural experience, when I travelled to Oaxaca, Mexico with Pedro for the *day of the dead*. My friend and I drank tequila with his siblings at the site of their parents' grave, in a cemetery lit with candles and packed with flowers. The oldest gravestones sadly observed the festivities alone, and so they would sit, alone for the rest of time, forever forgotten by the living.

I checked my email. No news. I hadn't heard from Angeline for too long, and I was getting worried. I tried calling her again, twice. I knew that accepting death was part of everyone's spiritual quest but given Angeline's mysterious silence, this was a topic I preferred to avoid. In fact, this topic was starting to freak me out. I had to leave Varanasi.

29 - Speaking in Globish

I caught a train to a city near Nepal with a plan to go tramping in the mighty Himalayan mountains. Nepal was on my way to China, and tramping seemed like a perfect activity to clear my head, plus it was great exercise too, and I always insisted on staying fit. Indeed, I was more determined to stay fit than ever because all the delicious vegan food in India helped me to appreciate just how much I came from a fast-food nation of unhealthy workaholics. I missed my regular soccer work-outs.

My new train-mates (from Spain) were also headed to Nepal in order to tramp the Annapurna Circuit trail. Thanks to their positive determination to attempt this trek in winter, when they invited me to join them, I accepted. I tried my best to participate in their conversation which was difficult because my mediocre Spanish from Mexico was no match for their speedy slang from Spain. They were patient and helpful but my brain got tired from deciphering so much backpacker banter, so I borrowed José's dictionary to review practical vocabulary, ready to embark on a new adventure, in Spanish.

Emerging from the Gorakhpur train station, locals hurried into rickshaws and tuk-tuks while my new travel mates and I stood gaping at the pandemonium, and as such we were a target. Hustlers swarmed to us pretending to be helpful. We ignored their blah-blah to focus on one question, "From where departs the cheap, local bus to the border with Nepal?"

The hustlers all lied, insisting there was no such bus. "But you are in luck," one of them said. "I have private car. I take you for only ten American dollars per person."

We found the local bus which was gratifying, but we were not yet good to go. Our bus driver insisted that we put our packs into an insecure and filthy compartment, his way to charge us for one more seat inside. Many of the locals had more stuff than us, and none of them paid extra, so we argued but we lost. We paid; after all, it was only about a dollar.

Soon we found ourselves at the international border where it was not obvious where to get our passports stamped, nor the correct rate to exchange Indian rupees for Nepalese rupees, but we figured it out. In the process we met two backpackers from Italy.

Davide and Mario's Spanish was poor and their English was worse, so they spoke what they called *Globish*. For example, when I asked Davide about his travel plans, he answered, "I follow flew."

"Do you mean, you go with the flow?"

"Yes. I go with flow."

Davide and Mario were also planning to tramp the Annapurna Circuit trail, so they joined us. Together we hired a private car to Phokara. Our driver made haste until the loud boom of gun fire caused all traffic to halt. "Maoists!"

We quickly abandoned our car to hide behind a brick wall for protection from bullets, and there we sat for hours, speaking in Globish, until finally the traffic began to move again.

We drove through a surreal scene of banana trees and road-side kiosks, all closed, with soldiers dragging two dead bodies towards a military caravan, with the ground nearby glistening with blood. Other soldiers directed traffic.

José said, "Fucking hell!" The rest of us nodded our heads in stunned silence.

At the next village, more military men ordered our car to stop for a curfew, so our driver arranged a place for us to sleep, then he escorted us to a restaurant that offered fried chicken and beer. I remained upbeat, happy that my European colleagues provided a distraction for my head, to not think about death but to tell jokes instead.

We continued to Phokara in the morning, and I was delighted to see the majestic mountain views, but I was also anxious about the increasing time with no news from France. Phokara was a base for backpackers so it was easy to get online. No news. My friends and I watched a comedy film about bowling in a bar, then I checked my email again. No news.

My hotel rented bicycles so I woke up early to ride. The man in charge, Lou, only had one bike and it looked ancient, so I asked if I could go for a test ride. Lou said yes, so I circled the block. The bike had a mechanical defect so I circled back. Lou was strangely nowhere to be seen so I returned the bike to its original place, then I walked in search of a better bike which I found a few blocks away.

I checked my email, then I rode through rice fields and forested trails. I rode into town to buy thermal underwear, a wool hat, and high-calorie snacks. No news. When I arrived back at my hotel, Lou ran towards me yelling, insisting that I stole his crappy old bike. He said I had to pay. He said that if I didn't pay he would call the police.

I said, "I did not steal your bicycle, so call the police if you must."

He did. They came. I told my side of the story through an interpreter. After much discussion in Nepalese, they all agreed I should pay for half the missing bike.

I said, "No way."

Lou said, "You will go to jail!"

I told the police my theory that Lou stole his own bicycle as an opportunity to extort money from an American. After much discussion in Nepalese, the top cop shook my hand while saying in Globish that I was free to go. He kept Lou for further questioning. I felt that my clear conscious created positive karma, whereas with Lou it was the opposite; his guilt showed through his body language. Karma or no karma, I was happy to be free, and happy that Lou got served.

That night I received an email from Angeline. I read it voraciously. She said she was sorry for taking so long to reply, that all was well, and that she loved me. Then I woke up. There was no email. Damn.

30 - Maoists

My European mates and I took a touristy minivan to the Annapurna trail-head where lovely people greeted us with smiles. Mostly these people were trying to sell us trinkets that we did not want, but their genuine charm was a nice way to start the day. My friends and I bought coffee and fried noodles, then we sat to contemplate our ambitious mission, three weeks of walking up and down mountains, then we hit the trail.

Going up, the endless stairs distracted my mind, the rigorous exercise tested my body, the mountain air nourished my soul, but I failed to find happiness. Indeed, I brought up the rear feeling grumpy. When my friends asked me why I was so quiet, I explained about Angeline's long-overdue reply, and to make matters worse, I said, I was suddenly disconnected from the Internet.

José asked me if I knew any of Angeline's friends, and I was surprised I hadn't thought of that. Angeline was an early adopter of a brand-new technology called *social media* but I wasn't, so I did not have access to her Internet *friends* but I did know how to contact her father. I knew his full name and place of employment. My instinct was to go straight back to Phokara to get on line but my comrades convinced me to continue. There was nothing I could do, news or no news, so I might as well tramp.

Davide summed up the weather with the only perfectly grammatical English sentence I ever heard him speak, "It's fucking cold." Endless uphill walking warmed us up, so did the afternoon sun, and with the sun came spectacular mountain views that helped me to find my positive attitude.

We encountered the Maoists just before the village of Ghorepani. We had heard that we would have to pay them baksheesh so this was not a surprise. The Maoist men had guns but they did not intimidate. On the contrary, the older one seemed friendly as he explained who he was with a British accent. He asked us what countries we were from, so we told him.

The Maoist declared, "Trekking in Nepal costs twenty American dollars for citizens of Europe, and one-hundred dollars for citizens of the USA." He looked at me.

I was used to haggling so I said, "One-hundred dollars? That's too much. And it's not fair. Our guide book says..."

The Maoist interrupted, "To pass, you pay. You come to Nepal as a tourist, so this small money means nothing for you, but for us, we are in an historic struggle to bring justice to our people, to free them from feudal oppression. Therefore, to pass, you pay."

I said, "I'm happy to pay twenty dollars, OK? But..."

The Maoist interrupted again but this time he looked angry. "We fight against the murderous King Gyanendra," he said. "And we fight against America. You say you bring democracy to the world but you bring only oppression, and in the name of God. Ha! And you call us terrorists because we resist, but America is the real terrorist! Citizens of Israel must also pay one-hundred dollars."

"Whoa," I said. "I do not support my government's foreign policy, so..."

"But you benefit from your government's murderous imperialism! Nobody from Nepal except the fascist King and his friends can afford to travel to America. You are rich. American tourists are all rich."

"A hundred dollars is too much money."

"It is not! To pass you must pay! You are rich because of American state terrorism, but you act as if you do not even know."

I looked to my friends for support but they looked back with stunned silence. Meanwhile the Maoist spoke to me with a condescending tone. "In 1953 your country removed the leader of Iran to help one oil company, proving that you do not really care about democracy. Hypocrites! Then you removed the leader of Guatemala for one *banana* company! How many South American presidents have died from an assassin's bullet or an unfortunate plane crash? You stole Hawaii. You enslaved Africans. You wiped out your own native people. And now you brashly announce to the world that you have the God-given right to invade Iraq and Afghanistan. To pass you must pay."

The force of his words left me speechless.

He continued, "And that's not the worst of it. Your institutions loan money to poor countries at high interest and you make them pay in dollars, but they do not have dollars, so you make them sell their natural resources to get dollars, and you don't even pay them a fair price! What's going to happen when the forests are gone? There is nothing free about your so-called free trade. That is why you are a rich tourist, such a young man, but able to travel the world. So please, do not tell me you cannot afford one-hundred dollars to visit our beautiful mountain villages."

José interjected, "Please wait. My friends and I, we talk private, OK?"

The Maoist men glared but stayed silent as we stepped aside. Meanwhile José told me in Spanish, "You should have said you're from Spain. They didn't ask to see passports."

I replied, "Good idea but too late. I'm OK with twenty dollars. I was expecting that, but..."

José said, "If we split the baksheesh six ways, it will only cost about thirty dollars each."

I said, "That's generous. Thank you. But I'm going back down. I just decided."

With that, my companions paid their baksheesh and continued their trek without me. They understood that my decision was not about money. I was just that anxious to contact Angeline's father. I watched my friends walk away until they were out of sight, and I felt sad, but I had to do what I had to do. I had to *follow the flew.*

I surveyed the scenery: majestic mountains and angry rebels. I was anxious but also in no mad rush, so I took advantage of my unique opportunity to interview Maoists guerrillas. I asked the older guy how he learned to speak English so well.

He answered, "I went to school in London, but then I returned to help my brothers in arms."

I asked the younger guy, "Do you hate me? Or just my government?"

He answered, "I hate you if you do not renounce your government. I hate you if you are a savage and inhumane capitalist. I hate you if you support the terrorist wars of your criminal president."

I said, "You should not hate people you do not know."

The Maoist men both glared but I felt compelled to engage them. They were educated and articulate, and I was curious to understand their point of view. I asked the older guy, "You explained what you are fighting against, but what are you fighting for?"

He answered, "We fight for justice for the people of Nepal. We fight for a new economic model, one that supports the small business, the rural farmer, and the artisan, because we do not have capital and we do not want capitalism. We must replant our forests. We need sustainable agriculture to live in harmony with our fragile environment. We have witnessed the complete failure of the so-called 'free' market to provide these things, a system that increases inequality and consumes resources for quick profits with no regard for the future. And these profits do not stay in Nepal! They go to America! Our problem is not a lack of resources but a lack of fair distribution. We know what to do, unlike the King who lives in a fantasy world."

The younger Maoist added, "We also fight for the fall of America so that all the world's people can be free to pursue sustainable economies. At first we applauded when New York was attacked with airplane missiles, but then we discovered your criminal regime designed the attacks as an excuse to launch new imperialist wars."

I said, "I don't think that's true. Sorry, but this is where I draw the line. I'm no fan of..."

The Maoist interrupted me, his voice threatening. "It is true! We know the CIA was involved. We know all about your corrupt relationship with Saudi Arabia. We understand the vast power held by your military-industrial complex. The strategic importance of Israel is also obvious. Your criminal leaders will stop at nothing to further the cause of empire, including murdering your own people. America must be stopped!"

"Whatever, but you must know that you cannot defeat America militarily. OK, maybe in Afghanistan, but not at home."

"Every empire has fallen and yours will be no exception. You will be defeated economically! Planetary resources are dwindling, your debt is skyrocketing, you rely on cheap oil, and global forces are growing ever stronger to resist you."

"I'm too ignorant of the facts in Nepal to pass judgment about your cause against King Whats-his-name, but I do assume that you're right about that. I assume that your cause is just, and I do hope you can bring peace to your people. I saw the result of your war the other day. I saw death. So I hope your Maoist leaders are good and wise so that your war is worth the cost. May you soon know peace."

The older man asserted, "You know nothing about war."

His stare no longer bothered me so I stared back, then I put on my backpack, then I turned to walk down the mountain.

The man said, "OK. You pay only twenty dollars. You go now, join your friends."

I said, "No thank you. I need to go see about my girlfriend."

I felt surprisingly at peace as I walked down ten-thousand steps. I repeated to myself often however, "There has to be an explanation." I stopped at a trail-side guest house only when it was too dark to continue.

When I finally arrived in Phokara, I scoured the Internet for publications from the Large Hadron Collider looking for Papa's contact details. I did not succeed in this mission, but I did figure out the standard pattern that the laboratory used for email addresses, and so I was able to send Papa a message. I told him that I was in love with his daughter, and I was worried.

While online I researched the alleged CIA involvement in the attacks of September eleven. I found a shocking number of conspiracy theories, but it made more sense to me that the airplane missiles were piloted by pissed-off Arabs. I remembered people asking after the attacks, "Why do they hate us?" The Maoists gave a better answer in a single diatribe than I ever heard on television. It was karma.

The Maoists made it clear that lucky-bastard Americans like me enjoyed our super-power status not because we were morally superior, but because of the winds of history. We won World War Two and then used that advantage to maximize the profits of empire. My encounter with the Maoists strengthened my determination to research the facts of history, warts and all. I felt stupid for having gone so long without comprehending the greed, the institutionalized greed, the profit motive baked into the corporate system. I no longer believed that America was benevolent, but instead that humans are always trained apes, and some apes are trained better than others. As a child I believed the institutionalized lies because I wanted to believe. I was gullible. I was human.

31 - Freak Street

I travelled to Kathmandu, the ancient city a few hours away by bus, a place that always captured my imagination, like Timbuktu I imagined, but with a mystical mountain air.

A German backpacker named Leonhard sat next to me on the bus, and despite his punk hair cut, face piercings, and tribal tattoos, he was nice to talk to. He said he was going to Freak Street and that seemed appropriate. Freak Street, he said, was named after hippies who called themselves *freaks* in the 60s and 70s, back when Nepal had a more liberal attitude towards drugs. My freaky friend had an acute sense of history when it came to hippies and freaks. He talked so much about Freak Street that when we finally arrived in Kathmandu, I decided to check it out too, especially given its prime location in the heart of the old city.

We arrived at Durbar Square, a plaza lined with pagodas, statues, and shrines, the Kathmandu of my imagination, peaceful temples from an ancient kingdom so different from the noisy traffic jams on the way into town.

Leonhard and I sat to watch locals buzz about, plus hippies in search of enlightenment, and tourists wearing mountaineering gear in search of that perfect photo or maybe a cappuccino with carrot cake. Other tourists were on their way home after shopping for thangkas, mandalas, and scrolls, wall hangings that radiated tranquility. I couldn't blame them. I was tempted to buy a souvenir myself.

Leonhard and I enjoyed our quiet viewpoint until two local kids insisted on selling us drugs. They were annoying so we left. My companion knew of a hotel nearby so we went to check it out. The place only had one vacancy, a double room, so we took it. This was no problem because I was beginning to like my freaky friend. He was weird but nice, and it was common for solo backpackers to share rooms to save money.

I went to check my email. There was no news, so I returned to my room only to find Leonhard rifling through my stuff! I yelled, "Fuck you, you freaking freak!"

The punk avoided eye contact as he gathered his things and left. Meanwhile I certified that I had all my valuables, slapping myself for bad judgment. I should have known better than to share a room with anyone who thought Freak Street was the number-one tourist attraction in Asia. I never saw Leonhard again.

I walked into the tourist district on a mission to swap my India guide book for a Nepal guide book, then to sip cappuccino, eat carrot cake, and read about Nepalese history. Then I walked in a random direction to explore.

An old man asked me where I was from so I answered, then I asked him to please show me the most interesting thing in our vicinity. The man, Sankhu, led me to a temple hidden behind an electronics store where devotees burned incense while others arranged flowers. Sankhu directed my attention to a wooden carving with sexual detail that reminded me of Khajuraho, a wooden man's *schlong* poised to penetrate a wooden woman. Sankhu said this was the most interesting thing in our vicinity.

A boy approached us to clean our ears. He wrapped cotton onto a stick as if we had agreed, then he repeated the price as if we were negotiating. Sankhu told him to go away.

We walked until we encountered a white man begging for money. The guy explained how a taxi driver just stole all his stuff. He said, "I had my backpack in the trunk, and when I stepped out to the street, the bastard sped away! So now I'm fucked."

I offered to buy the guy lunch, Sankhu too.

Sankhu said, "No thanks. I go now to visit my son."

That's how I traded a lovely local man for a desperate Argentinian named Gunther. Just after we ordered food, the guy began complaining about his sore neck, then he found out I was American so he complained about America, then he complained about the Jews. For some reason that I did not understand despite his rant, he hated Jews. I was shocked when he actually said, "It's too bad the Nazis didn't kill them all."

I snapped, "You asshole! Don't you know the Jews are just another culture caught in the winds of history? The Jews are not the problem. Your racist attitude is the problem!"

I stood up to cancel the food order, mumbling, "Great, another Freak-Street freak."

Back on the noisy street, I wanted to clear my head so I took a tuk-tuk to Bhaktapur, a peaceful place that Sankhu recommended.

The historic center had no motor vehicles and no Internet portals, but it did have exquisite Buddhist and Hindu temples in harmony with a plaza loaded with statues of mythical beasts. I stopped for coffee in a parlor filled with old men, none of whom spoke English, but they were all smiles. Our non-verbal dialog was the highlight of my day. I had no idea what they were on about most of the time, but they were hilarious.

32 - A Rolling Stone

The worst kind of news is the message that tells of the death of someone dearly loved. For me this news arrived as an email from Angeline's father. The tragic words burned me deeply, leaving me unable to read beyond the words, "drunk driver." My eyes swelled with tears, leaving me staring into a fuzzy haze of grief.

The pretty young woman at the next computer asked if I was OK. Her words pulled me back to reality, so I dried my tears with my t-shirt then I watched her read my email. Minutes passed before I was able to look her in the eyes. The only words I could find were, "Thank you."

She said, "It's OK. I'm here for you. OK? Don't worry. I'm here for you."

The manager of the Internet shop asked if I wanted anything to drink. He said not to worry about the bill. I said, "No thanks." I had trouble breathing.

As my brain began to function, I could see Angeline saying, "You don't remember the dinosaurs, do you? No. Because you were dead. It's a Yin-Yang thing." This sounded reasonable at the time but it was bullshit. A dark cloud hung over my soul.

I gathered the courage to read the rest of Papa's email. Angeline was cremated and her ashes were scattered. She would forevermore exist only in my mind.

The young backpacker with her hand on my shoulder did give me some comfort, but I felt horribly alone. Her name was Sara.

I said, "Thank you Sara, for your compassion. Will you please join me for a walk?"

She said, "Of course." Then she grabbed my hand and led me outside.

I asked her about her immediate plans, a selfish question because I wanted a friend. She answered, "I am so sorry. I fly home tomorrow! I've been travelling for exactly one year, and... I don't want to go home, but I have my ticket and I'm out of money."

I suddenly felt like crying, so I asked Sara to tell me about her time in Asia, a selfish question because I wanted her to talk, about anything, I didn't care. She told me that she flew to India upon completing her duty as a soldier in Israel. She was too pretty for me to imagine her as a soldier, and this made me curious. I realized that despite Israel being a tiny country, I had met so many Israelis in India that it was common to see restaurants advertising in Hebrew.

Sara explained, "The situation for Israeli soldiers can get really bad. Very stressful. Of course it's nothing like what the Palestinian people suffer, but it is stressful. Imagine mandatory military duty... So yeah, a lot of ex-soldiers, just as soon as we get away from all that shit, we come to India. For me, I like the yoga, but a lot of my friends just want to hang out somewhere cheap and smoke charas all day, and others only go to Goa to pop pills and dance at trance parties. I'm not a charas smoker myself, but I do appreciate the shanti-shanti attitude of the hippies, especially after..."

Sara stopped talking and she looked sad, so I changed the subject. I asked her about the Jewish holy book, just to make conversation. Sara explained how disputes over interpreting the Torah led to various sects, much like the Protestant split from the Catholics in the time of Martin Luther. She said, "The Torah forbids work on the Sabbath for example, but what constitutes work? Soldiers carry guns..."

Regarding the war between Israel and Palestine, she said, "It's a holy war, because when it comes to land disputes, people turn to the ancient texts to justify their claims. And religious zealots don't care much for details like water rights. But there has been so much violence on both sides, it's no wonder people are so stressed out."

Sara offered to buy me a book, so our mission became finding an appropriate bookshop. She bought me a book written by the Dalai Lama, the Bodhisattva of Compassion. It was a beautiful book with lots of pictures plus words of wisdom.

We sat together to sip coffee and talk about life for another hour or so, but eventually she said the inevitable, "I have to go. I fly home tomorrow!" Sara wrote her email address on a napkin which she gave to me saying, "Please look me up. I want to see you again. Come to Israel."

I put the napkin in my pocket saying, "You are kind. I want to see you again, too."

"You have the right attitude and that's everything. You'll be OK. You don't have a choice really. Do you?"

"You're right. I'll be OK. This coffee shop will be reclaimed by the Earth in a millennium or two anyway. You know what I mean? This place right here will become a swampland again, or a forest. So you and me, we have to live now, and happily too, because we're alive! Indeed, we should jump for joy because life is the very opposite of death. Live well, Sara my friend, and have fun. And don't worry about me. I'll be fine. I don't have a choice really, do I?"

Sara's smile made me smile, then she left me alone. It was inevitable. She kissed me on the cheek then she left.

I was too depressed to sit still, so I walked like a zombie until I got hungry, then I ordered a meal, then I stared at my food while the radio played a song by an American poet named Bob. He asked me how it felt to be on my own like a complete unknown. Not so good. I did not want to linger in Kathmandu feeling sorry for myself, and I had no direction home. It seemed too depressing to go to Paris to mourn, and inappropriate to follow Sara to Israel right away, even though that was tempting. Furthermore I knew there was no airplane to anywhere called happiness, so I decided to continue my trip to China as planned, like a rolling stone.

I did not embark on my world tour to relax in fancy hotels but instead to participate in the raw experiences of life. By travelling to Tibet in winter I figured, my survival would depend on my wits and therefore I had to remain strong. Despite these brave intentions, I lingered in Kathmandu for nine days feeling sorry for myself.

I told myself that Angeline was fine, that I was the one experiencing mental anguish. I wondered if she and I could ever have made a future together, but it didn't matter; she was dead. Every time I looked at her picture on my camera I cried, so I stopped looking. I never felt more sad and alone. I missed my music system.

When hunger compelled me to eat, I braved the street, barking at the hustlers and tuk-tuk drivers and everybody else. I was in no mood to socialize. I became angry easily, even to the point where I yelled profanities just because somebody honked a tuk-tuk horn for no apparent reason. I had zero tolerance for anyone who tried to sell me something that I did not want, and I did not want anything. One vendor grabbed my arm and this physical contact almost provoked me to hit the guy in the face. Later I saw this as a sign that I needed to chill the fuck out. Angeline was dead. Get over it.

I began to interact with locals differently, playing them for sport. For example if they asked me where I was from, I might say I was from my mother, or from Earth, or from none-of-your-fucking-business, or I might refuse to answer while allowing guesses, anything but the truth. One benefit of travelling alone was that I could experiment with different attitudes to see how they played. I could be a real asshole one minute and then quite gracious the next. Chill out, Raymond. *OM.*

33 - A Swiss Bank Account

I emerged from my self-imposed isolation when I realized that I was free to choose to be happy. My positive attitude was elusive but I knew that If Angeline's death taught me anything, it was to enjoy living while alive. Determined to move on with my own life, I set my alarm to get up early with everything prepared to make coffee, my plan being to sit alone inside my favorite temple at dawn.

I sat inside a particularly beautiful temple where colorful statues depicted Hindu deities silently watching over Kathmandu's humanity. I gave the night guard some coffee and he left me alone, so I was able to sit quietly in the heart of the city, in the most peaceful place in the world despite the ever-louder traffic noise outside. When a devotee eventually snapped me out of my trance, I went walking in search of fresh coffee and a guide book for China, in this case a pirated photocopy.

I walked to the Chinese consulate to apply for a visa. I needed a special permit for Tibet, they said, but they wouldn't give me one unless I was part of a group, so I left in search of a group. A travel agent directed me to a tour company where I purchased a seat on a bus. They photocopied my passport and faxed it to Beijing for approval.

I had to wait several days, so I visited the Internet place where I met Sara. The manager was the only person who knew me, and I needed to talk. He made tea, and his kindness helped me gather the courage to reply to Papa.

I also emailed Bastiaan to pass along the tragic news. My happy-hippie friend replied quickly to say that I should return to Goa, but I did not want to go backward; I had to move forward. My friend and I were in sync with future plans however, so we agreed to probably meet in Thailand in a month or two, after my loop through China. This made me smile, and I felt less lonely.

My brain created a fantasy about meeting Sara in Israel, an emotion I initially tried to shut down but eventually allowed as a way to trick myself into feeling less sad about Angeline. I wanted to send Sara an email, but I decided to wait until I was more recovered emotionally, with my perspectives more mature.

Instead I called Pedro.

He said, "Cabrón! I'm glad you called. Shep and I have become your personal, fucking, private-detective service, man."

"Dude," I said. "Angeline is dead."

My friend and I talked for hours about love and life until finally I asked him for his news, and I could hear him smile. He said, "You're not going to believe this, but first of all, Shep still hasn't gotten anywhere with that government database, but he is conducting research in the underground hacker networks on that, so stay tuned, but meanwhile... Shep got a copy of Pops's income taxes!"

"What? Really? How?"

"Ha. Shep now gets his taxes done with Pops's accountant, the same guy, and he gave Shep access to the office Wi-Fi network, so of course Shep dropped in some spyware, a keystroke sniffer he said, and with this he obtained the password for the office's file server. Check this out: Pops only inherited two-hundred-thousand dollars from your grandfather when he died."

"What? That's not even close to what he paid for..."

"Exactly. Check this out: Shep found a three-million dollar transfer from a Swiss bank account!"

"What?"

"Yeah. This is how your father paid for that fat house of his. Shepherd also notes, by the way, that this money landed in Pops's account just about one year after your grandfather died, coincident with Pops receiving his real inheritance money. It looks like Pops timed the transfer so that he had an easy answer for anyone who might ask how he suddenly obtained so much cash."

"Yeah, that's what he told me. Gramps died, so... Three million?"

After a long discussion, Pedro and I agreed that I should call Pops but not mention anything about what I knew, as this would give me the upper hand. We debated interview tactics, eventually deciding on the idea to propose a family reunion in Jerusalem, because assuming Pops couldn't fly out of the USA, it would be interesting to gauge his reaction.

I made the call.

My mother answered and it was good to hear her voice. I fought back tears as I told her about Angeline. We talked for a long time about life and love, until she told me to come home.

"Actually Mom," I said, "I have a different idea. Maybe you and Pops would like to meet me in Israel? I'd love for you to show me where you two met. We could go anytime, totally at your convenience. I'm off to China in a couple of days, but I can change my plans any time. What do you think? Let's go to Jerusalem!"

"Um, that's an interesting idea son, but... but I'll have to talk this over with your father, and you know how he is, not wanting to travel too much anymore."

"Mom, since when doesn't Pops like to travel?"

"Oh well, you know, he's getting old and he likes his comforts, and besides, Israel is so dangerous now."

"Mom, Pops is not too old, and you guys are rich! You can fly first class. Stay in a fat hotel. Jerusalem is safe. So come on, what do you say?"

"It's a good idea, but you'll have to get your father on board. He's here. I'll put him on. Meanwhile, what can I say? I'm so, so sorry about your girlfriend, dear. That's terrible. I'll pray for her."

"Thanks Mom."

"Do you have any friends. I don't want you to be alone now."

"Yeah Mom. I have friends. We're all going to China together."

"OK. That's good. Be safe, dear. I love you. Here's your father."

Pops said hello, then I gave him my news. He replied, "Oh shit. You should come home. Be with family. Come home."

"Actually Pops," I said, "I have a different idea. Maybe you and Mom can meet me in Israel? Mom just said it's a good idea. It would be great! You can show me where you two met, and we could go anytime, totally at your convenience."

"Well son... I don't know. I'll have to talk this over with your mother, and I can't get her to go anywhere anymore. And we're very busy these days."

"Pops, you're retired! And you don't need to go tomorrow. This trip can be in two months, or whenever. Mom just said she likes the idea!"

"I'll talk to her about it, OK? So call us back. We'll think it over. Where are you now?"

"I'm in Kathmandu, Pops. It's a fascinating city, but I'm not doing so good right now, you know? I really want you and Mom to meet me in Israel. It's something I've always wanted to do, my whole life, to travel with you two in Israel."

"I'll talk it over with your mother. OK? Call me back tomorrow."

"OK, I'll call you tomorrow. Goodbye, Pops."

"Goodbye, son. I'm really sorry about your girlfriend. I love you."

"I love you too, Pops."

I walked in a random direction and kept going, to the edge of the city and beyond. The exercise and ever-changing scenery prevented me from thinking too much.

Snarling dogs approached me. I felt fear and they became aggressive. I picked up rocks and they backed away. This gave me courage and they backed away more. I threw one rock and the dogs gave me all the space I needed to continue in peace.

Arriving at a village, I saw a naked boy flying a homemade kite, laughing with joy. This made me smile. Tired, I looked for a hotel. Finding none, I sat under a tree.

A boy with a soccer ball asked me if I needed a guide. I said yes, so he led me to a man who rented a room, then he led me to a woman who cooked eggs and toast. He asked for nothing in return, so I gave him a dollar.

I collapsed on an uncomfortable mattress where I slept intermittently until roosters crowed. Then I slumped all the way back to Kathmandu, stopping only for breakfast.

When I found a place that offered international telephone services, I called home.

I was angry with Pops for repeating the same lame reasons for not meeting me in Israel, but his attitude confirmed that he really was on the no-fly list, and he was determined to keep this a secret. I was tempted to call him a liar but I held my tongue. I said I was going to China and then Israel, with or without him, probably Syria too.

I asked him if he had ever been to Syria.

He answered, "No. The first time I went to the Middle East, I was in the military. The second time I had an Israeli work visa, and Syria would never have let me in as a tourist."

"Pops, you never told me you had a work visa. I thought you were just a soldier."

"No? Oh well, I had a job in Tel Aviv. I never told you that?"

"No, never."

"Oh well. Your mother persuaded me to move back to California when she got pregnant. We moved just before you were born."

"Interesting... What did you do? I mean, what was your job?"

"Ah, it was just a boring technical job. I was an engineer."

I tried to grill Pops for detail but he was not forthcoming, so I dropped it. Instead I scolded him for his lame reasons for not meeting me in Israel, then we said goodbye.

I called Pedro. He said, "The next time I see Shep, I'll tell him to make an addition to the Pops-research to-do list. We'll find out what he did for work over there."

I walked to the tourist district and ordered a steak. I was intent on keeping to my pseudo-vegetarian habits generally, but I had a strange craving for red meat. Angeline was dead, Pops had a Swiss bank account, and I was about to traverse the Himalaya mountains in winter. What a crazy life.

34 - Lost in Lhasa

My tour group consisted entirely of Germans. They all spoke passable English but mostly they spoke amongst themselves, which was fine with me because I wasn't feeling particularly social. I sat in the back of our minivan and watched the scenery go by, which was spectacular and that helped my attitude.

At the border with China, our driver took our passports then left us waiting along with monks wearing only robes in the freezing cold. I changed one-hundred dollars for the equivalent amount of renminbi, the people's currency, then I scouted out the scene. The Tibetan people all made me feel welcome even as they peddled trinkets, but the Han Chinese ran the show; they controlled the money and the guns.

My group and I traded our Nepalese minivan for a Chinese minivan near the Friendship Bridge, then we began our epic journey along the Friendship Highway into Tibet. The roads were surprisingly good, and where they weren't so good, ambitious construction projects were underway. China!

We stopped where the driver and his tour-master buddy wanted to stop, but this included sleeping in villages and eating in rustic restaurants, which I found entertaining even when the food was boring and bland. We got lucky with the weather to see Cho Oyu from Tingri town, a spectacular snow-capped-mountain giant. I also enjoyed visiting Kumbum Chorten, a site with ancient temples packed with a dizzying collection of colorful murals. We visited the Rongbuk monastery near the base of Mount Everest, an impressive site too, but our view was obscured by clouds. Mostly I was impressed by the fortitude of the farmers who somehow survived on the hills lower down.

One of our stops was unplanned, our vehicle broke down, but our tour guide and his driver buddy got to work as if engine repair was as routine as filling up with petrol. Meanwhile I walked around a nearby lake, and this uplifted my attitude tremendously.

When we finally rolled into Tibet's capital city, the tour-master said our hotel was crappy as a tactic to up-sell us to somewhere more expensive. The guy also tried to sell various side excursions at extra cost. I still hadn't made any connection with the Germans, so I asked the driver to drop me in any neighborhood that had cheap hotels. He said no, adding that this was illegal and therefore he could lose his tourist license. I offered him fifty American dollars. He tried to haggle for more money but he finally agreed, and just like that I was lost in Lhasa.

I entered what appeared to be a hotel (I was unsure because I was suddenly illiterate). The receptionist spoke just enough English to communicate that she did not have a license to accept foreigners, so I walked until I found a tea-house to warm up. Meanwhile I researched my guide book. I sat next to a man wearing a yak-fur coat, and I really wanted to talk to him but this was not possible, and that made me feel strangely excited.

It took a while, but I found a hotel that accepted people like me, had tea with the English-speaking manager, then I left to explore. My hotel was in a Han Chinese neighborhood which was interesting, but I wanted to see the Tibetan neighborhood more, and I wanted to walk because my muscles were still tight from the epic minivan ride, so I bailed in the direction of the Potala Palace.

Even wearing all my layers and walking quickly, I felt cold, but not too cold, because I was wearing all my layers and walking quickly. I toured the Potala Palace, once Lhasa's fortress of Buddhist power and an appropriate place to contemplate philosophy, I figured, so I sat for a spell in a prayer hall with a giant Buddha trying to think pure thoughts. The palace museum's treasures were interesting but I was more impressed by the imposing architecture with colorful attention to detail, and by the busy rush of pilgrims who took turns spinning every prayer wheel so that their improved karma would deliver them to a better future, or something like that.

I wandered for another hour until I encountered a temple where monks sat chanting. A woman offered me tea so I stayed until the ceremony was over, soaking up the warmth and the primordial vibrations. I also contemplated words that were carved into stone in English (translated also into Chinese and Tibetan). One carving read, "Commit no evils; engage in virtuous deeds; subdue one's mind thoroughly; this is the teaching of the Buddha." Another read, "You are the master of yourself. What other master could there be? Through calming yourself alone, you find this master that is hard to find." Yup.

I met a monk outside a restaurant with a sign in English. He made eye contact, then he whispered, "Excuse me mister. You have photo Dalai Lama?"

The old monk's face showed a child's hope so I asked him to join me for lunch. I insisted. Dan told me it was illegal to possess a photo of the Dalai Lama in China but this didn't stop me from packing the book that Sara bought me in Kathmandu. I told the monk that I would give him this book, then I told him again and again using different words until he finally understood. His appreciative smile displayed both great joy and bad teeth.

The monk was old enough to remember when the Dalai Lama fled into exile, and over lunch he told me about the destruction caused by the People's Liberation Army, and the steady erosion of Tibetan culture since, especially since the completion of a direct train to Beijing. Every day more Han Chinese arrived and things got worse for the Tibetans who were poor in comparison. Tibetan independence was impossible, said the monk, because the Tibetan territory had too many resources, the Buddhists were too peaceful, and the Chinese army was too strong. He said he was happy that at least the Communists no longer prohibited Buddhism, despite their controls on the number of monks.

The old man was eager like a schoolboy to hear my description of Dharamsala and the world beyond, so I told him stories while I escorted him to my hotel. Once there, I introduced him to the hotel manager while I fetched the Dalai Lama's book. The manager made tea, then we all sat together and looked upon the book's beautiful photographs while contemplating the words of wisdom.

When my new friend left with his treasure, I watched him walk down the street, then I watched as police approached him, grabbed the book, and threw him to the ground. Without thinking, I ran out the door to help. When the police stared at me, I stopped running. One of the cops pointed at me and yelled, making it clear he wanted me to approach, so I did.

The old monk said something that I understood to be in my defense, then a cop hit him so hard that he bled from his nose.

People on the street stopped and stared but nobody said anything.

I told the monk to please tell the police that this was all my fault, that I did not know the book was illegal. I insisted, "Tell them I gave the book to you as a gift. Nothing bad will happen to me."

The police glared while the monk translated. They argued for a while. Finally my friend said to me, "We go now police station."

An English-speaking cop interviewed me, then he delivered his verdict: the police would destroy the book, let the monk go free, and deport me.

A different cop escorted me to my hotel then left with my passport. When he returned, my document had Chinese characters stamped in red ink over my special permit to visit Tibet. The same cop then escorted me to the train station. Once there, he demanded money. He knew the English word for money, but not enough English to have any kind of dialog. When I removed my wallet, he grabbed it rudely then removed all the cash, some of which he spent on my train ticket, then we both waited quietly until I boarded that train, to where I didn't care. I had seen what fate wanted me to see in Tibet, and besides, it was fucking cold.

35 - Monkey See Monkey Do

I walked up and down the train looking for foreigners but there were none. I had no Chinese money and the food vendors did not accept dollars, so I went hungry. My only joy was that when I smiled at people, most smiled back. A few responded to my queries, but none spoke enough English to make conversation. One guy said, "Happy Birthday!" Another guy simply asked me, "Who?" Mostly I watched the scenery roll by, remote hills dotted with occasional villages populated by tough survivors.

I matched the Chinese characters on my ticket to characters in my guide book to determine that my destination was Xining, the train's first stop outside the Tibetan Autonomous Region, a city with a rich history given its location on the ancient Silk Road, a city lower in altitude than Lhasa and thus warmer. It seemed perfect.

As I disembarked the train, I spotted a white guy so I ran to him to ask if he could please change twenty dollars. He did more than that, he gave me advice.

Thomas John also known as TJ, from Chicago, scribbled some Chinese characters on a scrap of paper saying, "Show this to any taxi driver. He'll take you to the Monkey See Monkey Do café. You'll like it. The owner speaks good English and they make good food, plus the hotel across the street is good value. I'm on my way to Xian now but I'll be back in a few days. If you're still here, it'd be great to hook up. I don't often get to talk to other Americans."

The entrance to TJ's favorite café had artwork depicting monkeys sipping coffee; this was predictable, but that which I saw next was not: four Chinese guys smoking a joint. On the table was a pile of marijuana plus four cups of tea.

The fat guy invited me to sit, so I sat. The skinny guy offered me his joint. Feeling exhausted, I declined. I asked for coffee instead. The tall guy made coffee. The guy with glasses just smiled. Referring to the marijuana, I asked, "Is that legal?"

The skinny guy answered, "Not legal, but marijuana look like tea. Nobody notice, and if notice, nobody care. If police find, say make problem only for self. We make no problem for police, and police make no problem for us."

The fat guy added, "But be careful. More close Beijing, more police law. Here Xining, far Beijing. You know?"

I nodded to show understanding.

As best as I could tell, the guys' names were Jang, Liu, Wei, and Lee. I asked Lee how he learned to speak English so well. He answered, "Long ago I live in Yangshuo, many foreigner, very beautiful."

I told my companions about my arrest in California for weed. This prompted Wei to roll another joint. He must not have understood when I declined previously because he offered it to me. This time I accepted saying, "Monkey see, monkey do." Everyone laughed.

I added, "By the way, the guy who told me about your fine café, TJ, he said you have good food, and I haven't eaten since Lhasa..."

Lee recommended the primate pesto. It was wonderful and cheap. The joint was free.

The walls of Lee's coffee shop were painted with scenes of simians in human situations, a world of chimpanzee accountants, orangutans with perfect haircuts, and gibbon girls in love. Lee explained, "We all monkey, no tail, but monkey. Some good, some bad, most in middle." That sounded just about right to me.

Despite the coffee I needed sleep, so I stepped outside to beautiful snow flurries. It was pretty darn cold, so I walked straight into the hotel that TJ recommended.

The reception guy understood that I wanted a room, and I had just enough money.

I took a shower then collapsed on my bed. Feeling depressed, I resolved not to smoke any more pot. I didn't rule out smoking with a guru on a mountaintop, or maybe with Bas in Thailand, but in Xining without a compass, I needed all my mental faculties to find my way. I missed Angeline something fierce.

The hotel manager knocked on my door to give me a thermos of hot water.

As soon as he left, my phone rang. I answered, "Hello. English?"

A female voice said, "Massage?"

I did not want a massage girl, I wanted Angeline, so I unplugged the phone from the wall, then I flipped on the TV. The one channel in English documented the Japanese army invading the central homeland during World War Two. I flipped the TV off and fell asleep.

The next morning I found a Bank of China where my debit card worked to get cash. When I checked my email, there was a message from Papa with a photo of his daughter attached. She was beautiful. I forwarded the photo to Bastiaan. As he was online at the time, we chatted for a while, confirming our plan to meet in Thailand in about a month. This made me smile.

Curious about the so-called 'great firewall' of China, I searched the Internet for the words *Dalai Lama*. I was surprised to receive a page of keyword matches until I realized that none of the links worked. The only information I could find about the Bodhisattva of Compassion was the existence of forbidden pages on the World Wide Web.

I explored Xining's historical sites including a city mosque and a mountain temple. I watched a group of men playing a game that resembled chess, with elephant pieces instead of bishops. I took a dump in a most-disgusting public toilet. The insects seemed to love the stench but I did not; I did however love the adventure. China!

As a white guy in a city with no white guys, many pretty girls looked at me and smiled. This was great, but in a funny way it made me feel lonely because I could not talk to them. Overall however, the pretty smiles boosted my morale. They distracted me from thinking about Angeline, and so I began to move from mourning to acceptance. What choice did I have anyway? I wished that I spoke Chinese.

I rented a bicycle. I hiked up a mountain for the view. I tried different restaurants. I especially liked the places where I could walk into the kitchen and point at vegetables because the various chefs prepared them deliciously every time. When in doubt, avoid meat.

I visited the Monkey See Monkey Do café regularly to discuss human-monkey nature with Lee and his bad-English-speaking customers. This dynamic changed when TJ returned from his trip to Xian. I felt a special bond with him because he was a fluent speaker of English, which was weird. He told me about his trip and all the lovely people he met. Then he ordered the gorilla gado-gado.

Lee noted that TJ and I were both Americans so he pushed the idea that democracy was not harmonious because as he put it, "Election is stupid." He asserted, "Your president is chimpanzee." He said, "China better because Communist Party make plan for future without concern for popularity." Finally he added, "I like television because television train monkey for harmonious society, but not television for vote like America. That's stupid."

"Interesting," I said. "Harmony huh? I agree the needs of the many outweigh the needs of the few, but..." I was suddenly not sure if democracy was good or bad in theory. What makes one ideology better than another? I wasn't sure about the facts of the matter. I concluded, "But that doesn't make democracy bad in theory."

Lee said, "Democracy with one-and-half-billion people, bad in theory."

I pondered the vastness of that number, the phenomenal wealth of humanity, then I said, "I see your point, but... What do you think about censoring the Internet? Is this harmonious propaganda, blocking access to information about the Dalai Lama?"

Lee answered, "We have freedom of speech on Internet, but government must limit freedom to protect common good. Dalai Lama is not harmonious."

"OK. What do you think about the factories where they make all the cheap stuff to send to America? Aren't the workers virtually slaves?"

"Maybe you prefer die of hunger? How you say? Look at big picture. For example, China have too many people, so government make one-child rule. This no possible in democracy."

Instead of trying to argue with Lee's logic, I asked TJ his opinion. He answered, "Lee's right. China's monopoly of power allows them to do effective strategic planning. They're building infrastructure everywhere. And most people seem pretty happy about it all because the economy is growing. There's something to be said for a government that gets stuff done. Compare that to

America's dysfunction."

Lee said to me, "You see? TJ prefer China more than America."

TJ said to me, "It's true. None of the bad stuff affects me personally, and living here has advantages, the food of course, and the girls, man, the girls!"

The more my compatriot and I hung out together, the more we bonded as friends. He discovered that we both played an American sport called footbag (commonly known by the brand name Hacky Sack), similar to ball-kicking games all over the world, where the goal was not to win but to play beautifully while cooperating to defy gravity. My new friend and I played footbag with our Chinese colleagues joyfully.

One day we walked to the old market, a place I loved for the colorful human energy. TJ ate a fried scorpion then he said, "Chinese people eat all manner of bugs, because you know, if you don't eat them, they might fly away. Mmm... Delicious!"

I suddenly thought about Sasha, the woman I met in Brooklyn. I promised her that I would try interesting food so I ate a scorpion. It tasted like bug, but not as bad as I expected, actually quite edible.

I was shocked to see rhinoceros horn for sale, but for TJ this was normal. He said, "Some ape will buy this, thinking it will increase his sexual potency. Why? Because he saw some other ape buy it."

I said, "Yeah. Monkey see, monkey do."

TJ took me to a dance club to drink beer and flirt with girls. The city streets were lined with flashing neon lights and we went inside to party. Alongside China's optimistic youth, all fashionably dressed, we danced and drank and flirted until the time came to go to a karaoke bar to drink more. The KTV computer had songs in English, so I could sing (poorly) but my conversations with the girls never got much past, "What's your name?" We did however all speak the same body language on the dance floor.

All the curious stares made me feel like a celebrity, but I couldn't have a real conversation with anyone but TJ. He asserted that as I got unceremoniously deported from Tibet, I would not be able to extend my tourist visa, and therefore I needed to get my ass moving if I wanted to see more of China, and there was a lot of stuff worth seeing. I was tempted to stay in Xining because I was having fun, but I agreed with his assessment, so I bought a ticket on the night train to Xian. I also bought a postcard and mailed it home.

On the train I secured my backpack with my wire loop and padlock, then I closed my eyes in thought. I was born the son of my wealthy American father, and it did not matter from where his money originated, I was the lucky-bastard beneficiary. Angeline was dead but I was alive to enjoy an epic adventure that included Chinese dance clubs, primate pesto, and mind-expanding perspectives. I fell asleep with a smile.

36 - Travelling Light

Ticket Man pushed on my arm and this woke me up. He said something in Chinese to which I replied in English that I had no idea what he was on about. He said, "Ticket." This forced me to abandon my dream involving dinosaurs to find my wallet. I told the man to wait. Meanwhile I realized that I had to pee so I put on my shoes. That's when I discovered my wallet was missing because my backpack was missing! I sprang out of my bunk to look around desperately only to find Ticket Man staring me in the eyes. He repeated, "Ticket."

I scanned my surroundings, suddenly shaking uncontrollably. My voice trembled, "I don't have my ticket," I said. "It was stolen! All my stuff! All my stuff... Stolen!"

I yelled to nobody, "English? Hello! English please! Speak English?"

Several people in my vicinity stirred but none responded. Meanwhile Ticket Man's expression indicated that he really wanted me to show him my ticket. Suddenly freaking out, I ran down the corridor to look for my backpack as if whoever stole it might have left it somewhere obvious. As I felt my anger exploding, I noticed Ticket Man say something into his two-way radio, then he chased after me running.

I opened the door to the next carriage yelling, "English? Speak English?" Then I ran to the next carriage. No English. Ticket Man finally caught me by grabbing my jacket, then he grabbed my arm. I panicked and elbowed him in the chest to release me. This was a mistake. I escaped, but my nemesis caught me again at the next carriage door. Now he too was angry. He held my arm firmly while yelling some words into his radio.

I took a deep breath. "Please," I said. "My ticket was stolen, but I paid... Xian. Xian!"

Meanwhile a second Chinese-rail employee came running. He spoke with Ticket Man for abut one minute then he said to me, "You exit train, next station."

I said, "No! You don't understand. I bought a ticket but it was stolen. My backpack was stolen! I don't speak Chinese. I have no money. Xian. Xian!" I bowed humbly.

Ticket Man Two repeated, "You exit train next station, or I call police."

I briefly considered this option but I did not want to see the inside of a Chinese jail (and this seemed like a real possibility given that I elbowed Ticket Man violently, plus I just got deported from Tibet). My only other option was to ask the gentlemen as nicely as possible if they would please let me ride until Xian, but it was too late; these men did not want me to be their problem; they had already made their decision.

Just then, the train engaged its breaks for arrival into a station. I saw no option but to admit defeat, so when the train stopped I disembarked in a state of shock. I wandered out of the station like a zombie into a small town that was bathed in darkness, with the first rays of light signaling a new dawn. What the hell just happened?

I could not believe how stupid I had been for not having anything useful (like money) in my secret pocket. I let my guard down just when I needed it most, lured into a false sense of security by a stupid wire loop and padlock. I felt stupid for elbowing Ticket Man too. Stupid! No longer did I feel like a lucky bastard.

A rooster crowed just as morning forced the stars to fade. Fortunately I slept in my clothes, and I had my wool hat in my jacket pocket, so I was able to stay warm as long as I kept moving. I also had the eye-of-Shiva necklace Angeline gave me. She said Shiva would protect me from evil, but she didn't believe this was true.

I was determined to find someone who spoke English, or someone who would let me use the Internet, or someone to give me money. All I had to do was get to any big city from where I could find another Westerner, but Xian was too far to walk. When I realized that all I required was an English-speaking financial benefactor, I yelled obscenities to the wind. How could I be so stupid?

Roosters crowed with increasing frequency as people began to buzz about. I found a beef-noodle shop with locals having breakfast, and the food looked delicious, but I was unable to convince the staff to serve me for free. Nobody admitted to speaking English, so I walked on.

To every person I asked, "English?" When this didn't work, and it never did to any useful degree, I tried my bad Chinese, but this was not sufficient for dialog either. Most people seemed kind and curious but nobody helped me. I figured that with little disposable income, everybody's face-saving response was to not understand the foreigner babbling gibberish, even when they understood very well that I was asking for help.

Morning turned into day and I grew increasingly frustrated and exhausted, my initial hope shattered. I found exactly one Internet-portal shop but the place's sole employee would not let me go online for free. I stayed calm until he refused to let me use a computer even as a language translator for speaking with him, then I began to yell, then he made me leave.

Once outside I yelled more obscenities to the wind.

I loitered outside a convenience store where old men played a game called *go*. I tried making elaborate gestures to ask for food or money, and some of the men responded with words, but others laughed at me. This was irritating. If I had been in a better mood I might have stayed, but instead I redoubled my efforts to find a hero.

I sensed that most villagers were decent people, too caught up in their own lives to help a foreigner. I must have seemed to them strange at best, perhaps subconsciously seen as an enemy from an alien tribe, or maybe they simply wanted to save face while keeping their cash in their wallets. I sat under a tree feeling sorry for myself until my frustration turned into desperation as reality sunk in. I needed to find a place to sleep.

I knew that I could go to the police, but this was my last resort because the worst-case scenario was bad; I was officially a trouble maker. My only other idea was to sneak aboard a train and steal a ride to any big city. I couldn't figure out a way to reliably bypass the ticket-checking guards during the day, but late at night I figured I could probably sneak into the station via the shadows along the tracks, get on board a train, and then lock myself inside a bathroom. This became my new Plan A.

Meanwhile, inspired by a TV show about a guy who survives in the wild, I walked towards a nearby hillside to set up a comfortable nest behind a giant rock that provided shelter from the wind. I twisted branches from shrubs and I gathered leaves to mimic a bed and blanket. I tried and failed to start a fire.

The wind blew in a misty rain so I hid behind my rock. Meanwhile the weather got worse, and it was too cold to sleep. In my waking nightmare I imagined Angeline's car crash. I saw her crying for help, crying my name. Damn! I feared that I might not ever find true love again or worse, that I might freeze to death behind my stupid rock. As my reality became enveloped in darkness, I wept.

Finally I said out loud, "It's OK to be angry that Angeline is dead, and it's fine to be fucking angry that all of my fucking stuff just got fucking stolen. But get fucking over it!"

Deep introspection followed. My focus became anger management because hitting Ticket Man was a step too far. I worked on strengthening my impulse-control neurons by rehearsing violent scenarios from which I calmly walk away, ideally with everybody laughing.

I told myself that my passport and debit card were replaceable and I would simply have to deal with the hassle, and clothes were clothes; but I lost my camera with all my wonderful photos of Angeline, and I lost the napkin upon which a beautiful person named Sara wrote her email address. Shit. I never felt more sad and alone.

I attempted to meditate. I found that I could control my thoughts somewhat if I was sitting calmly but, I asked myself, what about those moments of surprising stress when passions are inflamed? I did not answer this question with logic, but never since have I allowed an angry impulse to veto my logical brain's appeals for calm.

That night I discovered a newfound curiosity to understand myself better, for example to know how I reacted to stressful situations such as having my girlfriend die, then allowing all my stuff to get stolen thanks to my own stupidity, then getting kicked off a train thanks to my own poor anger management, then enduring freezing rain behind a stupid rock. My death was unimportant to the Universe, I figured, but nevertheless the prospect of my inevitable demise was not uplifting. I told myself repeatedly and calmly to be the Buddha, to accept that my life was ultimately meaningless. But it wasn't! To me I had meaning.

That night I learned something about suffering. I learned that money does help one to be happy but a great attitude helps more. I was never going to be happy about my predicament but at least I was able to calm myself down. I was happy when the rain clouds dispersed in time for sunrise, and I was amazed that somehow I stayed awake all night, and then I was delighted when the sun brought the warmth of a new day.

I walked into town in search of English or maybe beef noodles, but after a frustrating hour of fruitless begging, I detoured onto a promising road into the farmlands, through fields devoid of crops, awaiting spring.

Dogs barked at me. Old women yelled at me, apparently telling me to get off their property. At one residence, I thought seriously about stealing clothes for extra warmth, but I didn't. At another residence I found a water well, so I drank as much as I could stomach. I always tried to appear friendly and I made gestures, but I received mostly blank stares and Mandarin chatter. A few people questioned me but with no words in common, they helped me not at all. Inspired by hunger, I walked all day.

I realized that I failed to inspire anyone to help me because I was trying too hard; I was frustrated, angry, and I lacked confidence. As I walked, I worked at calming down my mind.

My luck changed when I came across children playing. I spoke every word I knew in their language and they giggled, so I juggled rocks and they giggled more. I played the clown to their delight until their mother appeared and approached me. She said, "Ni hao."

I said, "Ni hao." Then I gestured that I was hungry, laughing at myself while she laughed at herself as we tried and failed to talk to each other.

The woman led me into her humble home, adorned only with a portrait of Chairman Mao. She stoked a fire, then she prepared a feast of noodles, eggs, and tea. Her smile filled me with joy. She spoke to me in Mandarin, and I told her in English just how much she was my hero. When I was done eating, I gestured that I needed money and a place to sleep, but either she didn't understand or she had no cash. I had no way to force the question, so I thanked her repeatedly then left.

Energized, I returned to town to beg from the men playing *go*. They were not unkind, but after an hour or so, I still had zero cash. I tried to communicate my desire for a warm place to sleep, but either they did not understand or they did not trust me inside their homes at night. As soon as I got frustrated by their lack of actual help, I bailed.

I tramped back to my improvised camp in search of dry twigs for fire kindling in case my mission to sneak aboard the night train went bust. As I explored the area I found a coin, valuable silver from China's past and surely a good omen. Money! I considered trading the coin immediately for Internet time, but I wasn't sure what message to send or to whom, because my situation was defined by its urgency. So I said a prayer to the remover of obstacles. "Hey Ganesha," I prayed. "Please help me get to Xian with this coin!" I didn't believe Ganesha would help me, but this was how I entertained myself.

As soon as night fell I entered the train station via the shadows. Despite the possibility of trading my coin for a ticket, I went with Plan A, to sneak on board a train and then find a bathroom. When a train finally arrived, I jumped onto the platform then walked casually through the metal door of a second-class sleeper carriage. Easy! I turned left looking for that bathroom, and this brought me face to face with Ticket Woman. She said, "Ticket." *Doh!*

I calmly presented my coin. "Xian," I said. "I want to go to Xian please. Thank you."

The woman said, "Mei yo."

"Do you speak English?" I asked, now suddenly feeling desperate. "This coin is silver. Money. Money. Xian! Xian!"

Ticket Woman said, "Mei yo," then she said something else.

Meanwhile a young lady approached, dragging a wheeled suitcase. She studied my face then her eyes widened. "I speak little English," she said. "I can help?"

Yes! I asked my new hero to please translate my case. She did, then she translated the synopsis. "No buy ticket on train," she said. "Only in station, but station no take old money... But I think my grandfather, he buy old money from you, enough for ticket. My grandfather, he speak English good. Long time he live Hong Kong. I visit grandfather now. You come."

Yes! I wanted to kiss this fabulous woman but instead I thanked her emphatically. As we walked away from the station, I asked her about my new favorite subject, her. I learned that her name was Chan Lian, a university student visiting her family farm on a school holiday.

I said, "Ganesha works in mysterious ways. Glory be to Ganesha!" Chan Lian looked puzzled, so I added, "Never mind."

We walked away from the city down an unfamiliar path. Meanwhile I tried to pronounce my new best friend's name with correct Mandarin tones, which made her laugh. I didn't care about my bad pronunciation; I cared only about her fantastic English-speaking smile.

37 - Old Man Chan

Arriving through a gate into a decorative courtyard, Chan Lian raced ahead to announce our arrival. She returned with her grandfather, a senior citizen whose wrinkled face exuded wisdom. The old man studied me with a curious expression, then he said, "Hello."

"Hello," I said back. "It is very nice to meet you, sir."

He said, "It is nice to meet you too. We do not often receive foreign visitors. Welcome."

The man asked what I was doing in China so I told him about my world tour, quickly bringing the tale around to my predicament. I added that Angeline just died too, something I had not intended to say but I let slip out, probably because I was just that relieved to have a friendly ear.

The man answered, "My friends are mostly dead too, and I never have many possessions, so we are same. You cannot go back in time to be with dead girlfriend, and you should not live in past with memory. Your life now is about now, so I hope you enjoy Chinese tea."

It was the best tea ever.

The man introduced himself as Chan Ming. "But you call me Old Man Chan," he said. Then he put his hands together and bowed, laughing, "I like the way that rhymes."

He introduced his wife, a woman whose face was even more furrowed than her husband's. I couldn't pronounce her name so I called her *Wrinkles* in my mind. She said, "Hello Raymond. Nice to meet you." I quickly realized this was most of the English she knew despite having lived in Hong Kong; she never had much reason to interact with the British.

Old Man Chan asked me questions about me, patiently translating for Wrinkles. He also had private words with Chan Lian, my unlikely savior, a girl who always smiled. Regarding my predicament, the old man said that my lock must have made my backpack appear valuable, then he said, "Weak defense can be worse than no defense." Then he reprimanded me for elbowing Ticket Man, but not directly. He said, "One must always resist violence." Then he told me not to worry, that he would help me.

I said, "Thank you so much. And regarding the incident with Ticket Man, yeah, I've given that a lot of thought already, and lesson learned. Anyway now I need money. I do have a silver coin that should be worth enough to pay for a train ticket, so if it's not too much to ask, can you please buy this coin from me? Or if you could please give me a small loan, just enough to travel to Xian (actually Beijing would be better because they have an American embassy and I need a new passport). If you can help me with that, I promise I'll pay you back double, no triple."

The old man smiled. "This is possible. Another option is you earn money. You work here with me if you have no urgency, if this is acceptable? I need help to fix fence. My boys think farm life is boring, all live in cities, and I have heavy work to do. My grandchildren help, but, but I do not want to bore you with family drama."

I said, "Sure. Yes. Deal. Just tell me what you want me to do."

The old man answered, "Drink tea. You keep coin as souvenir." Then he said, "By the way, how old are you?"

I answered, "Twenty five."

He said, "When I was your age, I was twenty seven."

When I looked puzzled, he laughed. Then I sipped my tea, delighted to be on a family farm with friendly farmers, plus chickens, pigs, and a vegetable garden. Perfect.

I asked my esteemed host to tell me about his adventures in Hong Kong. He began by laughing. "Once upon a time," he said, "there was small boy who think farm life is boring so he travel to Hong Kong with his uncle, for exciting life..."

Young Mr. Chan got a job at the shipping docks and eventually became a manager. He learned how to fight Kung Fu. He studied English. He met Wrinkles at a beef-noodle stand, then they got married and raised two children. He had a good life in Hong Kong but returned to the farm during the Cultural Revolution after receiving word from his sister that their parents desperately needed their help. The old man told me how he coached his children to say to everyone, no matter what, that they were returning to their village because they loved Chairman Mao and wanted to work for his prosperous and modern China. He told me about the brutal war for ideas that followed. He told me that he had since learned to appreciate boring farm life in peace.

Chan Lian said to me, "Grandfather make good money in Hong Kong, but only thing he buy for farm-house is refrigerator."

The old man protested, "That's not true. I make other maintenance. Anyway, now I want to buy clothes-washing machine also. Your grandmother deserves modern luxury, I think."

Chan Lian said, "When I visit farm, I am clothes-washing machine."

The old man and I discussed world affairs while Chan Lian and Wrinkles prepared dinner, sautéed vegetables and rice. When I asked him what he thought of the Communist Party, he answered, "I do not get involved in politics. If I criticize government, I only bring danger to my family. I am not communist and I am not capitalist. I am humanist. I try to do what is right, not what is profitable. Even here in humble village, people charge too much for vegetables, money money money. I prefer traditional way, except of course for refrigerators and clothes-washing machines."

When Chan Lian served the table, the old man said to me, "Sometimes you must feel something missing to give value. Raymond, you recently had difficult adventure, so now you must value simple dinner with humble farmers."

It was the best dinner ever.

Chan Lian gave me a tour of the house. She gave me a towel then showed me where to take a shower. I took a glorious shower, then I found my hosts to say goodnight. Chan Lian escorted me to my bedroom, then with her intentions as obvious as her crooked teeth, she sat next to me on the bed.

I said, "Thank you for helping me Chan Lian. You really saved my ass. Please thank your grandfather also. Please tell him that I look forward to helping him with farm work however I can."

My unlikely hero put her hand on my shoulder in a way that left no room for misunderstandings, a sexy gesture. I protested, "Chan Lian, I barely know you! Oh, and I'm really looking forward to getting a good night's sleep. I can't remember ever being this exhausted."

"Soon you know me better," she answered. "You sure you no want sex? Very good for healthy sleep. No worry, I have condom. Do you have big penis?"

I didn't want to disrespect my hosts but I couldn't refuse her. Chan Lian seemed so beautiful at that moment, her eyes smiling with such enthusiasm, I said yes. My hero rode me with a sexual prowess that brought me to ecstasy and beyond, and with that, all the stresses from my ordeal drained away. When she left me, she said, "Sweet dream, nice American man." I slept until the roosters crowed.

38 - Ki Gong

As I walked to the bathroom to pee, I saw Wrinkles and Old Man Chan practicing Tai Chi in the courtyard, my favorite place on the farm because it exuded antiquity in both architectural style and detail. To me this was the most traditional courtyard in all of China, even if it wasn't. I watched my hosts in admiration of their delicate movements, casual yet precise, smooth but forceful. I admired their physical prowess.

At the breakfast table while eating the best noodle soup ever, Wrinkles spoke to me in Chinese and I spoke to her in English. We got along famously. Mostly I thanked her repeatedly for her kind hospitality and patience in putting up with a crazy foreigner.

I asked the old man about Tai Chi. He said he was just a humble practitioner, but he was willing to show me the basics if I was keen. I was keen. Indeed, this seemed perfect!

But instead of discussing Tai Chi, the old man steered our conversation to the job at hand: fence repair. He explained how we were going to fix the fence the old-fashioned way, by hauling wood with help from a donkey cart borrowed from a friendly neighbor. But first, he said, it was most important for me to teach English to his granddaughter.

As soon as we left the breakfast table, my student Chan Lian escorted me to her bedroom and began undressing. I protested but her shirt was already off. She said, "Teach me dirty words." The sight of her breasts aroused my animal instincts, so I began her lesson with the word *titties*. Then after a quiet quickie, we discussed grammar and pronunciation; this was more productive but not as much fun.

The first day of fence repair was easy, and it was fun to cruise around with the donkey cart. All I did was help to load and unload wood, but I understood why the old man wanted younger hands to help.

Just as we finished our work for the day, Old Man Chan told me, "We would be honored if you can stay here for one month, because this is the next opportunity for Chan Lian to take time from university, to escort you to Beijing."

I said, "Yes certainly. Let's plan on that then. One month.

Thank you so much."

This seemed like a long time, but I was happy to go with the flow. I did not require Chan Lian to escort me to Beijing, but I made no argument. I could tell the old man was setting me up as a potential grandson-in-law, and I did not mind because, wow, what a great opportunity to do a deep cultural dive! More than anything I felt grateful.

The next morning my new guru woke me up and gave me loose-fitting clothes. He told me to get dressed and meet him in the courtyard in ten minutes. There he instructed me to stand with my feet shoulder-width apart, my knees slightly bent, and my arms hanging only by gravity, grounded like a tree, while he and Wrinkles practiced their Tai Chi form. I watched the couple flow through their movements while trying my best to stay completely still, which was difficult so early on a cold morning.

Wrinkles said something that maybe meant she was going to make noodle soup for breakfast, then she entered the house. Meanwhile the old man scrutinized my disposition. "First you must learn to breathe," he said.

I thought I already knew how to breathe, but I was wrong. My guru showed me exercises to control energy flows that I previously never perceived. I was amazed at how little I knew about breathing. My guru instructed me to imagine a fiery ball of energy centered around my gut. "This is *Ki*," he said, "the dynamic energy of your living spirit, your core energy. You must dominate your *Ki* before you study Kung Fu."

"I thought you were teaching me Tai Chi," I said.

"Correct. You study Tai Chi Chuan, Yang form, but the man who learns Tai Chi with precise control also prepares for Kung Fu with speed and power. We have time together so I will try to prepare you. I will show you *Ki Gong* exercise also, most important to dominate this *Ki* energy, to allow your *Ki* to flow through body like water."

Old Man Chan demonstrated the first few transitions of his Tai Chi form, then it was my turn. He corrected me with gentle pushes, and I was able to mimic his motions more-or-less before breakfast. I sensed his delight as a teacher to have a student, so after breakfast I asked him if we could train some more. He made the second lesson all about breathing.

And so began our daily training. Soon I could imagine my *Ki* energy flowing, and I could see how the concepts applied to fighting, not that I was keen to fight, but I was very keen to have this unique opportunity to study with a venerated master in a remote Chinese village, something that seemed like the epitome of the travel-adventure experience. I was also keen because I saw our training as a meditation; to get it right I had to calm my mind. I trained as hard as I could, and Old Man Chan seemed encouraged by my progress, but never satisfied.

As for Chan Lian, she found a way to get me alone for sex every day of her visit, four days in a row, but then her studies beckoned and she returned to Xian. We were friends and we were lovers, but we were not in love. No problem. I had no qualms about practicing the art of pleasure, and the sex helped me recover emotionally from my recent traumas. Chan Lian was my hero, and while she was away I missed her. I knew that I did not want to marry her however, implying that soon I would likely never see her again. As with Angeline and my ex-girlfriend Maia I wondered, if I never saw them again, did it matter if they were alive or dead? Either way I had to move on, as travellers do.

When the old man and I finished the fence project, to celebrate, we drank tea.

From then on we practiced martial arts relentlessly, focusing on the art of his favorite Tai Chi form (a complete set of transitions designed to cover all the important movements). The old man taught me movements from a Kung Fu form also, but mostly we focused on Tai Chi so that I might complete all the form's transitions correctly before my eventual departure.

The old man showed me defensive tactics too, such as how to take a hit to avoid injury. Also he showed me how to penetrate an opponent's defenses to incapacitate. I hoped I would never have to use such tactics. Indeed, I would have to be in serious trouble to break someone's knee with a sneaky kick, or to strike someone hard in the throat (and then run away), but that wasn't really the point.

The old man and I often sat to sip tea and discuss anything and everything. He seemed as interested to learn from me as I was to learn from him. He often quizzed me about Western ways. He was also intrigued by India.

When I asked him about Angeline's Yin-Yang theory, he answered, "Yin and Yang apply to all of life, not just Tai Chi and physics theories." I asked if this made Yin-Yang the essence of Chinese philosophy, to which he replied, "No. Philosophy is Western idea, logical and precise. Yin-Yang is flexible like green bamboo. It is adaptable." I asked him to elaborate, so he explained, "Give power to positive energy and resist negative energy. Recognize if you are jealous or angry. Emotion is normal, but first you must think. For this purpose I make my grandchildren go to school, to train their minds, to pursue virtue and resist vice. Demand much from yourself but little of others."

With such fascinating company, time flew by.

The old man made sure I stayed busy by helping with household chores, practicing martial arts, or explaining my knowledge to him over tea. It did not matter if we discussed politics, culture, or *Ki* energy, I was always fascinated by his perspective. Seldom did he allow me moments of laziness because laziness was not a virtue, but I cherished my down time so that I could simply think things through. My routine was anything but boring, but after a month, as the date for Chan Lian's return to the farm drew near, I became anxious. Old Man Chan and Wrinkles were awesome companions, and I was grateful to have them as friends, but I needed to get a new passport, and I needed to access the Internet to let people know I was alive, and I needed to travel the world. It was time to go.

Chan Lian arrived early on a warm afternoon, and I was delighted. I suggested we leave immediately for a long walk because I had a destination in mind; I wanted to give my silver coin to the woman who fed me when I was hungry.

As we arrived at the farm house, the woman recognized me and waved. Soon we were all sipping tea with Chan Lian translating as I explained the circumstances that led me to beg for food. When I gave the woman my coin, she held it to her chest and cried.

Chan Lian and I walked back to the farm via town, past the men playing go. They waved at me with smiles, so we stopped to to say hello. Chan Lian translated as we discussed the inherent difficulties of non-verbal communication. I was tempted to call the men out for not having helped me, but I didn't want to cause them to lose face. Instead I pointed out that smiles were universal.

Back at the house, after a quiet quickie, my girlfriend displayed a ravenous curiosity about America. She seemed fascinated by what she called the paradox of Western values: liberty and democracy contrasted with inequality and crime. It was not an easy thing to explain. When I asked her about China, she always focused on negative aspects such as small-town gossip, jealousy, and corruption. I realized that this negativity made it hard for me to love her. When I asked her what she thought about the Dalai Lama for example, she called him a terrorist separatist and a bad man, lusting for power and hellbent to have his own Kingdom. Sigh.

The day before Chan Lian and I left for Beijing, the oldest Chan of the Chan clan told me, "The youngest daughter of my youngest daughter is a woman now, but she has no master." By master I knew he meant husband. I knew that he knew I was shagging her.

I said, "She's a nice girl."

He said, "Chan Lian is intelligent and hard working. She will make an excellent wife."

I looked him in the eyes to say, "I am honored that you see me as a potential husband for your granddaughter. Really. But I see the selection of one's life partner as one's biggest decision, not to be rushed. Maybe Chan Lian would make a perfect wife for me, and if that's our destiny then I welcome it, but I think one should only marry for love."

The man said, "You are wise. I do not understand modern ways, especially American ways, but no harm to ask. I am old. I must yield in favor of new generation."

I said, "The new generation has much to learn from you."

He said, "Yes and no. Modern children prefer to learn from television. I do not like television. This is the opposite of meditation. Television gives people thoughts so they do not have to think. This leads to lazy habits and poor character. But children love television. What can this old man do?"

I shook my head. "I think you must accept that change is inevitable, and find happiness in the fact that you provided a good education for your grandchildren."

"You are right," he said. "Are you sure that... maybe you want to marry Chan Lian and live on humble farm?"

"I cannot," I said, then I felt sad.

39 - Husband and Wife

On the train to Beijing I felt liberated with no backpack. Gone was that paranoia that accompanied having things worth stealing. Chan Lian brought only a change of clothes and the essentials of personal hygiene. Easy. In the restaurant carriage over tea, she proposed. "Grandfather say you make good husband," she said. "You want marry me?"

I told her that I was honored, but I could not marry her because I was on a mission to explore the world. She said that this was understandable but it did no harm to ask. No worries.

Arriving in Beijing, we went to the tourist district to find a hotel, something that seemed like a trivial goal, but no; Chinese people were prohibited from sharing rooms with foreign people unless married. It took an hour to find the back-alley hotel manager who believed our lie in exchange for cash. Chan Lian told him we were husband and wife.

We made love, took showers, then took a taxi to my home country's embassy.

In the room dedicated to American Citizen Services, a consular officer gave me an Affidavit Form to fill out, to describe the circumstances under which my passport was stolen. The man made me sign this form in his presence, then swear out loud that everything it said was true. He told me to wait while he verified my previous passport through the Passport Verification System, and to clear my name through the Name Check System.

Chan Lian and I waited, with nothing to do but look at life-sized portraits of my chimpanzee president and his vice chimp-in-chief, both with cynical grins that seemed strangely appropriate for my bureaucratic moment.

A Chinese man asked me to enter a sound-proof room for an interview, but it was not he who appeared on the other side of the bullet-proof glass, but an American woman who glared at me through wire-rimmed glasses.

"Raymond Love Junior?"

"That's me."

"You do realize that you overstayed your Chinese visa?"

"Yeah. Someone stole all my stuff, and it took me a month to get enough money to buy a train ticket."

"That may be true, but the Chinese authorities will not be sympathetic."

The woman reprimanded me for not filing a police report, then she said, "It will take us three days to issue you a new passport, then you must leave China. You can apply for a new visa, but only from outside of China. You should start looking into plane tickets."

"That's going to be difficult seeing as I don't have any money."

"Do you know anybody who can wire you money electronically?"

"Yeah, my father can do that."

"Good. He can send you money care of this embassy. I'll give you the necessary information. Now, go get your picture taken, second room on the left down the hall, then return to me with a completed Passport Application Form."

I asked the woman from where I could call Pops, so she gave me written instructions for dealing with Chinese public telephones. I said, "That's all well and good, but I still don't have any money." The woman gave me one-hundred dollars worth of local money along with yet another form, then she gave me a document to show the police should they stop me.

As I had to call Pops, I tried to think of a clever way to get him to confess his secrets. Why was his name in the Terrorist Screening Database? And why did he have a Swiss bank account? And what did this have to do with his job in Israel? But I needed his help, so I decided not to call him a liar.

Mom answered the phone and it was good to hear her voice. I gave her my news, about which she commented, "Everything happens for a reason, dear. It's all part of God's plan."

I said, "Mom, do you honestly think I got robbed to fulfill God's plan? Do you think Angeline was killed for a reason?" Sigh. "Never mind, Mom. I'm sorry. I love you. But I need help. OK? I need money. We can talk about God later. Can you please put Pops on? I need him to wire me some money."

I told Pops about Ticket Man and Old Man Chan, quickly skipping ahead to the part where he himself was about to walk into his local bank to wire me money. I gave him the embassy's account details.

Before I left home, I gave Pops power-of-attorney over my bank account for exactly this kind of emergency, so I asked him to please instruct the bank to send me a new debit card too, care of the American embassy in Bangkok. Pops said he would, then he told me about the time someone stole his passport in Turkey.

This gave me an idea. I said, "Turkey is a Muslim country, right? Did you know there are a lot of Muslims in China, too? Especially along the ancient Silk Road. Speaking of Muslims, I've been wondering how it must have been for Gramps to marry a Christian woman. It must have taken great courage and love."

Pops said, "Indeed. I remember your grandfather once said, 'Raymond,' he said, 'Christian or Muslim, it does not matter. We all worship the same God of Abraham.' In some countries this could have been a life-threatening stance, but not in the USA."

"That's interesting, Pops. So anyway, how did Gramps make all his money?"

Pops hesitated. "Well you know, he was a lawyer, and he, he settled some pretty big corporate lawsuits, you know, and these gigs paid pretty well."

I could tell Pops was lying, but I couldn't think of a way forward without giving away my game. Instead I asked him to please send me ten-thousand dollars. He made me promise to pay him back. I thanked him, and that was the end of the call.

During my month off-line, Bas sent me three emails. The first one said he was poised to arrive in Thailand. The second one had the subject, "I'm in Bangkok. Where are you?" The third one said, "Hey man, I'm getting worried." I replied, hoping that I wasn't too late, hoping to see my friend soon.

Concerned about banking fraud and identity theft, I logged into my bank's web site and sure enough, there had been a spike in spending just after I left Xining. Fortunately this triggered my bank's anti-fraud system which blocked further transactions. I was happy because I was expecting worse. I called the bank's hot-line to request a new debit card in case Pops forgot.

Chan Lian and I went to see Tiananmen Square, the plaza where the Communist / Capitalist Party once slaughtered pro-democracy protesters, the famous plaza with a giant portrait of

Chairman Mao hanging over the entrance to the Forbidden City, previously the home to emperors. We went inside. The palace was interesting to explore despite the shockingly bad air pollution. Every sign with tourist information had a footnote that said, "Brought to you by the American Express Corporation." I wondered what Chairman Mao would have thought about that. To me, this seemed ironic.

We visited the Great Wall as a day trip. Getting off the bus, the site was crawling with tourists, with a cable car for the fatties who were too lazy to walk up the stairs. I marched Chan Lian away from the crowds, and the further we walked, the fewer people we encountered. After fifteen minutes we were alone to enjoy stunning views of the site in all its majesty. The wall was great. From this perspective I understood a universal truth: to escape a horde of tourists, walk up a steep hill.

Back at the embassy for the United States of America, I collected my new passport and ten-thousand dollars, less the cash they already gave me and other fees.

Suddenly flush with cash, I celebrated by taking Chan Lian to a shopping mall, much like an American mall but with a different breed of credit-card-carrying, tailless monkeys. The consumer frenzy was identical. I bought a small backpack, emergency clothes that did not match my style, plus a heating element for boiling water (for coffee). Tempting as it was, I did not replace my digital camera, but I did get my hair cut and trimmed my beard. For Chan Lian I bought perfume and a CD player with speakers that ran on rechargeable batteries. I gave her two-hundred dollars to shop for music. She was delighted because pirated CDs were ubiquitous and cheap in the black markets.

The travel agent asked, "Where do you want to go?"

"Bangkok," I answered. "One way."

"When do you want to go?"

"The day after tomorrow."

The youngest Chan of the Chan clan cried, but then she got tough. She was a strong woman who would live a good life and she knew it. I gave her five-hundred dollars to buy a clothes-washing machine for her grandparents, making her promise to thank them for their kind generosity. Then I gave her another two-hundred dollars out of spontaneous generosity. Then I gave her a kiss goodbye.

When I boarded my bus to the airport I was excited. Bangkok! Reflecting on my time with the Chan clan, I knew that I learned something profound, something that would require the rest of my life to fully understand, but this seemed barely relevant as I embarked on a new phase of my journey, indeed a new phase of my life. Thailand!

40 - The Oldest Profession

Arriving into Bangkok, at passport control, my immigration officer demanded proof that I was vaccinated against yellow fever, or else he said, I would not be allowed to enter Thailand. I told the man that I was vaccinated, but I didn't have any proof handy. He said therefore he could not allow me to pass. *Doh!* Fortunately before I left California, I took digital photos of my important documents and emailed these to myself. With hindsight, this was an excellent idea because ten minutes later I was on my way.

I hurried towards a sign that said, "Nothing to declare." Then, Thailand! I changed money, bought a guide book which I flipped through quickly, then I stepped outside to the hot, humid street. I immediately felt sweat on my brow and I loved it.

I told my taxi driver to take me to Kao San road, a neighborhood that my book described as good for backpackers. The driver replied, "You no want Kao San. Too dirty. Tourist ghetto. You prefer Patpong. Beautiful girls! I take you there. I know good hotel."

Out of curiosity I looked up Patpong in my book, a destination for sex tourism inaugurated during the Vietnam war primarily to serve American soldiers. I said, "Just take me to Kao San road, please." He did, and I enjoyed our scenic ride into the heart of the mega-city. Bangkok!

I got a cheap room in the tourist ghetto, then I explored the scene, enjoying my anonymity as I watched locals working in bars, restaurants, tattoo parlors and travel agencies. I enjoyed watching the tourists too. I noticed a few salty old ex-pats, but more common were the Westerners who seemed as if they just embarked on their first overseas trip ever. Some of the tourists looked just like me. Others seemed interested only in alcohol.

A man approached me with a menu of pretty girls, literally a menu. Another man tried to sell me marijuana, but my instincts told me he was a police informant. Instead of wacky weed, I bought a miniature statue of Ganesha to enhance my wisdom and remove obstacles, or so I enjoyed thinking.

A girl with a perfect body paraded by, and I followed her with my eyes. A woman said, "You want her? Only fifty dollar." Instead

I bought delicious pad-thai noodles from a street vendor. I was hungry, after all.

Then I got a Yin tattoo, nearly identical to Angeline's tattoo, but located higher up on my back, a permanent reminder of my eternal soul mate, but not always in my face.

I sent an email to Angeline's father to tell him what I did. I also emailed Pops to thank him for his help. I received one email from Bas explaining that he went to Cambodia to visit the ancient temples of Angkor Wat, which he said were awesome and I should go, but he was no longer there. He met a girl named Sophie and went with her to her village. He asked me for news, so I told him about my tattoo.

As I needed supplies, I went to the city's largest shopping mall, crowded with credit-card-carrying, tailless monkeys of the Thai variety. I bought flip flops, a hat, sunglasses, and a minimal first-aid kit, just enough to get to a hospital or pharmacy in case of emergency. Then came the hard part, new clothes that suited my style. I refused to wear anything with an obvious brand name, because I was not a walking billboard for any corporation, so I only bought beach shorts. Then I toured a temple with a giant reclining Buddha, an impressive site packed with colorful artwork. Cool!

Next I went to the American embassy to see about my new debit card, and as a bonus there was also a package from home. Mom sent me a miniature Bible with a magnifying glass to make out the tiny font, plus a box of chocolate brownies. Later as I ate those brownies, I teleported to a time when my parents were my heroes, before I grew to see them as normal human beings. Despite the brownies and the cash, I was angry with them because they lied to me while making lame excuses for not meeting me in Israel.

I walked in a random direction until I got hungry enough to order pad-thai noodles.

While I waited for the chef to work her culinary magic, I heard a female voice say, "Hey Mister. You want massage?" I was standing in front of a massage parlor.

The girl was gorgeous. "Hmmm," I answered. "Maybe. How much?"

"Only ten dollar. I make really good massage."

I made a list of why not? Then I followed her inside. She gave me a great rub down, but avoided my private parts. On numerous occasions however, she came very close. When I got excited, she asked, "You want happy ending?"

"You mean sex? For free?"

"No, not free silly. No money, no funny! Only ten dollar."

Why not? The massage girl removed my underwear, then she took off her clothes too. She applied a condom, slid on top of me, and with all the tenderness of a long-time lover, she massaged the last part of my body that she had yet to touch. Happy ending indeed!

When we finished our funny business, Massage Girl surprised me by making tea. We had a nice conversation. I asked her about Thai politics and she asked me about China. I told her that Chinese people were more human than I expected, and less Chinese.

Since I had just gotten laid, I decided to check out the infamous Patpong district without being distracted by my animal instincts to procreate. The neighborhood was crowded with kiosks selling everything from t-shirts to switch-blade knives, plus strip clubs packed with drunken tourists.

I walked into a bar and bought a beer. What a show! Busty babes took a bubble bath, then lesbians wearing leather licked each other, then a girl shot balloons from across the room with a blow gun inserted into her vagina.

One of the hookers introduced herself to me as Violet. She sat next to me and just then, an obese Western man walked into the bar with a beautiful, skinny girl. This shocked me. I said to Violet, "That seems wrong, that couple, but maybe my attitude is a result of my own cultural biases. What do you think?"

She said, "Normal. Business. You buy me drink?"

"As soon as I am certain that you and I are destined to have a stimulating conversation, then I will happily buy you a drink."

She stood up. "OK. I go order drink."

"Wait! You did not understand me. I did not say that I was going to buy you a drink, not yet."

She looked sad. "You no buy me drink?"

"Ask me again in five minutes."

Violet said that I was boring, then she left me alone, which was just as well. I sipped my beer and watched the naked women on stage, growing lustful as I admired a particularly beautiful dancer's bouncing boobies.

Meanwhile I pondered the morality of sex tourism, thinking no harm, no foul, especially in the enlightened age of the condom. The key for any man who might indulge therefore, was to ensure that there was no harm. I imagined my mother sitting beside me, quoting the Bible to prove that sex outside of marriage was a sin, but that was all theoretical because it would have been impossible to ever get Mom to enjoy a beer in Patpong. There was just no way.

A man with long hair and a big nose sat next to me. He said, "A lot of gorgeous women, huh?" He was talking to me.

I asked him, "Are you talking to me?" Then I smiled. "Um, yeah," I said. "I never knew girls could do that with ping-pong balls."

The guy said, "Yeah. Just wait until the blonde one smokes a cigarette."

As I let my imagination run with that idea, Big Nose added, "By the way, what do you think of that one? She's beautiful, don't you think?" He pointed to a full-figured lady outside. I nodded my head affirmatively.

"Ha!" he said. "She's a he!"

"What?"

"Yeah, a lady boy. I know from personal experience."

"Huh?"

"Yeah, that one tricked me. I don't usually go for the boys. I've since learned to pay more attention. Always look at the Adam's apple, man. That's how you can tell. But I fucked her anyway, um, I mean I fucked him." He laughed.

Despite my disgust at Big Nose's vulgarity, I scrutinized the individual in question; she really was a he.

"If you want to know," Big Nose added, "this isn't the best place to pick up girls. It's too expensive. I come here for the show. Anyway, don't get me wrong. I'm not trying to hit on you or anything, man, but if you want, my hotel is pretty close to here, if you know what I mean." He winked.

I said, "No thanks." Then I looked away.

After an uncomfortable silence, Big Nose said, "Don't do that, man. Don't just ignore me. I'm actually a fucking direct-blood descendant of Chief Seattle."

I replied in my unfriendly voice, "Do you think that if you met the Dalai Lama in a bar, do you think he'd say, 'Hey, I'm the fucking Dalai Lama?' I don't think he would."

Big Nose drank from his beer. "Yeah," he said. "Cambodia, man. That's where to go for the best girls. I'm going back soon, if you want to tag along. They've got cheap drugs there too. Grass is basically free. People are more concerned about getting rolling papers. Can you believe that? And they've got heroin too, but be careful with that shit, man."

Just then another Western man approached. He sat down next to me saying, "I see you've met Chief Talks-out-his-ass."

I laughed, "Yeah, unfortunately."

"Did he hit on you yet?"

"Yeah, unfortunately."

The guy said to his friend, "See? You just turn people off with your bullshit. You need to learn to be subtle."

I finished my beer in one gulp, then I said, "If you'll excuse me, I have to go pee."

Instead I hailed a taxi. I was disturbed, certainly not because of the bar girls whose job it was to be pretty, but because of Chief Talks-out-his-ass; that dude freaked me out.

I went straight back to see Massage Girl, and not just for another quality shag, but because she was the closest I had to a friend. I wanted to ask her opinion about sex-tourism over tea. On the way I asked my taxi driver what he thought about the scene. The man answered, "Focus on positive things." I couldn't get him to say anything negative, even though I could tell he had a lot to say.

When I asked the same question to Massage Girl, she answered, "People should die!"

I said, "Huh? Who do you mean? Who should die?"

She said, "Father who sell daughter as sex slave should die! Man who refuse condom should also die! Some black-market criminals and politicians too. As for Chief Talks-out-his-ass, maybe he should die too. I don't know. Maybe he is just a gay man who only want some sweet Raymond love, you sexy boy."

I told my masseuse that Big Nose was just another trained ape, then I gave her a tip and departed back to the noisy street. I knew that I would never go back to her, but I also knew that I would never forget the Thai girl with green eyes.

41 - Full Moon Party

Feeling anxious to leave the noisy, traffic-congested city, I travelled to an island called Ko Phangan, an island that was about to have a full-moon party. I took a train then a ferry, both packed with young Europeans eager to participate in a beach rave. I succumbed to the buzz. I grew excited too.

I continued to the party beach on the back of a motorcycle with a wildly imprudent driver. As he passed on blind corners and accelerated into the unknown, I trusted my fate to the Gods, or so I enjoyed thinking. The trip was scenic, and I was the first tourist to arrive from the ferry, which helped in finding a vacant room.

I joined a pick-up soccer game at sunset, then I sat with my Irish teammates at a beach bar, which was fantastic. I had forgotten how much I missed drinking beer and talking shit with the boys.

The next day I found a tailor to sew secret pockets into my new clothes, and inside my new backpack too. I knew this wouldn't prevent someone from stealing my entire pack, so for cases like sleeping on a train or walking in a dangerous neighborhood, my plan was to spread my cash around to minimize the risk. This made me think of Pops, because he originally gave me the idea to use a decoy wallet. I was damn curious to know what he was up to.

I called Pedro.

My friend had good news and bad news. The good news, he said, was that Shep figured out where Pops worked in Tel Aviv, as a Senior Technical Adviser for a weapons manufacturer. He said, "We think Pops was advising the IDF, the Israeli Defense Forces, and in that case, he would have earned a good salary, but not millions, because he wouldn't have received commissions on sales."

I said, "Interesting..."

Pedro said, "Yeah. The bad news is that Shep still hasn't gotten into that database of truth, but he says he's making progress. He exploited a vulnerability in a Homeland Security web server, he said, to get a *command shell*. With that he was able to drop in a *root-kit*, a set of hacker tools. I don't understand his techno-jargon, but he knows what he's doing. He said he's taking his time though, better to be careful, to make sure he doesn't leave an audit trail."

"Interesting."

"Yeah, so anyway, Shep said he's stuck on that line of attack for now, so he's looking into maybe an easier way to just read out some data. He said there must be a browser-based tool for field agents to query the various watch lists, and it might be possible to sniff out a log-in credential, or crack a password file. I dunno, but it's progress. That's good news too!"

Anxious as I was to know the truth, instead of calling Pops, I rented a motorcycle, to relish in the freedom provided by personal petrol power. It was a lovely day after all.

I followed a sign to a waterfall, parked the bike, then walked along a concrete trail to a viewpoint. From there I descended a muddy track to the base of the falls where I went for a swim. When I returned to the viewpoint, I chatted with the tourists snapping photos. The view was lovely, but the splendor of the falls was at the swimming hole, past flowers and butterflies. I knew the tourists would not go down the trail because it was muddy, and I was happy they were so trained because I was able to enjoy the pristine pool in solitude. This encounter made me wonder how many people on Earth there were whose feet never touched dirt.

I met my Irish buddies again for soccer, then we watched the full moon rise. The boys all took ecstasy pills and they invited me to join them, but I declined. I was high enough already, high on life, plus I had just taken a siesta so I was rested and ready to go.

As night fell, the beach came alive with lights and music, especially techno-trance, but also reggae and rock-n-roll. I enjoyed flirting with random girls, the sport of making witty conversation. This seemed to me like fishing, throwing out lines and hoping a good-eating female would take the bait. I saw girl fishing as sport, unlike the pay-to-play scene of the big city. I went fishing for just fun, to see if I could catch myself a beauty.

It didn't take me long to get some fish on the hook: two ladies from Argentina. One of them was playing with glow-in-the-dark juggling balls. When she took a break, I asked if I could give them a try. She said I could, so I juggled for a minute, then I offered to buy her and her friend a cocktail.

Maria and Cristina spoke English with me but Spanish with each other. I understood most of what they said, but I didn't let on until Maria said, "I think we should invite him to the party."

I said (in Spanish), "What party? Aren't we already at the party?"

The ladies seemed shocked, so I added, "You never asked me if I speak Spanish."

Cristina laughed, "Yes, we should bring him to the party."

The ladies led me away from the beach to a private gathering with dim lighting and soft music. They introduced me to Ricardo from Spain, then they kissed each other, a slow and sexy kiss. They were lesbians! Ricardo put his arm around me, then his hand moved slowly down towards my rear end. I instinctively jerked away.

I tapped Maria on the shoulder, saying, "Remember me? Um, I'm not gay."

Ricardo looked disappointed as the ladies burst out laughing. I wanted to convert them all to heterosexuality to continue partying on my terms, but I didn't see any way to make that work, so I said goodbye and left. I caught the wrong kind of fish.

I bought a beer then wandered around to observe the piranhas and sharks, prostitutes trying to latch onto single guys, and men who befriended tourists to make money, somehow, anyhow. It struck me as funny that no gay guys had ever hit on me before ever, and then twice in one week. Boom. I wondered if this had anything to do with my shopping-mall clothes until I realized this was silly, but nevertheless I suddenly wanted cooler clothes. It struck me that I could have said yes to Ricardo as a student at the University of the Open Road but no, I liked girls. I drank my beer and wondered how trained-ape theory might explain a gay gene. Then I wondered about something else.

It was easy for me to make fleeting acquaintances but nobody as interesting as my lesbian friends from Argentina. I ended up hanging out with my Irish buddies who were shockingly talkative from their ecstasy pills, until they got annoying. By this time the party had turned into a drunken riot, with European youth vomiting into the sea, but I didn't care. I was feeling too happy just to be alive. I said to everyone I met, "Life is good."

42 - Not Lucky, Blessed

My Irish friends invited me to join them for scuba diving on the next island. I always wanted to see the life of an alien world, so I accepted. I sometimes dreamed of swimming underwater, magically able to hold my breath (and fight off big sharks), so when I finally donned the gear and made the plunge, I loved it.

After a week my friends departed but I stayed. They were in a hurry to get home but I was not. Sweet. My hotel had a kitchen, a trade-a-book library, DVD movies, and Internet access. My cabana had a hammock with a view, plus the beach was perfect for swimming. Alas nowhere is perfect, the mosquitoes were annoying. I practiced the art of ignoring them (and applying bug spray at dusk).

I also practiced meditation to see if I could control my monkey mind. I found that staring into a candle flame helped me to focus, but that seemed like cheating because for me the benefit came from thought control on demand, ignoring mosquitoes for example. I practiced meditation to improve my ability to stay calm no matter what, to train my neurons to improve their higher-order thought-management functions, to catch my emotions growing in strength before they could take over, and then to focus on my breathing.

Via email I agreed with Bastiaan to meet in Malaysia on a specific date, and I was happy to have a plan. I was also happy about the existence of Thai locals who understood the art of making coconut curry. Delicious!

I received an email from Robert "Mr. Suit" Onassis asking me if I made it to China as planned. I was surprised by his gesture of friendship, just as I imagine he was surprised by my lengthy discourse about the Communist / Capitalist Party's divergence from Marxist theory.

I had just read the Communist Manifesto by Marx and Engels, a deceptively small work. I didn't agree with the authors' idea to abolish individual property, nor did I believe the bourgeoisie would inevitably fall to the proletariat, and I thought it was extreme to prohibit religion, but the book made it clear that capitalism did not balance all concerns.

Robert, my unlikely pen-pal, replied, "If Yang is Capitalism, then Yin is not Communism but Catastrophic Environmental Collapse."

I reminded Robert that he should run for political office. Then I walked into a dive shop. I was in the mood to swim with fish after all, to pretend I was a ten-eyed flying monster on an alien planet.

An American family joined me on my dive boat. I found it amusing that even on dry land, the daughter wore a dive mask over her long blonde hair. I said to her, "You're a lucky girl, to be able to scuba dive in Thailand!"

"I'm not lucky," she said. "I'm blessed! And I'm not a girl. I'm a boy!" *Doh!*

The mother said, "Don't worry. It's the hair, but he insists we don't cut it."

I apologized to the boy, then I asked him his name. He answered, "Chris."

I asked him how old he was. He said, "Ten."

I said, "When I was your age, I was twelve."

Old Man Chan's joke inspired a chuckle, and I felt redeemed.

Chris's parents were named Richard and Lynn. As our boat sped to our dive site, we chatted about our mutual home, California. Lynn wore expensive jewelry including a diamond-studded Christian cross; Richard wore a name-brand polo shirt; but aside from being overdressed, they seemed nice. Their social status seemed irrelevant as we engaged in light banter.

Richard said, "If I had your free time, I'd go to Malaysia. I've read about some world-class dive sites there." He listed off a few places.

Lynn said, "Yes, but we won't go there, not to Malaysia. They have too many Muslims."

I studied her face to see if she was joking. She wasn't, but I still asked, "You're joking, right?"

"No," she answered. "We won't go to Europe either. The Muslims are breeding. But Thailand is OK. We don't have any problem at all with the Buddhists."

Richard nodded his head in agreement, seriously concerned

about getting blown to smithereens the minute he stepped off a plane in Hamburg or Kuala Lumpur.

I said, "I suppose you're entitled to boycott any country as you see fit, but I'm pretty sure that most Muslims are ordinary people going about their lives in peace. I agree with your main point, though, yes, Muslims do breed. In fact, if they didn't, there wouldn't be any Muslims at all, would there? Except perhaps for converts, but then, who would ever convert to a religion that prohibited sex?"

Richie Rich scowled, then he asked if I was, "one of those Hollywood liberals."

I answered, "Seriously? I mean, wasn't Jesus a liberal? Blessed are the poor? If Jesus were a politician, he'd reach out to Muslims in the spirit of tolerance and good will. And Jesus wouldn't have invaded Iraq either, for example. Blessed are the peace makers."

The man said, "Sorry Roy, but you've got it all wrong. The dictator over there, Saddam, he had weapons of mass destruction, and we brought democracy to those people. If we did things your way, the Arabs would have nuked New York by now, and Jesus wouldn't want that, now would he?"

Lynn added, "God bless America."

I said, "Interesting. If what you're saying is correct, then God really is a conscious being in the sky, and that means I need to rethink, well, everything. I mean, does God want us to destroy planet Earth with unsustainable growth, or is that the Devil?"

Just then, a wave from another boat splashed us, causing Lynn's mascara to run. I had to work hard to not laugh. I mean, who wears mascara to go scuba diving anyway?

My California colleagues reminded me of Mom and Pops. I knew there was no winning a political debate with them, but we were trapped in a boat together, so I gave it a try. They argued against "big government" and "liberal bias" just as their "fair and balanced" television shows trained them to do. They blamed the lazy poor for wanting handouts, saying that they should all simply get jobs (as if there were an abundance of good jobs).

I said, "Look, Dick... May I call you Dick? The rules of capitalism dictate that the winner takes all, and that's bad economics. And there's no compassion or justice! Did you know the number-one cause of social strife around the world is not poverty but inequality? Money has to circulate from the wealthy to the poor somehow, and the poor spend everything they get, so it goes around, and if this cash flow is managed wisely, it benefits everybody, including the rich who don't need more money, but do enjoy low crime and happy neighbors."

Richie Rich glared. "You know Roy..."

"Raymond."

"Sorry. Raymond. Liberal politicians convince the poor they're victims. But you never hear them say the words, 'personal responsibility.' You never hear them tell the poor that it's their responsibility to study hard in school. Liberal programs like welfare only encourage those people to be lazy."

"Seriously? Interesting. Hmmm... Correct me if I'm wrong, but I'm guessing that you went to a private school. Yes? And your white father helped you to find your first job. Yeah? Or did you simply inherit all your wealth? Or, did you grow up in a ghetto with overcrowded schools, with your father in jail and your mother with AIDS, in a neighborhood with high unemployment, drug dealers, pimps, and street gangs?"

"The Lord helps those who help themselves."

"You didn't answer my question."

Lynn snapped, "That's enough! We don't want to argue with you. One should never debate politics. People get upset."

I replied, "You're upset. I'm not. And the boy seems fine. Your husband said that one of the reasons we invaded Iraq was to install democracy, but isn't debate the essence of democracy? We shouldn't get upset with each other, but we should be outraged at the media machine that spews lies and propaganda. And besides, I'm not criticizing you personally, I'm criticizing the bad ideas that you learned from TV."

Richie Rich glared at me. "Look, Raymond," he said. "You may disagree about why we went to war in Iraq, but the fact is, we're there, and we must win. Fact is, an American defeat would be a victory for Al Qaeda and for Iran, and Jesus wouldn't want that, now would he? The war against Muslim extremists is the central struggle of our time."

I said, "I agree with you that religious extremism is a bad

thing, but that's also true for Christianity. And besides, the more we fight this so-called war on terror, the more we create new extremists, and Lynn is right, the Muslims are breeding. Look, we can never win a war against an idea with bombs. And by the way, isn't the central struggle of our time to create a sustainable economy? Isn't our primary struggle to prevent corporate greed from destroying our fragile planet? Don't we need to eliminate soul-crushing poverty?"

The man scowled, staring at me silently, so I asked him, "Are you happy?"

He did not answer, so we arrived at a verbal truce. We also arrived at our dive site. I donned my gear and took the plunge. Soon my brain became filled with calm and awe. When I found a lobster under a rock, because my brain is funny, I imagined I was a monster on another planet, flying, with ten eyes.

There were things I knew that I knew, like the existence of lobsters, plus things I knew that I didn't know like the limits of my possible knowledge. I also knew there was no convincing my compatriots that my talking points were superior to their talking points, because they had casually developed, unscientific worldviews. The laws of physics can be tested in a lab, I thought to myself, but what about politics?

I saw a sea snake, and this made me think of the Loch Ness monster, funny because I didn't believe the beast existed despite being plausible. I did not believe in the Loch Ness monster because there was no evidence. I believed in lobsters. I also believed that human beings were trained apes, and this fact dominated politics more than economic theory. Nevertheless I redoubled my determination to research the evidence and the historical truisms, to understand anything pertinent to the debate. Regardless of the political forces at play, the best plan for governing planet Earth I figured, must always be a plan that was consistent with the facts. Science in, religion out.

As we motored back to the island, I encouraged Richie's rant, curious to discover any valid arguments that I never heard before. I questioned the man about his evidence, and I did not accept anything he heard a television pundit say as valid. I also questioned myself about my evidence. The first time I ever had opinions strong enough to get into a political argument was that day with Richie Rich, but unlike him, I never got upset. I took him on for sport.

Back on dry land, I addressed the boy. "You're lucky," I said, "to go diving in Thailand! The fish were amazing, eh? Did you see the sea snake?"

He replied, "Yeah, that was cool! And I'm not lucky, I'm blessed!"

I said, "Woo-hoo for you! By the way, you can learn a lot from the Buddhists."

43 - Travellers versus Tourists

On the island of Ko Samui I splurged on an air-conditioned room. Fancy places didn't usually tempt me, but I was in the mood to sit by a swimming pool and sip a piña colada. I observed that the tourists at my hotel were from a different tribe than the backpacker crowd I was used to. None of the tourists were travellers.

Not all backpackers were travellers either. Many professed a desire to explore but spent most of their time smoking marijuana with other backpackers, or eating chocolate cake at a German bakery. I enjoyed chilling out with other backpackers too, but I respected more the volunteers, wanna-be monks, and roadies who avoided their comfort zones to grow themselves or help others. I concluded that most backpackers were future tourists who were held back only by their lack of money.

One example: I witnessed a backpacker refusing to pay for her hotel room because it had ants. Ants! "Your website does not say you have ants," she said, and therefore she refused to pay. "You should use poison!" Sigh. Tourists! My room had ants too, but I never ate food in my room so there was no problem.

I observed that travellers tried to communicate in the local language, whereas tourists expected everyone to speak English. Also travellers went with the flow, whereas tourists had itineraries, and they booked tours. Travellers endeavored to make discoveries about the world, and more importantly, discoveries about themselves, whereas tourists sought to have all the comforts of home, even when visiting ten cities in seven days, seeing a lot but discovering little. Travellers made local friends, but tourists only knew natives with a service to peddle. Travellers quit their jobs to take advantage of opportunities for adventure or love, but tourists had more money than time, anxiously trying to relax before racing back home to work. Travellers were fit, and tourists were fat.

I observed that tourists were common, but travellers were rare. And I was a newbie, wanna-be traveller, ambitious to explore further. While I enjoyed the occasional swimming pool and piña colada, I preferred gallivanting around India the hard way, and I loved the freedom that came with living out of a backpack, with no boss and no schedule. As I observed tourists with big cameras that made them targets for con artists and thieves, I made a decision that I had been struggling with since Beijing; I decided not to replace my stolen camera.

With this in mind, I watched a rent-a-car pull into my hotel's parking lot. The tourist couple that emerged wore matching trousers that converted into shorts with zippers. From this clue, I guessed they were American. This was confirmed when I heard them speak. The couple had so much stuff that they had to make multiple trips from their car to their room. The guy dropped his beer mug, the one he bought in Germany. It broke. He yelled, "Shit!"

I thought of Old Man Chan, a man who bought exactly one modern convenience, a refrigerator. The tourist couple seemed as if they were from another planet, especially when they emerged from their room wearing swimming suits with matching ultra-light towels. The couple sat near me then introduced themselves. Harry had curly hair, and Sally was not wearing makeup. They were charismatic. I grew to like them. They were nice.

Harry told me how a Thai guy just stole their passports (a cute girl caused him to divert his eyes for a few seconds, and that was long enough for the thief to grab his day-pack and run). I felt sorry for my compatriots so I explained the logistics of getting new passports, then I told them about my analysis of travellers versus tourists.

Sally said, "You're right. What strikes me the most, after having visited places like Africa, after seeing the things they struggle with, and the things we Americans worry about, trivial things, it just doesn't make any sense; I mean, how do you compare worrying about food to worrying about a fictional character on a TV show?"

Surprised I asked, "You travelled in Africa?"

Sally said, "Yes! We love to explore the world. That includes America by the way, a country founded with a great idea, albeit inefficient, OK dysfunctional, but travelling helps us to appreciate just how good of a life we have. We live in Boulder, Colorado. It's safe and clean with gorgeous mountain scenery. If we get sick, we have a world-class hospital. If there's a fire, the firemen arrive within minutes. And we have pretty good schools."

Harry added, "We get that people who hate America have genuine grievances. We get that people see us as the Evil Empire and the Great Satan. You know the golden rule? He who has the gold makes the rules, and of course this leads to corruption and arrogance. But don't let me go off on a rant. I'd rather have one of those piña coladas."

I jumped into the pool to cool off, and while I was underwater I saw with stunning clarity the culture that formed so much of my personality without my knowledge or consent. I saw the relentless television campaigns designed to convert me into a patriotic consumer of mostly superfluous stuff, a lifetime of propaganda that made me biased towards having the tourist mindset. I saw the endless bad headlines designed to make me afraid of the world (but everything was OK inside the bubble). As I swam underwater, I was delighted that Gramps made me dream of adventure.

I decided at that moment to go somewhere off the tourist trail with great scuba diving. I had one week before my encounter with Bastiaan, just enough time to visit a remote island called Sipidan. But first I rode an elephant. Despite being touristy and despite feeling guilty from supporting the beast's captivity, I let Sally talk me into it, and I was glad I did because it was just that cool to ride an elephant. My new rule was to not act like a tourist, but the more rules the less free.

44 - You only Live once

At the border to Malaysia, one sign dominated the scene, written in twenty languages, in red: DEATH TO DRUG SMUGGLERS. I had no drugs but the sign still gave me the heebi-jeebies. As Massage Girl stated so clearly, some criminals probably deserved to die for the good of society, but I saw this as ethically debatable, and as such, the sign affirmed to me that most moral codes were cultural not absolute.

I changed money then sat under a tree to wait for the bus to Penang. From there I flew to Tawau on the island of Borneo, from where I caught a bus to Semporna, from where I took a boat to the island of Mabul, from where I arranged a boat to Sipidan.

Previously I thought of Borneo as primitive, a land of jungles, headhunting tribes and wild orangutans, but from my airplane window I saw logging, mining, and palm-oil plantations. I saw that greed only has to prevail once to prevail forever when it comes to ecological destruction. I also saw jungle, and with that hope to preserve a natural balance.

The first time I heard the *muezzin* it caught me by surprise. The Muslim call to prayer, exotic, even surreal to my ears, was blasted across the land five times daily from loud speakers mounted on every mosque's minaret. In populated areas this reminder of Islamic dominance was inescapable, and the faithful obliged. But for me this pseudo-singing quickly became annoying. It seemed arrogant for clerics to require that everyone listen to unappealing noise, especially at five in the morning. I imagined a quieter Malaysia in the era before electricity.

In contrast to Thai women, most Malaysian women wore head scarves, but that didn't make them less beautiful. Indeed, I saw Muslim women wearing clothes that could only be described as sexy. I never understood the connection between covering one's hair and God, but the veil served another purpose: whereas I instinctively saw gorgeous Thai women as potential girlfriends, these Malaysian women seemed off limits. The veil seemed to say, "I do not practice premarital sex, period, and especially not with infidels." At first I felt uncomfortable around these women, but as I began to meet them randomly on my journey, I realized they were generally friendly, indeed charming human beings, prisoners of culture.

In the town of Mabul I met André, a scuba instructor also on his way to Sipidan, so we travelled together. Later we swam together as dive buddies.

André escorted me to his favorite underwater canyon, and the alien life was stunning. We saw turtles, rays, eels, sharks, and colorful corals beyond my imagination. Awesome. Then while swimming about thirty meters deep, my regulator malfunctioned. I breathed sea water into my lungs! I gagged, and I could not breathe! I tried desperately to suck air from my regulator, but it gave me only water. I panicked.

I had a backup breathing apparatus, but even though I trained for the possibility of using it, I already coughed all the air from my lungs, and I was in no position to fumble around. I was too deep to sprint to the surface. I was about to drown.

With precious seconds ticking by, I kicked hard to sprint to André. I gave him the hand signal for "trouble" then I stole his regulator from his mouth.

My coughing prevented me from getting a breath, and I could not answer André's quizzical gaze, but I saw that he found his backup regulator, and that eased my mind a little. I gave him the hand signal for "go up."

I knew that I would die if I didn't get oxygen, so I focused my brain on not coughing. I drew in some air, then coughed it out. Shit! I tried fast and shallow breaths desperately, and this worked somewhat, better than nothing. As my dive buddy and I ascended, painfully slowly, I repeated to myself, "You have air and you're going up. Stay calm. You have air. Stay calm. You're going up."

I was never more happy to see blue sky. I coughed up sea water, a horrible sensation, but I was alive. If André had been two meters further away, I would not have reached him. I might have used my backup regulator and ascended by myself, but there was no way I would have ascended so slowly, with such discipline, and therefore I probably would have died from a build-up of nitrogen bubbles, a fatal condition called "the bends."

André filled a balloon with air to signal for our boat, then while floating in the tranquil sea, I calmed down enough to tell him what happened. "What could have caused my regulator to malfunction?" I asked.

"I don't know," he said, "but I am going to investigate. All I can say is that professional divers travel with their own regulators for a reason. You're lucky to be alive."

I inhaled sea microbes into my lungs, something potentially life threatening, so I departed immediately for a modern hospital in Penang. I did not imagine I would ever go scuba diving again, not because I was afraid of dying, but because I was fond of living, and one only lives once. I preferred snorkeling anyway, less gear, less money, same fish.

45 - Aloha in Aloha out

At the Tawau airport I queued behind a German man wearing black socks, black shoes, and a flowery aloha shirt from Hawaii. He wanted to catch the next flight to Penang, but he did not ask politely, he demanded, "I must get on this flight!"

The ticket agent, a petite woman wearing a blue hijab, told the man to please have a seat. Instead the man repeated his demand more loudly. The woman typed into her computer, then she said, "I'm sorry sir, but the flight you desire is sold out."

As the man walked away mumbling curses, I realized that I wanted a seat on the same flight. "Hello," I said. "Salam. I have a ticket to Penang in a few days, but I need to get to the hospital there, for urgent medical treatment, so I'd like to change my ticket for the first available flight please. Thank you." I smiled my friendliest smile.

The woman asked for my passport and my existing ticket, then she went to work. When she gave me a boarding pass for the same flight the German guy wanted, the woman behind me said, "Nice job! Aloha in, aloha out."

"Huh?" I replied. "I'm sorry, but I don't get your meaning."

"I live in Hawaii," she said. "Aloha means love, the warmth of sincere smiles. That German guy might be wearing a Hawaiian shirt, but he has no aloha. I bet the Muslim girl bumped him just to teach him a lesson, but I doubt he learned anything. This just goes to show that if you ever get into trouble in Asia, the worst thing you can do is get angry. Instead smile, smile, smile, especially if things get difficult." Good advice!

I travelled without incident to a surprisingly modern hospital where the triage staff put me in front of a doctor quickly. The guy prescribed antibiotics to kill the ocean microbes in my lungs, then a nurse escorted me to my room where she attached an intravenous drip into my arm.

I flipped on the television. The one channel in English broadcast twenty-four-hour news with stories about terrorists, blockbuster movies, and a celebrity sex scandal. I flipped the TV off. I breathed deeply.

I finished my novel then fell asleep, but I awoke often gasping for air. I could visualize myself floating in the ocean, with my lungs filled with water, with a minute to go before everything faded to black forever. I thought about how Angeline must have felt at her moment of death: very sad, I imagined. Every time I awoke, I forced myself to think of something good; for example I was happy about meeting my friend Bastiaan soon.

Despite the intravenous needle in my arm, I tried to practice Tai Chi. I also began reading the mini-Bible Mom sent me.

"In the beginning God created the Heaven and the Earth," it said. "And the Earth was without form, and void; and darkness was upon the face of the deep." Darkness in the ocean deep! I was traumatized.

God created Adam then warned him, "Of the tree of the knowledge of good and evil, thou shalt not eat of it. For in the day that thou eatest thereof thou shalt surely die." Fascinating.

Mom was instructed by her elders that the literal truth of these words was never to be questioned, but Mom wouldn't know a scientific theory if it was served to her for breakfast. She believed the Grand Canyon was proof of Noah's flood (God's first genocide), and she believed that He made Adam, penis and all, and then later decided it might be a good idea to create a woman too, so He made Eve from Adam's rib as an afterthought. To me, this didn't make Him seem especially clever.

"And on the seventh day God ended His work which He had made; and He rested on the seventh day from all His work which He had made." I figured that God should have spent that seventh day on empathy and intelligence, plus He could have worked on His writing skills too.

The book of Genesis listed many things that God created, but none of these was precious air. The text also ignored ice and polar bears, consistent with a human author from the Middle East. The book mentioned Earth but no other planets or galaxies, and it described a bizarre ether called *the firmament*, consistent with a human author who had no clue whatsoever about astronomy.

I read the entire book of Genesis, then I skimmed Deuteronomy and the Gospel of Luke.

It must have been easy for the Spanish conquistadors to convert the Aztecs, I figured, because the Mexican God demanded human sacrifice and the reward was corn, whereas the Spanish God sacrificed himself, and the reward was Heaven. That must surely have seemed like a better God. The Spanish had guns and steel weapons too, plus evolved resistance to smallpox. The Aztecs were allowed to go to Heaven, but only by confessing their sins to the Spanish priests. The holy sacrament of marriage allowed them to have sex. Nonbelievers, no matter how good, were doomed to Hell.

I fell asleep, and in my dream I saw religion as a great white shark gobbling up smaller ideas, then I saw Jesus and Buddha fighting over who's teachings delivered superior inner peace. This vision of the two messiahs in a Kung Fu fight was hilarious, and the nurse who woke me up to check my vital signs was gorgeous. Beholding such beauty, I realized that life was especially precious with no fictitious after-life.

In my next dream I saw Buddha explaining that one's morality has nothing to do with one's faith, and everything to do with one's actions. "Some apes call this karma," he said. "Aloha in, aloha out."

46 - No God but Allah

I awoke gasping for air, wanting to see the future, and *voila!* I had a roommate.

"Good morning," he said. "I see you fell asleep reading your Bible..."

I smiled, "Good morning. Um yes, the Bible, yeah, it's my favorite book."

I did not know immediately why I lied, but as I surveyed my surroundings, I realized that I was in no mood to debate philosophy, but I was curious about Islam, so I probably said the right thing. Meanwhile my roommate held up his book for me to see. "No problem," he said. "We both worship the one true God." His book was a beautifully decorated *Al-Qur'an*.

We exchanged names and reasons for hospitalization. My roommate told me that he was studying Arabic so that he could read his book in the same language that Allah himself communicated to the prophet Muhammad, his namesake, peace be upon him.

I did not know the original language of my book. All I could infer from the first pages was that my translation was commissioned by King James in the seventeenth century.

Muhammad's eyes reminded me of Old Man Chan's eyes in that they were wizened from a million smiles. The man quizzed me about my religious beliefs so I said very little, using the opportunity to quiz him back about Islam. For example, I asked him why his book mandated that women should cover their hair.

"No, no," he smiled. "No mandate. This is cultural reasoning. Back in the days of the prophet, peace be upon him, back when he was governor of Arabia, his house was the government house, and his wives covered themselves as was the custom of the day, to protect their privacy, to reduce the shameful desires of lustful men. Men are weak."

I admitted, "That's true."

Muhammad laughed and praised Allah, then he said, "Al-Qur'an makes prohibitions against theft, alcohol, sexual intercourse before marriage, and other sins like that. Wise clerics have also made interpretations over the centuries, and these, along with the pillars of Islam, define *Sharia law*. The veil is not part of Sharia law. We believe culturally however, that women should dress modestly. A man's wife is his wife, yes? Not to be shared in public."

"Ah," I said. "OK. No sharing of the hair. I get it. And what are the pillars of Islam?"

"I am glad you ask. First is the *Shahadah* which we must recite in prayer. The words mean, 'There is no God but Allah, and Muhammad is the Messenger of Allah.' Second, we face the *Kaaba* five times per day and humbly submit ourselves in prayer. Third is the *Zakat*, whereby all Muslims give to charity according to one's wealth. This is our most important social duty. And four, we should all visit Mecca at least one time; this is the *Hajj*. Finally, we fast during the holy month of *Ramadan*."

"Thank you for explaining."

"There is no problem. You may ask me any questions as you like."

"OK. Do you believe in Jesus?"

"Yes and no. Al-Qur'an does not affirm that Jesus performed miracles or that he was born from a virgin, but it does affirm that he was a prophet like Abraham and Moses... With no disrespect intended, your Bible was drafted at the Council of Nicaea in the year 325, where elite clerics voted for the texts to be included, and the word of Allah cannot be determined by a vote! Furthermore, the original texts from your book have all been lost, and this leaves grave doubts about their authenticity, but Al-Qur'an is verified and reliable history."

"Thanks," I said. "Good to know. So, what do you think about Buddhism?"

"The Buddhists are not of the book, but here in Malaysia we are tolerant and there is no problem. The monks teach lessons of peace."

I liked my roommate, I liked his smile, so I took advantage of the opportunity to discuss something that had nothing to do with malfunctioning scuba regulators. I asked him what he thought about suicide bombers.

"Al-Qur'an allows for war in defense of Islam," he said, "and this is known as *jihad*. Israel's occupation of Palestine is one example because this is a religious war. But I must be clear to you. Islam prohibits suicide and the killing of civilians, even in war, so the suicide bomber is not a true Muslim. The suicide bomber believes he will become a martyr and go to Paradise, but this problem is not caused by Islam; this problem is caused corrupted generals and clerics who manipulate their ignorant brothers."

"Yeah," I said. "As soon as religion becomes a political force, it loses all the good bits."

"Exactly. For most Muslims, jihad is war against one's own sinfulness, the process of improving one's spiritual self. Therefore it is not fair to criticize Islam based on the actions of guerrilla warriors fighting for survival. Islam is the world's most peaceful religion, and Malaysia is proof. Here we have a technological sector and our economy is growing. This is important as we do not have oil. We study English too, since this is the international language. This is Islam! We have no tribal mindset, and we are open to all good ideas from the West."

"Such as science..."

"Yes, exactly. Science is good."

"What about evolution?" I asked. "Do you believe in Adam and Eve?"

"Yes, of course. Al-Qur'an confirms the story in your book of Genesis. Islam and science are like hand and glove. Evolution is not science since it cannot be proven. Man did not come from a monkey."

I saw no point in defending evolution so I changed the subject. "When I crossed the border into Malaysia from Thailand the other day, I saw a sign that said, 'Death to drug smugglers.' What do you think about that?"

Muhammad answered, "This must seem harsh to you. I understand. But we do not have the same social problems that you Americans have in such abundance. We have order and we intend to keep it that way. The death penalty eliminates the drug problem including the crime it causes. It is not common that someone is so stupid to traffic drugs that we have to send him to the gallows. This is not a problem in practice."

My roommate explained the difference between *Sunni* and *Shiite* Muslims, "After the prophet's death, peace be with him, the

Sunni followed the correct teachings, but the prophet's son-in-law, Ali ibn Abi Talib, made himself to be holy *Inman* with authority over all spiritual matters. His followers are the Shiite. Please note, only the Sunni follow the one true path."

The most beautiful nurse interrupted to serve breakfast, and my roommate never took his eyes off her, as was understandable because she was stunning. Muhammad had two wives and he was looking to see if he could afford a third. When I asked him to elaborate, he referred me to sixth century Arabia, when the wealthier men were encouraged to take in widows from the tribal warfare of the day, thus multiple wives were AOK with Allah.

The next time I saw my doctor, he said I was out of danger and free to go. I felt strange because I did not want to go; I was enjoying my conversation with Muhammad, but I left anyway, in search of my one true path.

47 - The Happy Hippie

Thanks to the magic of email, I knew that Bastiaan arrived in Georgetown on schedule, so I caught the next bus, walked a few blocks, knocked on his door, and there he was. My friend gave me a bear hug, then his eyes watered. "I'm so sorry about Angeline," he said.

The sadness of our shared loss and the happiness of our reunion made for a bittersweet moment. Just before I might have cried, Bas broke the silence. "There's a restaurant around the corner with the best fried potatoes I have ever seen in Asia, real Nederland style, with homemade mayonnaise. Are you hungry?"

As we walked into China Town I explained how I almost drowned, to which my friend commented, "It's not a real adventure unless you risk your life. No risk equals no adventure. And by the way, I am happy to see you alive."

I told my friend about Ticket Man, Chan Lian, and the rest of the Chan clan, thus explaining my mysterious disappearance from his point of view. Then as we entered his favorite local restaurant, Bas told me about his new girlfriend, Sophie.

"It breaks my heart that I can't just live with her and travel freely," he said. "What shit the governments of the world have put on all the occupants, imaginary lines that separate us from each other. But I can't trade my freedom for a life in Cambodia, not even for love."

He told me about Cambodia, "Wonderful people, terrible government. Everybody I met was nice, charming in fact. The problem is that we can't get Sophie a passport. The bureaucrats in Phnom Phen insist on documentation that doesn't exist, and even if we do manage, you know, it would not be like a European passport. Every visa would represent a pain in the ass. Anyway long term, the only way for us to stay together is to get married. Meanwhile I gave Sophie some money to study English, and she's looking into getting a birth certificate. But I'll be honest, It was good for me to leave, to gain perspective, because this all happened pretty fast."

"I see. So what's next?"

"I'm not sure. Cambodia gave me a thirty-day visa so I stayed thirty days. I could have renewed this for another thirty days, but then you came back on the radar, and I'm glad you did. Perfect timing. And not just because you speak fluent English, although that's great, but frankly it's rare for me to meet anyone who loves the open road as much as you, a real traveller who does not complain, someone who I can stand being with for more than about a minute."

I said, "Thanks! That's good to hear. I'm happy about travelling with you, too."

My fine furry friend, the happy hippie from Holland, ordered beer and fried potatoes with extra mayonnaise. My doctor told me not to drink alcohol until I completed my dose of antibiotics so I ordered pineapple juice. Delicious!

Bas said, "So where was I? Ah yes. Sophie's aunt and uncle are so happy, really just happy to be alive. They survived the genocide and now they have their own restaurant where they make almost no money, but they smile all the time. They make great food. Anyway Cambodia... There are guns and drugs and prostitutes everywhere, and you can't go into the jungle because of land mines, but Angkor Wat is wicked! And the people are lovely, charming in fact."

I smiled. "It's so good to see you, my friend."

Bas smiled back. "Yes," he said. "It is indeed."

He showed me digital images of Sophie, ancient temples, Sophie, and elephants with Sophie. She was a very lovely woman.

Our beverages arrived. We clinked our glasses. We drank.

Bas said, "Anyway, I've been studying evolution ever since Angeline explained this science to me back in Goa, and I've concluded that the great apes are most-interesting beasts. So now I'd like to suggest to you, because we're just across the Straights of Malacca from the island of Sumatra, which is home to wild orangutans... So might I suggest to you that we go there next?"

I replied, "Sumatra eh? Done. Man, we are on the same page! I want to see wild orangutans, plus gorillas and chimpanzees too, in Africa. Ever since Goa, I've been pulling together my own trained-ape theory of human nature, and I can't imagine a better way to gain insight than to go hang out with our closest cousins. Plus you know, Africa! What world tour would be complete without touring

Africa?"

Bas said, "Gorilla and Chimpanzees, check. Africa, yes."

I said, "Great. I want to visit Israel and Syria too, by the way, so let's fly to Tel Aviv from Jakarta and then enter Africa via Egypt. Then why not continue south by local bus all the way to Cape Town?"

My fine furry friend said, "Done. When are we leaving?"

Plans might be what make the Gods laugh, but I was happy to have one. Africa!

48 - Escape to Sumatra

Bastiaan and I sat in our hotel's roof-top garden to enjoy the evening air and to admire the view over China Town, plus the greenery of potted plants. My friend told me about the time a car crashed in front of him in Goa, killing the driver. He said he would have been killed too if he hadn't been distracted by a pretty girl, causing him to miss a step. He said, "It's funny how the Universe works, don't you think?"

That's when Louie appeared. At first he seemed normal. He was short but muscular. He had bad teeth. "Hi," he said. "I dunno if you guys noticed, but this hostel is all coupled up. You blokes are the only single guys as far as I can tell. So anyway, I was thinking of goin' out and gettin' loaded. Wanna go along? I know a fuckin' great bar."

Bas said, "Maybe," then he indicated for Louie to have a seat.

Louie said, "Cool. Hey, if you guys wanna smoke up before we go, I've got some spliffs rolled with some fuckin' great hash."

Bas nodded his approval, so Louie fired up a spliff. Meanwhile I assured myself that there was no danger, so I relaxed and enjoyed the sunset. I didn't smoke because I didn't like tobacco with hashish, but I did say to Louie, "I don't know about you, but something about the death penalty gives me the heebi-jeebies. What the hell are you doing with drugs in Malaysia?"

Louie said, "It's cool here. Don't worry. It's cool. Don't worry."

This made me worry.

I asked Louie what he was doing in Malaysia, the standard question. He replied, "Just a beach holiday. Yeah. Just a beach holiday. I'm from New Zealand, and we do have beaches, but they're mostly cold as..."

I had a bad feeling about Louie but for some reason, call it thirst, we took a taxi to his fuckin' great bar. As we stepped out to the hot, humid night, Louie said loudly, "Hey! I have another spliff. Let's go burn it before headin' inside."

I herded him away from the taxi saying, "Are you crazy? You don't know me, and you certainly don't know that taxi driver, man. He heard you. And in case you haven't noticed, that shit is very much illegal here."

Louie told me not to worry, then he lit his spliff.

Unimpressed, Bas and I entered the bar which was pretty great. It had a tree growing up through the roof that created a rustic ambiance of tropical delight. The music was not too loud, and everybody seemed happy. Bas and I ordered beers. Meanwhile we watched the taxi driver watching Louie smoke his spliff in the shadows.

I decided to drink one beer despite being on antibiotics, and as I took those first refreshing swigs, Bas told me about the time a snake bit him in Sri Lanka.

Louie joined us and ordered beer. He said, "I told ya this place was fuckin' great!"

For a moment everything seemed normal, but then Louie gulped down his beverage with haste, proclaiming with a wild look in his eye, "There's gonna be a fight."

Bas said, "What the hell are you talking about, Louie?"

Louie did not answer, so I added, "Louie, what's going on?"

Louie said, "I'm OK, so fuck off." With that he walked over to a group of local twenty-somethings and he grabbed the cutest girl's ass. She screamed. One of her friends pushed Louie forcefully, then Louie hit the guy in the face, knocking him to the ground.

The crazy Kiwi engaged five Asian guys with moves I recognized as Kung Fu, and for a while he seemed to be winning, that is, he delivered more blows than he received, but by the time his adversaries stopped kicking him, his right eye was swollen shut and his left arm was visibly broken.

The bartender said angrily to Bas and me, "Get your friend out of here now!"

Bas swatted a mosquito before replying, "That crazy asshole is not our friend."

The bartender looked unimpressed so I added, "Don't worry. We're here to help."

Bas called Louie, "a fucking tweaker." Then we escorted him away. The guy was obviously in severe pain but I failed to feel sympathetic. Nevertheless I asked our taxi driver for help. His name was Ashraf.

"Allah teaches us to forgive and to be compassionate always," he said, "so I will help this foolish boy, even though I do not think he deserves it. Mostly I want to help you help him." Ashraf addressed the tweaker, "So listen to me boy, if the police ask me I will not lie. I will tell them you have drugs. I could smell your hashish cigarette. So you are in big trouble. If you stay in Malaysia, they might send you to the gallows. Do you understand?"

The tweaker said, "I know. I fucked up. I'm sorry. I just wanted to practice."

I wanted to practice my minimal Kung Fu skills too, but I also wanted to not be an idiot.

Ashraf said, "I recommend that you leave Malaysia tonight. Did you tell anyone the name of your hotel? No? Good." He addressed me, "Get him cleaned up, and for the sake of Allah, make sure he does not have any more drugs! I will wait. Then I will drive you to the border with Thailand."

Bas said, "That's a generous offer so thank you, but this asshole is not our friend, and I don't want to sneak across any borders. I am willing to help, but I'm not willing to take any risks myself. Plus we want to go to Indonesia, not Thailand. When is the next ferry to Sumatra?"

Ashraf answered, "Six o'clock tomorrow morning. I can pick you up at five. The police will not likely find you so early, so it should be OK. But this foolish boy will attract attention with his face like that! You need to get all the blood off him, with clean clothes."

Louie said, "Yeah, get me to Indonesia, please."

With that, Ashraf drove us to our hostel.

Bas and I dragged Louie into the shower. We made sure he got clean, then we escorted him back to his room where I demanded, "What other drugs do you have? I mean it. If you want our help, then hand over all your drugs, right now."

The tweaker gave me a velvet pouch containing a chunk of hashish, rolling papers, tobacco, a lighter, a pipe, and a metal box containing white powder. Bas recognized this as methamphetamine, a drug he called, "extraordinarily nasty shit." Bas flushed all of Louie's drugs down the toilet, then he threw the pouch of paraphernalia onto the roof of the next building.

At the designated hour, my friend and I dragged Louie out of bed to meet Ashraf who was punctual. He drove us to the ferry port, then he bought ferry tickets to minimize the number of people who might see Louie on the street. He earned his tip.

The moment of truth came at the immigration check point. Bas and I went first but we kept our eyes on the scene, standing close enough to hear Louie explain how he fell down some stairs. Liberty achieved, we approached him to see if he needed any more help.

"Nah," he said. "I can take care of myself. Thanks. I owe ya both my life."

"Good," I said. "By the way, do you believe in Heaven?"

"Nah."

"Reincarnation?"

"Nah."

"Well," I said. "If you believed in Heaven then I'd say, live well so that you might have eternal bliss, and if you believed in reincarnation then I'd say, live well so that you don't return as a street rat or a cockroach, but instead I say, live well because you only live once. The next time you fuck up, we won't be around to save your ass."

Bas added, "Yeah. In other words, try not to be such a stupid monkey."

49 - Globalocity

My friend and I had no plan for the city of Medan, Sumatra's largest city, so we went for a random walk. Our first mission was to get Indonesian money. We found a bank and our debit cards worked. Easy. Next we risked street food for breakfast because it looked clean and fresh, fried eggs over rice with hot sauce, plus sodas with ice. The vendor promised the ice was made with potable water and we believed him.

As I ate my eggs and sipped my soda, I observed a modern yet traditional metropolis in a mad scramble to the future. As I tried to imagine the city in a time before traffic jams, before the place became known for decay and corruption, a boy approached Bas and said, "Hello mister! You need help? No worry, you don't have to pay. I work for tips... Call me Ishmael. I am number-one local guide."

Bas said, "Yeah? OK. Where can we find the wild orangutans?"

Ishmael answered, "Easy. You go Bukit Lawang. I can show you minibus stop, close to here."

The minibuses did not depart until they got full, and ours was not full so we waited. Meanwhile two musicians with guitars sang in English. One guy had metal spikes in his ears and the other wore a Bob Marley t-shirt. They sang well, so I gave them the last of my Malaysian ringgit when they passed the hat.

Ishmael pointed out two women with rotten teeth and blood-red gums. He explained the cause was a lifetime of chewing betel nuts for the intoxicating effect. Bas called this a disgusting habit, then he prepared to light a cigarette, so I said to him, "Yes. It does seems stupid, doesn't it? To destroy your own health just to catch a buzz?" My friend looked at me as if annoyed, then he put away his unlit smoke.

Ishmael correctly guessed that I was from North America and Bas was from Holland. Impressed, we gave him a tip and he walked away whistling a tune.

Our minibus was almost full, so we boarded. The last seat was filled by a gray-haired backpacker wearing leather boots, airy trousers, and a t-shirt from Pakistan. His backpack was adorned with world flags. He had sapphire blue eyes. As Westerners do on Indonesian minibuses, we greeted each other in English. The guy's name was Peter.

Bas asked him where he was going.

Peter answered, "I'm already here. Wherever I go, here I am. Everywhere I go is home. Welcome to my humble home. Ah, but where am I going *next* you ask? The jungle. My plan is to camp with wild orangutans. I was here in Sumatra years ago, and this was my favorite program."

Just then a truck honked its horn near to our ears without a good reason, something which is always annoying, but this particular horn broke the record for decibels of loudness, a horn so loud that it seemed criminal. Peter added, "Also, I need to get some jungle time man, because... all this intolerable city noise! I'm seriously ready for some peace and quiet. I've been on the road a long time."

I said, "Yeah man. I hear ya. We're going to the jungle too, for exactly the same reasons. And by the way, welcome home."

Peter said, "Thanks."

Our minibus was full, so it departed.

Peter told us that he was sixty-one years old, and still he was a wanna-be rock star. His wild hairdo and his energetic style made him look much younger. Bas and I quizzed him about his life enough to learn that he worked as a history professor in Sweden, but then his wife died, so he sold his house and hit the road. We agreed to join forces for a jungle trek.

I asked him, "How long have you been travelling? How many countries have you visited?"

He answered, "*Globalocity*. Global velocity! The road is my destination. I travel with ferocity!"

He smiled. I liked him already. "Since I left Sweden," he added, "my velocity has been eighty-three countries, plus or minus four, in seventy-five months."

"Plus or minus four?"

"Yah. This depends on how you define the word *country*. Also, how do you define being *in* a country? Does the airport count? If you sleep through a country on the train, does that count? Does

Hong Kong count? It's China, but it's not China; it has its own currency, culture, border security... And what about Puerto Rico? It's part of the United States, like a colony, but they have a separate Olympic team and they speak Spanish. Does this count? What about Scotland and Wales? I was in the Soviet Union which is no longer on the map. And meanwhile, Timor Leste has only been an independent nation for a few years."

"The Vatican?"

"Not much more than a big church."

Peter told exciting travel stories, but our minibus ride was more memorable for the near-death sensation as our imprudent driver sped too fast down crowded roads.

In Bukit Lawang, we found a hotel along a river-side path, then we went out in search of beer, to refresh our energies and to celebrate being alive.

In a rustic bar with a scenic view, Peter described his previous trip to Sumatra, noting how shocked he was by the population explosion since (but happy about the widespread availability of potable water). He told me that the word *orang-utan* meant *jungle-people*, then he explained how perilously close the great apes were to extinction, a depressing topic but as he put it, "If we don't talk about the Earth's urgent problems, then there's no chance whatsoever of solving them."

My new friend from Sweden understood human history, and therefore how political power came to be structured dysfunctionally. He also knew about science, its limits, and how to separate facts from opinions via a disciplined method. He taught me a new word, epistemology, the nature of knowledge, and I was delighted. He explained the limits of human linguistics, especially with words as tricky to define as *fact*. "Philosophers can debate this stuff forever," he said, "but my point is that we can know things if we build our belief system on top of humanity's science, not humanity's literature. And isn't that the goal of philosophy? To understand why things are the way they are, consistent with absolutely all of the evidence?"

As darkness fell, our bar filled up with backpackers and a local guy started playing guitar while another guy started singing remarkably well, then the bartender handed out bongo drums.

Peter bought drinks for me and Bas, then he removed a classical flute from his vest pocket and joined the band, playing rock-and-roll woodwind with an Indonesian twist.

50 - The Jungle

We first saw the orange beasts in cages. They seemed sad, perhaps because they did not understand they would soon be free. Former pets and orphans, they awaited release from quarantine into Gunung Leuser National Park, their last safe haven in Sumatra. Minutes later we saw more furry apes travelling via their tree-canopy highway to a platform loaded with bananas, a daily feeding provided by the orangutan rehabilitation center.

I surprised myself by how excited I became upon seeing these creatures alive and free in their forest home. I admired their athletic prowess as they moved from tree to tree. Unlike monkeys, they seldom jumped, instead relying on their body weight to bend the tree branches. I felt an immediate connection with these furry critters, because speech and tree-climbing abilities aside, they were us. These were the people of the jungle.

Peter explained that orangutan DNA was ninety-six-point-four percent the same as human DNA, then he put things in perspective. "Back when I taught history," he said, "I told stories of human ambition and greed, sometimes of love, the stories of Julius Caesar and Napoleon Bonaparte. But, do you know the most important fact of human history? Evolution, the story of life itself, the story of how humans split from the other apes to walk upright, and how that changed everything."

Ah yes, the jungle! My friends and I hired a guide named Jaka for a three-day trek. Jaka was my age but smaller and stronger, a jungle man. He carried our food and camping gear. The rest of us brought day-packs with extra clothes. Bas also brought the hammock I gave him in Goa, and a Frisbee, Peter brought his flute, and I brought a wad of hundred-dollar bills as a light-weight precaution against the theft of our stuff stashed in town.

The transition from private land to jungle was abrupt, from civilized to wild in twenty meters. Suddenly we were in a world of plants, birds, and bugs, all very much alive. This jungle had gigantic ants, too. Cool.

Atop the first hill we encountered a monkey sitting by the trail. I paused to enjoy a moment of eye contact, friendly, curious, and calm. Then he sprang at me! Big teeth and sharp claws! If his purpose was to show me who was the boss, he succeeded. He was the boss.

Jaka laughed, "Welcome to jungle!"

Rain turned our walk into a muddy ordeal. Jaka zipped down the trail wearing flip-flops, but for the rest of us the track was hard going. After a while, our guide pointed out tiger tracks in the mud, adding, "Do not be afraid of tiger. I never see tiger, whole life. Never. Tiger afraid of people."

I wasn't convinced that tigers were afraid, only that they were good at hiding in the bush, so I no longer brought up the rear. This made me remember something that Gramps once said, "More snakes see you than you see snakes." He wasn't referring to serpents necessarily, but also to con artists and thieves. Gramps was a wise man.

Suddenly Jaka yelled, "Run!" It's never good when one's guide yells, "Run!" This is especially true in a tiger-infested jungle on a muddy trail with snakes and spiky plants. The urgency was hornets. We were near a nest. They attacked. We ran.

Bas got stung several times, so we stopped to rest as soon as we were clear. Jaka knew a plant that alleviated hornet-sting itch, so he procured some. Meanwhile my friend whipped out a joint made from wacky weed that he bought in town. He said, "Pain killer."

The happy hippie offered his joint to Peter who declined saying, "No way. I'm crazy enough without that shit."

Jaka shared in the joint, but he never drank alcohol because he was Muslim. He said, "I think Islam is good. I follow rules more or less."

Jaka had little knowledge of the modern world. He said he never owned electric toys that imprison the human spirit, and that's what I liked about him. He was closer in lifestyle to his ancestors than his neighbors, in a good way. He said, "My grandfather never go to city, and he die happy, but then logging company clear jungle and force family to move. My father, he die unhappy and young. That's why my big wish is to always live in jungle, but I cannot! Near Bukit Lawang there is only national park and then palm-oil plantations. At least I can make money from crazy foreign tourists like you. Anyway, you can live in jungle. Western tourists have money. You can buy land and build bamboo shack, make very nice vegetable garden."

Peter said that if he told his "civilized" friends that he was going to live in the jungle, they'd say he was crazy, "mad as a box of frogs." He said, "My friends at home live in a plastic environment bombarded with sensory overload. True, it is a bit more comfortable." Given that we were sitting on tree roots with insects buzzing about, this seemed funny.

Bas said, "The television tells me to buy a bigger television, but I don't miss the constant advertising trying to incite me to buy shiny objects that I don't need and can't afford. We've been seduced by golden trinkets, and in order to buy those trinkets we must work as slaves to our credit-card bills. I'd rather spend my money travelling. Despite the hornets, I love the jungle. Ahhh... The wild." He puffed on his joint.

I suddenly felt like climbing a tree.

Jungle Jaka sliced open a vine containing potable water, then he offered me a drink. Jaka took it for granted that this particular vine had water, just as I knew for example that American convenience stores have bathrooms, but to use them one has to ask the clerk for the key.

The rain stopped so we pushed on to camp. Bas set up his hammock and fired up another joint. Peter called him an addict. Bas ignored this to ask me, "Want some?"

I couldn't say no because there was nothing to do but contemplate life from a different perspective. As I sat down to relax, the ganja buzz hit my head. I felt less muscle ache from tramping which was relaxing, but simultaneously my brain became easily distracted by thoughts which were creatively different, plus euphoria. I had to stand up and walk to the edge of the creek, then I had to walk somewhere else, such was my body buzz. With nothing else to do, we all played Frisbee. Then Jaka prepared dinner while the rest of us watched monkeys watching us watch them. Then came the birdsong at sunset. Awesome.

The next day we encountered an orangutan mama with her baby clinging to her fur. The great ape hung from a tree with one hand while eating a mango with the other. My friends took pictures until eventually Mama climbed down to the ground and walked towards us. We all froze. Meanwhile I observed myself becoming more observant, fully in the moment with only my animal instincts to guide me. Mama grabbed my day-pack, and I let her have it.

The great ape casually climbed a tree while holding my pack with her left foot, then she paused to think. She unzipped the main compartment and removed my water bottle, then she unscrewed the top off the bottle, smelled the contents, then threw the bottle to the jungle floor. She proceeded systematically, unzipping every zipper and analyzing every object. Finding nothing of interest, she threw everything away.

At one point, the jungle rained green bits of paper with pictures of Benjamin Franklin. Bas laughed as I collected my money. He said, "Orangutans might be intelligent, but they don't know the value of a dollar!" With that, he lit a cigarette.

Peter said to me, "Wild apes are smarter than we give them credit for, and humans are dumber. Take for example Bastiaan's cigarette habit. He knows it's dirty and bad for his health, not to mention all the land that could be used for growing food, but there he is..."

Bas interrupted, "Ease up! I'm not done evolving yet." He puffed his smoke then started singing, "I'm a monkey. He's a monkey. She's a monkey. It's a monkey. Aren't you glad that you're a monkey too?" Everyone laughed so Bas repeated his verse. Then we all joined in, and as we sang, I could imagine the orange apes humming along as best they could.

The next day we saw more wild orangutans, but to my disappointment, they weren't humming Bastiaan's jingle. I wasn't really disappointed. The scene was amazing to watch: humanity's closest cousins, naked and vulnerable, playing with their babies while hanging upside down, holding onto tree branches with their feet.

Our trek ended at the bank of a raging river. Jaka's friend Django met us with inflated inner-tubes strapped together with rope to make a raft. Jaka secured all our stuff inside a water-proof bag, then we careened down the rapids back to town.

The toilet in my hotel room was a hole in the floor, and there was no hygienic paper, but I was used to hand-and-water ass cleaning, and I was conscious of the fact that the flush toilet was a recent innovation for ape-kind, along with the hot shower, written language, shoes, and money. I realized that my culture's addiction to electric gadgets, despite the nature channels on television, made it difficult to see the true nature of nature. Later it occurred to me that the place where I felt most alive was exactly the place with the most variety of things that could kill me, the jungle.

51 - Not Tarzan

Peter, Bas, and I travelled to Lake Toba by local bus, a full-day ordeal worth every minute of discomfort in order to arrive at this scenic paradise created by a volcanic mega-explosion. Upon arrival at the lake we boarded a ferry to an island the size of Singapore, an island where Peter knew a hotel with stunning views, welcoming people, and a damn good coconut curry.

The first thing I did was swim in the clear, refreshing water. Next I smoked a joint with Bas on our veranda. I was surprised he had marijuana because he recently told me that he decided not to travel with it because of police checkpoints. At the time I told him it wasn't worth the risk. But he brought ganja with him after all. He explained that in case of a police checkpoint, the only thing that might have gotten him busted was fear. "Police smell fear." He said that he wasn't afraid himself, but he wasn't sure about Peter and me so he lied to us.

He said to Peter, "You're right though, marijuana is not the answer, unless the question is, 'Hey Bastiaan, what do you want to smoke?'"

A man paddled past our veranda in a canoe, selling fish and magic mushrooms. We declined so he paddled on. That's when Bas and I invited Peter to join our trek to Africa.

Peter answered, "Africa by bus? Wild gorillas and chimps? Sure. Count me in. I've always wanted to go to East Africa. Why not Ethiopia?"

The next day we all bought one-way e-tickets to Tel Aviv for the last day allowed by our thirty-day Indonesian visas, then we wandered around our touristy Christian town in search of a bar to celebrate our freedom, which we defined as our ability to act spontaneously.

As we wandered, Peter tried to convince Bas and me to never have children. He said, "People ask me all the time how I manage to travel so much, and I tell them, no children. And to people like you who say they want to live free, I tell them, no children. The world has too many fucking people already anyway, literally."

Children! Trained-ape theory predicted that I would find love, and then, could I realistically abstain from procreating? I had never thought about this before, me, a father? Yikes!

The first bar that Peter, Bas, and I encountered blasted electronic music too loudly, so we gave it a miss. The second bar had no music at all, so we walked on. The third bar played classic rock, but not too loudly. We ordered beer.

The bartender was furrier than Bastiaan, with a gray beard and chest hair visible through his rock-and-roll t-shirt. He said, "I think I'll join you. Cheers! It's Tuesday so it's a beer night! No it's Wednesday, isn't it? Yes. It's Wednesday. In that case, I'll have a beer!"

George introduced himself, then he asked us to list our names and nationalities. We replied honestly, then he said to me, "You had me fooled. Interesting." With that I knew he was an American also. When I called him on that, he replied, "Yes, but just because I live in Sumatra, I'm no master of the beasts and savages. I'm no Tarzan. Actually Lake Toba is quite civilized." With that, he knocked over his beer.

As George cleaned up his spillage, Peter asked him how he came to own a bar in such a remote corner of the world. The man smiled. "I'll tell you tomorrow. That'll be Thursday, a beer night!"

Peter told us about a guy he saw killed for spilling beer in Colombia, shot by a miscreant so macho that he was willing to kill for pride. Then Bas told us about the time someone stole all his stuff in Jamaica at gunpoint. This led me to describe my adventures in China. This led George and Peter to tell more stories from China.

George said that China's government was only Marxist to the degree that it prioritized the needs of the many over the needs of the few; otherwise it was capitalist, so it was closer to being socialist than communist, but in a uniquely corrupt way.

I asked Peter, "Sweden is socialist, right? What do you think?"

He answered, "Yah, socialist. Sweden has capitalism too, but we don't allow profits to trump all other concerns. It's a mixed model. We have retirement pensions. We have universal health care. Sure some people are lazy and live off the state, but this is not expensive compared to war machines, and it's easy to pay for with smart taxes. Sweden is socialist yes, but that's just a word. The governing principle is not any ideology really, but good economics and human-oriented policy. Look at the statistics: Sweden has low inequality and high happiness."

George said, "I'll drink to that! And because I like you guys, the next round is on me."

We clinked our beers, and as we drank, the radio played a song of protest against the Vietnam war by a singer named Country Joe.

George said, "You want to know why I bought this bar? I'll tell you. I used to work as an economist for the International Monetary Fund." He looked me in the eyes. "You've heard of that, right, the IMF? It was a great gig, with an excellent salary and all that. For my job I screwed over Indonesia's economy... Look, I'm not exactly proud of this, so first let me give you some background..."

George hit his beer. "After the Great War," he said, "the IMF and World Bank were established to provide monetary stability and to rebuild the so-called 'first world' democracies of Europe. I was excited to work in this field after I saw the Marshall Plan in action. You've heard of that, right, the Marshall Plan? We gave free money to Europe to rebuild (we did the same for Japan) and these countries became our strongest allies and trading partners. This was fantastic! I was a believer in America. I thought, let's do the same thing for the third world!"

Bas said, "I'll drink to that!" We clinked our beers.

George continued, "Yes, but the Fund's mission changed. We abused our power. We began forcing countries to enact policies with no scientific basis, policies that failed miserably, really stupid policies."

I said, "Oh shit. What kind of policies?"

George answered, "Here in Indonesia, the Fund forced cuts in education and food subsidies, then forced the privatization of key industries, even when these only created monopolies with no benefits for the people. This was not like the Marshall Plan at all; this money was not free, and it came with strings attached, big strings called 'structural adjustments' that we imposed on debtor nations. These were designed for two purposes, to ensure our loans got paid back with interest no matter what, and to open third-world countries up for first-world exploitation."

I said, "Oh shit. What caused the Fund's change in mission?"

George answered, "Greed found a way... After the Great War,

free-market capitalism became like a religion, because communism was the new evil enemy, see? The commies were atheists for Christ's sake! And thanks to all the relentless propaganda, most Americans came to believe that the so-called invisible hand of the free market can do no wrong. It's a great bullshit story, right up there with the one about the magic super-man in Heaven who listens to prayers."

Bas yelled, "Bullshit!"

George smiled then he hit his beer. "Yes. So anyway, my organization wanted to loan as much money to Indonesia as possible, because the machine profits wildly from all those interest payments, see? My job was to demonstrate that the Indonesian economy would grow so quickly (thanks to our investment money) that the government could pay back their loans easily. I knew this was bullshit, but I was just doing my job, you know? We only showed graphs with arrows pointing up, because you know, up is good and down is bad. I'm oversimplifying a bit, but you get my point."

I asked, "What did Indonesia do with all the loan money?"

George answered, "Mostly to fund projects run by American companies to construct infrastructure needed by other American companies to extract oil and lumber for export to America, plus arms to protect American interests. The dictator Suharto, he got rich from all this. Now he's dead, but the people still have to pay back the debt, and in U.S. dollars too, but Indonesia can only get that much foreign exchange by selling their oil and lumber." Sigh. "Meanwhile the pencil-necked geeks in New York and Washington say that every time a forest gets chopped down, that this is good economics, see, because some company is making a profit. They have a graph that points up." Sigh. Beer.

Bas looked angry. It was the first time I ever saw him look angry. We all drank and listened to U2. Then the lights went out and the music stopped, a blackout. We shared a moment of silence. Yang was reaching its maximum.

George said into the darkness, "The corrupt assholes with all the money promote economic models that are flat-out wrong because they only consider money, without even a hint of a balance with nature. Our models must subtract when we cut down a forest, and we must subtract when we crash a fishery or deplete an aquifer, and we need to friggin' subtract for war! But of course they use the wrong models on purpose, so there's no hope. We're already witnessing the largest extinction since the dinosaurs, and we're just getting started. The orangutan has little time left. Basically we're talking about the worst parts of the Bible, the Apocalypse, Armageddon. But I don't care. I'll be dead soon enough."

When the lights came back on, a sappy love song filled our ears, and this seemed so out of place that we all laughed, then we all drank beer.

Peter said, "Sorry George, but I disagree. I think a better world is still possible. Just imagine a global government for example, and not the United Nations with its veto system, nor the IMF where the rule is one dollar, one vote. I mean, imagine if there was only one central bank, and one army too, then..."

George interrupted, "Horse manure!"

Peter said, "OK, you're right, never mind. I got carried away. But I think a global government is a natural and necessary step for humanity, at least meaningful cooperation, especially to manage shared resources. Can you imagine the Earth in a thousand years without it?"

George said, "Yes. I can imagine Earth without humans quite easily. And for humanity to get to this utopia of yours, with a benevolent dictator or whatever, first there's gotta be some kind of catastrophic event so big that it convinces everyone that any alternative is worse, maybe a nuclear war, who knows? Meanwhile I predict that every country on Earth will become like Indonesia is now, only worse, with the rich hiding in fortresses and visiting each other by helicopter, while the masses suffer in decay. But I don't care. I'll be dead."

Peter said, "But George, it doesn't have to be that way! China has more than a billion people and China is making progress. If the number-one problem is overpopulation, then let's build family-planning centers. Let's educate the girls. You see? Another world is possible."

George said, "Possible, but not very bloody likely! God wrote it in stone: thou shall not plan your family. I think we should send every AIDS orphan in Africa to the Vatican. Then maybe His Santissimo will come out in favor of condoms."

Bas said, "But every sperm is sacred."

George said, "I'll drink to that."

We all drank.

I broke the silence. "So George, you never told us why you bought the bar."

The big man answered, "Oh yeah. I quit the Fund after the Asian financial crisis of 1997. Capital flight at the click of a mouse, with zero friction. So stupid. Boom! Crash. The friggin' geeks in New York and Washington made a mess of it again. The subsequent chaos made land here incredibly cheap, and since meanwhile I fell in love with a lovely local lady, well, the rest is history."

Just then, three women walked into the bar, permanently disrupting our pseudo-intellectual chatter. Three sisters from Australia, bubbly and cute, began telling jokes and travel stories, often with sexual innuendo. Peter tried to explain how the history of Indonesian economics was a perfect example of American imperial power, but the ladies were not interested; they just wanted to have fun, and we did have fun. Indeed, we partied until late, and when we finally left the bar, we agreed to meet the next evening for more. This marked the end of a memorable day, the day Peter agreed to join forces with Bas and me for a trek across Africa.

52 - Marvels of Evolution

I woke up with a hangover, jumped in the lake, then joined Bas to sip coffee on our veranda. He told me about his conflicting emotions: he missed his Cambodian girlfriend Sophie but he also wanted to sleep with Victoria, such were his animal instincts. I confessed that I wanted to sleep with Elizabeth, as I too was an ape. Peter jumped in the lake then he joined us. He said he liked Regina. We sipped coffee and discussed freedom, which we defined as the ability to go with the flow, or not.

Bas asked me, "What's that on your forehead?" I knew what he meant. I had a strange bug bite that was growing larger every day, a legacy of our jungle trek. I decided right then to do something about it. First I sterilized a knife, then I performed surgery in front of my bathroom mirror. I made a tiny cut, then I squeezed out insect eggs and puss (this was messy and gross), then I jumped in the lake. And so began a lazy day...

My friends and I met the Australian sisters at George's bar that evening as arranged. George made sure we always had enough beer, and we all got drunk again. Meanwhile the single boys flirted with the single girls. In the cool evening air, we swapped stories and laughed at life. Elizabeth and I hit it off, and that was especially fun, so I invited her to join me the next day for a motorbike tour of our island. She said yes.

Happy to have a date, I procured the best-quality motorcycle available for rent, then I met Elizabeth for lunch, then we hit the road. We stopped to see craft markets, Batak villages, and stone Gods from an extinct religion (the Batak people since converted to Christianity). We had fun but I felt no spark, no magic chemistry, so there was no point in pursuing a physical relationship, especially as she and her sisters were poised to fly back to Australia in two days. Thanks to a new technology called *social media* however, we would forever be Internet friends.

Elizabeth complained that her holiday was too short, but she had plenty of money. I figured that she merely lacked the courage to put her life on hold, to put all her stuff in storage and just go, so I did my best to encourage her. I promoted the freedom that only comes with a one-way ticket, then I told her that she should sell her house.

Over coffee, Bas confessed that he slept with Victoria. He smiled the smile of a man who just got laid, and that made me feel envy, an animal instinct. Peter said that meanwhile, he and Regina, "discussed literary classics."

Bas said, "Really? The classics? That's fascinating. Do you want me to score you some Viagra?"

Peter said, "Ha. I'm not so old, my dear friend. No, Regina is a lover of the arts. She can discuss the chivalry of Chaucer and the allegory of Milton!"

Bas said, "Wow. No way. Milton?"

Peter said, "You know not what you are missing, my friend. But alas, most people would rather have sex and laze around smoking dope than discuss extraordinary literature."

Bas said, "True enough. And you, my friend, know not what you are missing. How shall I say this? Victoria has it going on in the sack."

Peter said, "Ah humans, marvels of evolution, animals that sometimes have deep thoughts. The tragic irony is that we've been too successful. We're running out of planet!"

Bas said, "If humanity is doomed, shouldn't we concentrate on having fun?"

Peter said, "Touché. But the surest way for evil men to triumph is for good men to do nothing. Humanity is *not* doomed if we act now. Protesting greed is my creed, man, and I might add, I have fun doing it."

Bas said he'd drink to that, then he brewed another round of coffee.

Meanwhile Peter told us about his visit to Seattle, USA, in 1999 to protest against the World Trade Organization. He said, "The mainstream media only showed stoned hippies and anarchists breaking windows, but Seattle marked the birth of independent media on the Internet! We no longer have to get our news from the corporate *thing*. And that's great because we can fight back against this monster better when we're armed with information."

I said, "It's no wonder the protesters are so angry."

Peter said, "Oh, they have many reasons to be angry. Did you know that some 'free trade' treaties (such as NAFTA) allow corporations to sue governments to overturn laws that threaten their 'expected future profits'? Seriously. Corporations can now sue governments in secret tribunals, and they have successfully abolished laws that protect the environment and public health. This is bad. As of when did corporations obtain a sovereign right to profit?"

He explained, "The *thing* feeds on money. The *thing* has banks on Caribbean islands. The *thing* is immortal. And no matter how heinous a crime the *thing* commits, we cannot put it in jail, but we can limit its powers with new laws and treaties. This is why I sometimes volunteer as a political activist, not to be anti-globalization but pro-humanity, because World War Three has begun, and this time it's the humans versus the *thing*."

I suddenly felt like swimming, so I walked to the water's edge. I said, "It's a jungle out there, but short of a nuclear war or an asteroid, I think humanity will survive. We're pretty adaptable." With that, I became a fish.

While I was underwater I saw with stunning clarity how the *thing* was a marvel of evolution, a mutation of corporate law, and like an invasive species of strangler vines, it was destroying previously harmonious ecosystems. My interest in politics spiked. I wanted to understand how humanity might cage this *thing*, or at least return balance to the ecosystem, so I began to quiz Peter relentlessly.

53 - Culture Shock

My friends and I had a plane to catch a thousand miles to the south so we departed down the trans-Sumatra highway, a poor-quality winding track. We stopped to explore volcanic regions and tribal villages so much however, that we eventually became pressed for time. That's how we decided to fly from Padang, Sumatra to Yogyakarta on the island of Java, trading grueling days of long-distance buses for cultural centers and archaeological sites. This saved us money too because the flight was cheap.

Peter had been to this region before so he acted as our tour guide. First we visited the ancient Hindu temples at Prambanan and Candi Sukuh (by motorcycle), both with fascinating scenes from ancient life (including sexual detail) carved into stone. Oh how times have changed.

I loved wandering through ancient temples with my friends, and touring the volcanic highlands too, with that air of freedom that only comes from the open road. I also loved swapping stories with locals who generally made us feel welcome (except for the hustlers who made us feel like walking wallets), especially when sitting in a market with old women selling vegetables, where the sights and smells were little changed for centuries, and the price was negotiable. I loved eating in restaurants crowded with locals where the food was always tasty and cheap. I loved the rough edges, and I loved the fresh fruit. Who knew that mangosteens could taste so sweet?

Regarding touring by motorcycle, the crowded chaos did intimidate me at first, until I internalized the rules that Peter summarized concisely, "Don't worry about what's going on behind you. Use your turn signal. Don't be stupid. And most important of all, don't hit anything in front of you. This implies that it is OK to cut across traffic rather boldly if oncoming traffic can see you clearly; they won't hit you. There is order in chaos. Go with the flow. And watch out for people going the wrong way, but they'll be all the way to your left, so the general rule to keep left has an exception in this case. If you need to go the wrong way, keep far right."

Regarding finding a bed every night, it did help to have a guide book but we rarely slept in a recommended hotel. Our book was useful in finding hidden gems along our route, and useful in understanding the history and the layout of cities, but popular hotels were often expensive, so we preferred to walk around in a good location and negotiate for empty rooms.

Regarding buying water, almost never. I boiled two liters every morning as part of my coffee routine, plus Bas and Peter both carried filter pumps. We observed that most tourists drank expensive mineral water, but restaurants bought five-gallon jugs of boiled water for almost no money, and they let us top up for free.

Regarding *sarongs*, these masculine skirts were required for all men to wear in order to enter sacred places, and I learned to love mine. I bought a cotton sarong with a cool batik design which I wore when entering temples (as required). I also used it as a sleeping sheet, a beach towel, and as a layer against the high-altitude cold atop volcanoes.

The undisputed archaeological highlight of Java for tourists is Borobudur, the world's largest Buddhist stupa and a site rivaling Machu Picchu as the place with the most foreigners crowded in per square meter. The traveller's challenge used to be getting to places like Borobudur (with no direct flights, no ATM machines, no Internet, no guide books, and no English), whereas for us the challenge was getting away from all the people, to soak up to vibe, to appreciate the masterpiece of ancient craftsmanship in peace and quiet. Our solution was to arrive with the sunrise and then relax with home-brewed coffee while waiting for the entrance gate to open.

It seemed odd to visit a Hindu temple with no Hindus, and then a Buddhist stupa with no monks in a land of Muslims. Peter explained how these religions coexisted for centuries until the mega-eruption of the Krakatoa volcano in 1883 changed everything. "Krakatoa allowed the Islamic militants to take over," he said. "They exploited the fact that so many people blamed Shiva for the devastation. The Buddhists and Hindus who survived this chaos were then mostly either forced to convert to Islam or flee to Bali."

"By the way," he added, "the tsunami that devastated Sumatra in 2006 was big enough to stop the civil war in Aceh. No country has more active geology than Indonesia. The last time I was here I felt a strong earthquake. Geology, man..."

Peter always knew the history of such things, and I felt lucky to have him as my travelling companion. I never imagined I'd meet a guru from Sweden, but then again I never imagined Bastiaan either, a happy hippie who constantly made me laugh.

At Borobudur, a fabulous site that was crawling with tourists like ants, my friends and I scrutinized our fellow Westerners. After travelling away from the tourist zone, I felt culture shock when we arrived squarely back on the beaten path.

I was shocked the first time I walked into a restaurant full of white people focused on electronic gadgets instead of each other, many wearing inappropriately immodest clothing for a Muslim region. These tourists seemed selfish and sloppy, they spoke loudly, and they lacked humility, especially when they flaunted their wealth in front of people who worked so hard for so little. I was shocked by those tourists who took photos of local people as if they were zoo animals without asking permission first; and I was shocked whenever I saw a foreigner haggle so much when buying something that the vendor barely turned a profit.

Peter said he was shocked by the pace of change caused by too many people. "Even Bukit Lawang is getting crowded," he sighed. "And worse. Some places that became famous for pristine beauty are now so crowded that they are famous only for being famous. Ha."

Borobudur however, was famous for being awesome, a site packed with fabulous stone carvings that told an epic story without words, the story of Buddha, a reminder that even long ago enlightened leaders could build great monuments with slave labor.

Leaving the site we were forced to walk past hundreds of shops, many selling the same cheap tourist junk. Peter lamented that this so-called art was all inferior to the skilled craftsmanship he remembered from his visit to Borobudur years before, not because he wanted to buy anything he said, but because he liked to look at art, not copies of copies of copies. He called this phenomenon, "cultural death by mass tourism."

The good news we figured, was that hordes of tourists were generally easy to avoid, but if we got stuck with them somewhere like Borobudur, watching them excitedly photographing each other poorly always made us laugh, especially when all the men wore identical, touristy sarongs (loaned to them upon entering the sacred site). I was happy that I owned a cool sarong.

Observing tourists made me feel conscientious about any behaviors that could be tagged as American, especially as I was about to go to the Middle East. I encouraged Peter and Bas to coach me towards internationalizing my English, for example saying *trousers* instead of pants, *torch* instead of flashlight, and avoiding words like *dude*. I worked hard at sounding not-American on demand, a good exercise in self control and cultural understanding. I was happy that I did not own any electronics.

Our final stop in Indonesia was Jakarta, the center of money and politics, a sprawling city with too many people, a city where we observed the nation's elite casually strolling through air-conditioned shopping malls. I was still sad about losing my good travel gear in China, so I bought new trousers and sunglasses to console myself. Arriving into Jakarta made me feel excited, with a renewed sense of adventure: Israel, Syria, Africa! Oh yeah...

54 - General Lipshitz

As my friends and I boarded our magical flying machine, to jump across Asia in just a few hours, we agreed that we were the luckiest people alive. We were born in the golden age of world travel, the age of jumbo jets and abundant petrol, plus we had the money and *chutzpah* to explore our world, and there were still wild gorillas to see.

The airline offered free magazines for passengers, and the cover of one grabbed my attention: "Chinese Soldiers Kill Tibetan Monks." I read the article, then the next, then the next. I was oddly hungry for Americanized news; it was all bad, but it was packaged in a familiar format which was strangely gratifying. One article was about terrorists in Yemen, promoting fear, and another mentioned radical anti-globalization protesters without saying why they were protesting, only that their views were radical. I once read such prose assuming that well-informed authors were striving to educate the masses, but I since learned to see the bias: these authors had editor-bosses who were employees of magazine-corporations that were wholly-owned subsidiaries of the *thing*.

I said to my friends, "My father reads this magazine religiously and his politics are somewhere to the right of Genghis Khan. He probably thinks socialism is a disease... By the way, did I ever tell you that he and my mother met in Jerusalem?"

I explained all about my parents including the latest word from Pedro. My friends were intrigued by the mystery so they helped brainstorm new ways to get information, and we came up with one idea, a plan for investigating Pops's former employer in Tel Aviv, a plan that required me to cut my hair and buy business-casual clothes.

I loved getting on the airplane in Jakarta, but I loved more getting off in Israel, the land where I was conceived. My friends and I arrived to a dry climate with a different air. We arrived at passport control. Our immigration officer was a mutant, literally; he had six fingers. He also had piercing green eyes. I asked him to please *not* stamp my passport because I planned to visit Syria in the future. He obliged by stamping a blank piece of paper instead.

My friends breezed through customs but security agents

stopped me to scrutinize all my stuff. This wasn't a big deal, but it was annoying.

When I finally stepped outside to breathe fresh Israeli air, I found Bas smoking a cigarette. I said to him, "Peter's right. You are an addict."

The happy hippie took a puff, then he said, "But this is not a problem because I can quit any time. Nothing for you to worry about." He exaggerated an expression of bliss. "Ah, yes. Mmmm. Life is good." He took another puff.

Peter said, "Quitting cigarettes is like breaking up with a pretty girlfriend who's otherwise completely wrong for you. There's an upside, she's pretty, but there's a bigger downside, she's otherwise completely wrong for you."

Bas admired his cigarette. "Yes, she is pretty, isn't she?"

Peter said, "You do agree, logically, that you'd be better off not smoking. No?"

Bas scratched an Indonesian bug bite, then he said, "If logic prevailed, then we'd all be robot computers. Boring!" He took another puff.

Peter insisted, "You didn't answer my question."

Bas said, "OK. I admit to that. Yes. I would be better off not smoking, logically speaking. Are you happy now, Mr. Spock?"

Peter said, "So... Are you a man or a monkey? I dare you to quit right now!"

I looked Bas in the eyes and added, "I double dare you!"

Bas scoffed, "I'll show you who's a man and who's a monkey!" He put out his smoke, then he exaggerated an expression of macho manliness.

With that, we took a taxi to our hotel where we promptly all fell asleep, exhausted from our trans-Asia flight. When I awoke, my friends were both snoring so I took a shower, left a note, then went for a walk, the first time I ever saw the Mediterranean Sea. The water was cold and infested with jellyfish.

As I sat to watch the waves, I missed Angeline and felt sad. I also missed Sara, the girl who helped me in Kathmandu. I had no way to contact her but her memory made me smile. I imagined bumping into her by chance in Jerusalem, inspired by the smallness of the world.

I walked into an Internet shop and called Pedro, and he had news! Shep figured out how federal agents accessed the anti-terrorist watch lists over the Internet. "Now he's working on logging into the website of truth using legitimate credentials, then he can search for Pops's record. So how does he do that? Right? Well, I don't understand much, but Shep did explain how he's targeting government agents to see if he can sniff out a password or hijack an authenticated session. Fascinating stuff... Did you know there's a 'dark web' where people publish attack scripts? And they get good money for new exploits. I had no idea our technology was so vulnerable! But as I said man, Shep's the man, and he seems optimistic!"

I thanked my friend for his good news, then I told him I was poised to investigate Pops's old company. Then I walked back to my hotel and broke bread with my friends, then with their coaching, I reinvented myself as a Christian tourist.

I travelled by taxi along American-style freeways past strip-malls with American-branded fast-food restaurants to a business park at the edge of town. Tel Aviv reminded me of southern California with familiar retail stores, architectural styles, and dry climate, but I did not feel at home. Despite the writing in Hebrew, I was surprised by the lack of Jewish symbolism, and despite the ubiquitous military, I felt safe. Excited as I was to be in Israel though, I missed Indonesia. I missed the fresh food and the bird song in the jungle. I missed the green.

At the designated building, I asked my driver to wait, then I walked through the revolving door. From outside, nothing but the company's name indicated it was in the business of war, and upon entering the grand lobby, my eyes were drawn to green plants and water fountains. Everything seemed normal but I happened to know, thanks to Shepherd the hacker, that this company was distinguished amongst defense contractors in Israel as the one that had been in business the longest.

The receptionist was American, and she wore too much make-up.

"Hello." I said. "I'm sorry to bother you, but my father used to work here, and I happened to be in the neighborhood, so is it possible that maybe you can direct me to one of the old-timers? Please? I'd really like to meet someone who knew my dad."

"What was your father's name, and when did he work here?" she asked.

"Raymond Love. I know this is a long shot, because he worked here twenty-six years ago, but..."

The woman smiled. "You're in luck. Here comes General Lipshitz! I'm pretty sure he's been working with us that long."

I followed her eyes to find an elderly man descending the grand stairway, a man with a paunch so large he needed suspenders to hold up his trousers.

The man approached saying, "Raymond Love? I know I know that name... Yes! Raymond. You look just like him! Raymond Love... I'll be damned. You're his son!"

I told the general about my world tour as my excuse to be in town, and he was sufficiently interested to invite me to join him for coffee. As we walked towards the corporate cafeteria, he described Pops as enthusiastic, good at his job, and active socially. He met Mom at a party, he said. When I asked what Pops did for work, the general said that Raymond Senior was a member of the technical staff, but he couldn't remember any details.

General Lipshitz provided fascinating insights but none seemed useful in my poker game with Pops. It's not every day that one gets to sip coffee with an Israeli general however, so I asked many questions, including about the company's business model, and I got him to admit that every battle was a profit opportunity. He said, "A war with Iran would be a major windfall."

Over lunch I reviewed the case with Bas and Peter, then I told them my secret: the next day was my birthday. This of course was cause to go drink beer.

Peter queried, "Did you know? The very next day after Israel became Israel in 1948, her Arab neighbors all attacked. Israel struck back in 1967, taking the Golan Heights from Syria plus the Sinai Peninsula and the West Bank. A few years later, Egypt and Syria attacked back, but Israel won. A few years after that, Egypt made peace, but then someone killed Egypt's president Muhammad Anwar Al Sadat. That's just about when you were born, so maybe you're the reincarnation of Muhammad Anwar Al

Sadat! But even if you're not, when Israeli troops moved into Lebanon, your parents moved to California."

I said, "Yup. Mom was pregnant with me, after all."

55 - The Most Holy Neighborhood

Arriving into the Old City of Jerusalem, history came alive. My friends and I walked through the fortified wall at the Damascus Gate into a crowded bazaar that seemed unchanged for millennium, except for tourists taking photos of course, and plastic souvenirs. Tourists are tourists, but the local people wore their religions on their sleeves the old-fashioned way, and they used beasts of burden to carry their loads. In the labyrinth of narrow alleys that followed, it was a miracle that we found a comfortable and cheap guest house easily.

We happened to be near the Church of the Holy Sepulchre, the site of Jesus's resurrection, or so it was written in the tourist brochure, so we went inside. The ancient architecture was interesting but I was fascinated more by the pilgrims, mostly Americans, queued to see the precise spot where somebody once said that Jesus stopped being dead. I had fun trying to convince these tourists that I was from Mexico. It helped to be with two Europeans to confuse the context.

Later in a shop across the lane, as my friends and I admired plastic statues of Jesus's mother, Bastiaan's face suddenly turned pale, then he darted towards a nearby restaurant. Curious, I followed, and I had to sprint to keep up.

Bas said to the headwaiter, "Please, where is the bathroom?"

The man forced a smile. "The bathroom is for paying customers only. Are you going to dine?"

"No," said Bas lurching. "But this is urgent."

The waiter repeated, "The bathroom is for paying customers only. I am sorry sir, but I must ask you to go somewhere else."

"In that case sir," Bas replied, "I must ask you to go get a towel."

Bas sprayed vomit across the floor, carefully avoiding innocent customers. As I laughed out loud, Peter said to the waiter, "I guess you should have let him use the bathroom, eh?"

The waiter stared silently at the mess on the floor. Meanwhile all eyes were on us. Then a female voice said, "Peter?" The woman's expression betrayed disgust from the vomit, plus bewildered recognition.

Peter said, "Gurli?"

Gurli said, "Oh my God! Peter! Holy shit! It's so nice to see you!"

Peter's long-lost friend Gurli stood up to give him a hug. Tall, blonde, pretty, and about Peter's age, she carefully avoided Bastiaan's spew, then she hugged Peter so excitedly that I could see both of them throwing off magical sparks of love at second sight.

Meanwhile Gurli's lunch partner, a lady closer to my age and also pretty, smiled at me, then she waved at me giggling. I waved back, and I had to laugh. Peter introduced Gurli, then Gurli introduced Adi, then Peter introduced Bastiaan and me. Everyone laughed except the waiter. Then Bas took his leave because he could feel diarrhea coming on quickly, he said.

As Gurli and Adi still had to pay for their meal, Peter and I escorted Bas outside, a moment Peter used to explain, "I haven't seen Gurli in thirty years! I'm amazed she recognized me. We used to go out. She's nice! In fact, at one point I thought I might marry her!"

With that Bas left towards our hotel looking unwell, then I asked Peter a question, but before he could answer, Gurli appeared, running to give him another hug. This left me standing alone with Adi. She asked me, "What's wrong with your other friend?"

"I don't know," I said. "It must have been something he ate."

Adi was taller than me by a hair. She seemed friendly but serious, with intense eyes that showed determination, perhaps forged from a life where nothing came easily. I could imagine her as an Israeli soldier, but I felt attracted to her nevertheless. She had an athletic body and a cute face. She worked as a real-estate agent. I complimented her earrings.

Adi and Gurli offered to guide Peter and me on a tour of the Old City and of course we accepted. Peter and Gurli had to catch up on their lives. I knew they would soon again be lovers. I also knew that I would be in Jerusalem longer than originally planned. I wondered if Adi had a boyfriend.

Gurli worked in Israel as a translator for Arabic, English, and Danish, her native tongue. She said, "I work freelance gigs so I don't make a steady income, but who cares when you get to travel the world?"

I never saw Peter look happier.

We all walked to the Western Wall, the last remnant of the world's first temple for God, the retaining wall for the Temple Mount. We passed through metal detectors into an area crowded with tourists, soldiers, and the Jewish faithful. Men with curly locks wore black hats. Many people stood against the wall to pray; some stuffed folded scraps of paper into cracks in the wall with chewing gum, prayers no doubt.

We visited the Dome of the Rock and Al Aqsa mosques, built where King Solomon's temple once soared, then we sat in the shade to enjoy the panoramic view.

Adi explained what it meant to be a "Jewish democracy," where Zionists do everything possible to protect their voting advantage, including having many babies. She said, "A Jewish democracy is where any Jew in the world can become a citizen, but Muslims living in the West Bank aren't even allowed to pray at Al Aqsa." As we looked over the most-holy neighborhood, Adi vented her frustration at the never-ending conflict, and the stress this caused for all concerned.

Gurli said, "The road to peace begins with tolerance, because tolerance leads to trust, and trust leads to collaboration, but meanwhile, that's the number-one problem in the Holy Land, intolerance."

I joked, "We should not tolerate intolerance!"

Adi laughed, then she said, "Or maybe the problem is too much tolerance? If I said I had an invisible friend from outer space, you would call me crazy. Yeah? But if I say Muhammad flew to Jerusalem on a winged horse, or Jesus turned water into wine at a dinner party, well then… Do I really have to tolerate a stupid idea just because it's an old idea? Isn't it a good thing to call bullshit on flying horses and magical dinner parties?"

I was suddenly more attracted to Adi. She had spunk. She went on to say, "Nothing undermines peace more than blind faith in the impossible, uncontaminated by evidence, and maybe we should not tolerate this. Whenever people believe that God is on their side in a war, um, they're wrong."

I replied to this by quoting an Israeli named Sara, "It's a holy war, because when it comes to land disputes, people turn to the ancient texts to justify their claims. And religious zealots don't care much for details like water rights."

Adi said, "Exactly."

Peter said, "Maybe the problem here isn't a lack of tolerance but a lack of fact checking. I mean, to believe in supernatural saviors is to fundamentally misunderstand how things really work, and that's bad. How can we make a lasting peace without this common understanding? Therefore we must be free to call bullshit on stupid ideas, yes, especially those held by the moderate majority. For example, let's call bullshit right now on land being holy."

Gurli stared at Peter for a while, then she said, "You haven't changed a bit, have you?"

Peter smiled. "I have gray hairs now."

The former lovers swapped stories until Adi announced that she had an important real-estate appointment. So we all walked to her car, detouring along the path allegedly taken by Jesus to his crucifixion. Peter said there probably was a man named Jesus, a man who challenged the authorities of his time, so they killed him, and ever since the winds of history blew a cyclone over the holiest of neighborhoods, by the book.

Gurli asked Peter, "What are you guys doing tonight? Adi and I are planning to visit some gay Iranian friends, and I'm sure they won't mind a few special guests." She gave her business card to Peter saying, "Call me."

Then, after a long goodbye complete with hugs and cheek kisses, the ladies got into Adi's car and sped away. Adi! That third cheek kiss was real.

Peter and I walked to our room where we found Bas smoking a cigarette. He said, "I know, I know, I'm a monkey. So you don't have to say anything, but, um, the nicotine helps my stomach, um, with the nausea. What? Did you honestly think I was going to quit forever on a moment's notice? Wait. Don't answer that. Anyway, it's not my fault, these things I do. There's an invisible puppet master in the sky. I'm a puppet."

I asked my friend how he was feeling, and he answered,

"Much better, thanks."

"Good," I said. "Do you want to go out for dinner tonight with the ladies you almost puked on, and a couple of gay Iranians?"

56 - Dinner with Gay Iranians

The exterior of Massoud and Gad's house was unwelcoming, a sturdy wall topped with glass shards and an electric fence. The interior however was impeccably decorated. Our hosts were convivial and merry. They served hors d'oeuvres with wine. Everyone flaunted their sexuality, flirting because flirting was fun, even while discussing politics.

With Adi, I had a fish on the hook but perhaps only one opportunity to reel her in, or else she might swim away. I stepped up my flirting while initiating physical contact, looking for any non-verbal agreement to get even more physical. The party energy helped, especially given that Peter and Gurli were officially back together, plus Massoud and Gad were gay indeed, sometimes kissing in the kitchen, and Bas seemed unfazed by being the odd man out.

The food was marvelous.

Our hosts spoke just enough Globish to have a conversation. For example, Massoud asked me, "America booom booom Iran, nuclear power?"

I said, "I certainly hope not."

He said, "Hmmm. Stupid. No booom booom. Stupid."

I agreed, then he asked me if I believed in September-eleven conspiracy theories.

I answered, "Every theory is a conspiracy theory. The question is, who were the conspirators? I think the job was done by pissed-off Arabs, but maybe the CIA tricked them into thinking they were working for Al Qaeda. Huh? Yes? This seems easy if you're the CIA. But I don't know. Peter however is a history professor..."

Peter responded, "OK then, here it is: Saudi Arabia used to be poor, then they found oil. The King didn't have an army so he made a deal with America. Now the King rules by enforcing Islamic fundamentalism, but in an ironic twist, it's the religious extremists who see his deal with America as a deal with Satan. We know the September-eleven terrorists were sworn enemies of the King, determined to expel the infidel army... Or as you say, pissed-off Arabs."

I valued my friend's ability to explain the great games of

diplomacy. I also valued Bastiaan's jokes, Adi's good looks, and Iranian culinary delights.

After dinner, Gad brought out a water pipe for smoking opium. He said the flowery goo came from Afghanistan. We all imbibed except Peter, who insisted, "That shit'll make you crazy." He was wrong; the small dose merely mellowed our minds.

Adi explained how her friends came to reside in Jerusalem. She said, "There's not much tolerance for homosexuals in Iran, and they're rich so they could just move. I know because I was their real-estate agent." She said to me, "Come, I'll take you on a tour of the house."

We visited the study and the master bedroom. She showed me the walk-in closet. I pulled her to me, but she pushed me away saying, "Not yet. Not here." Then she escorted me to the guest room, saying, "Now. Here."

I kissed her madly then grabbed her breasts, a little rough like I could tell she wanted it. I unbuttoned her pants. She pulled off my shirt, then she pushed me towards the bed. I loved the lust, and I knew she did too because she was a screamer.

Our friends greeted our return to the kitchen with a round of applause. I knew that Bas felt envy however, because later he said, "So I get sick and you get the girl. I know, I know, it's your karma. In your past life you were a chimpanzee, but a kind and gentle chimp who always thought of the other chimps first. Before that you were a pig, but a righteous pig, and before that you were a rat. You had to repeat rat several times. You started out as sea slime, but now you're you, Raymond Love, recipient of sweet *kutje*."

Later I asked Adi, "Can you please maybe help to find a date for Bastiaan?"

She said, "I'll see what I can do."

It's moments like these that cause travellers to procure better medium-term lodging in the city.

57 - Tea with Suicide Bombers

We said we wanted a cultural tour so Adi crammed us into her car and drove us towards Palestine. When Israeli soldiers scrutinized our passports, she told them we were Christian tourists so they let us pass. We drove through a gate in the so-called *apartheid wall*, an imposing barrier that cut across rocky fields dotted with olive trees. We drove into Bethlehem but the scene did not resemble the city I remembered from my childhood: humble shepherds plus kings from afar bringing gifts to the infant Jesus. Instead the scene resembled an impoverished Arabian city in the desert, with graffiti protesting Israel's brutal military occupation. Bethlehem! Not what I expected...

We arrived at the famous Nativity Church which was surprisingly plain, but it did have one highlight: under the altar was a chamber with a metal star bolted to the floor at the precise spot where somebody once said that Jesus was born. Adi showed us the church's various rooms much as she would show a home to a potential buyer, and of course I encouraged her.

Next we drove to Adi's favorite restaurant where our jovial host, Abdullah, escorted us to a table as he told a boy to fetch tea. We sat. We drank tea. We ordered hummus with pita bread. We discussed the military occupation, the obvious topic.

Abdullah said, "In Palestine we have little freedom for movement, not to Jerusalem, not even within West Bank. And Gaza is prison! Good peoples must stand up to bad peoples. We must resist Zionist occupation every way possible. Please try the hummus."

Bas asked, "Every way possible? What do you mean? Suicide bombers?"

Abdullah answered, "Not suicide. Suicide is desperation. Our martyrs are not desperate. They die for Islam... You must try this hummus. You never eat hummus this good in your life." The hummus was awesome, loaded with garlic and dripping with olive oil.

Abdullah left us to eat our snack, then Adi explained her take on the complex factions and shifting alliances in the fight for the desert called Palestine.

Bas commented, "I do love the hummus, but I hate suicide bombers."

Adi said, "Who doesn't? But what would you do? What would you do, Bastiaan, if you were treated like a prisoner, your home destroyed and so on, just because you're a Muslim living in a Jewish democracy? What would you do if you find yourself on the wrong side of the guns? If the enemy takes away everything you love? With no job, no hope, with life only suffering?"

Bas said, "OK. OK. I see your point, but I still hate suicide bombers."

Adi answered, "Who doesn't? Anyway, you said you wanted a cultural tour so... If you want to meet someone radical... Abdullah is all talk. I know someone radical, someone who I'm sure actually likes suicide bombers."

We all indicated our curiosity, so Adi led us to a nearby mosque, the first time I ever stepped inside an Islamic house of worship, a clean and peaceful space decorated with geometric patterns. Adi said something in Arabic to one of the men, something like, "Say, do you know where I can find Mahmed?"

The answer was yes, so we followed the man's instructions to a nearby coffee shop where Mahmed sat smoking a sheesha pipe with friends. The cleric stood up, obviously delighted to see Adi. He welcomed us warmly then we all sat together.

Adi introduced us as European friends thinking of volunteering to build houses for innocent people made homeless from the war. We never discussed this, but I understood her tactic to get on Mahmed's good side, so that he would speak with us openly.

The cleric said, "In the name of Allah, most gracious, most merciful. Peace be upon his messenger. I am glad you are here! *Alhamdulillah*. We need international volunteers. Israeli soldiers do not fire on Jews or internationals, and we can always use help with home construction... What do you drink? Tea? Coffee?"

We all indicated tea, except Bas who ordered a cappuccino.

When Mahmed stood up to call the waiter, Adi whispered, "You guys don't have to build houses. I met Mahmed when I got home from India, when I volunteered to build houses, to ease my conscience, you know, from things that happened while I was a soldier."

Mahmed championed the cause of home building. My friends and I did not make any commitments, but we did express sympathy towards the innocent victims of war.

When Adi asked for news regarding the fight for Palestinian liberation, the cleric replied, "Last week I was in Hebron where I saw with my own eyes destruction of home, belong to Mustafa family which is two parents and seven childrens. Israeli soldiers break door because nobody home. They send in dog. They throw out beds, television, clothings, everything, then they destroy home with bulldozer. It is hard to describe, to witness this war crime. How can we turn away from this? To see our land desecrated? What do we tell Allah on judgment day when he asks us what we have done? I tell you now that we will win victory or martyrdom. The Israeli soldier is not invincible, and I know peoples who can prepare the sacred explosion. Al-hamdulillah."

Bas said, "Sacred explosion? Wait a minute, Mahmed. Are you saying that you support suicide bombers? I hate suicide bombers." Bas glared into Mahmed's eyes.

The cleric answered, "I understand you. Nobody like if innocent peoples die, but our childrens grow up in this violence and poverty. They tell me they want to be martyr. They tell me they want to kill Jews and Americans. With childrens, I insist they must first memorize Al-Qur'an, Allah be praised, but with grown mens... We have few options to fight back against this Zionist brutality."

"But, doesn't Allah forbid killing innocent people?"

"Generally yes, but this is jihad. We must defend Palestine of course, but more important, we must defend Islam. We will never know peace until Allah reigns supreme over this land. If this means innocent peoples die, then this must be. We have a fatwa."

"What's a fatwa?"

"Whenever we have a difficult matter such as this, we must turn to our supreme clerics for spiritual guidance. In this case the Zionists want to destroy Islam so we must accept the casualties of jihad. We know Israel, she will lose, and American Devil, she will not get what she wants in the Middle East."

Mahmed explained how the United Nations resolution number

242 named Israel as a criminal aggressor under international law, until she returns to her 1967 borders. For Palestinians to fight back, Mahmed said that killing innocent people was OK because his supreme leader said it was OK. After all, he had a fatwa. Mahmed saw the West as morally corrupt, and he was right about that, but he failed to see his own immorality and corruption.

Walking back to Adi's car, Peter said, "The Palestinians should study people like Gandhi and Martin Luther King for leadership skills. They won their struggles through non-violence. Maybe all the Palestinians need now is a strong leader."

Gurli said, "Yeah, someone like Jesus."

As we arrived at the car, Bas joked, "No hope? Become a suicide bomber. Great pensions! We offer free health care, too, in the afterlife, and virgins!"

Next Adi drove us to see a Jewish settlement built illegally on some of the best Palestinian land. Unfortunately the Israeli soldiers did not let us enter the town because, they said, it was not a tourist attraction. This scene seemed surreal to me. Why like this?

We drove to the Dead Sea, a special place to swim because the water is so salty that humans can float effortlessly. Swimming there was fun. Adi and Gurli coated each other in mud, which they claimed had special healing properties.

I let Adi coat me with mud too, which was slimy but sensual. She and I had an understanding: as the status quo was easy and fun, she would be my girlfriend for however long my friends and I stayed in Israel. This made me warm up to the idea of volunteering to build houses, which seemed like an interesting cultural experience anyway. I was delighted to have Adi as my temporary girlfriend, but I knew it wouldn't last. She did not want to trek across Africa, and she was too rude and rough for me sometimes, and she smoked cigarettes, and she was bigger than me and this seemed weird, but no worries; life was about moments and we were having fun. I enjoyed my mud bath.

Thanks to this tour of Palestine, I realized that to comprehend the Middle East, one has to study the history and go there in person, and as I acquired this education, my interest in the politics grew. I began to see not just problems, but solutions. I saw that it was possible to achieve peace in theory because the obstacle was not a lack of negotiating points (such as swapping land, or designating Jerusalem as a *global city*), but instead a lack of courage to close the deal, with political leaders afraid of giving away too much perhaps, or afraid of their enemies, or afraid of their own people. It was easier to understand the fear on both sides after meeting Mahmed; that dude was scary.

I explained this analysis to Peter and he said I was dead wrong. "Fear certainly plays a role," he conceded, "especially fear of suicide bombers, and of course cynical politicians promote this fear in order to convince the public to vote a certain way. But if you want to understand Israel's political fight, follow the money (and the water rights). Who profits wildly from the status quo?" General Lipshitz came to mind, then my chimpanzee president's corrupt cronies, the alpha males of global politics. Damn. "To understand the Middle East," Peter added, "one has to think like an imperial overlord, protecting one's strategic interests just as a chess player protects his king, with little concern for the pawns in the fight."

On our way back to Jerusalem, we drove through Jericho, the oldest continuously-inhabited city on Earth. Jericho's ancient ruins were not spectacular but it was interesting to see the wrath of time. Next we drove to Ramallah for ice cream, the perfect cold dessert after touring a hot desert. In Ramallah I observed Muslims and Jews enjoying ice cream together peacefully.

58 - Doing God's Work

Adi invited her friend Shay out for drinks. Like Bastiaan, Shay had dreadlocked hair and a tattoo made in India, and sure enough, they became instant friends. Shay was born a Jew but converted to Bahá'í, Bastiaan's new favorite religion. He explained to me how Bahá'í promoted the unity of all humanity and the oneness of all faiths, teaching morality lessons from Muhammad, Jesus, and the Buddha.

Adi drove us to Haifa to visit the Bahá'í shrine of the Báb. Beautiful gardens! After so much brown desert and concrete jungle, it was nice to see green.

I caught Bas smoking and I gave him shit for it, as friends do. He said, "Ah yes. I did quit cigarettes, but this is a spliff. From now on, I hereby pledge to smoke tobacco only as a vehicle for smoking hashish, and Shay set me up with some good Moroccan. Want some?"

Most tourists who lingered in the Holy Land were pilgrims who believed. My friends and I stayed because we all had hot girlfriends, but I was fascinated by the history and culture too. I found it ironic, all the talk about the miracle of life in a land of perpetual war, with little green. My favorite color was green. I missed Indonesia where I felt alive in the jungle, with wild beasts, relaxed humans, and exotic fruit. But the Israeli jungle was an adventure too.

One day I asked Gurli to teach me basic Arabic. She answered, "Most important is *enshallah*, which means Allah willing, used when speaking about the future. *Al-hamdulillah* means thanks to Allah, giving him credit for everything in the past. And for dealing with pesky street hustlers, *imshee* means go away, and *haram-aleyko* means shame on you. But it's best to just ignore the aggressive ones. Pretend they don't exist. Do not make eye contact. But if you want, you can call them sons of camels; they hate that."

Gurli was funny like that, and I knew what Peter saw in her. Indeed, the couple got along so well that Gurli decided to join our trek across Africa. Adi and Shay decided to join us too, but only as far as the Red Sea in Egypt for a beach holiday. And so we planned the next leg of our trip, over mint tea.

We had to skip Syria because the ladies could not get visas. Much as I wanted to understand my grandfather's culture and meet distant relatives, I was resigned to wait for better flow. Meanwhile I emailed Pops to ask for details about my great uncles and second cousins so that whenever that flow flew, I would have people to visit. I missed the extreme freedom provided by travelling alone, but it was worth compromising this in order to share a trip across Africa with friends.

After much debate, we decided to fly to Ethiopia from Cairo, skipping over the Sahara desert. From there we would fly to Rwanda to see wild gorillas and chimpanzees, and then continue southward by public transportation, *enshallah*.

We made a plan to depart in three weeks, as soon as Adi could clear her schedule.

Meanwhile Shay's friend Jess introduced us to a Palestinian women who just lost all her worldly possessions. While she had been celebrating at her daughter's engagement party, Israeli soldiers reduced her home to rubble. The woman was wearing festive clothes that could not have been more inappropriate for her gloomy mood. I had a hard time looking into her eyes, such was her sadness. We decided to help her.

Peter, Bas, and I joined a volunteer home-building crew. We had enough time to help build three houses, but the first one was the most gratifying.

I used to work as a carpenter in California so my skills came in handy. One of the men on our crew used a jig saw to cut rebar, a steel rod used to support bricks. The rusty saw was a mechanical defect waiting to happen, and I could imagine shrapnel flying in all directions, so I stayed clear whenever rebar was cut. Mostly I worked with the wood as a framer.

One day, we walked by kids playing in a trash pile, singing a song which Gurli translated as, "We will die for Palestine." The kids threw stones at us, laughing. I was shocked at how common it was for people to throw stones, mostly at dogs. One of the construction guys threw stones at every boy who approached the site, his way to say, "Stay away."

I noticed myself getting used to Palestinian poverty, even the children raising younger children instead of going to school. We humans get used to things, especially when surrounded by proud and warm-hearted, tough survivors.

An old man told us we were "doing God's work" by volunteering. He invited us into his humble home for mint tea and lemon biscuits, saying it was in the tradition of the prophet to be hospitable. It was not easy doing God's work, but it was fulfilling to help innocent victims of the war, and a great way to dive deeply into the culture too.

I met a Jewish elder in Jerusalem who told me, "We are surrounded by enemies. It is suffocating." When I asserted that not all Arabs were his enemies, he replied, "Yes of course, but I am not afraid of the nice ones."

The old man defended his government's war posture, he said, to ensure the survival of his people against annihilation from suicide bombers and crazy dictators with nuclear weapons. To him this justified his government's treatment of the Gaza Strip as a prison. He said the only way for Jews to live in peace was to have a purely Jewish state, despite Israel being a democracy. He also supported the expansion of Jewish settlements into Palestinian territory. When I politely called him out for his extreme politics, he told me about Hitler's Holocaust, an abomination of history that he remembered vividly. I replied by asserting that two wrongs don't make a right.

Every Islamic believer with whom I discussed religion and politics asserted that Islam was about goodness, family, charity, hospitality, and peace, and from what I could determine, most of these people tried to live up to ethical high standards, and good on them! But when I questioned them directly about blasphemy, most said that blasphemers should be executed because this was the sharia law, with no room for debate because supreme clerics had already determined that not even a cartoon drawing of the prophet could be tolerated.

In the holy land, a land full of dangerous ideas, my opinion was irrelevant.

Blasphemy was a hot topic for Gurli because she knew people in Denmark who were injured in riots after a newspaper published some cartoon drawings. She said, "If the Muslim community threatens Western journalists with violence for breaking a religious taboo, then this is not asking for our respect but demanding our submission. Sorry, but we're talking about Denmark here. No way. If the Muslims want to live in Europe as normal citizens, then they must be open to criticism."

Gurli and I shared the wish that Allah would grant Muslims the freedom to practice their faith without any coercion, including the freedom to abandon whatever beliefs they find to be inconsistent with proven facts, and including the freedom to laugh at intelligent satire.

Many people asked me where I was from, and I gave different answers depending on the situation. If I admitted to being from California, most people did their best to politely ignore me, with no joy; and if I said I was from Jalapan, most people seemed curious but unsure how to respond; and if I said I was Brazilian, most people wanted to talk about soccer or samba, joyfully. I noticed that when haggling over the price of anything, it was always best to be from a poor country. For this reason, and to protect my personal safety, I continued to work at hiding my American origins; for example, I stopped saying the word *soccer*, saying *football* instead. One day I wore my Indonesian sarong then wandered through Old Jerusalem asking the street sharks to guess my country. None guessed correctly.

One day I found a wild flower which I gave to Adi. This brought out her beautiful smile which usually hid in hibernation from the cold stresses of war. Much as I liked her, I did not love her. I missed Angeline. Sigh. I hoped that my sorrow from her passing was a seed that would someday grow into wisdom.

When the time came to move on, I was relieved. Adi was a great temporary girlfriend, and we all had fun at her favorite dance clubs and coffee shops, but there's only so much fun one can have in a dusty desert surrounded by stressed-out people with guns, inside a conflict zone where both sides were right, and both sides were wrong. Bas summed up my mood perfectly. "Woo-hoo!" he said excitedly. "We're going to Africa!"

59 - High Stakes Poker

I got an email from Pedro saying, "Call me." I called. He said, "Shep disappeared, man! The government grabbed him! Because his computers are gone too. I mean, that's the only explanation that makes any sense. He got caught trying to break into that database so the CIA grabbed him, or something like that. All we know for sure is that he's missing. His girlfriend is totally freaking out."

"Oh shit," I said. "That's bad."

"Yeah, bad. You should call Pops. I don't know, but I'm starting to freak out too. I know it's a long shot, but maybe Pops knows something that can help?"

I called home but Pops wasn't there, so I talked to Mom. I told her about Adi. I told her about Israel. Then I envisioned a tactic to catch her off guard.

"I've been reading that Bible you sent me," I said. "Thanks! It's really interesting, you know, to actually read it. But I have some questions."

"Of course dear," my mother said. "Ask away."

"Great. How do you know that God really exists?"

"What? Because the Bible says so."

"But wasn't the Bible written by ancient humans? Wasn't the book as we know it commissioned at the Council of Nicaea in the fourth century?"

"What?"

"Mom, answer me this... I know that you've denied evolution all your life, but did you know it's a fact? Like gravity. Mom, I love you, but if the Bible were the literal word of God, it would be your duty to stone me to death. It's in Deuteronomy. I memorized the passage: 'Thou shalt stone him with stones, that he die; because he hath sought to thrust thee away from the Lord.' Mom, if the Bible must be obeyed, then you must stone me to death. Or maybe you know, it's just an old book?"

"Oh Raymond dear, I'm so worried about you. I knew it was a bad idea for you to go on this world tour of yours. Satan has clouded your mind. Please listen to me; you must ask God for forgiveness and repent."

"OK, I will. You're right, Mom. Jesus is with me."

When my mother began praying for my soul, I felt bad about hitting her with that Deuteronomy reference, but I succeeded in getting her flustered. The moment was right to pounce. "Mom," I said. "What exactly did Pops do in Israel to make so much money?"

"Huh? He... He was a marine Lieutenant. Why?"

"He wasn't a Technical Adviser for the IDF? Mom? Why hide that?"

"What? Your father, he's very modest about that. How do you know that?"

"Pops is modest? Mom, what's the real reason you didn't meet me in Israel? It's not too dangerous and you know it. I know about the Swiss bank account, OK? I know about the no-fly list. You have to tell me the truth."

"I... I don't know what you're talking about."

"Mom, where did Pops get all his money? You have to tell me the truth!"

I could hear Mom gasp, then she started to cry. "Your father and your grandfather... No. You'll... You'll... I'm sorry we lied, son, but... I'm sorry. You'll just have to ask your father about these things. Please forgive me. It's for your own protection. Come home."

My mother hung up on me. Undaunted, I envisioned a poker game and I was holding good cards, so I decided to bluff. I called Pops on his mobile phone.

"Hi Pops," I said. "Do you have a minute? I need to ask you about something."

"Junior? Sure. Go ahead. I'm driving the Ferrari to Pismo Beach..."

"Great. I hope you're doing great, Pops. It's too bad you and Mom couldn't meet me in Israel but I understand, what with being on the no-fly list and all. But at least you have a fat Swiss bank account. And General Lipshitz told me a lot of things, too." Silence. "Pops, I'll come straight to the point. Where did you get all your money? And don't lie to me. Don't tell me you inherited it from Gramps because I know that's not true."

"Lipshitz? What the...? Look son, first of all, General Lipshitz doesn't know shit. But if you must know, look, I told you I inherited money from Gramps because I didn't want you to think, you know, big arms dealer. I'm sorry I lied about that. Really. I should have told you. I'm sorry."

"Pops, I know that's not true, OK? You have to be honest with me!"

"Um, I'm going to hang up now."

"No! Listen! I have a friend. He hacked into a government database to find out more about you, and he disappeared, Pops, his computers too. The CIA got him."

"Uh oh. That's bad. Look son, I don't know anything about your friend, but if he was trying to hack into a CIA database, there's a fair chance they caught him... Sorry son, but I don't know, and there's nothing I can do. Sorry, really, but I have to hang up now."

I called Pedro.

He said, "Fly home."

I said, "That's tempting. I would, except that I have big plans now, in a word, Africa. Besides, if Shep disappeared because of Pops, then the CIA or the FBI or whoever has him. And if he disappeared for some other reason, then it has nothing to do with Pops, and that's worse, because if the Feds have him, that means he's alive."

"Yes, but if you confront Pops in person, he can't hang up on you. Fly home."

"That is tempting, but I have a better idea. You've known Pops for years. You confront him. Corner him in a public place. Tell him you know what I know."

"I dunno. I don't think..."

"What do you have to lose? He can't hang up on you, either."

"OK, I'll do it, for Shepherd."

60 - Survival Tactics

The instant we put on our backpacks our excitement spiked. On the road again! Gurli abandoned her translation gig in order to travel with Peter, and this amplified their enthusiasm. Crucially also, Adi and I maintained our playful, sex-holiday dynamic; we were young and free and we knew it.

We entered the Kingdom of Jordan, and immediately everything seemed peaceful compared to the strife that plagued her most-holy neighbor to the west. Arriving into the city of Amman, we quickly adapted to the traveller's routine of walking around in search of good food or anything interesting. We explored ruins from ancient Rome, the culture that invented indoor plumbing. Then, as Holland was just about to meet Denmark in a football match, we procured a bar with a television. Bas and Gurli bet on the game.

Travelling with three attractive females, Peter, Bas, and I became virtually invisible. Gurli and Adi always stood out because they were both tall and pretty, even when Gurli wore local-style head scarves (because she liked that look), plus Shay's hippie hairstyle could never be ignored; all eyes were on the women.

We found a bar and ordered drinks, non-alcoholic of course because this was a Muslim bar, then we sat with the men near the big-screen TV but not for long; the manager made us move upstairs to the "family area."

Despite being in a secular urban center, we were forced to acknowledge our cultural context. Some women in the "family area" did not wear head scarves, and others smoked sheesha water pipes, but the culture undeniably catered for men as a rule. Compared to the Muslims I met in Southeast Asia, the Arabs seemed more strict. For example, I almost never spoke with Arabian women, but in Indonesia I did so frequently.

Peter asserted that despite the sexual segregation, Jordan was one of the more progressive Arab countries. He pointed out the trendy clothing stores, with young couples outside displaying their affection publicly.

Shay countered this narrative to ensure we wouldn't get the wrong idea as tourists. "There's still far too much sexist bullshit here," she said. "And this has nothing to do with God."

Bas joked, "Which God? The temptress wearing black leather boots?"

Everyone laughed except for Shay, who stared into her lover's eyes. "Families own their women until they're married," she said. "Then their husbands own them, and then they have to wear burqas in the desert, black ones. Do you have any idea how hot that gets?"

Shay then said to Peter with a nicer voice, "That's not progressive."

Bas previously told me that Shay was obsessed with women's equality issues, and he liked to take her on for sport, thus her defensive reaction. "If you men do not see women as equals," she said, "then you do not have to respect us. You can have us for sex then expect us to cook and clean for you."

Bas replied, "Ease up! The cave men hunted while the cave women raised the cave babies. The cave men..."

Shay interrupted, "The cave men hunted while the cave women invented the seed. We are capable of much more then motherhood, you know."

Bas said, "Ha. You made my point. We are not equal. I, for example, have a dick."

Shay glared until Bas proclaimed that women were smarter, then he praised the King for ensuring that Jordanian blokes had a place to chill out and watch sports without the lady folk around. This made Shay laugh.

Peter said, "Excellent! We all agree! Sex roles have been crucial for our species' survival, and every culture has a different way to deal with boobies and babies. Many cultures still have arranged marriages, and I for example, use condoms. And the burqa? Well, a man's wives must remain faithful for the man's DNA to go forward, right? Here is a culture that takes this natural programming to an extreme, that's all. Think about it: all humans gossip about who is sleeping with whom, and about which alpha male has more power, which affects who is sleeping with whom, and all this, the mating game, is programmed into our brains. The rest is cultural. The interesting question to me becomes, what do we all have in common?"

We all thought about this for a while.

I realized that religion had a survival tactic too: go along or go to Hell. The Christians recently burned heretics alive, and there was still a death penalty for blasphemy and apostasy in Islam. I explained to my friends how religion was the great white shark of ideas.

Bas said, "Did you know that gorillas have a different survival tactic?" He looked at Shay. "The alpha male sleeps with all the females... all of them!"

Shay replied, "More interesting are the bonobos, where sex is controlled by alpha females. Bonobos have more sex and less fighting than chimps, more in-group empathy and less out-group enmity. Therefore the new world government should have women in power, not the testosterone-dominated bullshit we have now."

Adi said, "Amen, sister!"

Gurli asked Peter, "Do you think we'll get to see any bonobos in Africa? I like bonobos."

Peter answered, "Maybe, but wild bonobos only live in the Congo, and we can't just turn up in the Congo. The fighting there is just too dangerous. Once we get to Rwanda, we can do some research and then make the call."

Holland won the football match. This made Bas happy because his tribe won. I was happy because I was in Jordan. And I was happy because I finally understood the psychology of sex roles ala trained-ape theory. Love is a form of in-group empathy, while war is blatant out-group enmity. Humans are complicated.

I fell asleep trying to generalize this lesson, and I realized to my surprise that I was a racist, not intentionally, but my brain naturally matched patterns and took shortcuts that made me treat people from different races differently, a subconscious bias towards trusting people who looked like me while fearing the unknown. This same, natural bias also ensured that I was a sexist. Despite knowing many brilliant women, I knew far more poorly-educated women who seemed less intelligent because they were trained to study only church doctrine and motherhood. And the human brain is good at making generalizations. Fortunately travelling the world expanded my neural training so that I was less likely to judge unknown individuals based on stereotypes.

That night I had a dream where Pops was a spy with a sexy Russian agent trying to kill him on a train. When the lady spy turned out to be Mom, I woke up; this was too much for my brain to handle. I put my arm around Adi, thinking we might make love, but she seemed annoyed that I woke her up. With this I knew it was time to break up with her soon, and the timing was perfect; I booked a flight to Ethiopia and she didn't. In my next dream I was with Angeline.

61 - Space Aliens

Lost to all but the Bedouins for a thousand years, Petra was Jordan's premier tourist attraction, a site packed with ancient Nabataean monuments carved from solid rock. My friends and I woke up early to wander through the ruins at sunrise, to appreciate the history without being distracted by tourists, fabulous and fun exercise.

The next day we travelled by ferry across the Red Sea to Egypt. We stayed one week in Dahab, a town famous for a good beach and great scuba diving. Everyone wanted to go diving except for me. I knew I was destined to die soon enough, and this helped me avoid the trap of thinking I had something to lose, but after my near-drowning experience in Malaysia, I did not want to scuba dive. I donned a snorkel one time to admire the colorful, alien life, but that was it and that was enough.

Instead, while my friends went diving, I took advantage of the time for fitness training alone in the desert, with yoga and *Ki* breathing mixed with abdominal crunches to strengthen my core, plus rock juggling for improved concentration and dexterity. While meditating I had an epiphany: there's a hard limit to self knowledge because most biological processes are subconscious.

My friends and I went on a camel expedition to camp on a remote beach with Bedouin guides. I was impressed by the camels, wonderful beasts that endured the desert by eating thorny plants while carrying tourists, all without complaining too much. I was also impressed by the Bedouin man who baked bread in the sand without the bread being sandy. We all sang songs around the camp fire except for Peter who played his flute.

One of our Bedouin hosts offered twenty camels to buy Gurli from Peter, but Peter declined. This was all in jest, but it did make me laugh.

Our plan became a countdown for our flight to Ethiopia out of Cairo. First we visited Luxor, the site of the spectacular temples of Karnak and the Valley of the Kings, the place where ancient Pharaohs were entombed along with material comforts for their infinite afterlives.

To get to Luxor we travelled by ferry to the continent of

Africa, then we continued by bus. Africa! I enjoyed seeing the Sahara desert. The endless sand seemed lifeless but I was still happy to see it, and I was happier still when we arrived at the Nile river. The green near the water's edge provided welcome relief to my tired eyes.

We boarded a felucca sailboat for a sunset cruise. Our captain Muhammad said, "American tourist, Israeli tourist, same every other tourist. All welcome! We have faith in Allah, and what force can stop Allah? America cannot stop Allah. Israel cannot stop Allah. Al-hamdulillah." The sunset was gorgeous, and we all had fun swapping stories with Muhammad, but mostly I enjoyed simply resting on the water after a remarkable day in the desert.

In Cairo we visited the great pyramids of course. Upon arrival we ignored the onslaught of hustlers to marvel at the greatest sight of Egypt: hordes of tourists descending from tour buses, especially the women in high-heeled shoes trying to walk in the sand. One woman had leopard-spot pants and a fluffy blue sweater; as she tried and failed to ward off the hustlers, Bas took a picture of her to show his friends back home.

We descended into the heart of one pyramid via a tunnel into a grand chamber. A guide was mandatory for this. Ours insisted that we weren't allowed to take pictures until we were alone, then he said while holding out his palm for baksheesh, "OK, you take picture, but hurry."

Bas asserted that the engineering of the pyramids was proof that ancient space aliens were involved in their construction. He claimed that the granite blocks of the king's chamber could only have been lifted into place with anti-gravity levitation, and that it was impossible for prehistoric monkey men to have done the job without this technology.

Peter responded, "Oh man, that is wrong on so many levels..."

Bas said, "Come on, admit it. The pyramids were built by space aliens."

Peter answered, "I'll admit to no such thing!"

I sat back and enjoyed watching Peter defeat Bas with logic. Peter explained how the great pyramid's largest blocks were actually lifted into place using ropes and counter-weights, then he lectured Bas on the physics of space travel.

I had just read a book about black holes, dark energy, and other mind-bending topics. While scientists debated why the expansion of the Universe was accelerating, I found comfort in the fact that we could measure the Universe expanding in a uniform, mathematical way. Einstein did not formulate a theory for everything, but he did prove that nothing with mass could possibly accelerate to the speed of light because this would require infinite energy.

Peter explained the practical implications. "The distances involved are unimaginably vast," he said. "A journey to even the nearest star would take thousands of years and would require a gigantic spaceship. So if space aliens ever made the journey to Earth, hypothetically, they would either still be here (and we would know) or they would have left behind some physical evidence, but there is no evidence. Pyramids, conspiracy theories, and personal anecdotes are not evidence."

Bas said, "Sorry mister smarty-pants, but haven't you ever heard of a warp drive? And what about worm holes? Teleportation, man!"

Peter said, "All science fiction. No technology can overcome the laws of physics, and despite the popular misconceptions, we know these laws shockingly well. The good news is that with billions and billions of stars, space aliens surely exist *out there*. The bad news is that these aliens are very, very, very far away."

We toured the Egyptian Museum to see the fabulous treasures crafted by ancient humans. To get there from our hotel we learned a new taxi-driver scam: agree to a price, and then upon arrival insist that the price agreed was per person (Cairo taxis are never priced per person). We argued with our driver and won. Sigh.

Outside the museum, a black man greeted me, "Welcome to Africa!" We were in Africa technically, but Cairo was culturally in the Middle East so it didn't feel like Africa, at least not the Africa I imagined when I imagined Africa from afar. I returned the man's greeting with a smile, pleased by his gesture. Africa!

A salesman approached me saying, "Hello friend."

I asked him, "Do you know me?"

He admitted, "No."

I said, "Then we are not friends."

"I am Abdul. What is your name?"

"Raymond."

"Nice to meet you! Now we are friends. Please look at ancient scroll, in my family many generations. Very good price."

"Ancient huh? I don't want to deprive your children of their heritage."

"Oh no! Children want video game more than old scroll."

The scroll was made from papyrus with a nice copy of hieroglyphics from Tutankhamun's tomb, suitable for framing. I asked, "How much?"

Abdul said, "You have good eye, my friend. One-hundred dollars."

I walked away saying, "Sorry, but I have no intention of buying this."

Abdul chased after me. "OK. Fifty dollars." I shook my head. "OK. Twenty dollars. My children are hungry. I need sale today... OK. Ten dollars."

"Five dollars. That's my final offer."

"Eight."

"Six."

"Seven."

"Done."

Just after Abdul and I completed our transaction, Gurli said, "Nice job. I thought Americans didn't know how to haggle."

I answered, "Stereotypes are made to be broken."

My new friend Abdul showed me photos from his pilgrimage to Mecca during the Hajj, a phenomenon I was interested in seeing first hand, but only Muslims were welcome, and I was not prepared to convert.

Abdul invited us to a wedding party in a Berber village. My friends and I had no other plans that evening so we accepted.

First we went to Abdul's house where he showed off his hospitality by ordering his wife to whip up some food. Then we went to the village square, a plaza filled with men smoking sheesha and drinking alcohol while another man with an electric speaker incited the crowd to donate money. Surprisingly for a wedding party, Adi, Gurli and Shay were the only women in attendance (the bride had a separate party indoors).

The guy sitting next to us offered us all free beer so we accepted. Then a boy appeared out of nowhere insisting that women should never drink alcohol. When I asked Abdul what he thought, he said it was OK for foreign women to play by different rules. Regarding the Muslim men drinking in public, he said this was a wedding party and therefore alcohol was OK.

Abdul suddenly insisted that my group owed him a hundred American dollars for the dinner his wife made for us. He was seriously insistent, and when we refused to hand over so much cash, he got angry. He screamed that he brought us to a party and gave us food but we gave him nothing in return. With that, I lectured him on the meaning of friendship. I told him that I had been planning to give him a generous tip but his crappy attitude made that impossible. Then my genuine friends and I bailed. As we walked away in search of a taxi, Abdul chased after us yelling obscenities. Sigh.

Peter said he was not surprised because with relatively poor local friends, no matter how friendly, there was always that money thing, almost always. From Abdul's perspective we were fabulously wealthy so to him a hundred dollars must have seemed only fair.

The next day was my last day together with Adi, so we planned only to relax.

A guy at our hotel recommended a restaurant for lunch which we could not find, so we asked a guy on the street. He said he knew where it was, so we followed him straight to his brother's shop. Normally we would have left immediately but a cute boy served us delicious mint tea. Adi liked the shop's perfume selection so I bought her a bottle as a gift, then we bailed.

That night, my girlfriend and I wandered around a chic retail district holding hands in the cool evening air. We ate ice cream while laughing at the irony of women wearing burqas while window-shopping for sexy lingerie. We made love, then we fell asleep in each other's arms.

Adi and I said goodbye after breakfast. This was a sad moment, but we both knew it was time.

Peter, Gurli, Bas and I took a taxi to the airport.

With time to kill before our flight, I mailed my 'ancient' scroll to California as a present for Mom and Pops. I wrote them a short but loving note too, because this seemed like an appropriate gesture; it was their wedding anniversary after all.

Meanwhile Gurli met three women from Saudi Arabia changing into Western clothes in the bathroom. She explained, "They're on a shopping trip for things that are hard to find in Saudi Arabia, things like sexy lingerie."

Just then, a lady walked by wearing a hijab veil which was normal, but she also wore pink furry boots with a matching pink purse. Gurli said, "If you look behind the veil, what you'll find are ordinary women, prisoners of culture. This one, for example, has no fashion sense."

Bas said that from the perspective of space aliens, this pink-loving woman was a space alien, then he took a picture of her to show his friends back home. Then we boarded our plane to Ethiopia.

62 - Goat Meat

We left Addis Ababa's modern airport in a dilapidated taxi with exotic music playing that made the driver's imprudence seem surreal. We drove past grand monuments, cheaply improvised store fronts, and shepherds walking their goats through traffic intersections. The unintelligible scribbles of the Amharic language provided no insight, but our guide book informed us that the year had thirteen months, the clock's zero hour coincided with sunrise, and the official date was eight years behind the rest of the world. In Ethiopia, it was the year 2000.

Peter explained how Ethiopia managed to escape colonization during Europe's mad scramble for imperial power in Africa; thus the eight years of clock drift; the Ethiopian Christians were never governed from Rome.

That night we found a traditional restaurant where beautiful women offered us honey wine called tej. To eat, we used a flat bread called injira to scoop up yummy sauces with our hands, but before that, we washed up with soap. I avoided the goat meat, preferring the vegetable sauces called fasting food. Delicious.

We visited Africa's largest market, a maze of bazaars with donkeys hauling goods along rocky streets. I noticed zero other tourists as we perused the shops and chatted with friendly locals.

In a store selling antiques, Bas recognized the face on a bank note to be Haile Selassie I, also known as Ras Tafari, the last emperor of Ethiopia. The store's owner explained that Ras Tafari was a direct descendant of King Solomon and the Queen of Sheba. He said, "Haile Selassie I was the messiah prophesied in Revelations. He was the King of Kings and the Lion of Judah."

The man asked Bas if he was a Rastafarian because of the dreadlocks in his hair. My friend replied that his hairstyle was just a fashion statement, but he sympathized with the Rastafarians' positive messages for peace and love.

The store's owner was a Rasta-man. With short hair and a button-down shirt, he didn't have the stereotypical look, but he did believe in the book. He sang a song written by a Jamaican poet named Bob. "Emancipate yourselves from mental slavery," he sang, "None but ourselves can free our minds..."

Bas suddenly looked pale. "I don't want to interrupt your song," he said. "But I need a bathroom. Please help. It's urgent!"

Just then, Peter appeared with a dark stain in his blue jeans. I never saw him look more embarrassed. Bas said, "Oh shit."

The Rasta-man led Bas to a bathroom consisting of a hole in the ground behind a scrap-metal door. Peter went inside next to clean himself. Gurli had diarrhea too, but not as bad. It must have been the goat meat because I felt fine.

Later, while my friends lay in agony from intestinal cramps, I went on a walking tour of Addis Ababa, home to the African Union and much more.

The highlight of the national museum was the fossil skeleton known as Lucy, famous because her bones were significantly older than the previously best-known fossil of a bipedal hominid. I didn't understand radio-carbon dating so I made a mental note to study the science the next time I got online.

The more I studied evolution, the better I understood human nature. I was not an atheist (because I believed in the God of General Relativity, Quantum Mechanics, and Chaos) but I was not religious either; evidence-based belief is not religion. I knew the mainstream label for my belief system was *secular humanism*, but for pragmatic insights about living as a human being, I turned to *trained-ape theory*. I left the museum humming Bastiaan's jungle jingle, "I'm a monkey. He's a monkey. She's a monkey. Aren't you glad that you're a monkey too?"

I walked by a shop advertising an international telephone connection, so I called Pedro. He answered, "Cabrón! Hey man, I'm glad you called. I saw Pops!" This was exactly what I was hoping to hear, so I encouraged my friend to continue.

He said, "I followed him man, just like in the movies. I pretended it was a coincidence when I bumped into him. At first he was friendly. He said, 'Hey Pedro! Nice to see you.' Ha!"

"That's awesome! Go on..."

"Right. So I asked Pops if he worked for the CIA. Ha! Then he got really nervous. He said, 'Where'd you hear that?' I said, 'From Junior.' Ha! I said, 'I know everything that Junior knows.' He seemed to calm down after that. He said he doesn't know anything about Shep, and I believe he was telling the truth about that. So I asked him about the Swiss bank account."

"And?"

"Well, simply put, Pops stonewalled me. He said, 'I don't know what you're talking about.' But I'm convinced he doesn't know shit about Shep. He's up to something though, for sure. The way he got nervous when I asked him about the CIA. He's up to something. But I didn't find out shit... Oh, by the way, Shep's girlfriend got a lawyer. She's really scared. Shep's been missing for two weeks!"

"Damn," I said. "How can I help? I mean, I am tempted to fly home and confront Pops, but as you say, he doesn't know shit about Shep, so what can I do? I can't blow off my friends in Africa unless there's some way I can actually help, but I can't, can I? What do you think? Should I fly home?"

Pedro agreed that there was nothing I could do, so I might as well stay in Africa. We moved on to talk about space aliens, trained apes, and goat meat.

63 - The Historic Circuit

After three nights in Addis Ababa, my friends and I embarked on a promotion by Ethiopian Airlines called the "historic circuit," a series of short flights that allowed us to quickly visit several cities of interest, something that would otherwise have required several weeks of grueling bus rides on bad roads.

First we landed at Bahir Dar, home of the "magnificent" Blue Nile waterfall. The city had wide avenues and modern conveniences, but the countryside seemed stuck in the Middle Ages (except for corrugated-metal roofing, electrical wires, and plastic). We saw zero motor vehicles (except for our own taxi), but we did see donkey carts carrying agricultural products, and people walking barefoot down rocky roads. The Blue Nile waterfall was no longer magnificent thanks to a hydro-electric dam that diverted most of the water, but I was happy because the local people needed electricity more than we needed pictures of a magnificent waterfall.

Gurli was crabby because she still had diarrhea, she hadn't slept well, and the flies were getting on her nerves. The flies. She got more agitated when she stopped to photograph an old man, only to see him drop his pants and crap on the road. I wasn't surprised that she freaked out because I already knew her to be obsessively clean. Peter told her to harden up as only a boyfriend can, then Gurli vowed to be stronger.

Just then a group of boys approached us saying, "Please give money." One of them looked normal, albeit too skinny, but the rest had eyes that were eerily white; they were blind. Gurli gave them money.

My time in India prepared me somewhat, but looking into the eyes of blind children is not something one gets used to easily. I always knew that in the worst of times, Ethiopian children died of famine by the ten-thousands, but seeing the reality in person made it clear that even in the best of times, peasant families lived close to the margins of survival.

A boy approached us saying, "School pen?" Gurli gave away her pen. When she later began to grumble and rant, I understood. I sometimes felt jaded and cynical myself, but nobody ever heard me complain because I knew the difficulties of travelling in Ethiopia were nothing compared to the difficulties of being Ethiopian.

My friends and I took a boat tour of Lake Tana, home to several island monasteries with ancient murals of angels, demons, humans in Hell, and Saint George slaying a dragon. Our boat captain made sure we had an enjoyable voyage. He told us stories as we motored across the lake, and he introduced us to friendly monks who proudly showed off their island sanctuaries.

An Ethiopian woman joined our boat trip back to Bahir Dar, but I could tell she was not a local from her accent and her camera. The woman, Mary, explained that when she was a girl, Mormon missionaries paid for her to study in Salt Lake City (where she eventually married a guy named Brad), and this was her first visit back to her native country. Mary was a tourist.

She told me, a fellow American, "I'm really having a hard time dealing with the poverty. I mean, I don't know how these people survive. I guess they're just so ignorant they don't know any better, but I mean, they're so dirty! God! I'm so lucky I got out."

Our boat captain's expression hardened. He was probably somewhat ignorant (there were no great schools in his neighborhood), and he was somewhat dirty (there was no good sewage infrastructure either), but he was a nice guy.

Peter asked Mary, "So then, as a Mormon, are you here to sponsor a charity, perhaps?"

She answered, "Yes. Brad and I give ten percent of our salaries to the missionaries, because let's face it, only Jesus Christ can help these people."

Bas asked, "Really?" Then he put on his mean face. "I bet if you gave our fine captain a generous tip," he said, "I bet it would help him."

Mary ignored this to defend her church. She asserted that the missionaries provided many community benefits with their money, plus eternal salvation. Bas replied sarcastically. Peter broke the awkward silence that followed by giving our captain a generous tip. Meanwhile I enjoyed the fresh air as we zoomed across a beautiful lake at sunset.

My friends and I boarded our scheduled flight to the city of

Gondar, known as "Africa's Camelot" thanks to some old castles, but we did not land in Gondar. A goat ate an electric wire causing a building at the airport to catch fire, so we detoured to Axum, the former capital of the Axumite empire at the edge of the Sahara desert.

In Axum's central city we saw normal people going about their business, some working, some eating, and some merely trying to get more comfortable. We saw tribal women with elaborate tattoos. We also saw camels and donkeys carrying heavy loads.

Peter explained how an empire became a desert: Axum's booming population cut down all their trees, he said, leading to soil erosion and eventual collapse. He said, "Modern humans should learn from this history, because whenever civilizations chew through all their natural resources, they tend to go bye-bye."

We allowed a charismatic boy named David to guide us to some interesting ruins. He also took us to see the shrine that held the Arc of the Covenant, designed by Moses to house the Ten Commandments, or so it was written. David said, "King Solomon gave the Arc to the Queen of Sheba because he loved her, and she brought it here." He added that only a few monks were allowed to see the sacred relic.

Peter said, "If these monks could prove the Biblical account of Moses by revealing the sacred Arc, they would do so."

David didn't know about that, but he did know the location of a tella bar, home of hand-crafted beer which we all drank from metal cups decorated with images of the Lion of Judah. The beer was delicious, and the local drunks were entertaining. Two of the older women had Christian crosses tattooed onto their foreheads. Somehow this seemed charming.

When I asked David what he wanted out of life, tears came to his eyes. "All I want is two meals a day and a place to sleep," he said. "I swear to God that I want nothing more."

On our flight to Lalibela, the final stop on our historic circuit, I contemplated the poverty I had seen, in-your-face poverty, the kind of daily struggle that makes one appreciate that one is a lucky bastard.

Bas said a prayer out loud. "Dear Jesus," he said. "Please abolish terrestrial injustice and extreme inequality. Thank you.

Make it so that all the little animals have fulfilling lives, now and forever, amen. Thank you. Sincerely, your friend, me."

64 - The Genius of Lalibela

More than Petra, the Taj Mahal and the Great Wall of China, Lalibela's church for Saint George amazed me. Carved from solid rock with beautiful detail, this masterpiece of ancient architecture was not a ruin but an active place of worship, and it was carved straight down into otherwise ordinary rock. My friends and I sat to admire the site along with three barefoot priests plus Eddie.

The boy approached us timidly. "Hello," he said. "I want to practice English. Is this OK? So that some day I can become doctor. My grandmother says I am so lucky because we have faranji to practice conversation. Please can I talk with you?"

Gurli said, "Please have a seat."

Eddie sat.

Peter said, "You are lucky, and your grandmother sounds like a wise woman. Most children I meet only want a few coins which they spend foolishly."

Eddie said, "My grandmother is wise! She can read! You want to meet her? You can meet my brother Samuel too! He is official tour guide, the best. And you must have guide to see all of Lalibela's churches."

We followed Eddie to his humble home, roughly the size of a California kitchen. I was shocked to learn that eight people lived in this tiny space, sleeping on mats that they stashed away during the day.

Eddie's brother supported his clan by taking tourists on tours. His sister was pregnant from a man who raped her because he believed sex with a virgin girl would cure his AIDS. Both of Eddie's parents died of AIDS, thus his desire to become a doctor. Eddie explained all of this while his grandmother roasted coffee beans over burning wood, then she smashed the beans by hand, then she made the most delicious coffee ever.

We hired Eddie's brother Samuel to guide us around all of Lalibela's impressive churches. We took cheesy photos with happy priests, and we walked through ancient tunnels in total darkness. This was not the Africa I imagined when I imagined Africa from afar.

Samuel convinced us to hire a car for an excursion out of

town, to visit a church in a cave called Yemrehanna Kristos. As we drove into the mountains, I was happy to see trees. I was happy to see green. Samuel said the local people were lucky because they had wood. He said, "Lucky because when they die, they can be buried in coffins."

Gurli asked, "Lucky?"

The Yemrehanna Kristos church was crafted with exquisite detail, and it was refreshingly cool inside the cave. One priest delighted in posing for photographs. The rest ignored us as they prayed.

On our way back to Lalibela, we visited farming villages with simple huts inhabited by peasants wearing only robes. This glimpse into humanity's pre-history was a stark reminder that my culture's creature comforts were all superfluous.

In the car we listened to Ethiopian reggae music. It was good. The Ethiopian rap, however, left something to be desired. We listened to music and enjoyed the rural scenery until our car broke down.

Fortunately we were within walking distance from a village where Samuel had a cousin named John who offered us a place to sleep. John didn't speak English but he did have wood for a fire on which he grilled grasshoppers as a snack. To wash these down, he sent his brother to buy us a Coca Cola. This snack was not bad for people who like crunchy insects with warm fizzy soda.

When Gurli refused to eat the bugs, Peter whispered that it would be rude not to graciously accept John's hospitality. Then, when John brought out the main course, goat organs including the intestines and penis, Peter's expression said, "Oh shit, now I'm gonna have to eat this." Then his mouth said to Bas (as a dare), "As they say in Russia, don't be a pussy..."

When John put the organs on the grill, Bas stood up saying, "I'll be right back. I'm gonna go buy another Coke." I went with him to make sure he had enough money.

Most Ethiopian restaurants offered goat meat and injira bread. I always asked for "fasting food" to get veggies, but that option wasn't always available. There was a lack of veggies because the once-fertile soil had become a desert. The local solution was to have goats eat the scrub plants that did grow, and people ate the goats, including all the organs. For John this was normal, but for me, not so much.

Gurli said she was allergic to meat as a hastily prepared excuse to go hungry.

I did not want to eat goat penis, but I was called upon to do so. I realized that in order to know myself, I needed to know my limits through experience. One has to test oneself to know the truth. In this case the test was grilled goat penis, and I passed but barely, happy that we had plenty of fizzy soda.

We slept on the ground with thin blankets, a long night in the cold mountain air. That's why I was delighted when our driver appeared at sunrise with a functional car.

Arriving back in Lalibela, my friends all wanted to rest, so I set out to explore alone, but not for long. Eddie ran up to me yelling, "Raymond! Raymond!"

I said, "Shouldn't you be in school? Oh, never mind."

I was delighted to have this boy as my guide. He called out detail excitedly as only a boy can. He held my hand. This was strange for me but normal for him. Culture. He asked me all about America. He asked me how many wives I had. I changed the subject to Darwinian evolution because for Eddie to be a doctor, I figured, this was the number-one fact he needed to know. He soaked it up, and this encouraged me to tell him the truth.

He asked me, "Do you believe in God?"

I answered, "That depends on how you define the word God. The laws of physics? Hmmm. God is a metaphor, and yes I do believe in metaphors."

Eddie thought about that for a while, then he asked, "What is a metaphor?"

"Hmmm," I said while thinking. "A metaphor is an idea not a thing, and God is an idea, because to talk about all the complexity of the Universe, we can just say God. So for example, you will become a doctor some day if God wants, and I do not mean if a supernatural being decides it. Do you see? For practical purposes you have free will, so make this thing happen."

Eddie nodded his head so I continued, "Any definition of God that doesn't agree with the facts is wrong, so the question becomes, what is a fact? For this, study the scientific method. You say you want to be a doctor, so instead of worrying about God, I recommend that you humbly accept that we humans are animals on an animal planet, so study biology to understand how this animal machine works, and study evolution to understand how this biology came to be. Evolution is also key to understanding humanity's true nature as more-or-less intelligent apes."

Eddie thought for a while before saying, "Yes. God is a metaphor!"

We walked in silence, hand-in-hand until finally Eddie asked, "Raymond, why are white people better than black people?"

I laughed in surprise. "White people are not better than black people," I answered.

The boy insisted. "Yes they are! White people are rich. They are smart, healthy, and fat!"

"White people have more money, that's all."

"But why? Why?"

"Well," I said, trying to think. "White Europeans colonized Africa, you know, stealing black people to take home as slaves, so... This made white people more rich while making Africans more poor."

"But why did black people not colonize Europe? Why?"

Eddie's question seemed so obvious that I was surprised with myself that I never thought to ask it. And I did not know the answer. I said, "You're a smart kid Eddie, really smart, a genius! So I tell you what: my friend Peter used to be a history professor, so let's go ask him..."

We found Peter sitting in the shade of our hotel's courtyard, sipping tea. I summarized Eddie's question, "How is it that white people came to be the world's economic masters? In other words, why didn't black people colonize Europe?"

Peter said, "Good question! The short answer is that white Europeans had better technology, things like guns and steal, plus better resistance to certain diseases, but to really understand why things are the way they are, you must go back in time..."

My guru of historical knowledge said, "Actually this is interesting! The answer to Eddie's question can be found in the first pages of the Old Testament, but not by any conventional reading."

I said, "Oh?"

He said, "Yah. The story of Adam and Eve is located at the right place and the right time, the beginning of history, the very first modern city. Before this, all humans were hunters and gatherers. This historical Garden of Eden was a special place because it had more wild plants and animals suitable for domestication than anywhere else on Earth, and that was the birth of farming. Farming!"

Eddie looked puzzled. "OK," he said. "But what does this have to do with white people?"

Peter answered, "I'm getting to that. But first, the Garden of Eden became a desert because the growing population cut down all their trees, but Europe was next door, see, with good soil and plenty of rain, and so thanks to geographical luck, white Europeans became the world's most productive farmers. The European geography was also perfect for city-states to experiment politically, militarily, and intellectually, and that's how white power spread, with books and guns and eventually science and industry."

Eddie said, "Interesting."

Peter said, "Yah. Crucially also, white Europeans evolved resistance to the diseases that came from their domesticated animals, diseases like smallpox that killed everyone else, and this was a huge factor in the colonial wars... And that's why white people conquered Africa and not the other way around. Geographical luck, really. Does that answer your question?"

Eddie said, "Yes. Thank you professor Peter! I wish I could study more. I have to share books with my cousins, and candles are so expensive. I wish I had books, especially books about diseases."

My friends and I bought several books for Eddie and his cousins at the school bookstore. We also gave two-hundred euros to his grandmother to buy candles. She gave us more awesome coffee. The one thing we wanted to give that we couldn't give was fast Internet, but we were hopeful the government or an NGO would plug that gap soon enough.

As I sipped my coffee I was happy that I finally understood the historical roots of modern inequality. Once again I was reminded that I had the rare freedom to travel spontaneously not because I was superior in any way, but because I was born at the right place and the right time, and I was happy to know this truth. I suddenly felt my humility increase.

When it was time to say goodbye, Gurli told Eddie, "Lalibela needs doctors, so follow your dream. You can become a doctor if you work really hard, so study relentlessly!"

I said, "Yeah, make this thing happen."

Peter said, "That's right. Nobody but you is responsible for your future."

Bas added, "Yes. Believe in yourself. You can do it."

I saw my little friend about to cry, so I asked him, "Do you have any advice for us?"

He said, "Yes. Spend all your money helping children like me, because you might die tomorrow. We are the future."

65 - Doctors without Medicines

When I sat next to the old man, he stood up with fear in his eyes, then he approached a stewardess and spoke to her softly, clutching his Al-Qur'an. The stewardess responded by asking a white Westerner if he minded swapping seats. The Westerner agreed, so he stood up then he sat next to me, introducing himself as Olivier. I introduced myself, then Bas introduced himself, then the captain announced our departure to Addis Ababa.

Meanwhile Peter and Gurli sat two rows away, giggling like children.

I asked Olivier, "What was all that about? With the old man?"

He answered, "I am not sure, but my guess is that he does not want contact with infidel people like us. Maybe he believes we cause AIDS. No, seriously. I know this sounds absurd but most Europeans recently believed that all disease was caused by sin, and the cure was to drain blood, so we are only about three-hundred years ahead in terms of medical understanding."

As our airplane taxied down the runway, Olivier explained that he worked for an NGO called Doctors without Borders. At first he did not describe how he helped Africa however; he described how the African people helped him to grow personally, how the people inspired him with their humility and pride and courage and good humor.

I told him, "That's awesome. Nice to meet you. Keep up the good work."

Olivier said, "Thanks. What about you? We don't get a lot of tourists in Ethiopia..."

Bas said, "Maybe it's the flies."

Olivier laughed knowingly, because the little fuckers were annoying indeed.

Bas explained how he and I came to travel together in Africa, then he asked Olivier to elaborate about his job. Olivier said he was on his way home to France to essentially beg for more supplies. He said, "We do a lot of great work! But I also end up holding hands a lot. People die by the thousands, no millions, for want of things we Europeans take for granted. Malaria is treatable and bed nets are not expensive, but most Africans cannot afford these. Ah well, many people cannot afford even to eat. There might be a million AIDS orphans in Ethiopia alone."

As I tried to fathom the scale of the problem, Bas said, "Please let me play the Devil's advocate. I'm not trying to be insensitive, but if we could somehow save a million people from AIDS, wouldn't that increase the over-population and therefore make the food shortage worse?"

Olivier answered, "Not if we also delivered on education for girls and birth control, but AIDS is killing the teachers! Imagine if we also launched reforestation programs. Imagine if we provided seeds and technical advise on sustainable agriculture, innovations that repel pests and increase soil fertility. You see? Plus now thanks to the Internet, people finally have access to agricultural technology, but here again, we need more money."

Bas asked, "But if wealthy donors fund all these aid programs, won't corrupt politicians just steal the money?"

Olivier answered, "It's true that money is wasted and greed is human nature, so yes of course, sponsors must target their funds wisely. Sponsors should avoid aid programs run by philosopher kings who fly around Africa to investigate all the best hotels. Instead we should promote field workers who go from village to village asking, what do you need? Anyway, most aid programs are so underfunded it's criminal. Still, every day we see new infrastructure, new toilets and new solar-power circuits, and mobile phones! Oh my God, finally we can talk to the outside world from the bush!"

Bas nodded his head so Olivier elaborated, "Anyway, we Europeans have no moral high ground to accuse Africa of corrupt government. We drew the maps that created landlocked nations, divided ethnic groups, put warring groups together, and then we exploited the chaos to enslave the people and steal their resources, and then we just walked away, leaving the mess in the hands of incompetent fools and ignorant tyrants. And now there are fifty African countries, all struggling to survive, and some are making excellent progress, like Botswana."

With that, our airplane took off.

Bas broke the silence. "Maybe the missionaries should just pray harder. Wait. No. I have a better idea. Let's ask the Pope. He has lots of money. He can call 1-800-GOD. And if anyone knows how to raise money, it's God."

It was obvious that Bas was joking but Olivier remained serious. He asked rhetorically, "What kind of God would allow so much needless suffering?"

This was the moment I decided to abandon my spiritual quest, the moment I realized that whatever I was looking for, it had nothing to do with any God or spirit, and furthermore, spirituality was a metaphor. Since I began looking for *it*, whatever *it* was, I learned that *it* was not about death but about life and love. The thing that I sought was knowledge of myself and of the Universe, plus morality, which was about life, love, and helping to end extreme poverty in Africa. I steered our discussion towards trained-ape theory, the study of human-ape behavior consistent with modern science and our own egos, an exciting topic because we were on our way to see gorillas.

Bas and I introduced Olivier to Gurli and Peter at the Addis Ababa airport. This was our last night in Ethiopia before flying to Rwanda, a fact we used to justify our decision to enjoy an expensive meal at Olivier's favorite Italian restaurant, quite luxurious compared to what we were used to. Gurli wore her only dress.

With red wine in hand, Peter proposed a toast to the fact that the Italians, who occupied Addis Ababa during World War Two, didn't stay long but did leave behind quality cuisine.

Bas said, "And thank God for that. I'm hungry."

We clinked our glasses, then Gurli commented about our newly strengthened appreciation of European luxuries after getting stuck overnight in a village near Lalibela. This prompted Olivier to ask if we planned to visit the Omo River tribes. "I recommend you go," he said, "because if you really want to appreciate modern comforts, there's no better way than spending time with tribal people."

Gurli said, "Eating fried bugs and goat organs, and sleeping on the ground?"

Olivier said, "It does make one appreciate Gorgonzola cheese, doesn't it?"

We all drank our wine and ate our cheese. Ah yes, fine dining.

Drinking wine somehow reminded me that my expedition across Africa was temporary, like watching a movie, and then I was free to return to California or wherever. I never had more empathy for poor Africans, but this was far from living their reality every day.

I answered Olivier, "Eating bugs and organs was no big deal because this was only for one night, but still, the only way to truly imagine living in poverty is to experience raw survival first hand. Eating bugs is actually normal and Italian restaurants are not. We are animals and that's a fact. So yeah, I hope we do get to visit the Omo River tribes. After crossing Africa the hard way, one cannot have the tourist mentality. We are travellers. Bring on the bugs! To me this is a more meaningful religious experience than eating communion in church."

I explained to Olivier my traveller-versus-tourist analysis and he agreed, adding that travellers travel not just to learn, to have adventures, and to look at cool stuff, but also to strip away all of life's baggage, including the expectations set by friends and family, including all the comforts and all the bad habits, everything, until there is nothing left but one's true self. I added that we also travel to hang out with diverse and interesting people, with lots of free time to read and contemplate and discuss politics and the meaning of life.

Then, as Westerners in Africa inevitably do, we discussed the continent's problems, but not for long. Bas clinked his glass with a spoon. "You're getting depressing," he said. "And that's the problem with travelling in Africa. The conversation always turns to something depressing. Should we not be discussing this fine red wine?"

We talked about the wine. It was fine. Then we went over practical steps to lift African countries out of their poverty traps, one economy at a time, starting by forgiving the "odious debt" that poor countries owed to wealthy foreign bankers.

Olivier said, "The world should treat economics like doctors treat disease. Treat causes and not symptoms. Look at historical case studies to see which remedies have worked and which have killed the proverbial patients."

We had no shortage of great ideas to improve Africa, only a

shortage of political power, a vast fortune, and magic fairy dust.

Peter said, "Skilled missionaries convinced the warrior tribes to abandon their traditions in favor of Jesus, a God of Peace and Love. They put trained-ape theory into practice and so can we. We can educate girls for example, the number-one way to treat the cause of too many people. Educated girls have fewer babies."

We discussed the pros and cons of globalization, a force changing planet Earth faster than any force in history (not counting volcanoes and asteroids), a force that made world travel possible along with many other benefits, a force driven by corporations and therefore without morality or justice, a tremendous force with a ferocious appetite for natural resources. I felt powerless against globalization's enormous scale, but I also felt empowered by Olivier's optimism. Thanks to him, I finally understood the wisdom in the words: *think globally, act locally.*

Later outside, Olivier lit a cigarette and Bas stared as if hypnotized, so Olivier offered him a smoke, a decisive moment given my friend's pledge to quit.

Bas declined dramatically, then he made a joke about the Pope. Next he thanked Peter and me for helping him quit, then he begged, "But please never (never!) ask me to give up my sweet, sweet ganja. Thank you. OK? It's my only vice."

Olivier finished his smoke then hailed a taxi. His last words were, "I think that if you work for the happiness of other people, then you will know happiness yourself, and for me, this is where I find meaning in my life, and this is why I will always return to Africa. Au revoir."

On the flight to Rwanda, I quietly sat alone and contemplated everything. I was delighted to be a traveller, to see for myself and to meet others who had seen for themselves so much of the world. The stuff we talked about seemed important for humanity, not for a sports team or whatever.

Despite the constant difficulties associated with the traveller's lifestyle, for me these only enhanced my sense of being on an epic adventure while studying at the University of the Open Road. I felt that my research into religion and human nature was going well, and I was even beginning to understand macro-economics; there was one question however, that I figured I could probably only answer from home: what the fuck, Pops?

66 - Beauties and a Beast

I first heard of Rwanda in association with the genocide of 1994 when nearly a million people were slaughtered in a hundred days of insanity, but this was not the Rwanda of our first impression. We arrived into Kigali via a modern airport and good roads where we witnessed well-dressed people working towards a better future. Even the tough-looking, unemployed men seemed like they were standing around in a good way. Compared to the poverty of Ethiopia, Rwanda seemed downright prosperous.

I was delighted to see the lush, green vegetation. Green!

Our plan was to see wild gorillas, chimpanzees, and the culture of the country, then we planned to continue overland to South Africa, and I liked having a plan despite knowing that plans are what make the Gods laugh.

My friends and I dropped off our backpacks, then we walked in search of the governmental office for tourism, to book our date with gorillas. We knew the deal: three-hundred dollars per person for "morning tea" with the mighty apes, a lot of money, but a small price to pay to help save the beasts from extinction through tourism.

The government office was decorated with posters of volcanoes, chimpanzees and gorillas, but my eyes were drawn to a different scenery: two female tourists discussing their gorilla booking with the clerk. They were both seriously gorgeous.

As my ears tuned into their words, I recognized the words *money* and *expensive* in a language similar to Spanish, so I guessed the women were from Brazil. My animal instincts aroused, I approached them and said in their language, "Caro, ne?"

One of them responded, "Você fala Português?"

When I hesitated she added in English, "Yes, too expensive! We thought Africa was more poor than Brazil so therefore more cheap, but here is too much expensive! Three-hundred dollars for gorilla!"

I answered, "Yes, but when you're an old woman, you will forget about the money, but you can never forget visiting wild gorillas!"

As the ladies nodded their heads in agreement, my friend

interrupted. "Hello," he said. "My name is Bastiaan, hello, and this is Raymond. He's American but don't hold it against him. He's actually a nice guy."

The ladies introduced themselves. Isabela was pretty enough to cause a car accident, but Sylvia was even prettier. With European and African features plus slightly Asian eyes, her unique blend of DNA was exotic and striking, especially her eyes. And her mouth. I was drawn to her easy smile that reflected a natural way. She had nearly perfect teeth. She also had qualities that I could not name, special qualities; she was naturally hot. Her hair was curly.

After a moment of the usual where-are-you-from smalltalk, Peter, Bas and I paid the clerk. Meanwhile Gurli chatted with the Brazilian tourists, and she must have created some same-sex solidarity because they agreed to join our gorilla group, and as our booking was seven days away, they agreed to join us to track chimpanzees too. I saw this as excellent news.

To celebrate, we walked together in search of a suitable restaurant to share a meal and discuss logistics. We ordered food that was amazingly good, pure-veg curries with Indian spices. Meanwhile the Brazilian beauties told us their story of friendship and a passion for nature that led them to realize their shared dream to visit Africa.

They loved Mozambique, they said, especially because they all spoke Portuguese so it was relatively easy to befriend local women, and as such they enjoyed numerous family meals, which were great. They loved their safari in Tanzania too, especially the elephants; and they loved Zanzibar's white-sand beaches and interesting Muslim culture; but they did not love the poverty, the disease, the destruction caused by civil wars, nor the unexpectedly high prices; and they did not love having only ten days left before their flight home.

I wasn't very happy about that, either. After a year of travelling the open road, Sylvia was the first girl who seriously grabbed my attention (except for Angeline). And there she was, sitting in front of me, asking me what I thought of Ethiopia.

As I contemplated an eloquent reply, Bas answered, "Hungry blind children, skinny cows, flies, fucking flies, surprisingly good Italian food, amazing stone churches in Lalibela (you should go there), and people who impressed me very much with their positive attitudes."

I said, "Yeah. Proud people, tough survivors... Ethiopia taught me that rich people who complain are spoiled brats."

Sylvia said, "Spoiled brats? Yes. Brazil also has too much spoiled brats."

Over dinner, Bas and I quizzed our new best friends about their back stories. We learned that Isabela was a veterinarian who specialized in fluffy house critters; she called herself a pet vet. Sylvia was an expert in criminology who worked as a parole officer. The ladies were both charming but there was something about Sylvia, perhaps the way she butchered English with a smile. I couldn't name it, but I was mesmerized by it, and I could tell that Bas was enchanted too.

After our meal we escorted the ladies back to their hotel, agreeing to meet for breakfast the next morning. No longer strangers, we kissed each other on the cheeks, three kisses each, which was normal for Brazilians but unusual for me. Culture. I complimented Sylvia's shoes.

Bas and I shared a spacious double room. The bathroom had a bidet, a legacy of the Belgian colonial masters, but there was no water, so I tracked down the hotel manager who agreed to send a maid to our room with a bucket. I told him to make it two buckets. With that, Bas and I rinsed off the day's dirt. Later I asked him, "So, what's new with you and Sophie?"

He answered, "No news. She still doesn't have a passport. But I know where you're going with this... You like Sylvia."

I said, "You read me like an open book my friend. I am smitten... But tell me the truth, you like her too, don't you?"

He answered, "What not-blind, not-gay male wouldn't?"

Just then, the electricity failed and we stood in the darkness, a blackout. For the first time I saw my friend as a competitor, because even though I barely knew Sylvia, she seemed perfectly mysterious. Her exotic beauty conquered my imagination, making me keenly aware that she planned to fly home in only nine days. I was not optimistic because our group dynamics seemed too tricky, plus as the man said, "Pretty girls are a dime a dozen but try to find one who will give you good lovin'." Worth a try! Another man said, "Eat dessert first because life is short." Sylvia to me seemed sweet, and perfectly delicious for eating.

We all met for breakfast as arranged. As I got to know the Brazilian beauties better, I noticed that Isabela seemed more intellectual and Sylvia more charming (she touched people when she talked to them, not to flirt, but because that was her way). Unfortunately I did not speak with them much directly because mostly they spoke with Gurli or with each other in Portuguese, but no worries, everything flowed along with a positive energy.

With one week to go before our date with gorillas, our plan began with a tour of the local area. Even though it seemed gruesome, we started with the genocide museum, because as Peter said, "Those who do not know their history are doomed to repeat it."

We explored the museum in silence because what can one say when looking at skulls smashed in by a machete? Two local women broke down in tears, no doubt survivors. I had to choke back tears myself as I moved past them to the next hall, the one that explained how German colonizers created the Hutu-Tutsi distinction as an administrative tactic before the Belgian colonizers formalized it based on things like cattle ownership.

Next we visited a church out of town where Tutsis sought sanctuary during a Hutu raid but were slaughtered just the same (this was one of the few activities for visitors described in our guide book). As we taxied out of the city, even the steepest hillsides were cultivated for agriculture, with vegetation that masked the hard-working farmers with too many children.

The church's caretaker was speechless as he showed us a collection of cracked skulls and blood-stained walls. Gurli sat down to cry. When a tear rolled down the caretaker's cheek, Sylvia and Isabela cried too. We all cried, all of us with our inner sadness and our naked humanity on full display. Robots don't cry.

We walked back towards our taxi in silence until I said, "Stupid monkeys."

Isabela said, "Work of the Devil? That is not explanation. Stupid monkey is explanation."

After an uncomfortable silence, Peter said, "The real explanation for the genocide was simply too many fucking people (literally). Rwanda has volcanic soil and plenty of rain and therefore lots of food, but every generation Rwanda's farms got sliced up smaller and smaller until... What we see from the historical record is that violent fights between siblings over land inheritance grew steadily in the years preceding the crisis. And then, even after the Hutus killed a million Tutsis, tiny Rwanda is still the most densely populated country in Africa!"

Just then, a breeze blew in the sweet smell of flowers. I said, "Yeah well, we live on a planet ruled by poorly-trained apes. That's the bad news. The good news is that it's a gorgeous day. Let's go find ourselves some gorillas and chimps!" Everyone conceded faint but sincere smiles. Just then a bird began to sing.

As we entered our taxi back to Kigali, the driver said, "Rwanda is safe for *mzungu*. Do not worry. Genocide happen never again! You here see gorilla?"

Peter answered the man's question with more questions, eventually prodding him to tell us his story from the war, a fascinating tale of survival, a narrow escape into Uganda then an epic quest for food and shelter. The man boasted about Rwanda's recovery since, especially the community courts called gacacas, similar to South Africa's Truth and Reconciliation Commission, to promote healing and unity. He said Rwandans wanted peace more than they wanted revenge.

He sighed. "Genocide is difficult for you. I understand, is difficult. But these men no have education so when politician say, 'Kill neighbor and take house.' So they kill. They take house. The neighbor is cockroach. You see? Neighbor is cockroach, and you need house, so take. What these men did was not *humanity* but *animality*. But I promise you, never again. OK? Rwanda's education is getting better, all the time progress. You here see gorilla?"

The taxi driver answered one of my private questions, how did trained-ape theory explain the warm-hearted optimism and friendly nature of people who had recently seen so much suffering? Because many aspects of daily life were far, far better than before, and still improving quickly, and the people were proud of this fact. I pointed this out to Bastiaan, and he replied that Cambodia was much the same, a nation of proud people who understood the value of helping their community to be happy while working together to survive. This translated into hospitality towards foreign visitors in a good way. Be excellent to each other.

67 - Trained Apes

We attracted attention as mzungus generally, but especially at the city bus station. Amputees approached us to ask for money. So did other characters who seemed anything but trustworthy. One guy had an inflamed tongue blocking his mouth so he could only breathe from his nose. He grunted as he drooled down his t-shirt, his way to ask for money. We all gave him money, hoping it might be enough to pay for a doctor. Poor guy.

One man spoke with himself in French while frantically waving his arms. Sylvia said, "That man has crazy ideas in his brains."

A woman entered our bus carrying her boy on her back. This would have been unremarkable except that this boy was horribly crippled, mentally retarded, and fully grown, weighing more than the mother. Isabela said, "That is unconditional love. Most people I think, allow boy to die." We often saw extreme examples of poverty at bus stations, but this station had more shocking examples than usual.

Once we got going towards Butare however, our fellow passengers were welcoming, the bus was new and comfortable, and the road was excellent. We made good time, racing past a thousand green hills towards an uncertain future. Perhaps we went too fast though, because a passenger in front vomited from motion sickness, spraying Gurli in the face through her open window. Oops.

Descending from the bus, a boy approached us selling soft drinks. I bought six, allowing myself to be robbed of a few coins on purpose. I gave the rest of my coins to the woman with the crippled boy. She thanked me in French.

My friends and I bought fresh groceries to ensure a better quality meal than we could probably find in a restaurant, or so I suggested as a way to socialize. Nobody in my group ever complained about rural Africa's restaurant food, but we did lament the fact that better quality required little effort. Why not cook with fresh herbs for example? When the grocery store refused to give us a plastic bag for protection of the environment, my friends and I applauded the new law. Rwanda lacked road-side rubbish compared to say, India, and thus Rwanda's air also lacked that horrible pollution caused by burning plastic rubbish.

We checked into a hotel named, "If God say yes, then why you say no?" Then we made a delicious meal as a team while listening to Sylvia's music collection. Good times.

I flirted with Sylvia at every opportunity but gently, playing it cool. I flirted with Isabela too because why not? Isabela was also a talented and lovely lady, but she did not inspire my lust. I flirted with her mostly to see if I could make Sylvia jealous, and yeah, a little maybe, and worth a try.

Later as Bas and I prepared for bed, we found ourselves in another blackout. As we searched for a torch, the woman next door yelled out rhythmical pleasures. Bas asked, "Is that Gurli?" At first the moaning was funny but it got annoying after a while. Nevertheless I was impressed by Peter's endurance.

The next morning we travelled to the Nyungwe forest, home to wild chimpanzees. Our bus was so crowded that squeezing in was awkward, but at least my friends and I provided entertainment for the locals. They laughed at us and we laughed back.

We settled into the Nyungwe guest house then arranged for tracking chimps. This entailed giving money to a park ranger who then alerted professional chimp trackers by walkie-talkie. We set our alarm clocks, then we all went to sleep in order to depart at first light.

I loved the sense of adventure as we descended into the jungle, that special place where the abundance of life made me feel alive and alert. We walked through an old-growth forest into a buffer zone of trees designed to protect chimpanzees while simultaneously creating renewable firewood for humans. We walked through a village into another buffer zone then into some native forest with a tribe of chimps. This was four hours of strenuous walking on muddy trails, fun exercise.

The Brazilian beauties spoke mostly with each other in Portuguese, which I saw as irresistible sport. I kept my ears open to their conversation even while discussing other topics in English. I couldn't help myself. Bas and I both made every effort to engage the lovely ladies in conversation, but they seemed to prefer speaking with each other. They came to Africa to see wildlife together, and they were just aloof enough to seem tantalizingly off limits.

Thanks to walkie-talkie technology, we finally caught up with the chimpanzee trackers, and chimpanzees! The great apes stayed in the tree canopy but we did get close enough to see their faces for about a minute. Mostly we watched them fly. I envied their lives in the wild green, without humanity's gift of gab but with superior tree-climbing prowess. They were awesome, cruising along forest-tree branches as easily as I might walk along a city sidewalk.

Our guide explained, "Chimpanzees know that villagers hunt for meat so they stay away. Chimps have common sense."

This reminded me of Mutsuko, the woman who told me how Artificial Intelligence was hard because computers did not have common sense, but when it came to life in the swamp, even lizards had instinct, swamp sense. Mutsuko told me that above all, primate brains were good at pattern matching and predicting. Chimps knew to fear us.

A female ape peed in our general direction, but with quick action we escaped the yellow rain. We knew she was female from her swollen genitals. Peter, Bas and I laughed as our curvier companions celebrated their advanced evolution, specifically their ability to conceal their menstrual messiness with far less swelling, plus the invention of clothing. Classic moments like this help boy backpackers to bond with girl backpackers.

We finally abandoned the great apes to walk back to our lodge. Hours later, we arrived at the sealed road, happy about this milestone because we were exhausted. As we sat down to rest, our guide bailed towards the lodge about three miles away.

Sylvia and Isabela both had blisters on their feet, a real concern, so I flagged down the first vehicle that came into sight, a Land Rover with a white driver. I asked the man if he could please give us a lift. He said no, adding that he didn't have room. He had room, so I asked him if he would please take only the two beautiful Brazilian women.

The guy said, "Sorry, maybe next time." Then he drove away.

My friends and I stated at each other incredulously until Bas said, "Next time?"

I said, "What a friggin' ape!"

Sylvia said, "Spoiled brat."

Bas asked, "Or was he just stupid?"

I said, "Stupid or poorly trained. Some apes are trained better than others, and that guy clearly needs some serious re-training, with a focus on empathy I would say. I mean, what an ape!"

Isabela said, "I think this says it all."

I said, "Yeah. We humans talk better than our furrier cousins, but we don't climb trees as well. And anyway, talking is overrated. I've noticed that wild apes communicate extremely well using facial expressions and gestures."

Sylvia looked me in the eyes and said, "Brazilian apes are trained for dance samba!" Despite her blisters, she did a little dance, and her smile was contagious. She had a talent for creating smiles, and for an instant we were all in Brazil, singing simians dancing to tropical beats. Oh man, I thought silently, she's tough in a good way, never complaining, and she grew up on a farm so she understands food, oh man.

A minivan came into view so I flagged it down. To my surprise, despite the van being packed full, the girl's volley-ball team insisted on giving us a ride. We squeezed in awkwardly, and by the time we got to our lodge, we were all laughing at each other's jokes.

Arriving at our rooms just in time for sunset, feeling that rush one feels at the end of any endurance workout, Sylvia said, "I am ape trained to want hot shower!"

If I could have frozen that moment in time, I would have.

The highlight of my shower was the troop of mischievous monkeys that oversaw the affair. The lowlight was the giant spider by the toilet.

I sensed that Sylvia liked me, but she also liked Bas. I could feel my body reacting to unfulfilled desires, so I made myself think about mischievous monkeys instead. When that didn't work to calm my mind, I tried meditation, focusing on my breathing in the present moment. This did help. My brain however, did not forget what it had recently seen, and that night I had a nightmare. I woke up just as I was about to get whacked in the head by a machete. That which brought me peace again so that I could relax and then sleep was my memory of Sylvia smiling at sunset.

68 - Peace and Love

A white guy named Jethro gave us a ride from the Nyungwe lodge to Cyangugu, a city on the border with the Congo. I was getting used to African towns, but if I had flown directly to Cyangugu from California, it would have been a shocker. Barefoot people walked along the rocky road including women balancing big bunches of bananas on their heads! Most of the children smiled and waved, but not the adults, most of whom glared with eyes that had seen too much suffering. I was getting used to that too.

Jethro took us to his favorite Chinese restaurant where he explained how the Chinese were invading Africa, buying many of the best farms to grow food for China. "At least they're building infrastructure," he said.

Jethro witnessed great political change in his home country, South Africa, and this fueled his optimism despite the setbacks. Jethro believed in people power. He believed in a better Africa. Further encouraged after a trip to Ethiopia where he saw reforestation in action, he dedicated his life to the cause. He said the key to reforestation was local involvement, because everyone must know the benefits from a sustainable source of wood. Jobs in the tourism sector are also great, he said, especially if these enable great apes to stay alive in the wild.

Think globally, act locally.

As Jethro charged his phone with a hand-crank charger, a crucial device for work in rural Africa, he reminded me of Olivier in that his head was full good ideas but his wallet lacked money. At least for the Nyungwe project, tourists like us provided cash.

With regard to Ethiopia, Jethro said, "The biggest problem is the goats. They eat the seedlings, so we need fences, but fences are expensive, and if we fence off a large area, who owns it? This is the tragedy of the commons." Sigh. "Sorry, I take it back; the biggest problem is not the goats; the problem is a lack of money, mostly to educate local people. For example, simply by planning herd movements so the animals shit and piss over an expanded area, we can reclaim farmland back from the desert. That's just one example..."

We moved on to talk about chimpanzees. Isabela said she was disappointed with our encounter, "because we arrive only so close for them to pee on us."

Jethro answered, "I have a friend who raises semi-wild chimps at his ranch, only about a twenty minute drive from here..." As a result of our enthusiasm, soon we were on our way. First we checked into a hotel in Cyangugu, then we bought beer and ice.

As we drove, Jethro told us how he met Aboyami at the bank in Cyangugu. They were both loitering in the lobby because it was the only place in town with air conditioning. They since formed a partnership to help protect mankind's nearest cousin.

Upon arrival at a farm house, Jethro introduced his friend.

"It's a good omen you are here," the man said. "I was just resting under the visitor tree, and you are an international group. Yes, a good omen. Welcome to my ranch."

Aboyami's ranch backed up to a patch of native green just large enough for a tribe of chimps thanks to the hillside being too steep for agriculture. Jethro told us how he was pushing the government to formally protect this land by visiting politicians and writing letters, because Aboyami's project needed to become official to become sustainable forever.

Our host took us on a walking tour. First he showed us the many fruit tress he planted, everywhere they would grow, of every viable variety. He told us how he consulted a veterinarian, and he educated his neighbors against eating bush meat. Then he told us about the time an alpha male attacked one of his guests, so he had to shoot it, the most difficult thing he ever had to do. Since then for his family's protection, he shipped the strongest males with violent personalities to a professional sanctuary in Tanzania. He said, "If we encounter an aggressive male today, the main thing is to stay calm, and you must remain true of heart, because if you have a dark place inside, they will know it, and they will not like you." Next he told us about a female he named Desirée because she traded grooming for sex.

Aboyami was a Tutsi. He said he survived the genocide by escaping to Tanzania, an adventure where any mistake could have ended in death. He returned years later and began his work to protect the chimps. His daughter married an English diplomat and moved to London; she provided the funding.

We encountered two great apes in a mango tree. It was fascinating and fun to watch them eat, but I preferred to watch Sylvia smile and laugh as she watched them eat.

Aboyami's wife Akila served lemonade at the ranch house to compliment our beer. We all drank some lemonade and it was delicious, but then the men switched back to beer. It's hard to say why.

Meanwhile Aboyami explained chimp politics. He said, "Right now everything is peaceful. Nobody would dare take on Zeus and Batman together, but when Zeus gets older, I think Batman will team up with Caesar and go against him. Chimp politics are much like our own. Soon I will have to send Batman to Tanzania, I'm afraid."

Aboyami said that chimps were the only species other than humans to make deliberate war against neighboring tribes. He said chimps were capable of empathy too, but incapable of asking questions. He said, "Their ethical system is best seen in the way they share food. They get very upset when food is not shared fairly."

I realized that I also got most upset by unfair inequality, thus my interest in political solutions to share the wealth. Gurli pointed out that bonobos lived with more peace and love than chimps despite their DNA being extremely similar, because bonobo females were the bosses. I knew she was right, that the world would be a better place with leaders motivated more by empathy and less by testosterone, but I did not want to debate politics.

Instead I invited Sylvia to go watch the chimps in the mango tree. I told her jokes in Spanish, and I asked her to teach me Portuguese. She said it hurt her brain to speak English so much, so she appreciated the break. We established a playful dynamic, but we were not alone for long. The reality of travelling in a group meant that other people were always around to participate in the dance, people like Bas and Isabela. But no worries, visiting chimpanzees was never about the pursuit of love but the awesomeness of Africa, wonderful moments, the stuff of life.

69 - King Congo

Our hotel at Lake Kivu had a private cove that was perfect for swimming. Not only was this refreshing, but I got to see Sylvia in her bikini. Isabela too. Seeing so much feminine skin helped me understand the Muslim approach: hide it because it makes men horny. I preferred the Brazilian / Khajuraho rationale: celebrate this beauty as one of life's great pleasures. I could easily have stayed at Lake Kivu for weeks, but we had to move on because we had a date with gorillas.

The hotel manager charged me for three nights instead of two. Sigh. He showed me in his book where he wrote down our arrival date incorrectly. This was a scam I had yet to see, but similar to the scam where the manager agrees to a discounted price but forgets the deal when the time comes to pay. I noted the best way to defeat these scams was to always obtain a receipt for the first night paid with the correct date.

We departed towards the Volcano National Park (home of gorillas) on the bus to Ruhengeri, but our bus broke down so we waited under a baobab tree along with all the stranded locals. Another bus finally stopped and it was full, but somehow, amazingly we all squeezed in. This was uncomfortable, and the air reeked of underarm odor, but everyone's positive attitude made the journey not so bad.

To continue from the Ruhengeri bus station there was no bus, so we asked local people for advice until we finally agreed to pay fifty American dollars to a guy with rusty sedan. The road going up was crowded with men carrying firewood and pushing bicycles loaded with stuff, plus women balancing big bunches of bananas on their heads.

We checked into a hotel then explored our vicinity, and immediately we were surrounded by children who wanted nothing but photographs. Later they escorted us to the market where a woman told us she hadn't seen a white person in years. She said, "Tourists care only about African gorillas, not African humans."

I told her that most Westerners were probably afraid of exploring Africa, afraid of violent crime, afraid of the unknown. I told her that most tourists did not understand that Rwanda was generally quite safe during the daytime, because back home we only heard the bad news.

One man invited us into his humble home mostly constructed with bamboo and thatch. The man did not need to tell us his child was dying of AIDS, such were his infectious sores. The boy seemed sad; he must have known he was about to die. But the man remained upbeat. He made lemonade while telling fascinating stories about daily life. The man was a proud survivor, working hard to make the best of his life. "Why not have a positive attitude?" he asked. "This one thing is entirely up to you."

Later some cute girls wearing bright school uniforms escorted us back to our lodge. After that we dined in a restaurant named, "Ordinary Food." The menu said simply, "You eat what we eat." We ate simple vegetables prepared deliciously.

We began our gorilla trek early, not because this was the best time for trekking but because gorillas generally rest after breakfast. A park ranger explained the rules: sneezing was prohibited, so was spitting, and sick people had to stay behind because gorilla DNA is just that close to human DNA. Furthermore, we weren't allowed to use flash photography. The final rule was that if an aggressive male charged at us, we were not allowed to run. "Not to worry," said the ranger. "Gorillas are vegetarians."

Our guides hacked through the bush with machetes while using walkie-talkies to communicate with the gorilla trackers. The men were all armed, not to protect us from gorillas, they said, and not because they were worried about poachers, but because we were near the border with Congo where the ongoing war was the bloodiest on Earth since World War Two, a power struggle that made even chimpanzees seem peaceful.

I loved every minute of tramping through the jungle, and then suddenly I was face to face with the mightiest of apes. The big guy's name was Congo. He looked me in the eyes, and I looked back, trying to convey that I meant him no harm. I said softly, "Good boy. Good gorilla."

Congo's eyes were just like human eyes, except they were surrounded by gorilla. His harem consisted of eight females. No other mature males were in the vicinity, but there were several babies. The fluffiest one climbed onto daddy's back, but his patience was low so he sent the kid straight back to momma who displayed loving tenderness.

These were not the monsters of popular myth; these beasts were us, only bigger and furrier. I felt privileged to be in their company because they were amazing and rare. Then I felt sad that so few humans could ever visit their wild cousins, to experience their humanity in person. Then I felt happy again, after all, I had friends by my side to share this moment of wonderful, wild African awesomeness.

Our guides finally tore us away from the gentle family marooned on their island of jungle in the sky. As we descended the mountain, these same men quizzed Isabela and Sylvia about Brazil, because they were fans of the Brazilian national football team, or at least this was their excuse to make conversation with Brazilian babes.

I told Sylvia in Spanish, "I plan to visit Brazil by the way, soon, just after my friends and I complete our tour of Africa, maybe in three or four months from now. Soon."

She said that if I visited Brazil, then I would learn Portuguese quickly. This was not the answer I wanted to hear, so I hoped she was playing me for sport. We were becoming friends, but she did not invite me to visit her, and I could not get her to admit to having or not having a boyfriend (I refrained from asking this directly because I didn't want to put her on the spot).

I looked for every opportunity to flirt but my fantasy girl stayed close to her best friend. Meanwhile I admired her ability to gracefully deal with Africa's challenges, because despite blisters, beggars, bug bites, bad food, and broken-down buses, she never complained. As we arrived back in the big city, I was keenly aware that I only had one night left to seduce her, and this made me feel increasingly anxious, a gift from the Hindu God of Horniness perhaps.

70 - The Girl from Ipanema

My friends and I selected a clean and popular Indian restaurant for our final group dinner. We drank German beer, and we entertained ourselves with witty banter. I flirted with Sylvia relentlessly even while discussing criminology, but we had zero privacy to go beyond words. I waited patiently for any opportunity to change this dynamic, then the wind blew in a torrential rain. When Peter suggested that we go home by taxi given this rain, I touched Sylvia's arm and said, "One more beer?" She said something upbeat to Isabela, then Bas caught my eye and his meaning was clear: go man, go. Finally my favorite Brazilian girl and I were alone!

The radio was playing a Bossa Nova song and this inspired me to say, "Yes, I must visit Brazil soon, especially if the people are as romantic as the music."

My companion smiled with no comment, so I asked her about psychology to keep the conversation flowing. She told me that she liked to study dreams as a mirror into the mind. "People have crazy ideas in their brains," she said.

We drank one beer while swapping stories, then we drank another while discussing shared interests, then it was time to go. I knew there would be no awkward silence if I were to ever visit her in Rio. My only question was related to the sleeping arrangements.

We stepped into the rain to hail a taxi. I used the opportunity put my arm around my date, and she responded with affirmative body language. Our embrace was natural. Our energy was perfect.

We sped away in a taxi, but after two blocks the driver stopped on a dark street. He looked agitated. He pointed a gun! "Quickly," he said. "Give me your money. All of it!"

Sylvia trembled. She handed over her cash. I gave away my decoy wallet.

The driver shook his gun. "Out... Out!"

Suddenly standing in heavy rain, I grabbed Sylvia's hand and led her running to the nearest shelter, then as we caught our breath, I showed her my secret stash of cash, and that helped her to relax. I suggested we run further in search of a taxi or an open business. I told her the running would keep us warm. She agreed, so I made a guess which way to go, and we ran.

Luckily we found a bar a few blocks away.

We were immediately the center of attention, as per normal being mzungus. Despite the friendly energy transmitted by the locals, Sylvia squeezed my arm tightly as if afraid. I escorted her in the direction of the bartender saying, "Jambo! Can I please have two glasses of that?" I pointed to a bottle of cognac, thinking the spirit would warm us up.

The bartender said, "Quoi?" Then another man translated my drink order into French.

Sylvia and I walked to a warm-looking corner, accompanied by the same man, an old soak named Bamba who seemed genuinely interested in us. He asked me why two mzungus were out in the rain, so I told him about the mugging. Bamba didn't have a car, but he found someone who did, a man who drove us home about an hour later.

I invited Sylvia to my room, and to preempt any possible excuse for her to decline, I added, "Just some hot tea to warm up." Bas wasn't there, so I assumed he was with Isabela. Yes! Sylvia sat on the bed while I put water to boil. We talked about fear. She broached the subject because the mugging scared the shit out of her.

Suddenly the lights flickered out, a blackout. In the darkness I found her, and I hugged her with all my positive energy. Our first kiss came naturally, gently like I knew she wanted it. I knew we could only ever share one first kiss so I made it last, to show my girl that I was passionate yet patient, with both desire and respect.

She said, "Mmmm... Gostoso."

With that I put my hand inside her shirt to feel her skin. I was about to explode.

She said, "I don't know if this is good idea." Then she put her hand under my shirt.

I said, "I'm not sure either." Then I unbuttoned her bra.

The lights flickered back on, allowing us to see each other. Sylvia looked away, seemingly embarrassed. She said, "No, I'm sorry. I can't do this. I'm sorry." Then she looked me in the eyes. "How can I believe? You and me, we are from different worlds. Of course you can visit me in Rio, but I am not girl with fifteen years who believes in enchanted prince. You are American. I see all the time, American man with Brazilian girlfriend. Always promise love, then go home."

I said, "I will make no promise that I cannot keep. I promise." Then I sang the lyrics to a famous Brazilian love song, "Tall and tan and young and lovely, the girl from Ipanema goes walking, and when she passes, everyone she passes goes ahhh..."

Sylvia said, "That is sad song. The man, he does not get to love the girl." She sang, "Ah, por que tudo e tão triste? Ah, por que estou tão sozinho?" Then she spoke, "This means, why am I so sad and alone?"

I asked, "Doesn't the song go on to say that the world smiles and fills with grace and stays more beautiful because of love?"

Sylvia admitted that this was correct, then she called me by the nickname Xuxú, and then Bastiaan entered the room with Isabela. He knocked first, and he opened the door slowly, but that didn't soften the impact of his bad timing.

Isabela reminded her friend that they still had to pack for their flight home the next morning. Damn! After a few minutes of chatter, Sylvia kissed me good night, then Isabela kissed Bas good night, and then they were gone.

I had to work hard at not feeling overwhelmingly sad. Bas did his best to try to cheer me up.

He and I woke up early to say goodbye, of course. We knew the ladies booked a taxi for five a.m. so we waited in the lobby at four-forty-five with coffee. I didn't have any private time with Sylvia but I did tell her, "I am going to visit you in Brazil soon. Rio is going to be my next stop, after Africa. Soon!"

"Good," she said. "Visit me. I want to see you again, Xuxú."

We hastily exchanged email addresses, then she hugged me and kissed me on the cheeks three times, as Brazilian ladies do, then too quickly she was gone, and so I knew that I simply had to go to Brazil as soon as possible.

I asked Bas how things went with Isabela, and they had a fantastic time he said, but the experience brought home how much he missed Sophie. He wanted to go to Cambodia, and I wanted to go to Brazil. Instead, we went to Tanzania.

But first, with growing concern for Shepherd the hacker, I

called Pedro, and he had news! He was poised to send me an email, he said, then he added, "Shep's in jail. So that's great! I mean, he's fine, but he did get busted hacking into that database. They caught him, the bastards, but that's all I know. So far they haven't even let him call his girlfriend, but she got a lawyer who managed to track him down." Good news, bad news.

71 - The Africa of Dreams

I had to work hard at the international border to avoid the various money-changer scams, such as give mzungus the wrong change because mzungus are too stupid to count. In order to obtain a good exchange rate for my Rwandan cash, I had to simultaneously do math in my head, count money in two currencies, protect my stuff, and negotiate with fast-talking hustlers. Sport.

My friends and I procured a hotel only to discover that it doubled as a brothel for truck drivers. This was not the Africa of dreams but we remained upbeat. We were about go on a wildlife safari, because what African tour would be complete without seeing lions and elephants?

I missed Sylvia. Without her mysterious, seductive, and decidedly feminine presence, travelling suddenly seemed masculine and out of balance. I found it interesting to observe how my brain changed when my animal instincts were aroused. I slept poorly and I dreamed of sex. Even on a street full of fascinating characters, I caught myself imagining this girl I barely knew. My brain insisted that going to Brazil was my top priority. Meanwhile, all I could do was play it cool and enjoy the adventure that is Africa.

Our minivan to Arusha was designed to sit fifteen people, but I lost count at twenty-eight. Despite being squeezed to the point where I could not move my feet, and despite the foul smell of unwashed bodies, all the curious, local smiles somehow made this journey entertaining, even fun, as we bounced our way down rocky roads for hours. It was fun that is, until a cramp in my gut signaled an urgent need to squirt diarrhea. Thus I was relieved when a truck forced our minivan off the road. Nobody got hurt but our vehicle sustained major damage. This gave me plenty of time to take care of business.

As I cleaned my ass with toilet paper, which I kept handy, a pig suddenly appeared and began eating my excrement. The pig startled the shit out of me.

Gurli was most grumpy. It did not help that we all had to wait under a tree for hours with no idea when we might be rescued. It did help that Peter played the flute brilliantly.

A minivan finally stopped for us. The vehicle was already full of course, but everyone insisted that the mzungus should get on board anyway. In this case Bas and I sat on the roof with all our backpacks. This was fun but dodgy because falling off was a real possibility.

Two people finally disembarked, allowing Peter and Gurli to sit, so Gurli was happy but not for long. Someone stuffed a crate of frozen fish into the space above her head, and this dripped cold, fishy water onto her back. She got hysterical and demanded that the driver stop to rearrange the luggage, to prevent further dripping. He stopped.

We could not make it to Arusha before dark as planned so we disembarked in Singida. There were no taxis so we had to walk in search of a place to sleep. There was no hot water at our hotel, but there was cold beer at the Who Knows? café, so we were happy.

Bas and I clinked our bottles to celebrate our elevated karma, then he made a toast to our home countries, where most things just worked and efficiently too, where the streets were clean of rubbish, where competent workers were promoted ahead of family members, where the culture valued craftsmanship and deliciousness and quality, where Islamic mosques were not allowed to wake everybody up before dawn with amplified calls to prayer, and where it was unthinkable for anyone to stuff a crate of frozen fish above someone else's head on a public minivan.

Gurli said she'd drink to that, adding that this was a good segue for her big announcement. She then explained the logistics of how she just accepted a job offer from the United Nations in Geneva as a translator. Peter announced that he was going to Geneva too, because he and Gurli were going to get married!

He said, "Globalocity, global velocity! I've been around the world in eighty months. Now it's time for rest, relaxation, and Gurli's lovin' generosity."

Bas and I both said, "Congratulations!"

Peter said, "Thanks. I'm ready for this. It's time."

Bas wanted to go to Cambodia as much as I wanted to go to Brazil, so we agreed to follow our girlfriends too, after our wildlife safari of course. We agreed that if both our relationships went bust, we'd meet back in Tanzania to continue our trek to Cape Town, but inspired by Peter and Gurli, neither of us was willing to pass up a chance at love.

Getting off the bus in Arusha, I noticed safari touts, money changers, vendors selling trinkets, and tourists who seemed intimidated, but we were travellers, experienced roadies, and therefore professionals at dealing with the street sharks. We politely ignored them and went on our way.

We spotted a restaurant advertising "happy" pizza and we were hungry, plus Bas was out of wacky weed, so we stopped. He ordered extra "happy" on the side.

Later I read an email from Sylvia saying that she got home safely. She typed, "I miss you, Xuxú, my horny. Come to Brazil."

I walked into a travel agency and bought a one-way ticket to Rio de Janeiro, then I researched getting a visa online. Luckily Arusha had a Brazilian consulate.

But first, a wildlife safari...

My friends and I hired a guide, a cook and a Land Rover, then we hit the road, stopping first at the Olduvai Gorge, home of the earliest evidence for humanity's bipedal ancestors, fossilized footprints that were three-point-six-million years old, virtually indistinguishable from the footprints of modern man.

Next we visited a Maasai boma, a fortified village and livestock enclosure. The villagers lived in huts made of mud, surrounded by a fence of spiky plants to protect against the ferocious beasts beyond (especially lions). These Maasai villagers were accustomed to tourists because they lived near the sealed road, but they maintained their nomadic culture including a diet of meat, milk, and blood. Visiting them provided a fascinating window into humanity's prehistoric past, back when we lived in equilibrium with nature.

Finally we arrived at the Serengeti National Park, the Africa of dreams, that Africa I imagined when I imagined Africa from afar. We saw all the big animals plus countless species of birds. From our campsite, sleeping in a cage like a zoo in reverse, we could hear lions roaring in the night.

Our driver's name was Ikayo, and Juma was the cook. They were both top blokes. With humor and intelligence they guided us well, but the first time Juma served a meal, he walked away with Ikayo to eat separately. Bas was the first to point out that this was ridiculous, that we came to Africa to hang out with Africans, and that the elephants were incidental. Bas asked Ikayo if we could please eat together.

Ikayo resisted initially because he was confused. He said no tourist ever made this request before. Then I explained the difference between travellers and tourists, concluding that we were travellers. Ikayo replied that the biggest problem with tourists was that they saw the world in black and white, when the truth was brown. From then on, we all ate together. This was the Africa of dreams, especially given that as soon as I fell asleep, my brain was able to insert Sylvia into the narrative.

72 - The Lion and the Buffalo

Our final safari destination was the Ngorongoro Crater, the collapsed cone of an ancient mega-volcano, a giant caldera teeming with wildlife. From a distance we spotted a herd of elephants so we chased them down to watch them eat flowers. Then we witnessed a lion eating a buffalo, tearing the flesh apart, bloody and savage. Then we stopped for lunch.

Peter asked me if I thought it was good or bad that the lion ate the buffalo. I said it was good for the lion and bad for the buffalo. He said, "Incorrect. It was neither good nor bad. These words are only labels that humans use to communicate ideas. The fact is that the lion ate the buffalo, nothing more, nothing less."

Bas said, "Me hungry. Me eat. Kill animal. Kill. Food!"

I said, "Sorry man but you're not a lion, and I hate to say this, but you just reminded me of that crazy Kiwi, that tweaker Louie from Malaysia."

My friend protested, "What? You can't compare me to him, man, not Louie. No. You can't compare me to him. I mean, what an ape! I mean, some people are so stupid..."

Gurli looked quizzical so Bas told her the story of Louie, the guy who started a Kung Fu fight in a fuckin' great bar. I added, "Louie was stupid."

Gurli said, "Yeah well, stupidity is a stronger force than gravity. Gravity sucks on the physical body but stupidity sucks on the mind."

Peter said, "Let's take Bastiaan's cigarette habit for example. I mean, I'm glad you quit, but..."

Bas interrupted, "Smoking is not stupid! OK maybe a little stupid but I'm smarter now, and it's more of a personal preference anyway. Some people like Parmesan cheese but I prefer Gorgonzola better. Do you know what I mean?"

Peter said, "Yes I do."

Bas said, "Good. So let's take another example. We used to burn people alive in the name of Jesus, and we still stone people to death in the name of Allah. That's stupid!"

"What about hacking up our neighbors if they happen to be Tutsi?"

"Or having children we can't afford to feed?"

"But sex is free, and every child is a blessing from the one true God."

"Yeah true. That's a real problem."

"If you were born an ancient Viking, you would have been blessed by Thor."

"Maybe, but I wouldn't have believed I was blessed by Thor unless I was stupid."

"Religious examples are too easy."

"Is there a Hindu God of Stupidity?"

"Oh man, don't get me started about stupid..."

My friends ignored this request, they got me started. And so we embarked on our inevitable rant against stupidity. During our trip in Africa we shared many rants, for example against imprudent drivers, filthy bathrooms, lazy cooks, corrupt politicians, and so on, but we had yet to rant against plain-old stupidity. Bastiaan provided one example: in Egypt at the edge of the desert, we saw many vendors peddling useless trinkets but nobody selling cold beverages, or hats. This led us to conclude that the hallmark of being stupid is not thinking things through.

"Think of the average person's stupidity. Half the people are stupider than that."

We all brainstormed stupid examples until we began to wonder aloud if the problem with humanity was more ignorance or stupidity, noting that we can train apes to be not ignorant, but we cannot train them to be not stupid. Peter said, "The problem with humanity now, during our critical moment in history, is that we're allowing the corporate *thing* to take over governments, and that's a stupid way to run a planet."

"Imagine a global democracy where the top priority was education instead of profit..."

"That's a fantasy. Few apes dedicate time in their busy schedules to analyze the complex details of global economics (for this they read the newspaper at best), but we give them the all-powerful vote. Managing our economies and our ecosystems should be the job of subject-matter experts, not popular buffoons. Furthermore, even the best-trained super-apes get their information (and their gift ideas) from corporate sources, even on the Internet. Garbage in, garbage out. Monkey see, monkey do. Think chimpanzee. Let's face it, we're gullible, hard-wired to believe our respected elders even when it's complete bullshit. Therefore democracy is not the best possible system."

"Yeah, but it's the system we have. Therefore..."

"Therefore it's a global phenomenon. Global warming, global stupid. I should make a movie. Set in an apocalyptic future, the film will look back at now to examine why we didn't save ourselves. I'll call it, an Inconvenient Stupid."

"Make the movie."

"Let me spin this another way: ignorant people cannot know what it's like to have a great education. They don't know what they're missing. Poorly-educated people value humility above all else, so to them smart people sound arrogant whenever they claim to know something. Therefore..."

"Therefore it's not so much that people are stupid. And anyway, that's not even the problem, I think. The problem with humanity now is greed, especially since the emergence of the corporate *thing* because this has turned the drive for profits into an abominable machine. Most people who vote for crappy politicians in America for example, are victims of sophisticated and well-funded propaganda campaigns. Meanwhile the impoverished majority do not vote at all, because they've been sold the idea that all politicians are the same, that government itself is the problem. And you can't blame the youth when they don't understand. They go to schools where we teach them that Christopher Columbus was a very great man, you know, celebrating white imperialism. We also teach them that growing the Gross National Product is economic nirvana, forever growing, and that's stupid but that's not human; that's the *thing* talking via some of its human employees."

"True. I know people with zero formal education who are quite skilled in various fields, smart people! Therefore the problem with humanity is more ignorance than stupidity, plus institutionalized greed as you say. Take Einstein for example, a lot of apes are geniuses! The world is full of visionaries who lack only an education, and these are our future leaders. Put another way, it's easier to believe something than to know something. Most people are believers, not knowers, but this can be reversed."

"Therefore we must teach the children the truth."

"Yes."

"People don't want to know the truth, man. The truth is rude, war and corruption. People want to hear lies, sweet lies. Ignorance is bliss, man."

Bas said this last bit, prompting Peter to ask rhetorically, "Would you concede that well-trained apes fix problems, and empathetic apes spread joy, and we all are capable of humor and grace?" He looked Gurli in the eyes to conclude, "And one finds beauty in this truth easily, if one knows where to look."

Gurli gave Peter a kiss, then she said, "You are a well-trained and empathetic ape."

Just then, a pair of ostriches ran near our site. This brought us all back from the abstract world of ideas to the physical Africa of dreams, but not for long. Bastiaan fired up a joint which we all smoked, even Peter after Gurli inhaled first, then we all travelled back to the quintessentially human realm of abstract ideas. We agreed that optimism and pessimism were just words.

Soon thereafter, Peter and Gurli left for Europe. We didn't have a long goodbye, but we did share hugs and kisses, heart-felt handshakes, and promises to stay in touch. Peter's last words were, "Globalocity! Global velocity! Now it's time for a new adventure. À Dieu."

From then on I sometimes spoke the word *globalocity* too, both to remember my Swedish guru and to represent all of my adventures with just five syllables.

Alone for the first time since Sumatra, Bas and I walked in search of a bar. Accompanied by a congenial bunch of drunken locals, we stayed until a fight broke out.

I reminded my friend that he told me in Goa how he paid for his travel habit by working odd jobs, but Africa was not cheap, and I never saw him work (other than making palm-leaf hats for tourists in Goa). I was drunk enough to ask directly, "How did you make your money?"

Bas suddenly looked sad. "Ah yes, that. My uncle died, and he didn't have any children so..."

"Oh. Bummer."

"Yeah."

"Death sucks."

"Yeah."

"And it's not just Angeline and your uncle, but genocide and starving children and war, and friggin' water buffaloes."

"Yeah. That's life."

"Yeah, that is life. Sooner or later our bodies all get recycled back to dirt, and that's OK, that's reincarnation, and that's the divine truth or whatever you want to call it. We live in an infinite Universe. We live! And that's the divine miracle. Then we die, and that's why we should live courageously, because why not? Do not be afraid to die my friend, because if you play it safe, you might live a few more short years, but maybe not. The fact is..."

Bas interrupted me. "You're right," he said. "And by the way, my uncle who died, he was a drug dealer. Ha! That is to say, he was the managing director of a pharmaceutical company in Holland. Yeah. I'm actually fairly wealthy now. This is all recent news by the way, not my uncle dying but the money finally landing in my account. I wanted to tell you earlier, but I never got around to it."

The next day, feeling quite hungover, my friend and I found the bus to Dar Es Salaam. We stopped in a village near Mt. Kilimanjaro just long enough to buy a bag of peanuts and two pineapples from a woman with no teeth, but mostly we sat on the bus and watched Africa out our window like a movie.

Our taxi driver from the bus station was a Maasai man with holes in his earlobes and scars on his face that betrayed his tribal past. When the man claimed to support twenty people with his salary, Bas asked him if he could find a better job. The man replied, "Why would I do that? No matter how much money I make, my family spend all." This was an African story.

We arrived at our hotel sweaty and tired but nevertheless ready to go out again because this was our last night together for the foreseeable future. We both took showers, then we shared a pineapple, then we procured a restaurant that was both clean and popular with locals. The food was delicious and cheap. Next we walked into a bar named, "Why not?"

Our drinking mates were middle-class professionals who smiled a lot. They seemed worried only about paying for their children's private schools and getting to work on time after drinking the night before with mzungus. They all wanted better jobs. This was another African story.

In situations like this, I avoided talking about my life because I did not want to inspire envy. I told people that I was a carpenter on holiday, and that my story was boring. If pressed about my holiday, I said, "When the money is gone, the trip is over." That's all. Mostly I was curious about their lives anyway, so this was easy.

The next morning early, the happy hippie from Holland woke me up to say goodbye. His last words were, "I suppose I'm just a carefree soul, ready to eat whatever delicious fruit that life has to offer, and now that fruit is a girl named Sophie, a girl I only met because you got robbed in China. It's funny how the Universe works, isn't it?"

I said, "Yeah. The good news is that this planet we inhabit, and this reality we know as life, it's all for our entertainment. Have fun."

Bas left with the wind at his back just as a crimson sunrise brought in a new day.

I ate another delicious pineapple, then I did my laundry, then I explored Dar Es Salaam, enjoying my freedom to be spontaneous. I did not feel lonely and I did not sense danger, but I did feel a thousand eyes watching me, perhaps curious, perhaps looking for a weakness. I watched children playing, old people chilling out, dogs sniffing, and vendors vending. I talked to locals about their world, so different from mine, yet so very much the same.

For my final meal in Africa, I sought out a high-class Indian place where I ordered the special vegan meal because I was on my way to a country famous for beef, then I sat alone and contemplated my love life. With Angeline, I told myself, I was never sure if we could have made a future together because hers was a different world from mine. Sylvia however seemed ideal for my desired lifestyle. Both of these beauties took my breath away, but with Sylvia I saw one chance to make a long-term relationship work, so I boarded my airplane hoping that she might be the one.

But if not, I reasoned, this would have to be OK; I would simply have to travel further. I always wanted to visit Brazil, and even though I was looking for love with the girl from Ipanema, I was willing to settle for some good old-fashioned monkey lust.

73 - A Marvelous City

My flight captain announced our arrival into Rio de Janeiro, "the marvelous city," and from high above the urban chaos, the city did indeed seem marvelous. From my window I could see granite mountains with forested hills plus a mega-metropolis with golden beaches.

I raced through immigration and customs to emerge into Brazil, feeling that thrill of arriving into a new air. I was poised to seal the deal with my new girlfriend, and that added to my excitement, but mostly I wanted to see her smile.

I scanned faces searching, then I walked around scanning more. I did not worry because I knew there were a thousand reasons for Sylvia to be late, but I was anxious. Finally she appeared, her smile intoxicating, her run to me electrifying. She greeted me with a kiss, slowly teasing my upper lip. Then she stepped away and looked me over.

"I am so sorry I am late," she said. "The traffic can be murderous. Anyway... Bem vindo ao Brasil! It is nice to see you. You want we go to beach today?"

There's nothing like the rush of arriving into a new city, with a new culture and a new air, but especially with a new girlfriend. Everything seemed right in the world.

As we drove away from the airport, Sylvia pointed out favelas on the hillsides, shantytowns where everyone was a squatter. She lectured me on safety in her urban jungle, a city with malandros (bad boys) and endemic corruption. "Police no go to favela, understand? Too much important in Rio, do not act like gringo, for example do not show camera in public. OK? Be careful. Always dress like Brazilian man." She told me that most favela residents were good people trying to make an honest living, then she made me promise to take taxis at night.

We detoured from the highway to stop at her favorite fruit-juice stand. I wanted to try every exotic flavor but I went with maracujá, the fruit of passion.

Sylvia's apartment building was surrounded by a wall topped with broken glass and an electric fence. The parking garage was tiny, but her car was also tiny so no problem. The elevator up to her flat was rickety. My new home away from home was also tiny, with barely enough room for Sylvia and me in the kitchen, with a sofa and a coffee-table looking towards a television, plus a CD player and speakers, but no other electronics. The bedroom was barely big enough for the bed plus Sylvia's stuff. My stuff therefore had to fit neatly inside a tiny closet in the laundry alcove.

As I surveyed this scene, the first thing I noticed was that Sylvia's number-one product of consumption was shoes. She owned a lot of shoes. Before I could get comfortable, she gave me a t-shirt and a pair of flip-flops wrapped in a bow, then she said, "Get changed. We go to beach."

A minute later we descended to the busy street where Sylvia pointed out landmarks as my brain adjusted to black-market DVD vendors, boutique clothing stores, and chic cafés. We walked three blocks and then suddenly I saw the famous postcard view, beautiful Ipanema beach. Amazing. We sat on the sand in the sun, then we swam in the sea, then we sat in the sun some more. We drank fresh coconut water. Delicious.

Our bond tightened as we shared our life stories. Like me Sylvia was an only child. Her mother died when she was two, and her father, Papai, never remarried. Sylvia grew up on a farm but studied enough to go to private school and then university. She majored in psychology originally to understand her relationship with Papai, she said, but as a practical matter she focused on criminology to get a government job. She said her professional goal was to help individual criminals become better people. I studied her eyes in hopes of gaining insight, and I found beauty, intelligence and humor. Lucky me.

When she asked about my world tour, I told her about India, a mystical land with remarkable treasures plus gurus skilled in meditation and contemplation, seeking to learn not how to conquer the world, but how to live in peace. Then I told her about India's madness and filth.

When she asked about my tattoo, I told her about Angeline and her theories of physics.

When she asked how I made enough money to travel so much, I told her I was frugal, then I explained the meaning of the word frugal, then I told her about selling my house. I said that after my world tour I would look for a job, but I still had no idea whatsoever what that job might be. Meanwhile I was leaning towards getting a university degree in science, or maybe volunteering with an NGO.

Sylvia blamed me for making her want to travel more, she said, because she just spent all her savings in Africa, and if she quit her job she would probably never find another one as good, so therefore she was stuck in Brazil for the foreseeable future. She said this was OK because in a way she was on holiday in California. Then she asked me how long I planned to stay in Rio, so I told her I had a ninety-day visa, extensible one time for a maximum of one-hundred-and-eighty days.

She said, "You stay with me now, with one condition: I am very clean person, OK? No messy. I have kitchen rules, OK?"

I agreed while making a mental note to be as clean and organized as humanly possible at all times no matter what.

Meanwhile people with perfect bodies paraded along the beach. There were ugly people too but the stunning girls in string bikinis grabbed my attention. Sylvia said that she didn't mind if I looked at other girls because she looked too (eye candy), but I could tell that she did mind, especially when she added that Brazilian men knew how to be more discrete shortly after she first heard the word *Angeline*. I saw this flash of jealousy as good news.

Arriving back at the flat, as I relaxed into the sofa for the first time, Sylvia served me a very cold beer but before I could drink two sips, she sat on me while simultaneously putting the beer aside and kissing my lips. I kissed her back and the fire within me ignited. She kissed my neck and the fire burned hotter. I knew that we could only make love one time for the first time, so I moved slowly, occasionally closing my eyes to memorize the scene forever. Sylvia and I made love on the sofa, and it was beautiful, fun, and hot.

When I finally returned to reality, I found a cold beer within reach. Nice.

That evening my lover and I dined at a fancy restaurant to celebrate our passion, a churrascaria with all-you-can-eat meat grilled to perfection, plus the biggest, freshest salad bar I ever saw.

Sylvia wore her favorite shoes. She was amazing. I knew I was going to like Brazil; I was going to like Brazil a lot. I was Sylvia's and she was mine, at least temporarily, because nothing is permanent.

74 - Seven Sins

Sylvia had to work so I explored the city, Rio de Janeiro! First I visited the various postcard viewpoints to get a feel for the lay of the land. Then I truly discovered Ipanema beach, a perfect place to swim, watch people, play pick-up football, eat fried cheese with beer, and so on.

I called Pedro, and he gave me an update from Shepherd's criminal case. "Our brother is still locked away in a stinking jail, and still no visitors, but the bastards finally let him call his girlfriend at least, and the good news is that Shep thinks they're gonna let him go free. He has a great lawyer and they're negotiating."

Feeling as if I had nothing to lose, I called Pops. I told him about Sylvia, I told him about Shepherd, then I asked him about Switzerland's banks. Pops answered my question with a riddle. "All I can say is that if a thief comes to take away your life or your gold, you should give away your gold." I asked him to explain, and he said, "Come home." When I pressed him further, he repeated, "Come home," adding that he did not want to talk over the telephone.

I put going home on my to-do list, but I was in no hurry despite being damn curious. Knowing that Shepherd was OK, I lost my sense of urgency, especially as I was falling in love with the marvelous riches of Rio.

Sylvia taught me Brazilian body language and polite mannerisms, plus specific things to say and not say. Per her suggestion I bought clothes to look like a middle-class carioca (a resident of Rio). Also, I tried to not think in English. The epic journey to mastery of another language begins with simple words such as *brega* meaning *bad fashion*, things like pink purses with matching fluffy boots. Sylvia and I often made fun of *turistas bregas* on the beach, plus the heroic, tragic, comedy called humanity.

Most people understood me when I spoke Spanish, but I did not understand them because the Portuguese accent is so strong that I failed to understand even words in English. Therefore I studied relentlessly, and so I began to speak *Portunhol*.

When Sylvia went to work, I often went to the same spot on Ipanema beach to play football and then socialize with my football-mates (to make some male friends). If we went to the pub then we usually drank beer, but sometimes we sat at beach-front bars to drink caipirinhas instead (with lime, sugar, ice, cachaça, and magic). I understood little when these guys spoke with each other, but I could survive one-on-one with my mini-dictionary.

I learned that when Brazilians refer to someone's education, they mean that person's character, manners, and respect for others, something not taught in schools. In comparison I was told, Americans seemed educated in arrogance (statistically speaking), so I worked hard at increasing my humility while hiding my gringo accent by exaggerating my vowels.

Sylvia helped me to learn her language of course, but mostly we spoke in English in order to communicate most effectively, important while negotiating the details of living together in a crowded space for the first time. It helped that she enjoyed exploring tantric yoga positions while naked, inspired by Khajuraho's copulating statuaries. And it helped that she loved finding fresh flowers in the kitchen after work. Flowers always inspired kisses. Sylvia was a kisser.

Every day she seemed more comfortable with my invasion of her private space, especially as I worked hard at being meticulously clean, a house husband with cash to spend, and I asked for zero favors. With plenty of time to think, I analyzed my previous live-in relationship (with Maia) to review the lessons learned, and so I finally understood my jealous rage that defined our final argument: I was an ape.

Despite understanding this intellectually, I still felt jealous whenever Sylvia kissed other men (three cheek-kisses to say hello, part of the culture). Mostly I felt jealous when she spoke with her mysterious ex-boyfriends using language that I could not understand. And it bothered me that she used ambiguous words the few times she alluded to us as a couple. Therefore I reminded myself to play it cool, to let time decide not logic, to be the visiting friend from Rwanda in no hurry.

At first I insisted on taking my girl out for dinner every night, but then she insisted on cooking at home to save money. So I started cooking these dinners myself, or I bought take-away meals which I served with wine. On Saturday nights however, we always went out, and after two weeks we finally did so with Isabela, and it was nice to see her.

Isabela quickly became that friend with whom I could seek relationship advice, which I wanted because Sylvia was elusive about our future as a couple. Isabela told me that Sylvia was acting cautiously because I was a gringo tourist and therefore we had no future as a couple, because gringos always go home. But everything was fine, play it cool, *follow the flew.*

Eventually Sylvia began to call me her boyfriend in public, and with that I became less jealous whenever she seemed overly friendly with other guys. I was a rational ape, continuously improving my ability to tame my hard-wired instincts with conscious controls.

I bought a drum and signed up for lessons to learn some Brazilian beats. Sometimes I read non-fiction in Portuguese as a way to study. Sometimes I wandered randomly, and I particularly enjoyed sipping coffee with old men in corner cafés. These guys were patient and helpful with my ongoing linguistic transformation.

Meanwhile I made a lesson plan to correct Sylvia's most-common grammatical mistakes in English, important because this was our lover's tongue. She told me, "I like you teach English good."

My football buddies took me to see Rio's team Flamengo play Cruzeiro, the team from Belo Horizonte. The game was well played but I was more impressed by Maracanã stadium, or rather by the fans who filled it, an amazing display of football passion, with dancing and chanting. This was the most fun I ever had watching a sporting event. Cruzeiro won. The Flamengo fans were upset but I was not.

Sylvia stepped up her role as my tour guide by driving to secluded beaches and historic mountain towns on weekends. We ate delicious food (Brazilian cuisine is amazing), and no matter what we did, we had fun. We made each other laugh. Sometimes we witnessed incredible beauty. As time went by, I began to see her humanity, her inner sadness, her childish joy, and her lonely soul in search of a soul-mate. Sylvia was an only child who moved to the big city successfully; all that she needed was love.

My beautiful girlfriend usually watched a tele-novela called Sete Pecados (Seven Sins) to relax after a stressful day at work. This novela depicted the lives of wealthy Brazilians as they tried and generally failed to moderate their vanity, envy, wrath, sloth, gluttony, greed, and lust. Together we worked out seven virtues: humility, respect, kindness, patience, generosity, justice, and love. We thought prudence, self control, and courage also seemed worthy in this list, but that didn't matter.

Sylvia told me that Brazilian novelas often had strong female characters who used birth control, causing the average number of children per mother in Brazil to drop dramatically, a crucial fact in a land of overcrowded favelas. She said the government helped by ensuring that condoms and the pill were widely available. Then she asked me, "Do you think lust is a sin?"

I replied, "Yes and no. The lust of the rapist is a sin, if you want to use the word sin, and so is the murderer's wrath and the banker's greed, but not the natural attraction between men and women. I mean, if it weren't for lust I wouldn't be here. I followed my animal instincts to be with you, good old-fashioned monkey lust."

We worked out how the so-called seven sins were all survival instincts taken to extremes. Sloth was conserving energy to the point of becoming obese. Greed was accumulating survival-related stuff such as territory to the point where the richest ten humans owned more wealth than ten-thousand humans could spend in ten-thousand lifetimes. Normal every-day greed however was healthy and required. Likewise wrath was a way for apes to say, "Don't fuck with me!" And vanity helped apes to attract mates.

Sylvia's vanity certainly worked its charm on me. I did my best to charm her back, striving for humor as my preferred way to deal with tricky situations. We frequently had misunderstandings due to our language barrier but not so much from culture, because my attitude remained positive when it came to forcing myself to adapt to the details. Mostly I struggled with the language, so I signed up for a private tutor to speed things along. I asked my tutor to teach me charming things to say.

I began to understand Brazilian humor, and like the music, this was loaded with sexual innuendos and double meanings. For example, everyone laughed at me when I said I wanted to eat Japanese food because my choice of words actually meant that I wanted to have gay sex with a Japanese man (the verb to eat, comer, has two meanings, one sexual). Therefore my linguistic transformation required disciplined study, patience, and humor, mostly humor.

Despite my best efforts, my lover and I finally did have a few arguments, nothing serious, stupid stuff really. For example she yelled at me when I sat on the sofa with sandy shorts. Things like that. She also demanded that I use dental floss twice per day, which seemed extreme until I learned that Brazil has the world's highest use of dental floss per capita. I was able to negotiate with her on that one. Sylvia was a kisser so I bought mouthwash.

Crucially none of our disagreements were serious, neither of us yelled, and our make-up sex was great. Whenever she got angry with me for being sloppy, I apologized ten times, then I told her that she had big ears, or something like that, anything to change the subject with humor. Sylvia did not have big ears but I insisted she did as long as this was funny. Regarding her extreme fondness for kissing, I was usually keen but if I was not keen then I insisted her nickname should be Smootchies, again to change the subject with humor. Meanwhile I redoubled my efforts to adapt, an easy task because far more than bickering about petty nonsense, my lover and I made each other laugh. If I saw that she was sad, I tried to make her happy. And if I saw that she was bored, I tried to ask an interesting question, such as, "How do you think trained-ape theory explains humanity's love for music?"

To keep things positive, I trained myself to have exactly one answer for most situations, *beleza* (especially when Sylvia was in a stubborn mood). If she said yes, beleza, and if she said no, beleza (great). No worries. Whatever. The woman is always right. The only problem with this was that I never saw her dark side, and she never saw mine either, but whatever, beleza.

Time raced along quickly, and soon I found myself visiting the Brazilian federal police to extend my tourist visa. They gave me ninety additional days which was great, but after that I had a stark choice: get married, stay illegally, or leave Brazil and stay away for at least six months. I had zero guarantee that Sylvia would say yes if I were to propose marriage, and I had no inclination to do so anyway, nor did I want to stay illegally, so therefore leaving Brazil had to become my new Plan A. It was theoretically possible for Sylvia to travel with me but only if I paid all the bills, and even that implied getting married to satisfy her father, I figured, so I had little choice. The good news was that I still had wanderlust, so I began to imagine a six-month trip abroad, reluctantly.

Bastiaan had a similar problem with Cambodia. He could not stay with Sophie legally unless they got married, so he and I agreed that maybe we might meet back in Africa after all. He said that it was healthy for people in cross-cultural relationships to take breaks, suggesting that Sylvia also probably needed breathing room and time to think. Then he said, "By the way, I just shaved off my dreadlocks because my neck was getting too hot."

Meanwhile Sylvia was all that I wanted. My visa problem was a worry for the future. Confronting Pops in California was a worry for the future. I was happy to simply dive deeply into Brazilian culture (and Sylvia). I was only anxious about meeting her father. The way she spoke about him, the man seemed like a strict disciplinarian, a man suspicious and critical of her various boyfriends over the years. I had to meet the guy sooner or later, and I was keen to visit the legendary family farm, but this was a worry for the future.

75 - The Postcard View

The more I came to know Rio de Janeiro and the better I spoke Portuguese, the more I saw beyond the postcard view. Growing inequality provoked social strife, and with rising food prices things were getting worse. There was vigilante justice when the government failed. There were crack addicts, beggars, and people who lived from garbage dumps. Homeless children slept on the streets sniffing glue, which helped to eliminate hunger, I was told. Many children worked the streets instead of going to school, juggling at traffic lights, washing windows, or selling fruit. Kidnappings were common, causing the walls around the mansions to get built higher. It was legal to run red lights at night, and there was usually a beggar, a salesman, or a musician on the subway trying to make enough money to eat.

Despite this poverty, I relished the diversity of Rio's rhythms. It helped that Sylvia lived near Ipanema Beach so I did not see the worst of things often; this helped me to remain unafraid. I saw fear in the eyes of people who knew better however, so I was cautious. Mostly I saw a culture with a special, musical energy devoted to living life fully, in a land populated with proud survivors.

I visited a public hospital when my football buddy Dênio broke his wrist. The hospital scene wasn't as bad as war, but it was pretty bad. I saw people screaming in pain from gunshot wounds, with dedicated but overwhelmed staff trying to help. I felt sorry for the impoverished masses with suffering visible in their faces, but so it goes, fellow travellers, best of luck and may the force be with you.

Dênio told me (translated), "The Brazilian elite have private hospitals, but this is to be expected given the history. Our elites mostly have European blood, whereas the favelas are packed with the progeny of slaves. Most victims of police violence for example, are black."

Despite this inequality, Brazil did not seem racist to me because it was easy to be color blind in a land where most people were mestiços and mulatos, especially compared to the USA where racism was more extreme. I had to explain this to my friend because he only knew America from Hollywood movies. Then he explained a key fact to me: many Brazilian slaves escaped into quilombos (jungle cities) where they preserved their African culture including food, music, and religion. "To understand Brazil," he said, "you must understand Africa." These facts helped me understand America better too, because without quilombos, the North American slaves largely lost their cultural roots, a terrible thing indeed.

Dênio was my best male friend, important because despite Sylvia being amazing, sometimes I felt the need to drink beer and hang out with the boys. I met Dênio playing football but we only became friends after I asked him about his tattoo of Shiva.

He said (in Portuguese), "My grandfather was a trader from India, and he taught me about Lord Shiva. Like him I also want to destroy all that is evil." This of course led to profound discussions about philosophy.

My new friend invited me for a barbecue in his favela home, plus Sylvia too, of course, so we all met in the city when she got off work, then we bought groceries and took a shuttle up the hill. Guarding the entrance to the neighborhood, boys with automatic weapons stood silently while others openly sold drugs. While these people spoke with each other about Sylvia and me, I pretended as if I understood and I kept my mouth shut.

Dênio escorted us through a labyrinth of red-brick shacks, some menacing with bullet holes and barbed-wire barriers, others welcoming and colorful. My friend's house was humble but his view over Copacabana was fabulous, and everything he owned was spotlessly clean. He put on music, a variant of samba called pagode, then we all danced and crowed.

Like Indians, Brazilians adored cows, but unlike Indians they adored their cows on the barbecue grill, with beans and beer on the side.

Gunfire got everyone's attention but not for long. Dênio said that "lost bullets" sometimes rained down on the city, killing people at random, and this was stupid, but mostly the drug gangs fought each other not the peaceful majority. He said the drug boss paid the electricity bill so the residents protected him. He said (translated), "I don't believe in lost causes. I am a fighter, but I cannot fight the drug gangs, so what to do? Me? I go surfing at sunrise. That's when I get my best ideas. Children do not have to become drug dealers to make a living, but they do need help from adults, so we are building a new community center! It is our responsibility to create art and culture, no? If not us, who?"

I began going surfing with this guy as of the next morning.

Regarding the endemic corruption, he said approximately, "The road to my mother's village is still dirt even though the government paid to pave it, twice. Everyone knows the mayor stole the money. He bought a mansion for his mistress. And then he won re-election. Can you believe it? The son-of-a-whore threw a big party and the fools voted for him. Democracy?" Sigh.

Later he told me, "Sylvia is nice, and she likes you, I can tell. Brazilian women like gringos because latino men are all safados like me." I understood every word except for *safado*, so I asked; it meant *womanizer*. This made me realize that Sylvia was damn good at making me jealous, the way she casually touched male friends when speaking with them, giving them intimate cheek-kisses when saying goodbye, and so on, but the situation was not symmetrical. My only other female friend was Isabela.

I managed to get Sylvia jealous at Dênio's next party when a pretty girl named Graziela taught me sexy samba moves. I knew that Sylvia got jealous because she commented on it later. To me this was funny because she once told me that Brazilian men had more dance in their blood than American men, and they knew more about the art of seduction, and it was good for me to become more Brazilian and less American in that way. Just not with other women! Not even with my memory of Angeline.

"Angeline, Angeline, Angeline!" Sylvia and I often discussed philosophy, but if I spun the discussion towards mathematical physics (and especially if I mentioned my Yin tattoo), she cringed, and then one day she blurted out, "You still love her, don't you?"

"I love her memory," I answered. "And now I love you."

Sylvia did not return this sentiment with words, but her sincere smile made me happy. She was a happy person, and her positive attitude made it easy for me to love her. She was tough, and she did not let the world's problems get her down. She was jealous of Angeline.

As I felt increasingly at home living in Rio, I became increasingly cavalier (sometimes walking alone at night) until I finally got mugged. When the thief told me to give him my money or else, I calculated my options for stunning the asshole with a Kung Fu strike. Instead I said that I just spent a year in China studying the martial art. I told the guy that he did not want to fuck with me, then I calmly walked away. He yelled after me but he did not chase after me. I smiled, thinking Old Man Chan would have been proud.

When I told Sylvia about this incident, she hit me for being stupid. She said I should have given away my decoy wallet, then she made me promise to always take taxis at night. I did not argue with her logic, but I did say, "Sometimes a show of strength is all that's required to avoid a fight." With that she hit me again, for being stupid. Then she pounced on me like a kitten.

76 - The Love Illusion

I told Sylvia about theories of everything, and she told me about the criminal mind. She had great insight into trained-ape theory from her experience as a parole officer. Every day she met apes who let their passions overwhelm their logical brains to the point where they committed crimes. Most of her parolees were non-violent drug users whom she helped to find jobs, but others were more animal than human, and she worked to get them back into their cages.

We often discussed humanity's essential conflict, our short lives versus infinite chaos, a conflict with monks, monkeys, and random shit storms. The country Sylvia most wanted to visit was India, especially Varanasi, to witness this conflict directly, so I promised to take her there on our next holiday.

To celebrate this plan we dined at an Indian restaurant. Sylvia wore hippie jewelry that she bought in Bahia. She looked sexy. We ordered tikka masala and chai. For the second time I said, "I love you."

A new peace was born within me when she loved me back. I stared into her eyes and travelled through time. Gone was the heartache from Angeline as she was forever young. I kissed my partner passionately, confident that living happily in the present was the very best I could do.

I elaborated on my previous statement. "I love your physical beauty," I said, "of course, because every guy on the planet (who's not blind or gay) loves that. But moreover, I love your talent for creating smiles. I love your intelligent and benevolent brain. And I love the fact that you love me back."

She asked me, "Why are we so attracted to each other?"

I answered, "Cosmic energy."

"No, God wanted us together! Ha ha."

"Al-hamdulillah."

"God is love."

"No, God is the universal laws of physics, and this explains chemistry which explains biology which explains life which explains love."

This analysis got Sylvia going. She said, "No way. I do not

agree. I tried reading that short book about time, and it said *maybe* the *big boom* something, and *maybe* the black hole something, and maybe..."

I said, "When you put it that way, it sounds like humanity doesn't know anything, but the key to theoretical physics I think, is that the scientists know what they don't know. Nobody is debating the observable facts, the empirical evidence, because this data can be reproduced, and nobody is disputing the perfect accuracy of Quantum Mechanics either. Humanity's intriguing puzzle is therefore to explain all these facts with a single, elegant, mathematical framework (with a Yin-Yang symmetry I believe), and that's what these physicists are on about. Therefore we do agree! All I'm saying is that the purpose of love is the purpose of life itself."

Sylvia agreed, then she told me everything she knew about dopamine and oxytocin, chemicals in the brain involved in creating the love illusion.

Later she said, "I think most people, when they know they are about to die, they hold onto God for strength because they believe they will live again in Heaven. I think we need love as a reason to live, and God as a reason to die."

I said, "Maybe we stay alive out of curiosity, to see what's gonna happen next."

Just then, our waitress served our food and chai.

Sylvia said (in English), "I think you are right that truth is with science, but this is too much intellectual for most people. Science is old men looking to old rocks to find boring old fossils. Love is also truth, human truth, and this is more important than old bones." Long eye contact. "By the way, how did you get Love as your name?"

"My grandfather did that," I said. "Maybe because Love sounds American, but I don't really know. Gramps was an immigrant from Syria, and certainly Love sounds more American than Alzahabi, but I never asked him. Gramps was a funny guy so who knows? I wish that I asked him more questions. But I like Love as my name. I like it a lot."

Sylvia and I dissected the nature of knowledge, and we embraced our ignorance of many things because without ignorance there can be no joy of discovery. I never asked her if she wanted to have babies, for example.

She confessed, "When I was a little girl, I had fear of dark rooms at night, and fear of fantasmas. How do you say? Ghosts? Spirits?"

She asked me if I had been afraid when we got mugged in Kigali. I answered that if I were a cave man, I'd have been a hunter. "I still have fear of ghosts," she admitted.

"Fear is normal," I said. "To me, the interesting thing is how our brains create this mind-illusion, but you're the psychologist. Schizophrenics hear voices, right? Some people have seriously intense hallucinations. I myself wake up sometimes believing that my dreams really just happened. That's where you'll find the ghosts."

Sylvia said, "You are right, but please when you meet Papai next week, please pretend to be Christian, or at least not explain science. Papai is simple farmer and he will not understand. Love is my religion but Papai is Evangelical. He believes too much on his faith in Jesus."

I asked, "Baby Jesus or space Jesus?"

Sylvia laughed, then I added, "OK, but between you and me, religion has proven itself incapable of solving Earth's urgent problems, but science has a fighting chance."

"I agree, but not with Papai, OK? Remember, before religion there was only wild and crazy monkey men, and then came the ten commandments, and this was law of God, and this was good. Monkey men need morality."

"Sure, but we also need science because unlike religion, science adapts to evidence. And regarding morality, humanity has enormous problems right now, and isn't our greatest moral duty to solve these problems, with science? Praying doesn't actually help."

"I agree, but not with Papai, OK? And anyway, you're talking about politics, so who decides what is science and what is not science?"

We were diving in deep, so I ordered a bottle of wine.

I asked Sylvia to imagine a secular church with singing and community, but instead of repeating the same ridiculous communion ritual over and over, the priests would teach something useful every week, for example solar-powered circuit design.

That's when I realized my problem was not ignorance of science, just as it was not ignorance of Tongan basket weaving; my problem was that I was anxious about meeting Papai, and I had to make a decision: either propose marriage, stay in Brazil illegally, or leave. I had forty days to decide this question to satisfy the government but only nine days to decide for Papai.

I decided. The timing was good for Bastiaan to leave Cambodia also, so he and I agreed to meet in Kenya and then head to South Africa by land, with a possible detour into Ethiopia to visit the Omo River tribes. Sylvia agreed that I should travel with my friend on the condition that I return to Brazil as soon as allowed by law. I promised I would, then I pledged to pay for her holiday in India also, as soon as she could arrange the time away from work. This became our new Plan A. I also planned to swing by California on my way, to confront Pops in person because I was damn curious to know his game. To summarize, my plan was to make the Gods laugh.

77 - Another World

Pedro sent me an email with the subject, "Good News Bad News." The good news was that Shep was free from jail, home with his girlfriend, alive and well. Good news indeed! The bad news was that the big man stubbornly refused to divulge any details about what happened, insisting that he was sworn to secrecy. "All he says is that they caught him, they held him, and then they let him go free, and that's really annoying."

I told my friend about my planned visit home in thirty-eight days to confront Pops and Shep in person, and of course to just hang out and drink beer. This was good news too.

When I hung up the phone I felt like drinking a caipirinha, so I walked to a funky beach bar where I sat near an Iraqi businessman, a friendly drunk who spoke Spanish. The guy seemed friendly that is, until he said he wanted to kill Americans.

He said (approximately), "I don't care if my dictator is a nice guy, and I have nothing to gain from speaking out against him. I care if my streets are safe for women to walk alone. I care if my milk is delivered fresh every morning. Fucking Americans..."

I pretended to be Brazilian while pressing the man to admit that he preferred Western liberty and justice compared to a dictator's oppression, just for sport. I told him (in Spanish), "Please do not hate the American people. They are trained apes just like you and me. I think you would be surprised how many Americans work for the good of humanity."

The Iraqi accepted my premise so I confessed where I was born. At first he didn't believe me so I proved it to him. He was so drunk that he laughed so hard that he cried.

When I went to go pee, the bar's television displayed news about a giant American bank going bankrupt, big news, so the next time I got online I researched the story: as investors made decreasing profits in manufacturing, the real economy, they turned to the speculation economy by pouring borrowed money into financial derivatives, foreign currencies and real estate, whatever bubble was growing fastest, and the biggest bubble of them all was bursting!

This made me think of Mr. Suit so I wrote him an email. "Hey

Robert," I typed. "The sky is falling! Yang is reaching its maximum and must retreat!"

"You're right," he replied quickly. "This could be the worst banking crash ever!"

The amazing thing my pen pal typed next was that he was poised to fly to Brazil for a conference in São Paulo, plus a beach holiday with his wife Jackie, including two nights in Rio. I was strangely delighted to be able to catch up with this man I barely knew.

Sylvia and I met Robert and Jackie on the beach in front of the their five-star hotel in Copacabana. Jackie looked like a richer, older Sylvia and they got along great. Robert and I shook hands as if we were old friends, American-style handshakes. Sylvia ordered a round of coconut water while I explained about Bangalore Budi and fortune cookies.

A bit later, Sylvia suggested we go to Shopping Rio because Jackie needed to get her bikini area waxed, and she wanted a new bikini too because why not? But first we had lunch at the shopping-mall's food court, with fabulously fresh fruit, salads, and barbecued meats. The feijoada was also delicious, the best food-court food ever.

The ladies departed to do lady stuff, leaving Robert and me alone for the first time. I told him that he should discard his American-style bathing suit for cool surfer's shorts. He agreed to browse, but first we ordered coffee and discussed the smallness of the world.

"Indeed, it's really small!" he said. "Did you know our planet only has fifty-million square kilometers of habitable terrain? Not so much, a fact that's easier to comprehend while jetting from one continent to another overnight."

The smallness of the world framed our conversation. The crisis on Wall Street and the American presidential election were big news in Brazil. I just read a scientific report about global warming. Everything on Earth was more inter-connected than ever at the dawn of the age of the Internet.

I reminded Robert that he could be a viable candidate to run for political office. I even thought of a jingle for his hypothetical campaign: "Globalocity, global ferocity! Together we can cage the corporate monstrosity!"

Robert liked my jingle but he was not keen to get involved in politics personally. I told him that humanity was in a race against the clock, because the multi-national *thing* was poised to devour the commons, and extinctions are forever. I said, "We have exactly enough time to prevent the collapse of critical Earth ecosystems if we start working to protect them seriously today."

My unlikely friend agreed that the Wall Street crash could be good news if we somehow fixed our broken system during the recovery. "But even if we agree on some ideal future state," he said, "the big question is how do we get there? The elites will always back the status quo."

I told him, "Seriously man, you should become a congressman or something! As Gandhi said, be the change you want to see in the world. I only get one vote every few years, but you man, you can get elected! You can prevail with the right marketing I think, because you'll look good on television. Don't get preachy about economic theory and logic. Use trained-ape theory. Use emotion. You're a natural salesman. Just pretend to be Christian."

Robert looked puzzled. "Are you saying I should use the same tactics as the opposition?"

"Yes. Tell the people what they want to hear, and never let the truth get in the way of a good story. Here's an idea: print a million bumper stickers that say *Jesus was a Socialist*. Realign the Christians! But don't actually convert to Christianity, man, because it's not OK to make public-policy decisions based on myth and dogma."

Robert sipped his coffee. "I like your thinking," he said, "but the socialist brand has too much baggage. It's better to create a new brand. Global warming is not a problem only for socialists, right? Maybe a better tactic is to focus on the facts, not activism but factivism. Real facts are stubborn things."

"Yeah," I said. "I like your thinking too. The problem is that the bad guys claim their bullshit is all fact too. You know? With so much uncertainty and complexity, maybe it's better to focus first on priorities. Dollar for dollar, what's more important, another nuclear submarine or computers in schools?"

"Or maybe we should focus first on effective solutions, ideas that work. For example we could tax financial transactions. Even a tiny tax would create friction in the speculation economy while simultaneously raising revenues. Another idea is to establish a universal minimum income (not the same as a minimum wage) for everybody. Think about it: anyone who wants to buy more stuff can get a job, but every human deserves a place to sleep and food to eat. This idea is simple and fair and prevents extreme poverty, and we don't need to raise income taxes to pay for it either, not if we tax accumulated wealth."

I said with a smile, "Brilliant. Come on, admit it. Running for office is actually feasible."

Robert said, "To be honest, now is a good time to take on a new challenge..."

I interrupted, "In bed?"

Robert laughed, then he said that if he were a congressman, he'd focus first on changing the election rules in order to get better lawmakers into office, as a wedge to enable further reforms. "Start with the wedge," he said, "in this case term limits, public financing for campaigns, instant-run-off voting to promote third parties, and the elimination of a tactic called gerrymandering."

"But that's all theoretical," he added, "because I'm not interested in fighting the old machine. Washington is just too full of corrupt, hypocritical Christians, and frankly they piss me off too much. Where is the love? Anyway, I'd rather build something new."

Just then Robert got a phone call that he did not answer, but this gave him an excuse to show off his new toy, the first ever smart-phone, the original *iPhone*. I was most intrigued. Indeed I was shocked at how easily this gadget could access the virtual world beyond. I told my friend about the Goddess of Magic.

He responded, "I haven't shown you the best part yet! This bad boy has apps for children, educational apps and games, and that's what I'm talking about! That's the future! And that, my friend, is a business opportunity. Today marks a moment in history. For the first time ever, human babies will be raised since birth with interactive digital screens."

Pops bought our first computer when I was nine, and he never loaded it with cool games so I ignored it to play sports. Now all that hi-tech stuff was finally becoming interesting. Robert's device was very cool and I wanted one, but I did not buy one because I felt as if this gadget might be too cool. I was worried that I might spend too much time with it, and therefore not enough time with a certain special girl from Ipanema.

I said something about sexy bikinis as a way to prod my friend into buying cool surfer's shorts. He did. Then we wandered the mall until we found our lady friends. We complemented their new shoes and their taste in fashion generally.

Sylvia insisted that every tourist in Rio must see the view made famous by a giant statue of Jesus, so we took a taxi to the base of the old-school tram up the mountain.

We discussed politics because the global financial crisis was a bigger drama than any tele-novela, history in the making, the dreaded crash. With Yang engulfed in crisis, there was about to be historic opportunity. Would our leaders stand up to the challenge? Would the people demand change? We could hope, but the so-called experts on TV only wanted growth, never sustainability. Their corporate owners required continuous profits. The bottom line was the only line. And the experts were freaking out.

As we looked over the marvelous city, Sylvia said that a revolution was required to create a new corporate-legal system that prioritized people and planet ahead of profits. I told her that she might be right, but another world was possible, not a perfect world but a better one. While not guaranteed that humans could create a sustainable system, we all agreed it was worth a try.

That night we dined at one of Rio's top restaurants, Robert's treat. Delicious! When the subject of politics came up again, Sylvia said, "Political problem is too much difficult, so let's dance! Now. I mean it. Let's go dance, because dancing will make us smile, and this will make happy chemicals in our brains." We went dancing.

78 - Flowers for Yemanjá

Peter and Gurli announced their wedding in Denmark so Bastiaan and I agreed to meet there on our way to Africa. We also agreed to swing by Amsterdam because what world tour would be complete without seeing Amsterdam? Meanwhile Sylvia talked her boss into more holiday time after six months, so we made a plan to meet in India. This was all great but I was more anxious than ever about meeting Papai, especially as we departed towards his farm.

Papai lived in the Brazilian state of Espírito Santo. The drive only took six hours but we stopped at a beach town on the way to break up the trip, a romantic escape from the big city. We stayed in a family-run pousada with gardens that were the favorite of hummingbirds, with freshly baked bread and an endless supply of fruit.

I learned the Portuguese word for hummingbird was beija-flor, flower kisser.

My lover and I walked hand-in-hand down the beach to enjoy the sunset. Soon we encountered a group of local women performing an elaborate ritual, so we stopped to watch. Sylvia knew the women were worshiping Yemanjá, the mother Goddess of the ocean. All of these women were from an African race, and they all wore white, some with candles, others dancing, and others offering flowers to the sea.

We sat in the sand a discrete distance from the ceremony, close enough to observe the beauty but far enough away that our chatter would not intrude. Meanwhile Sylvia explained about Macumba and Candomblé, Brazilian religions that survived from Africa transformed over centuries. Different spirits had different powers.

Many slaves faked conversion to Christianity, she said, but they really believed in spirits that they associated with Catholic saints as a subterfuge, creating a bizarre mix of faiths that persisted despite being totally incoherent. She didn't say this quite so neatly, but her English fluency was getting better all the time.

"Most people believe whatever their parents believe, and their parents before that," I told her. "Religion and language are the quintessential elements of culture." Then I explained the meaning of the word quintessential. Then I said, "Before the various religions of Abraham spread across the world through wars of conquest, most people believed in Gods of volcanoes, Goddesses of love, and things like Thor. The cave people wanted to understand their Universe too, so they guessed."

Sylvia confessed that she hated Candomblé. Her eyes indicated fear and disgust so I asked her to elaborate. "African religions have many spirits," she said. "Yemanjá, Xangó, Oxalá... My uncle made pact with bad spirit. He wanted more money, maybe women too. I don't know."

She took a deep breath. "One time when I was a girl, I watch Candomblé ceremony while hiding behind trees in the dark. At first this was wild dancing and chanting with crazy music, but then I saw my uncle drink blood and eat chicken raw, and he made cuts on body for permanent! Then I saw another man with eyes white, talking in spirit language, and I saw one woman crawling on ground crying with voice like baby!"

I could see some of this horror still lingering behind her eyes, then she calmed down. "Now I know my uncle is trained ape," she said, "but at this time I was too much afraid so I run away! My uncle, now he is Christian. He went to church for exorcism and this was good, a good thing for church to do. He is better now. He is... How do you say? He is a very nice Jesus freak, but when he drinks cachaça he changes. I think maybe he is schizophrenic. I want to run tests."

I let our conversation fall into silence in order to marvel at the beauty of the flowers for Yemanjá, plus the moon rising up over the sea. The ceremony would have made a great photo but I was happy I didn't have a camera. Instead I memorized the moment so that I could have it with me forever.

As my lover and I walked hand-in-hand down the beach, I contemplated the significance of Yemanjá, the African mother Goddess. I wondered what it was like to believe that throwing flowers into the ocean could somehow inspire the Universe to protect me from harm.

Sylvia broke the silence. "What's going to happen in the future?" she asked.

I asked back, "With us? With humans? The Universe?"

"With us," she clarified.

"Our love matters," I answered. "Don't worry, we'll sort out our travel logistics."

"Good," she said. "And... with humans?"

I answered, "Well, scientists say that planet Earth is going to get blasted by the sun whenever it turns into a red giant, but a few billion years should be enough time for humans to colonize another planet, so the question becomes, will we go extinct sooner? Or maybe most of us will die but not all, say in a nuclear war? Maybe the rich will evolve separately with genetic engineering? Or maybe robots will take over to save us from ourselves? AI is just getting interesting..."

I stopped to think. "Maybe humanity's future holds nothing but miserable wars as too many people fight over too few resources, and frankly this scenario seems likely if we don't get our shit together, because mankind's greatest machines are still being built for war. What a waste of human potential! So maybe we're witnessing the beginning of the end of the golden age of humanity right now, but maybe not. Maybe places like New Zealand will remain nice, isolated islands with OK governments and few people, but on the other hand, more places are becoming overpopulated wastelands too, like Ethiopia, so I don't know. The future? It's a mixed report. Thanks to science and technology and infrastructure improvements, maybe a better world really is possible, for humans and gorillas. Certainly there's no shortage of good people out there fighting the good fight, people improving humanity's standard of living one village at a time, and these people give me hope."

I paused to think some more. "In other words, now is humanity's final exam. The future is up to us. But even if our political systems fail us, and even if an ecological catastrophe is inevitable with climate change and unsustainable consumption, then that will be bad for future humans but not for us; we'll be dead. The good news is that now is a great time to be alive. This is still the golden age of humanity. The good news is that empathy is in our human nature. The good news is that you and I, we have each other, we have love, at least temporarily because nothing is permanent."

I knew that love was based on elevated levels of dopamine plus neural circuits programmed for raising babies, and given that I was about to meet my potential father-in-law, this made me nervous. I explained this analysis to Sylvia, and she told me to tell Papai the truth, and the truth, she said, was love.

79 - Zé Violão

Papai's ranch was ringed with forested hills but its primary feature was a grassy valley loaded with cattle. The ranch included a corral for horses and an annex for cowboys, with only one technological detail visible, the satellite dish on the main house, a crucial device for watching tele-novelas and football tournaments. The front garden was full of flowers.

Sylvia parked her car then ran to hug her father. I shook the man's hand firmly while saying it was nice to meet him. I didn't understand a word he said next but it sounded nice. Sylvia rescued me with words that I also failed to understand. Then she introduced me to her aunt Divina, a widow who helped take care of Vovô, Sylvia's grandfather, a man who was blind and deaf from age. Sylvia introduced me to Vovô, then she introduced me to a dog named Barão, a smart old hound who knew to stay outside with the chickens.

Tia Divina insisted on showing me the house. She pointed out the kitchen's wood-burning stove, then she made it clear that my bedroom was on the opposite side of the house from Sylvia's bedroom. I think she added that sex outside of marriage was a sin, but I'll never be sure. Despite my much-improved Portuguese, the language barrier was still a barrier. I knew that my epic journey towards mastery of this language would take years, but I could speak enough for polite conversation, so I dove in, reminding myself that attitude was everything.

The first time we were alone, Papai told me about his father. It helped tremendously that I already knew the story. Vovô was one-hundred-and-seven years old and the son of a slave. He was afraid to take a shower for fear of catching a cold and dying, and he was starting to smell. Papai saw this as funny and we both laughed.

Papai spoke to me loudly so I told him that just because I was a foreigner, I was not necessarily deaf. We both laughed again. From then on he spoke to me slowly and without using slang. This helped a lot. I found the man to be more sophisticated and intelligent than Sylvia ever gave him credit for, but this should not have surprised me because she was sophisticated and intelligent. Despite Papai being taller than Sylvia, their genetic similarities were obvious.

Sylvia told me that she studied psychology to understand her relationship with her father, and she concluded that her childhood traumas had nothing to do with him, but with her mother's death, which she didn't remember. This tragedy left Tia Divina as the woman of the house, which was weird, brother and sister widowers living together. Divina had several boyfriends over the years, but Papai stayed single and this made Sylvia sad. He did his best to be a good father, but Sylvia still had to get away, and this made her sad too. I consoled her with the philosophy of infinity. She said that I made her happy, and on this point I tried my best. Her happiness was my happiness.

That afternoon we all sat on the front porch to sip coffee and eat cake while having a conversation about life, with Sylvia translating the subtle details. Despite being constantly scrutinized, my anxiety plummeted as I found Papai to be a genuinely nice guy.

He told me to call him José, his Christian name, but nobody called him that so it seemed wrong. Divina called him Zé, and I noticed other people calling him Zé Violão, because as Sylvia explained, he played the acoustic guitar in church. From then on I called him Senhor Zé.

Sylvia and I climbed a mango tree. We jumped on branches to get ripe fruit to fall, then we raced down to beat the pigs to the prize, mangoes as delicious as any fruit I ever ate. Tia Divina and Papai watched this scene from the porch. Sylvia gave them both mangoes.

We all ate our fruit, then Divina invited us to pray. With a solemn expression of hope and happiness, she read a passage from the Bible, then she asked her Lord to protect us and to bless us, "not just today Lord, but for all eternity." She squeezed my hands and looked deeply into my eyes. She told Sylvia that I would make a good husband because I had Jesus in my heart. She said that she loved me and that Jesus loved me too.

Tia Divina prepared a fabulously delicious dinner, then at seven o'clock we all watched Sete Pecados on TV.

Later, just as I was falling asleep, Sylvia joined me, whispering, "Shhh..." We made love in silence, then she left. At first light she woke me up again, this time with coffee in hand.

While I adjusted to being awake, she prepared two horses for riding. Then we toured the farm. Then we visited her neighbor, a man named Manezinho with eighty-eight years, a humble man who lived only one hour from the ocean by car but never made the journey. When I asked him why not, he explained that the journey was much longer than one hour by horse. Later he asked me if California was a city near São Paulo. Sylvia and I stayed for coffee, then we trotted and galloped home. This was the first time I ever rode a horse and I loved it.

Papai arrived in his truck followed by two men in another truck. They called for me to join them, not Sylvia nor Divina, just me. He said something about doing a man's work.

One of the cowboys mounted a horse then returned with a cow. Meanwhile the butcher produced a heavy hammer. He struck a blow to the cow's head, causing the animal to make horrible noises from pain. The second blow caused the beast to fall over, shaking uncontrollably. One more blow and the beast was dead. As I quietly freaked out, one of the men sharpened knives while the other drained the cow's blood onto the grass. This made me want to vomit but I saw Papai scrutinizing my reaction, so I forced myself to think of green salad. I repeated to myself the following words: green salad.

I expected a barbecue to erupt so I was disappointed to learn this was a cash transaction. The butchers loaded the entire carcass into the truck and drove away, except for the liver. Papai explained that most cuts from a cow are best aged, but not the liver, and it was the most delicious liver I ever ate.

Sylvia explained that her father didn't keep cash because he didn't trust banks. If he had money, he bought cows, and if he needed money, he sold cows. She told me that Papai sold a cow that day just to see my reaction however, as a test. She said I passed. She said I was lucky because Papai was being nice to me, because he was intimidated by me, because I was a man of the world.

She confessed that the last time she brought a boyfriend to the farm, Papai tested his character relentlessly. "Not only did he kill one cow, but he also made party and he invite all the pretty girls from church to dance. Mostly I think Papai only want my husband to be honest and nice and courageous and strong and good and sincere and loyal. So if he tries to test you again, just relax, be yourself."

That night Tia Divina made chicken, the most deliciously fresh chicken I ever ate, served with garlic rice, black beans in a meaty stew, fried manioc, and green salad. At seven o'clock, everyone watched Sete Pecados.

That night I dreamed Pops was a spy fighting evil communist terrorists. I was flying and I wanted to help, but then I saw Mom so I flew to her, but the landing was too rough so I could not help. Mom saw me and waved, but then she faded away. What a funny organ, that brain. The next thing I imagined was Sylvia smiling at sunset.

I awoke at first light, surprised to see the table set for breakfast. Nobody was around so I drank coffee and ate cake, then I walked outside to watch the sunrise. I saw cowboys milking cows in the corral so I walked to them and said good morning. Sylvia found me and her father followed. He asked me to try to milk a cow. I found it surprisingly difficult to get the momma to squirt, and everyone laughed at me.

After that Papai invited me to go for a walk, just the two of us. He asked me if I loved his daughter so I told him the truth. Then he said (approximately), "Me too, so if you ever harm her, I will kill you." As I contemplated my response he added (slowly), "But I do not think you will because I believe you are a good person, so just one more thing: you will *not* get my daughter pregnant before you marry her! Do you understand?"

I answered, "Sim, Senhor Zé."

A moment later a serpent appeared on the trail, a venomous coral snake with red, black and yellow stripes. The snake surprised me, then Papai surprised me more when he asked me to kill it. I looked the snake in its eyes, and it stared back, then I looked the man in his eyes, and he stared back. Meanwhile the snake stayed motionless as if awaiting judgement, life or death.

I said, "Sorry but no. This snake is too dangerous. And I think it's better to live and let live. Why kill without necessity? Anyway you have more experience, so..."

Senhor Zé grabbed a stick and approached the snake

menacingly, then he flicked the thing into some grass away from the trail.

From then on, he and I got along great. He asked me about America and I asked him about life on the farm. I also asked him about his church, just enough to determine that he was a regular on Sunday primarily for the community gathering, a genuinely nice event with friendly neighbors and beautiful singing, not because he believed in Christianity's particular mythology, but because he liked to play the guitar and socialize. Papai seemed patient as we worked through our language barrier. He was curious, he had good humor, and he was a damn good musician too.

That night he showed off his skill. He prepared a bonfire, then along with three cowboys, we sang songs, sipped shots of home-made cachaça from the next farm (Zé did not drink), and we told stories. On my entire world tour, this was my only exotic cultural experience where I felt completely at home.

My girlfriend and I returned to Rio de Janeiro with a sense of mission accomplished. We arrived on a sunny afternoon, took showers, then went to the beach to sloth. Later we splurged on a fancy dinner to celebrate my positive encounter with Papai.

I announced as a surprise gift for my lover that I would pay for her to fly to Denmark for Peter and Gurli's wedding, even if she could only get one week away from work. Later we would travel around India together too, as soon as possible. She kissed me.

Two days later I received a most important email, a message from a man I never met named Tyrone W. Shrubb. The subject read, "URGENT. About your father and mother." I clicked. "Dear Raymond," the message read, "It is with a heavy heart that I must inform you that your parents are dead."

I stared blankly at the screen feeling shock and disbelief, then I read some more, enough to determine that the cause was a car accident, it was someone else's fault, and that somebody got away. Immediately I felt a horrible sadness swelling within me, but I held back tears to read more, then I felt the loss, and the love, and the grief. In a quiet corner of an Internet café, anonymous and alone, I allowed myself to cry.

I suddenly thought of Angeline and then my Yin tattoo, my eternal reminder that life and death coexist in a Universe with male and female symmetries arising naturally. The infinite cosmos (commonly known as God) reminded me once again that my existence as a human was fleeting, and I suddenly knew that I needed to spend the rest of that existence with Sylvia, my destiny, my luck, and my balance, so I did something I never did before, I visited her at work. I told her my horrible news, then I asked her to marry me sometime in the not-too-distant future. This scene was not especially romantic, but that didn't matter when she said yes.

80 - The Land of the Free

I saw Shep immediately upon emerging from customs. I only met him once before, but he seemed like a great friend when he smiled and waved. I noticed Shep before I noticed Pedro because Shep was almost twice as large, a tall and heavy Hawaiian with tribal tattoos.

I hugged my friends then shook their hands, then we aimed ourselves towards Pedro's car with a plan to go meet Tyrone W. Shrubb, to get the keys to the house and go over the will.

I told my friends about my strip search going through customs. I did not blame the agent because he was only doing his job, however I did wonder how much evil committed in the history of the world was done by people just doing their jobs. Soldiers came to mind.

Pedro said, "Welcome to the United States of America."

As we stepped outside to breathe California air, my friends offered sincere condolences for my tragic loss. I was happy and sad, happy to be with my friends, and sad because my parents were dead and that was very bad indeed. I only had four days in Brazil to face the shock and the pain of saying goodbye, so I was still an emotional zombie.

I changed the subject. "So Shep," I said. "Inquiring minds have to know... How did you get caught? What happened?"

Shepherd shrugged his shoulders, then he said, "I'm sworn to secrecy."

I insisted, "Come on, man. Spill the beans."

The big man answered by putting a finger to his lips, so I waited until we were inside Pedro's car before I asked again. This time he answered, "They caught me. They held me. They let me go free."

I said, "That's it? Come on..."

Shep remained quiet, so Pedro said to me, "So far I've only got him to admit that the government grabbed him, the bastards, but all he ever says is, 'They caught me. They held me. They let me go free.' It's actually kinda spooky."

Shep smiled proudly, "Well, I did steal a look inside the Terrorist Identities Datamart."

Pedro looked perplexed. "What? You never told me... Cabrón!"

Shep said, "Surprise! I wanted to tell you and Raymond at the same time, but I never imagined it would be under these circumstances." He looked at me. "Or three weeks ahead of schedule. Sorry again brah, for your loss."

I said, "Thanks."

He said, "So yeah, well, I finally figured out how to run queries by hijacking a legitimate login (using the same website that government employees use), and the first thing I did was search for Pops, and sure enough, he has a record! Yes sir. Our favorite database has Pops tagged as quote, a terrorist sympathizer, unquote (that's a technical term, sympathizer). The database also lists some of Pops personal connections in both Israel and Syria. And it says the case is quote, under investigation, unquote. But that's it. I bet there are other databases out there with more information (maybe a paper file too), but for now..."

"Cabrón!"

"Sympathizer?"

Shep nodded his head proudly. "That's everything interesting. I mean, there's more data in there, like Pops's driver's license number and stuff, but..."

I said, "I don't know how to thank you for sticking your neck out like that! I really appreciate it! Thanks a lot. And wow! That's really interesting... Sympathizer?"

Shep said, "Don't mention it. This is what I do for fun. Plus all this no-fly-list stuff is interesting too. But anyway, we still don't know shit about what Pops actually did."

I said, "Soon we'll have the keys to the house..."

Everyone smiled in anticipation.

I said to Shep, "Come on, man. Tell us. Spill the beans. How did you get caught? What happened? And they threw you in jail without charging you with a crime? What's up with that? Don't they have to charge you with a crime?"

Shep answered, "They actually followed a process that's been almost legal ever since congress passed the PATRIOT Act... So shit, OK, I guess I can tell you two guys, but don't ever tell anybody else! OK? Seriously... So anyway, as they say, curiosity killed the cat. Once I got access to that database, I couldn't resist searching for myself, and that was stupid because everything I did with that web-app got logged. I pointed a big, fat, digital finger right at myself. *Doh!*"

"Oh no."

"Oh yeah. Anyway, that's how they identified me so quickly. Then they threw me in jail, without charging me, and then I got a lawyer, and then all I can say is they made me an offer I couldn't refuse. Long story short, I have a new job that pays twice as much as I used to make."

"You took a job with the CIA?"

"The NSA actually, but that's just between us, OK? Seriously. They didn't torture me if that's what you're wondering. I'm a computer geek. They used logic. I have skills they need, and I have a squeaky clean background. I was raised a Christian. Plus I'm a minority, the only pure-blood Hawaiian the NSA has on staff, and certain government bureaucrats like that kind of thing."

As Pedro negotiated the corners of the LAX parking garage, Shep explained his hacker tactics in more detail. First he acquired the names of local field agents who might have authorization to run database queries, then he followed them around to look for a vulnerability, and he found one. An agent named Jack liked to surf the web using a certain coffee shop's free Wi-Fi, so Shep set up a man-in-the-middle attack, which he said was easy. With this he was able to watch all of Jack's unencrypted network traffic.

The big man explained, "As soon as Jack logged into his government account using OpenVPN, I knew I had him because OpenVPN has a vulnerability that I know how to exploit (it's a bug in OpenSSL actually). This is a vulnerability that allows me to steal session keys. In other words, as long as Jack was logged into his work account, I could also run database queries, hijacking his session. Of course it took me a while to set this all up (I had to write some scripts), but then all I had to do was wait for Jack to log in again from the same coffee shop. I drank a lot of lattes, but my patience paid off! First I searched for Pops, then I searched for myself which was stupid, and then, well, I couldn't resist trying to gain permanent access by dropping in a root-kit, and this set off a trip-wire alert for anomalous activity, and about a week later the

Feds came knocking on my door."

I thanked Shep again while Pedro paid the parking fee. Then as soon as we were away from airport security cameras, Pedro whipped out a joint saying, "Don't drink and drive... Smoke and fly!"

I laughed, "Ha! You just reminded me of my friend Bastiaan. I must get you two together some day... at the wedding! But for now, I'm sorry my brother, I don't want to put a damper on your celebration, but I'm not so keen to smoke just now."

Pedro put his joint away, saying, "No worries. Later."

Just then a car passed us with a bumper sticker that made us all laugh when we caught the double meaning: Jesus ain't driving.

Shep asked me from the back seat, "So Raymond, my brother, tell us more about your trip! Where all did you go exactly? India? Brazil? Africa?"

I said, "Yeah. First I went to India where I visited Pedro's friends Dan and Dana."

Shep interrupted, "I know them! They're awesome."

I said, "Yeah. They are. I hung out with them to pick up some spiritual vibrations, and to improve my karma. Yeah. Then I went to Nepal, then China where... man long story!" I told my friends the long story, concluding, "You guys must come with me to Denmark for Peter and Gurli's wedding! Sylvia will be there! And I'm buying first-class tickets..."

Pedro said, "Thanks! I can't wait to meet your fiancée."

Shep agreed enthusiastically, then he asked me what I thought about Africa.

"Going there was a humbling experience," I said. "I learned that as the son of my wealthy white parents, if I ever complain I deserve to be smacked upside the head. Yeah. The African people amazed me with their warmth and courage in the face of mind-boggling adversity. For most people on Earth, life is a daily struggle. We are the lucky ones."

Shep nodded knowingly, then he asked me where I liked best.

"That's easy," I said. "Brazil. I loved the culture, Sylvia, the food, the music, Sylvia, football on the beach, Sylvia... Seriously, Brazil was my favorite country. The people have a special, musical energy. They dance. And did I mention the food? It's really great."

Pedro zipped onto the freeway. It was a gorgeous day. We sped down the road for about ten seconds before traffic came to a screeching halt. Shep said, "Welcome to Los Angeles!"

The car in front of us had a bumper sticker that read, God bless America. With nothing to do but offer commentary, Pedro said, "That should say, God bless Mexico." We all laughed.

Another bumper sticker displayed the words Land of the Free printed over an American flag. "Democracy makes a great brand," I said, "with justice for all and a man on the moon, but I'm not proud of empty rhetoric. Land of the free? Maybe land of the lawyers is more accurate. It's true that Americans have many freedoms, but the more rules the less free. Anyway, personally I feel more free now than ever, with all the money I'm about to inherit."

Pedro said, "Yeah man, you are a lucky bastard."

I said, "Yeah but my parents just died, so I don't feel very lucky just now, but if you ever catch me complaining, do smack me upside the head."

Pedro said, "We're with you, bro. The American dream, you know, the big house, the big car. I didn't swallow that pill. But America is not so bad. I have a student loan. In most countries if I wanted to study, they'd tell me to come back whenever I saved enough cash. And furthermore, if America weren't king of the world, man, it'd be somebody else."

"You're right," I said. "I'm not anti-American, I'm pro-Earth. But I am suffering from culture shock and that's weird. Everywhere else felt like an adventure. Being home is weird. Everything here looks the same and smells the same. It's me that changed. I eat healthier now, way more veggies. I take shorter showers. I'm interested in politics now too, world politics, and the facts on the ground that argue for progressive policy. Yeah. While I was away I researched the facts of history, warts and all... And I think it's true that one has to leave one's home culture to understand it. You know? If you're inside the box, you have to leave the box to see the box."

"Yeah, man."

"Yeah. And you know it's funny, overseas there are different ways of life in all the little details. Culture. The way people make coffee is different. The electrical outlets are different. There are even people who refuse to use toilet paper! Most of Africa still uses cassette tapes for music because they haven't yet upgraded to digital. And most countries don't have mega-stores that you can only drive to by car. Those I don't like. In most of the world, you buy stuff from a real person, the store's owner. You haggle."

Shep said, "Welcome to the consumer zone, with cars built like tanks, and twelve kinds of chocolate-chip cookies in the pharmacy."

I said, "Thanks bro, but I prefer the jungle, the way it makes me feel alive, like our ancient ancestors walking barefoot and always alert. All of this consumer crap is unnatural. Everyone should go travelling, I think, to see how the world really is, out there, because for Americans especially, it's not exactly a good thing to grow up expecting to receive a free Christmas present every year. Do you know what I mean?"

Pedro said, "Yeah man. It sounds like you found what you were looking for."

I said, "Well, I didn't find enlightenment, if that's what you mean. That's too hard. But now that I think about it, I guess I do feel more enlightened. I did hang out with a lot of gurus. Before India I didn't know what to believe, but now I believe in Yin and Yang, at least as a metaphor. I believe that mathematics is the language of God, the natural laws of physics, but morality is cultural. Morality is not about God, it's about people, and gorillas, and justice, and racial equality. You know? We're all in this together. And another thing: we all end up in the same place, dead. Life is not about the destination. It's about the ride."

My friends nodded their heads so I elaborated, "If I went on the road hoping to find something, I reckon that I've had it with me all along. I found myself. The open road is a guru of self discovery, a great teacher. And I found love! But even more than with Sylvia, I think the most important relationship that we all have is the one we have with ourselves. To know oneself is to know joy and bliss! And on that, I'm still searching, learning all the time. So yeah, I guess I found my purpose also, which is to live well, to be mindful and conscientious within, and considerate of others always."

Shep smiled, "That's awesome brah. You're right."

Pedro said, "You should write a book."

I said, "Interesting idea."

Shep then asked me, "By the way, are you registered to vote? The election is in a few weeks..."

I answered, "No, not yet, but I plan to get right on it."

"Yeah man."

"Imagine, a black president..."

"Yeah. This could mark the end of an era. That guy, with his background as a community organizer, maybe he can unite the world with new treaties to protect the commons. Maybe he can modernize the global governance. Maybe he can take on Wall Street too, because with this gigantic banking crisis, now is the perfect time to demand change."

"Yeah, but is the man a miracle worker?"

"Even if he's a saint, how much can one man do?"

"His enemies will unite in opposition."

"Of course they will. Does the man have balls of steel?"

As Pedro turned the car onto a familiar lane, we talked about the audacity of hope.

I started to get anxious as we approached Mom and Pops's mansion, my mansion, an emotion that intensified as we pulled into the driveway. My first reaction when I saw the property was that it really was a lovely place. I saw it with new eyes.

Shep said, "Welcome Home."

Tyrone W. Shrubb was waiting for us. I never saw the guy before, but who else would be waiting for me wearing a suit and carrying a briefcase? As I emerged from Pedro's car, the man approached me to shake hands. "Hello, Mr. Love," he said. "I'm Tyrone. I was your father's attorney and friend."

"It's nice to meet you," I said. "Please call me Raymond."

"It is nice to meet you too. I'm sorry it has to be under these circumstances. I am truly sorry about your loss. I will miss your mother and father... But now I think it's easiest if we get straight to business. I only require one minute of your time."

"Thanks."

"First of all, with respect to the will, you get everything." Tyrone handed me the will saying, "Notice on the back of page two there's a safe combination and a computer password... And here are the keys to the house." He handed me the keys saying, "I think that's all you need urgently. Do you have any questions?"

"No," I said. "Not now, but I'm sure I will later."

"OK," he said. "Good. Here's my card. Call me anytime, day or night." He handed me his card saying, "Whenever you're ready, I'll come back here, or if you'd rather come to my office, that's fine too. Whatever makes you more comfortable. Again Raymond, you have my deepest condolences. Do you need any cash?"

"No," I said. "I'm good."

Tyrone said, "OK." Then he remembered that he still had to show me how to enable and disable the house's security system, so he showed me, then he said goodbye.

As soon as Mr. Shrubb drove away, the rest of us went straight to the kitchen to fetch beer, then we sat on the back porch overlooking the ocean. I sipped my magic brew and smiled with delight, because while I was overseas I forgot how much I liked hoppy American ale.

I made a toast. I said, "I hope that Mom and Pops's last vision in their heads, just before the lights went out, was a vision of Heaven on white fluffy clouds, with bare-breasted angels flying around. They believed in Heaven so I hope their brains took them there, so that they died happy." We clinked our beers.

I smiled a bittersweet, hoppy smile as I sipped my brew. Sigh. Life.

My friends and I could have sat on that porch for hours, except that curiosity compelled us to Pops's office and the safe; after all, we knew the combination, 12-45-78, not obvious but easy to remember. Inside were perhaps a hundred gold coins plus important-looking papers including the title to the Ferrari, but nothing that spoke to the mystery. I thanked Lakshmi, the Goddess of Wealth, then I tossed one gold coin each to Shep and Pedro, as it seemed right and proper for them to share in the booty.

We searched the office thoroughly but found not one clue.

Frustrated, we fetched fresh beers then returned to the back porch because the view over the Pacific coast was amazing, but we didn't sit for long. Shep was keen to get into Pops's computer so we went back to the office. Pedro and I discussed a world of topics while Shep typed furiously in a mysterious language. He came up with nothing useful.

When I went to go pee, I found the papyrus scroll that I bought for Mom and Pops in Egypt hanging in the bathroom. I suddenly felt like crying. Then I got a flash of inspiration! I splashed water on my face then ran back to the office proclaiming, "It's a decoy! We might have to rip this house apart, but we'll find Pops's real safe, I'm sure. Let's go!"

Sure enough, behind a bookshelf in the master bedroom, Shep found a loose panel hiding a locked metal door. After celebratory cheers I tried the combination, the only combination I knew, and it didn't work.

My friends and I drank beer, hoping for inspiration. Nothing. So I told the story of getting robbed in China, Old Man Chan and Chan Lian.

Meanwhile Shep studied the will. After a while he said, "Pops's computer password is dr1wss2p. That's password spelled backwards with the numbers 1 and 2 where the vowels ought to be. Try the combination backwards."

I did, and it worked. Yes!

Pops's real safe was full of ancient and rare coins sealed in plastic slabs designed to preserve their numismatic value. Seeing this treasure made me realize that I would never have to work a crappy construction job for low wages ever again. The safe also had a folder with miscellaneous papers. One sheet in particular grabbed my attention, a single sheet neatly folded down the middle, with a single word hand-written on the outside. The word was, "Junior."

I read the note out loud. "Son, You are reading this, so damn! I must be dead! Shit! Maybe I'm not just being paranoid. Anyway I saw your friend Pedro the other day and he startled the shit out of me. And this got me thinking, so I know this is weird, but I need to make sure you know a few things, and we can no longer trust electronic communications."

Shep interrupted to say, "That's mostly true. We *can* trust encrypted messages if we manage our own encryption keys properly."

I continued reading, "I'm sure the spooks listened in on our phone calls, for sure the ones from Israel, and your mother says she said too much, and the fact that some hacker got caught snooping into my records is bad. And your phone calls, not good. Look son, I'm sorry I lied to you, but I hope now you'll understand. The truth is your grandfather and I sold information to Syrian intelligence, and not for any love of Assad I must say, but really to keep an eye on Israel, because let's face it, their leaders are even more paranoid than I am. Don't get me wrong, I am pro-Israel, so how to explain? Nobody gives Assad any credit for this, but the man has been a force for stability in the region by keeping Syria's super-crazy assholes in check. He's secular. All of this has nothing to do with religion but with Palestine and the Golan Heights, you know, the excessive military bullshit. Two wrongs don't make a right."

I stopped reading to say, "That's Pops."

Pedro said, "There you go."

I continued reading, "And I'll be honest, the money was damn good too. Anyway, I retired from all that when you were born, but your grandfather kept at it. He was a true believer. He took risks. And I'm sure it was the spooks who killed him because they visited me. Of course I lied, and they didn't have any actual evidence so they left me alone, but they did put me on their stupid no-fly list which has been a real pain in the ass, I must say. By the way, your grandfather had some other business on the side so go to Switzerland. And that's about the size of it. Again son, I'm so sorry I lied to you, but I was afraid to say too much over the telephone. I hope you can forgive me. Love, Pops."

After a long pause, Pedro said, "Holy shit. We killed your parents."

I said, "No. Mom screwed up. They've been bugging the phones, right? Mom admitted to lying. She said Pops and Gramps were working together, then she hung up on me, for my own protection." Sigh. "I suppose that for spooks, it's easy to deal with a problem like Pops. Make the problem go away, right? They've killed presidents before. They killed Gramps. Make it look like an accident, right?"

I bit my lip to stop from crying, then I flipped through Pops's papers, my papers, consoling myself with swigs of beer. A statement from a Swiss bank showed a balance of more than five-million dollars. Another document described a safe-deposit box, in Zürich, Switzerland. I distracted myself away from grief towards bewilderment. Mom and Pops were dead, Gramps was a spy, and I was a millionaire. Wow.

I said, "Gramps came to America just after World War Two, changed his surname, and married a Christian woman, all so that he could raise a Christian-American soldier, designed from the beginning to be ideally suited to spy on Israel."

"Pops must have been a very valuable asset."

"And he didn't have to do much. General Lipshitz said that Pops was active socially. I can see him hobnobbing with the military brass over beer. He would have been good at that. Nobody would ever have suspected his loyalties. And then all Pops had to do was tell Gramps. Easy. Plus Pops was a member of the technical staff, so who knows what else he had access to?"

Pedro said, "The spooks know about you too, dude, so you better watch your ass."

I said, "Well, if they've been tracking me, then they must know I'm no spy. But Gramps, he must have sold Pops on the idea of spying just after Israel took the Golan Heights from Syria in 1967. That would have been the perfect moment. Pops was just the right age."

"Pops was hardly a peace activist."

"You're right. He was just another ape, so for sure the prospect of easy money helped to push him over the line. But regarding Gramps, I think he did what he did because he wanted to prevent World War Three, you know, to promote a balance of power. I believe he was a visionary not a psychopath. Yeah. I believe Gramps made Love not war."

Pedro finally lit his joint which we smoked with pleasure while playing billiards in the recreation room. Then we sat on the back porch, contemplating the electrified air of an impending storm.

I was sad that my parents were dead, but I knew that I would shed no more tears. With a fresh beer in hand, I made another toast. "To Mom and Pops," I said. "Bon voyage fellow travellers, so it goes, and thanks for all the booty."

Pedro commented, "We never considered the possibility that maybe the spooks didn't kill your parents (you know?) that it was just a plain-old car accident? These are not unheard-of in California, you know, car accidents. Actually, they're pretty common."

I said, "You're right. In fact, now that I think about it, I can't imagine the accident was anything but random chaos, bad luck, because Pops just wasn't that important, not enough to justify cold-blooded murder. I mean, he was just a run-of-the-mill mole as far as I can tell, and no longer active. All he did was liberate information. And seriously, can you imagine some CIA middle manager ordering a field agent to kill Mom? There's just no way."

Shep agreed, "Especially for a hit on United States soil. No way."

We all drank beer, then Shep broke the silence. "So, anyway, now you're a millionaire! Whatcha gonna do?"

I smiled. "Let's take the Ferrari out for a road test."

Shep shook his head. "No, I mean, whatcha gonna do with all your money?"

"Oh." I stopped to think. "Yeah, good question. I need to convince Sylvia to quit her job but that's going to be easy now, because I'm certain that she'd rather travel than work. America won't give her a visa without a ton of paperwork, but we can both go to Denmark for our friends' wedding, so yeah, let's go to Denmark! I must know what's inside that safe-deposit box too, and Zürich is pretty close to Copenhagen by train, so let's go there too!"

My friends looked at each other, then replied in unison, "We're there!"

I said, "Sweet! And to answer your question Shep, I don't have any big plans for the money yet, but I do want to help the world, you know, to do my bit. So I think maybe I'll set up a scholarship in Ethiopia, for girls. And maybe I'll go back to school myself, to study science! And maybe I'll donate to a community center in Rio or Brooklyn. Who knows? But mostly I want to live and love because life is a short and beautiful thing. Every day I'm alive is a good day. And I still want to travel a lot. I still haven't been to Syria for example, and Sylvia really wants to go to India. But first, Zürich!"

"No," said Shep. "First, you relax and enjoy your Ferrari car and your fat new home."

"Oh I will," I concluded. "But home is where the heart is, and this house is not where my heart is, so it'll never be my home. My backpack has become my home, and then there's Brazil! So I'm gonna sell this house, I just decided, and then I'm gonna go on another epic journey, to elsewhere and beyond. Globalocity!"

Pedro said, "Yeah man, you go. And first stop, Europe! Thanks for inviting us. You should invite Dan and Dana too. I can picture it now, all of us together at the wedding, with Sylvia and your other roadie friends of course. I can imagine it now, the party..."

Globalocity!

Raymond's real-life human avatar ***DC Leberknight*** once bicycled across Central America, then he moved to Tokyo. ***David*** taught computer science in Colorado, then he married ***Lili*** in Brazil, then they toured Africa by public bus. The happy couple eventually moved to New Zealand because it's a great place to live, but their adventures continue... Check out ***David and Lili's World Tour*** online, a travel blog. ***Global velocity!***

Thank you for reading about the adventures of Raymond. If you enjoyed the ride, please take a moment to leave a review at your favorite book store. ***Thanks!***

www.ingramcontent.com/pod-product-compliance
Lightning Source LLC
Chambersburg PA
CBHW051329020726
47501CB00007B/1984